BUT ONE REPLY

ROBERT L. DECKER

But One Reply

Robert L. Decker

Noble Six Hundred

PREVIOUSLY IN
NOT TO REASON WHY

Love, Honor, Courage, and Faith in an Unpopular War

I n *Not to Reason Why*, readers met Zack and Ruth, a young couple torn apart by the Vietnam War. He, a rising fighter pilot; she, a determined teacher. Their love was tested across oceans, prison camps, and political divides as Zack struggled to return from North Vietnam—and Ruth fought to bring him home.

Their story unfolds between 1967 and 1973, a time of deep turmoil in America. Those who served made even deeper sacrifices. Zack and Ruth's journey laid the emotional and moral foundation for those facing the war's final, desperate moments.

To read the full story of Zack, Ruth, and their companions, pick up your copy of *Not to Reason Why* by Robert L. Decker today, available on Amazon and Barnes & Noble.

PRAISE FOR
NOT TO REASON WHY

★ ★ Bronze Award @ ReaderViews.com ★ ★

★ ★ International Impact Award ★ ★

★ ★ Hemingway Award Finalist ★ ★

"… the reader absorbs the 620 pages with nary a hint of boredom."

"Most people reading about Vietnam focus on the ground war,
but Mr. Decker does a wonderful job bringing the
deserved attention to the air war."

"There is more truth here than in any history book I've ever read."

"The emotional depth, ethical complexities, and personal narratives
in this book are what make it a compelling read."

———•———

BUT ONE REPLY

This War's Ending Was Inevitable
Did honor and loyalty still matter?

In this sequel to *Not to Reason Why*, the reader meets three of its main characters again: Sue Guerri, her husband Rick, a former Air Force pilot, and his fellow ROTC instructor, Jeff Nickerson, now an intelligence officer in Saigon. The trio finds themselves tangled in another battle. This one is far from the streets of a college campus; it is South Vietnam in the spring of 1975.

As South Vietnam crumbles under the advancing Communist forces, Rick and Jeff are called once again to help in what may be the final chapter of the war. Sue is with them—as is danger. New faces share their call to action:

» **Marcel Dubois.** A former French Foreign Legion paratrooper who has been a Hmong freedom fighter for twenty years. He thrives as a guerrilla leader.

» **Lieutenant Colonel Bill "Dobie" Starbuckle.** A Special Forces veteran who suspects unfinished business lurks in the jungles of Southeast Asia.

» **Captain Eugene "Clicker" Cruthers.** An ex-Marine fighter pilot. Rick joins him near Saigon to train Vietnamese pilots.

» **Mai.** At first, she is only a house girl for Clicker and Rick's family. Later, she becomes Sue's only friend in this foreign land.

» **Lieutenant Colonel Ngo Tinh.** He eagerly accepts the help of Vietnam War veterans Clicker and Rick as he leads his pilots in the defense of their besieged country.

» **Ashley Peabody.** Publisher of a soldier-of-fortune-type magazine. He knows more about this war than his last big story reveals.

» **Master Sergeant Jimbo Atkins.** Also a Special Forces veteran, he flees a North Carolina jail to resume his favorite pastime: killing Commies.

The characters meet in Southeast Asia as the dominoes fall while the American people—and a polarized Congress—idly watch.

Rick must decide which is more important: risk his life and fly another mission or save his family and flee?

Clicker came for the jets—and for the women he loves. But now he must choose between escape and honor.

For Dobie and Jimbo it might be just another adventure. Perhaps it's something deeper: the unbreakable code of brotherhood.

When a comrade calls for help, a soldier can give *but one reply.*

———•———

But One Reply

© 2025 Robert L. Decker

All rights reserved.

ISBN: 979-8-9937335-0-0

First Edition

Published in the United States

Noble Six Hundred LLC

noblesixhundred.com

This story is dedicated to
the 58,318 American men and women
who are remembered on the
Vietnam Veterans Memorial wall.
Their brothers and sisters in arms still grieve for them.

CONTENTS

SOUTHEAST ASIA MAP

TIMELINE OF THE FALL OF SAIGON

December 1974	People's Army of Vietnam (PAVN) captures Phuoc Long province (60 miles north of Saigon).
March 5, 1975	PAVN attacks Army of Vietnam (ARVN) north of Hue (390 miles north of Saigon).
March 10, 1975	PAVN attacks Ban Me Thuot. President Thieu withdraws ARVN from Central Highlands.
March 25, 1975	ARVN troops abandon Hue; PAVN captures city and attacks Highway 1 to Da Nang.
March 30, 1975	PAVN captures Da Nang (about 360 miles north of Saigon).
April 1, 1975	World Airways airplane leaves Saigon carrying orphans.
April 3, 1975	President Ford announces Operation Babylift and orders a C-5 to Saigon to evacuate orphans.
April 4, 1975	Operation Babylift begins with the C-5 departing Saigon. Pan Am Airways announces flight of orphans from Saigon.
April 17, 1975	Khmer Rouge captures Phnom Penh, Cambodia. Cambodian genocide begins.
April 21, 1975	PAVN captures Xuan Loc 40 miles east of Saigon. South Vietnam President Thieu resigns.
April 23, 1975	Defense Attaché Office at Tan Son Nhut clandestinely evacuates a group of Vietnamese employees.
April 28, 1975	A-37s flown by North Vietnamese pilots attack Tan Son Nhut Air Base late afternoon.
April 29, 1975	PAVN shells Tan Son Nhut around 3 a.m. The helicopter evacuation begins midday.
April 30, 1975	Last US helicopter departs the Embassy at dawn. PAVN captures the Presidential Palace in Saigon. President of the Republic of Vietnam orders the ARVN to surrender.
May 14, 1975	CIA evacuates Hmong General Vang Pao by helicopter from Long Tieng, Laos.

PROLOGUE

Spring 1995

Rick sat in the dark living room, but the real darkness came from within. The room's gloom came from the closed drapes and the twilight outside the window. Rick's inner darkness came from the sadness deep in his soul. He felt exhausted, physically and emotionally.

Hushed voices of his three adult children around the kitchen table floated into the living room. Their conversation came in pieces. He could discern their different voices, although the words were unclear. Rick took small comfort in knowing that Sue had instilled a strong sense of loyalty among them. They would need that close bond now. This afternoon, they had buried their mother.

The last three months had drained Rick and the children. At fifty-two years old, Sue had lost her battle against breast cancer. Rick and the children had tried to make her comfortable during her last month. Teri, their youngest and only daughter, had left her spring semester at Texas A&M to come home. Teri's older brothers had taken time from their young careers to help. But Teri had helped Rick carry the heavy load of caring for Sue. Providing comfort against the scourge of cancer was always a losing battle.

Rick suspected his children were asking questions that only he could answer. As they had grown up, he sensed they recognized their tight bond stemmed from something in a shared past. Lee, the oldest, and Teri understood they were adopted from Vietnam. The children knew that the family had left Vietnam in a hurry when Teri was a baby. But Sue had never wanted to tell them more of their history. It was too painful for her. She wanted only to focus on loving them and working for their futures.

Rick knew one question the children might ask had no answer: *Why had this happened?*

It was the question to which Rick had no reply.

Sue had asked a similar question at another tough time in their history. She had found her answer then.

The hushed conversation paused. Rick heard pages turning. Then, the talking resumed. But it wasn't a conversation. He could tell they were asking each other questions, but the tone suggested that no answers came. Then, chairs scraped along the hardwood floor. They were coming to ask him the questions. Rick downed the swallow of bourbon in his glass.

Lee led them in. He carried two small, old photos. David and Teri each held two magazines. Rick recognized the photos and the magazines. They had found them in Sue's trunk at the end of their bed. It was in that trunk, folded inside wool blankets, that Sue had hidden her sad memories. Lee had discovered the envelope in a drawer years before. Sue had walked in before he had opened it. Now, the children had found them again.

After twenty years, the time had arrived to tell them how they had become a family. But it was more than just their family story. To tell it right required that he relate the intertwined stories of four families. Those magazines told parts of those stories.

———•———

DON'T ASSUME I'LL BE HERE

O n a cloudy December afternoon in 1974, Rick Guerri pulled into the parking lot of his small apartment in College Station, Texas. He had the same pit in his stomach that he had felt three and a half years earlier. Then, the news of getting back to flying the Thud, the F-105 fighter-bomber, had excited him. He knew then that Sue would not be happy about it. To say that she had not been happy was an understatement. For the first time, he had heard her use the F-word.

The news about this job wasn't like returning to the Thud as a Wild Weasel pilot. He wouldn't be flying the dangerous mission of hunting surface-to-air missiles over North Vietnam. After all, the war in Southeast Asia had ended, sort of. He turned off the ignition of his old GTO.

How can I ease into telling Sue? That was his immediate task. After a minute of thought, he knew. *Might as well do it straight.*

The job didn't exactly thrill Rick either. It did not require a master's degree in electrical engineering. But he had opened too many "we'll keep your resume on file" letters. He hadn't found any engineering jobs available. The few aerospace recruiters during his first semester at Texas A&M had not warned him that job prospects would disappear. Rick recognized they probably had no clue then as well.

His plan to go back to school had been straightforward. After earning a master's degree, he would get an engineering job designing new airplanes or new cockpits. Then, maybe he could work his way into flight testing. Staying with his undergraduate major seemed like a good move. Airplanes were going to become much more electronic. An Air Force fighter plane being developed had "fly-by-wire" flight controls. The pilot's control stick did not use mechanical cables and levers to move the control surfaces. The side-stick in the jet was essentially an electrical switch.

Despite two new Air Force jet fighters and one Navy fighter, budget cuts had slammed the aerospace industry. Even commercial aviation suffered. Airlines could no longer count on Air Force contracts ferrying men and women to and from war. America's Vietnam War had been over since January 1973, nearly two years. The decline in business had hit the commercial aircraft makers as well.

As a result, no aerospace company was hiring engineers. Spending cutbacks had pushed thousands of engineers into low-paying jobs. Many were pumping gas at the disappearing full-service gas stations in Southern California or Northwest Washington.

This job offer meant one important thing: Rick and Sue wouldn't have to live on a college student's budget. Sue's job as an assistant manager in a department store fell short of their two incomes before Rick left the Air Force. Now, he had an excellent job offer.

While it wasn't an engineering job, he would at least be flying supersonic jets again. The downside was the location. It was in South Vietnam. He would be gone for three-month periods, with a month at home in between. When Rick had resigned from the Air Force, Sue had been happy to leave behind the separations and uncertainty of military life. He knew this job would not seem that much different to her.

Sue was certain to bring up the airline job question again. Rick had grown tired of answering that airline question. His answers to Sue's frequent inquiries had become curt and impatient.

Graduate school had placed unanticipated stress on their marriage. The strain of living off her salary had taken its toll. Rick had carried a heavy academic load so that he could finish as quickly as possible. He had underestimated how rusty his mathematical knowledge had become. Auditing undergrad math courses had increased his study load. As a result, he had worked only a crummy, low-paying, part-time job for one semester. Bearing the financial load and caring for David, their young son, wore on Sue.

At least with this job offer, the financial strain would end. It paid much better than the Air Force, even accounting for the double-digit inflation. With four days until Christmas, he could now afford a decent present for Sue. He hadn't been able to buy her a pretty piece of jewelry for two years. David, their nearly four-year-old son, could receive more than just three cheap presents.

Steeling himself for a tough conversation, Rick walked into their two-bedroom apartment. Living in the cramped quarters had not been easy, either. It was quite a downgrade from their spacious four-bedroom house with a big yard. He dropped his briefcase inside the door. Sue came in from the kitchen. She studied him warily for a second. She noticed his face was not beaming as she had expected with a big job offer.

"So, how did the interview go?"

"They offered me a job."

"In engineering?"

"Not exactly."

"Meaning …?" Sue's internal radar warned her to steel herself.

"No engineering openings exist right now. They need instructor pilots. They are paying more for pilots than for engineers."

"Teaching whom?"

"Foreign students," Rick hedged.

"Where? In California?"

Rick said nothing.

"Arizona?" Sue continued.

"No. South Vietnam."

"South Vietnam?" Sue's voice showed growing anxiety.

"Yes."

"Is that war over? Occasionally, the news suggests it isn't."

"The peace agreement remains in effect."

Rick knew it was a weak answer. Technically, it was an accurate statement. Sue scrutinized Rick. "How soon do we have to leave?"

Here it comes, Rick thought.

"I go to California to learn to fly the F-5 right after New Year's Day."

"How long is the training?"

"It depends on how quickly I learn. Maybe a month or six weeks."

"Then …?" Sue pressed.

"I leave for South Vietnam as soon as possible."

"You leave …" Sue replied. "When do David and I leave?"

"It's not clear if you're going. I've negotiated three-month periods, coming home for a month in between. They don't seem to contemplate families going with the pilots."

"You asked …" Sue prompted after a pause.

"Not exactly. It was clear from everything they said."

"Well, you call them and clarify it. Tell them your wife and son will join you."

"Living near Saigon for you and David might not be the best idea."

"Because it's too dangerous?" Sue pressed. "But the war is over."

Rick knew he could not admit to any danger in the job. He wasn't sure how to phrase his objection to Sue and David coming along. Sue sensed his dilemma.

"If it's too dangerous for David and me, then it's too dangerous for you. I don't want you to go. You can find another job. Apply to the airlines."

"As I've said before, I'm not interested in an airline job." *Here we go again,* Rick thought.

"I still don't understand why you are hostile to flying for the airlines," Sue countered. "Maybe it doesn't pay well for a couple of years. But then the pay becomes fantastic. And we can fly anywhere in the world for free."

"I don't want a union job," Rick countered, louder than he intended. "You only advance based on seniority. And I don't want to fly a big jet straight and level for the rest of my life. It's like being a bus driver."

Sue placed her right hand on her hip. Her piercing, dark eyes framed by her black hair displayed a fierce determination that belied her petite frame.

"If you insist on taking this job and going without us, it can mean only one thing. We are not important to you. So, buster, you need to understand one thing. If you leave, do not assume David and I will be here when you return."

Rick looked at his wife. She wasn't bluffing. And he knew she was right. There was no choice between this job and her and David. They mattered much more to him. They were his life. Flying fast jets was a dream job when no one shot at you. They had survived two long separations with people shooting at him in that fucked-up war.

To answer her, Rick walked to Sue and pulled her close in a tight hug.

"You and David are my life," he said. "I love you. I'll call them tomorrow to clarify."

Sue wiped a tear from her cheek. She kissed Rick.

"I love you, too. But I couldn't stand another separation."

———•———

CAUCASIANS?

Marcel Dubois checked the direction of the sun flickering through the underbrush in the mountains of Central Laos. Glimpses of it shimmered through the leaves as the wind shifted. He quietly crawled to his left under a large elephant ear plant. He didn't want the reflection from his field glasses to give his position away to those on the distant cliff. Wiping the sweat from his eyebrows, he peered through the eyepieces. He twisted the knob to bring the distant figures into sharp focus.

Marcel studied the figure on a ledge below the top of the cliff, who leaned over with his back to him. The loose clothes and crude hat made identifying any features impossible. Marcel shifted to another figure on the other side of the ledge. This one looked to the right. Again, the ragged clothing obscured any physical features, and a hat shaded his face. The only other figure in view was too far back in the shadows.

A key question plagued Marcel. Were they Caucasians? Marcel could not tell. They shuffled, hunched over. He could only guess that they were emaciated under the loose pants and shirts.

Marcel shifted his scan to the face of the cliff above and below the ledge. High above, he could see the bottom strands of a rope ladder. Below the ledge, rough rocks and boulders hampered access to the cliff. Access to the ledge had to come from above. The rope ladder suspended above led to only one conclusion: those on the ledge were prisoners. He needed a better look at the plateau above the ledge. A different vantage point would also answer another important question: did a cave provide some shelter for the prisoners?

Marcel realized that the chattering birds in the trees had suddenly gone quiet. He lowered the field glasses. To his left, the clear, descending whistle of a babbler sounded. Looking toward the sound, he spotted the face of Keej, his Hmong guide and brother-in-law. Keej subtly nodded. Then he disappeared.

Marcel shifted his gaze down, then froze in place. Only his eyes shifted from side to side to spot what concerned Keej.

Minutes passed before Marcel spotted leaves moving on the game trail a hundred meters below. Several figures passed a slight break in the vegetation. Marcel counted five figures in Pathet Lao uniforms. He guessed more were in the patrol whom he had not seen.

Twenty minutes passed before a low rustle of leaves came from behind Marcel.

"We need to go," Keej whispered in his Hmong dialect.

Marcel nodded and slipped back from his vantage point into the thick jungle. He followed Keej through the underbrush, trying to stay as quiet as his guide. Marcel still marveled at the stealth of these native warriors. After fighting with them for twenty years, Marcel still could not match their skill in the jungle.

Marcel had met Keej after the French debacle at Dien Bien Phu. The battle had been the last gasp of the French armed forces in the war to retain their colony.

Soon after Marcel had completed paratrooper training with the French Foreign Legion, he stood in the troop door of a battered airplane. Looking at the jungle below, he knew then that he was jumping into hell.

Volunteering for the paratroopers had not been his first choice. The Legion had been rougher than he had expected when he had walked into the recruiting office in Paris. He was sixteen years old, running from the Belgian police. The French Foreign Legion had seemed attractive compared to Belgian or French jails.

Growing up in Belgium, he spoke French. That made the first year much easier for him than for the foreign recruits who spoke no French. His training corporals only harassed recruits in French. At least he had understood their screaming orders. When he had completed the training and his first assignment in Morocco, his corporal approached him.

"The lieutenant says you should volunteer for parachute training."

Marcel had promised to think about it. A day later, his corporal asked him about his decision. When Marcel demurred again, the grizzled corporal gave him a piece of advice.

"If you disappoint the lieutenant, your life will become hell."

The next day, with the lieutenant standing in the background, the corporal provided a glimpse of his future. Marcel had joined a group of prisoners shoveling out the outdoor latrines. He had reconsidered and promptly volunteered for parachute training.

That decision culminated in his first combat jump into the valley of Dien Bien Phu, French Indochina. Heavy green vegetation of the jungle below gave way to a clearing. The green light next to the door flashed on; the jumpmaster supplemented his guttural cry with a strong shove. Marcel flew out the door.

His paratroop regiment had fought bravely for five months before the decisive battle. Marcel had crawled out of the defeat into the jungle and mountains. He barely survived sneaking west when he encountered a group led by Keej's father. Pulled from his hiding place, Marcel was prepared to die. He feared the Viet Minh had tracked him down.

He realized he might survive, though, as he listened to his captors converse. From the little Vietnamese that he knew, Marcel realized they spoke another language. Their clothes were not like the Vietnamese either. They fed him and treated his infected boils and insect bites. They did not tie him up. As they prepared to move on, Keej's father motioned to the jungle, then in the direction they were preparing to walk, trying to explain something to Marcel. He guessed they were giving him a choice. He could go back into the jungle on his own. Or he could follow them. So, Marcel had stayed with them for nearly twenty years now. He had married Keej's older sister in the intervening years.

After another twenty minutes of crawling through the forest, Keej stopped. Marcel slid next to him.

"I'd like to get a better look at that ledge," he whispered in Hmong. "I'd like to know how many are there and if there is a cave."

Keej nodded and pointed up to their left.

"Up."

Marcel nodded. He followed Keej to the left, where they started a steep, slow climb. Remaining quiet required them to creep through the wet, slippery vegetation. The prior day's rain made the climb very difficult. Marcel's feet slipped on the brush underfoot. He had to avoid snagging his feet on the branches and vines. Pulling a foot free from an entanglement made too much noise. Years of traveling in the thick jungle made Marcel thankful for his small stature. He had hated being small as a boy. The larger boys had mercilessly tormented him at school. Now, it was a distinct advantage in the forest. He cradled his M16 in front as he crawled. Slinging it onto his back would cause too many snags.

Another hour passed before Keej stopped. He pointed across the small valley. Marcel saw they were still slightly below the level of the ledge on the cliff. It was a good vantage point. He took his binoculars from his pack. Keej crawled several feet away and lay in the bushes to watch.

The distance prevented Marcel from seeing any facial features of the prisoners. He studied them through his glasses, again from the shade of the bush.

Marcel counted three figures on the ledge. As he suspected, the cliff opened into a cave about the height of a man. The figures all appeared to be about the same height. He could see smoke curling up from a small fire. One figure stood with his back to Marcel, looking up the cliff. Marcel moved his glasses up the cliff to the top.

Another figure started lowering a bundle on a rope. When it reached the ledge, the figure at the bottom removed the bundle. The figure high above moved as if pulling up the rope. Then he lowered another bundle.

Marcel surmised that a meal had arrived. He shifted his gaze to the fire. Two other figures added small pieces of wood from the first bundle and built the fire. One figure carried a cooking pot to the side of the cave. Marcel saw the glint of a slender stream of water as the prisoner filled the pot. The prisoner carried the pot back to the fire. Contents from the second bundle went into the pot. Then the prisoners cooked their meager meal.

Marcel shifted his search to the plateau above the ledge. He could see only three figures. Likely, the patrol that had passed them headed there. That made too many for him and Keej to chance a closer look.

Marcel crept over to Keej.

"Take a look," he requested. "Are the prisoners Caucasian?"

Keej peered through binoculars for several minutes. He shifted his gaze among the figures across the narrow valley. Finally, he lowered them and handed them back to Marcel.

"Hard to tell. All look the same height. Foreigners always seem to have one taller." He shrugged.

Marcel frowned. He wished he could get up to that ledge to make sure. But that was impossible.

The Americans had been asking for the past twenty-three months since the peace agreement ended their Vietnam War. One friend had been very persistent.

"Are there any Americans still held in Vietnam? In Laos? What have you seen? What have you heard?"

The prisoner lists provided by the Vietnamese Communists contained gaping holes. As a result, rampant rumors emerged of abandoned prisoners. The Americans failed to understand. The more they asked, the more they would hear about remaining prisoners, even if none existed. Vietnamese and Laotians could earn money by saying, "Yes."

Now, the rumors had become even more insistent. Word circulated that a North Vietnamese deserter had an Air Force Academy class ring to sell. The deserter claimed to have stolen the ring from a prisoner of war. The prisoner had not been on any list supplied by the Communists.

———•———

DOBIE

———⊢———

Lieutenant Colonel Bill "Dobie" Starbuckle, retired US Special Forces, pulled the hood of the poncho over his head. Rain rarely bothered the veteran jungle fighter, but the drizzle had turned into a drenching. The Laotian rainy season had ended, so this heavy afternoon rain was unusual.

He approached the small hut on the edge of the village, initially walking past it. Then he pivoted and crossed the muddy road at an angle. His eyes searched the area on both sides of the road and past the hut. No one was around. Every sensible human had sought some shelter from the deluge.

The retired Green Beret did not expect that anyone had any interest in him. But it paid to remain alert. An American traveling out of Vientiane, the capital of Laos, was unusual. At five feet eight inches tall, his thin physique did not stand out among the native population. His tanned complexion, unobtrusive nose, and black, close-cropped hair helped him to blend into the scenery. Dobie favored dressing like the locals, especially when traveling away from the city. He also favored eating like the natives, too. He preferred the squash, sweet potatoes, and carrots in the local diets. A Green Beret doctor had once noted the prevalence of carotenemia among those eating the local diet. Dobie figured it helped him blend in.

Dobie crossed the road and entered the hut. It was a teahouse of sorts. The faint odor of ammonia told Dobie that a back room served more serious habits. In the flickering light of the lanterns, he spotted his old compatriot in a corner, facing the door. Two cups of tea were on the table.

"*Sabai-di baw?*" Dobie greeted Marcel.

Marcel smiled.

"Adding a little Lao to your language skills?" Marcel's English still contained the accent of a native French speaker.

"Probably enough to get me into trouble."

Dobie reached to shake Marcel's hand as he sat down.

"Where's Keej?" Dobie asked as he scanned the corners of the small room.

"Outside, watching,"

"I didn't see him."

"Exactly," Marcel responded with a slight smile.

"How is the family?" Rather than get right down to business, Dobie wanted to check on life among the Hmong.

"Doing as fine as we can expect."

"Trouble up north?"

"Always."

"But everyone is healthy?"

"For now," Marcel stated. "But not all in the village are so fortunate."

"Casualties?" Dobie inquired.

Marcel nodded.

"Are the deliveries of rice and other needs reliable?" Dobie continued.

"Less so than usual. The village chief has decided to grow some rice instead of only poppies. But we've had to move to find a place to grow."

"Prudent idea of growing some rice," Dobie agreed. "Trends for the future are not encouraging. Waiting for a handout of food from strangers is never good. Especially from a government. Ask any American Indian."

"We see an increase in supplies coming across the borders from the east and north. It has pushed us south and west. Preparations for an offensive, it looks like."

"While your supplies have declined," Dobie added.

Marcel nodded.

"And the Pathet Lao has pushed us west of the Plain of Jars along the Nam Xong River," Marcel added. "Too many to find enough space on hills to grow rice or poppies. The soil is not as good, and it's warmer than our mountains. Much illness."

"How about moving further west?"

"Not good. There is much trouble among the Chinese, Shans, and others."

"Not a viable option, then," Dobie acknowledged, sipping his tea.

"Some of us hope the Americans don't make the mistake the French made with our people in Tonkin."

Dobie noted that the former Foreign Legion paratrooper referred to the Hmong as if he was one of them. But living with them for twenty years and marrying a Hmong leader's daughter made Marcel one of them.

Not wanting to make any assumptions, Dobie asked, "Which mistake?"

"Taking the Hmong for granted."

"How so?"

"The French forced the Tonkin Hmong to sell their crop to the Tai people. Tais paid very low prices for the crop. So the Hmong came to hate the French more than they hated the Viet Minh. The Hmong lugged all that heavy artillery through the mountains that surrounded Dien Bien Phu."

"It sounds like working with your general is not going well," Dobie ventured.

Marcel nodded, glancing around.

"We have no one else to sell our opium to. While he pays a respectable price, we know he sells at a good profit. He grows rich while we die. Many villages have no more young men."

Well, Dobie wondered, *maybe working with me will look good.*

He decided it was time to get down to the business of this meeting.

"Any intel to report on my current interest?"

"Keej and I investigated two sites we heard about," Marcel began. "With so much activity, we could not get to a third. Only one had anything curious."

"Such as?" Dobie encouraged.

"A Pathet Lao unit held three prisoners on a ledge in front of a small cave. Guards were high above, who lowered food and firewood to them. Other patrols were in the area."

"American prisoners?" Dobie prodded.

"Couldn't tell."

"Not forced to work," Dobie replied, "suggests they could be high-value captives."

"Perhaps."

"Aren't prisoners usually forced to work?" Dobie pressed. "To grow their food, at the minimum."

"Yes," Marcel agreed.

"Where was this?"

"Around twenty klicks south of the old Lima Site 85."

"Far from Sam Neua, where we know they hold local prisoners."

"Yes, far southwest of there."

"So they could disperse prisoners away from known locations," Dobie suggested. "Any reports of prisoners remaining around Sam Neua?"

"Too dangerous to get any closer. The activity there continues to increase. Supplies are going there as well as south."

"So nothing definitive to base any action on," Dobie stated.

"There is one other piece of info," Marcel went on. Dobie's ears perked up. "I have heard of a deserter from the North Vietnamese Army who has a ring to sell."

"What kind of ring?"

"Supposedly a class ring from a US military academy."

"Really?" Dobie leaned forward. "That would be very unusual for an American POW to have a class ring with him."

"I thought so, too," replied Marcel. "Except this ring has a name inscribed on the inside."

"What name? I can check it against known MIAs."

"The deserter claims the name is not on any of the POW lists provided by the North Vietnamese."

"How would he know who was on the lists?"

Marcel shrugged. "The name on the ring is something like Catuin Rooso. During interrogations, the deserter gave different pronunciations and drawings of the script. He also said the number 63 was on the side of it."

"Did he have the ring?"

Marcel shook his head.

"He claimed to know where it is and that he could get it, for a price."

"Of course," Dobie nodded. "Did he say how he came to see the ring?"

"Claimed that he took it from the pilot after capturing him. It looked like gold, so the deserter thought he could sell it. Taking something from a captive and not turning it in is a big no-no. So the guy has kept it hidden."

"What supposedly happened to the captive?"

"Unknown," Marcel admitted. "The deserter's unit turned the prisoner over to another squad."

"When and where was the prisoner captured? That could help validate the name against one of the MIAs."

"All he said was in Laos in early 1968."

Dobie thought for a few seconds.

"What do you plan to do with this info?" Marcel inquired.

"Let me check on the name and the year on the ring. An old friend is back in Saigon in an intel slot. You remember Captain Nickerson?"

Marcel nodded.

"In Saigon, the Americans have an MIA unit that is negotiating to get info on the remaining MIAs."

"How's that going, I wonder," Marcel mused.

"You can guess. I hear the Gooks only read propaganda statements at every meeting and give zilch. A ring with a name matching an MIA case will interest the American team."

Their conversation paused for several seconds.

"Any changes to comm procedures?" Dobie asked.

"Do you still have a contact to pass a message through to me?"

"So far," Dobie replied. "But the spooks are getting a little harder to work with, especially on MIA questions. I need to buy radios for us. Then we can talk directly."

"The spooks may fear Special Forces tripping over the transportation business they run for us."

"Could be," Dobie agreed. "The North Vietnamese aren't the only ones who don't want Special Forces stomping through your jungles. Did your product get to market last spring with no trouble?"

"It seemed to take longer. Profits are reduced with all those Americans gone. Hence, the decision to plant some rice along with the poppies."

"I'll be in touch," Dobie stated. "To avoid talking about a ring on an open frequency, let's call it Tinkerbell."

Marcel nodded. "We should change our radio call signs."

Dobie thought.

"I'll be Pan," Dobie said.

"Then I'll be Hook," Marcel chuckled.

"How about setting a time to talk," Dobie continued, looking at his watch. "Let's use 0639 Zulu."

Marcel nodded.

"Let's broadcast in the clear, 'Let's talk.' Then be on the usual primary frequency at the next 0639."

Dobie nodded.

"Good luck on your trip back."

"You take care, as well."

Marcel rose and walked to the hut's door. Dobie finished his tea. He raised his cup to the Lao behind the counter along the wall. Another cup arrived.

He knew he had time before his ride back to Vientiane would arrive. *Might as well stay dry a little longer*, Dobie figured.

Dobie watched a patron walk through the door. The customer did not look around, but he went straight to the door to the back room. Dobie knew what it was for. He had smelled it the second he had walked in. People frying their brains on opium or heroin fascinated Dobie.

How did they think that creating a bigger problem in their meager lives solves any other problem? But Dobie recognized that reasoned thought evaded an addict.

Dobie finished his tea. He could hear that the hard rain had eased. Waiting in the wet trees beside the road for a long time was less attractive than sitting here. Yet, it would allow him to listen to a quiet jungle after a rain. He rose and headed for the door. He walked back down the road to the pickup point for his ride.

Over the last twenty months, Dobie had spent no time in the jungle. Like any skill, understanding the sounds of the rainforest required constant practice. He also did his best thinking while sitting quietly against a tree. Dobie found the curve in the road where his ride would pick him up. It gave a good view in both directions, eliminating any surprises as his ride stopped. If someone was on the road in one direction, the pickup could move around the curve.

By the time Dobie found a tree off the road with brush around it, the rain had stopped. He lowered himself to the ground, keeping the back of his poncho under him to use as a seat. He was early, which was good. Improved light told Dobie that the rain clouds were dissipating high above the tall trees.

As he sat there, he listened to the sounds. His experience had taught him that birds made the most useful sounds. During his tour with the Montagnards in Vietnam's Central Highlands, Dobie had learned the names of birds and their calls. He knew the English word for only a few of the bird species. The "Yards" had taught him not only the calls but also the different message in the call. A mating call differed from a warning shriek. It was crucial to recognize the difference. People sneaking through the brush toward him would not cause a bird to sing a mating call. Monkeys were useful in the same way. The shriek of a monkey warning of an intruder had alerted him to trouble on more than one occasion. His Yard friends had also taught him to recognize a poor imitation of a call. A Yard companion recognizing a human making the call had saved his hide twice.

As Dobie listened, his mind turned to Marcel's info. The cave with the prisoners would require more information. Could he convince Marcel or Keej to lead him there? The presence of nearby Pathet Lao troops raised the danger level. Some troops would guard the prisoners. However, the movement of other patrols would create a major challenge. What could he offer Marcel to make it worth the risk?

One skill that Dobie had learned over his tours in these forests was figuring out what motivated its natives. They were no different in that regard than people anywhere. The Hmong had a strong loyalty to their family first and to their village second. Food and sustenance topped their hierarchy of needs in the harsh jungle environment.

The mountain peoples of Indochina were useful allies in the war because other inhabitants had harassed them. The Communists had a penchant for stealing the crops of the mountain people, whether it was rice or poppies. That the Viet Minh before or the Viet Cong today called it a "people's" tax was irrelevant. So, the Montagnards and the Hmong were eager allies when given the chance to kill Communists.

Enticing Marcel to search for remaining POWs required some thought. Dobie had no resources of his own to offer. One potential source was a magazine publisher, who asked the opinions of many in the military. He kept asking if the rush to peace had abandoned American POWs in Southeast Asia. The publisher, a special ops veteran from World War II, wanted to bring any remaining POWs home. Financing a rescue would guarantee him the story. The circulation of his magazine, *Direct Action*, would skyrocket.

But were live POWs still held in Laos or North Vietnam? If there were survivors, time was their enemy. They would remain alive only so long. Gaping holes in the Communist lists meant one thing. The Communists knew a lot more about the MIAs than they admitted. Dobie figured the probabilities favored POWs in Laos rather than North Vietnam. Most unresolved MIAs resulted from the bombing of the Ho Chi Minh Trail in eastern Laos or the Plain of Jars in central Laos. Marcel's location of the cave with prisoners could hold captives from either location.

The ring intrigued Dobie. One obvious question argued against its authenticity. Why would a flyer have it with him, especially in Laos? Flyers in the covert war would sanitize their uniforms and possessions before missions in Laos. Yet, Dobie knew command posts routinely diverted planes to targets of opportunity.

The ring had to be investigated. Even if its owner was dead, it would confirm the Commies knew what had happened to him. Dobie recognized that bringing back some evidence of any MIA was second in importance to a live POW.

Dobie sat for several minutes, paying attention to the jungle. Its peaceful silence changed as a few birds began to sing as the rain stopped. He could see streams of light high in the trees above him. The afternoon rain shower gave way to the sun. He slid his poncho off as the warmth from the emerging sun penetrated from above. He shifted his shoulder holster so it wouldn't chafe on his skin through his damp undershirt.

Dobie inhaled deeply, savoring the odors. Wet hardwood leaves mixed with decaying branches on the forest floor. The musty smell combined with the fragrant blossoms, giving the jungle a unique scent. Yet the rain had left its clean scent behind. Dobie had spent countless hours in the pine forests of North Carolina. The mix of pine needles and sand was no match for the floral fragrance of the tropical forest.

Why was he here? The question cropped up often during his frequent, idle moments. The simplest explanation was that he sensed unfinished business in Southeast Asia. As a twenty-five-year lieutenant colonel in the Special Forces, the Army had told him he was no longer needed. He would never make a full colonel. He had pissed off a general at the wrong point in his career. His Army pension, though modest by civilian standards, met his inexpensive habits.

He could have worked for a US company in a security role. While stateside desk jobs were available, he would loathe them. Working security for a contractor in Southeast Asia was a better option. But that meant dealing with another chain of command.

On his own, he was free to define a mission. Finding any American abandoned by the sleazy politicians was a noble cause. He could correct a grievous wrong perpetrated by the politicians. He would also dictate how to accomplish the mission. No REMF, rear echelon motherfucker, would tell him with no explanation. Importantly, no staff weenie would tell him how *not* to do it. Constraining rules of engagement usually endangered lives.

The nagging question, though, often plagued Dobie. *Are there American prisoners that need rescuing?* Dobie concluded, *There could be.* In reality, no one would know unless someone went looking. Dobie knew that the government, including the military, would demand undeniable proof. The likelihood of finding such proof was close to zero.

His next step had to be to talk to Jeff Nickerson. Jeff could confirm the name on the ring. He might also provide some intel on the activity in northern Laos and along the Trail. Dobie knew the Air Force and Navy flew reconnaissance flights. A few planes had gone down, adding to the MIA list. Their shoot-down locations could be a starting point.

As soon as he got to Vientiane, he would find a way to Saigon to meet Jeff. He couldn't discuss what he needed to know over the phone. His retiree ID card provided access to Air Force cargo flights. Failing that, he would try Air America, the CIA's airline. He still knew a few old hands who did freelance work for the spooks. As a last resort, commercial flights still operated. But that cost money, and carrying his Colt .45 could be a problem. Commercial flights coming out of the Golden Triangle also received special attention.

Once he gathered more information, he would decide on a course of action. Then, he would contact the magazine publisher. Any operation required equipment and supplies, as well as personnel. Dobie felt confident that a couple of former Special Forces veterans would be easy to recruit. He needed to locate his prime recruit. Marcel and Keej would be his biggest recruitment challenge.

A bird's warning call interrupted Dobie's thoughts. Then the forest became quiet. A battered jeep wound its way down the rutted road. As it approached his position, the driver scanned both sides of the road. Dobie looked both ways. Satisfied that no one was around, he stood and stepped on the edge of the road. His ride stopped momentarily as Dobie climbed into the jeep. Then, it continued on its journey to Vientiane.

———◦———

CLICKER UNDERSTANDS

Former Captain Eugene "Clicker" Cruthers, United States Marine Corps, slammed the front door of his house in Bien Hoa, South Vietnam. He threw his flight bag near the stairs and placed his helmet bag next to it. His skin was hot and sweaty, and he was angry. He needed a shower, but he wanted a drink. He had to think.

Mai, his diminutive Vietnamese house girl, padded in from the kitchen. Clicker's furrowed brow and clenched fists were her first clue about his frame of mind. The surefire way to know his mood was the source of his nickname. He clicked his tongue rapidly. She knew the habit from working at the Bachelor Officer Quarters at Chu Lai seven years earlier.

Clicker tried to smile at her. It didn't work.

"Would you like a drink, Captain Gene?" she asked. Mai continued to address him that way, even though he had encouraged her to call him Gene or Clicker.

When Clicker had arrived at Bien Hoa six months earlier, he had gone to Chu Lai to find her. He had last seen her in 1972 on his final cruise in the South China Sea. Clicker knew she was dependable and needed a good job. She supported herself and her seven-year-old son, Lei. Mai's immediate family had died in the twenty years of war. Survivors of her extended family had scattered around the country.

Lei's father had been a US Marine lance corporal. He had died in the fighting in Hue, Mai's hometown, during the Tet Offensive in 1968. Another Marine pilot in Chu Lai had known the corporal and got Mai the job at the BOQ. The Marine pilots had adopted Mai as their little sister.

"Yes, I would, Mai," Clicker responded.

"I'll bring a gin and tonic to you on the porch."

"Make it a strong one, please." Clicker headed up the stairs to change out of his stuffy flight suit. He took a quick shower, thankful that he wasn't staying in Marine quarters with undependable warm water. Minutes later, he was back down in comfortable shorts and a tropical shirt. Before Clicker headed to the porch, he grabbed a folder from his flight bag.

He sat in his favorite wicker chair and put the folder on the table beside it. Mai brought him the drink.

"Thank you."

"Will you need a refill soon?"

Having managed the house for six months, Mai was familiar with Clicker's habits after a hard day. One other pilot had lived with them in the house, but he had finished his year's contract and had gone back to the States. Clicker had told Mai another pilot was coming soon. Soon meant tomorrow. Clicker had to meet him at Tan Son Nhut Air Base in Saigon.

"Don't worry about it. I'll fix myself any refreshers. Just fix dinner when you and Lei want to eat. I'll get mine when I want it."

Mai bowed and smiled in response. She padded back to the kitchen.

Clicker sipped the drink. Mai had made it strong in a tall glass. Clicker took a second sip and reached for the folder. It contained basic information about the pilot. He opened the company envelope, expecting the worst. Scanning the information produced a pleasant surprise.

The pilot looked highly qualified, maybe even a little overqualified. Clicker read the basic information in the file. A new master's degree in electrical engineering from Texas A&M University. Bachelor's degree in engineering from the same university.

Couldn't find an engineering job, Clicker concluded. *Why else would he return to a war zone? Poor bastard probably doesn't know it's still a war zone,* Clicker mused. He continued reading.

A former Air Force F-105 pilot, he saw. The Thud pilot wore the Air Force's 100-Missions over North Vietnam Patch with two tours in Thailand. His second one was in 1972 as a Wild Weasel pilot, a surface-to-air missile hunter.

The guy must have balls, Clicker concluded. He knew killing SAMs was a dangerous assignment filled by volunteers.

Then he saw the note that caused Clicker to pause. The guy's wife and four-year-old son would join him in two weeks. Clicker scratched his head after he read that.

They have no clue the war is not over.

Clicker sipped his drink. He had grown fond of Vietnamese women. It was one reason he had taken this job. *Still, a "round-eye" woman would offer variety to the scenery*, Clicker thought.

He recognized he was already making assumptions about the wife. Living in the same house with the husband could make any rendezvous challenging. But she apparently found fighter pilots attractive.

Clicker searched the folder, hoping to find a picture of the wife. He only found a grainy photo of Rick Guerri, no snapshot of the wife.

He put the sheets back into the folder and drained his drink. Time for a refresher, he decided. As Clicker fixed a fresh gin and tonic, he thought about this new guy. A Texas Aggie was a good thing, he knew. They would have similar backgrounds. As a graduate of the Virginia Military Institute, Clicker would understand an Aggie. State military schools had similar curriculums. Clicker held a low opinion of graduates of The Citadel, South Carolina's military academy. It was almost the same opinion he held of Annapolis graduates. Most were insufferable, except for the ones who were Marines. He assumed West Pointers were the same. Clicker was unsure of Zoomies, Air Force Academy graduates. He had never met one of those. Hopefully, the academy was new enough that they hadn't yet become entitled jerks.

Clicker sat back down in his chair and took a drink.

Sip, he reminded himself. After the last two days, he felt like guzzling it.

Clicker wasn't only an instructor pilot to the South Vietnamese Air Force F-5 pilots. He was also the manufacturer's technical representative in South Vietnam. As such, he also became involved in maintenance issues. The South Vietnamese Air Force often relied on his mechanical engineering to address problems. But this last problem did not require his engineering knowledge. He wasn't sure what skills it required.

A damaged F-5 had been sitting on the tarmac at Pleiku, 225 miles north of Bien Hoa. Battle damage over the Ho Chi Minh Trail had caused an engine fire, forcing the pilot to shut it down. With military aid to South Vietnam cut in half by the US Congress, the South Vietnamese needed every airplane it had. The jet needed fixing so it could fly again. A mechanic had inspected the jet and reported that it needed a new engine. That meant heavy maintenance at an airport that wasn't equipped for it. A new engine with tools and equipment had to fly to Pleiku.

That was the problem. Driving there was not an option. A transport aircraft was not available to send mechanics, an engine, and their equipment to Pleiku. It had been the answer for two days.

A Vietnamese colonel had offered a Huey. The helicopter was too small to carry everything. A larger Chinook helicopter would work, but the answer had been the same as for a cargo plane.

The longer the fighter sat at Pleiku, the higher the likelihood that local thieves would strip it. So far, the Vietnamese Army Rangers had protected the plane. They understood its importance to their fight. But any hotspot could demand their presence at any minute.

Clicker knew the "no aircraft" response was bullshit. At least one Chinook stood on the Bien Hoa ramp every day. Lieutenant Colonel Ngo Tinh, the squadron commander of the damaged jet's pilot, also knew it was bullshit. He had talked to the helicopter squadron commander. He had called Tan Son Nhut to search for a transport aircraft. With Clicker going to Tan Son Nhut to pick up the new American pilot, the colonel gave Clicker the name of a crew chief to contact. Sergeant Khắc managed the maintenance of a C-123 cargo plane. Colonel Tinh knew the crew chief, as he was a second cousin to Colonel Tinh's wife. The sergeant was expecting Clicker.

"Sergeant Khắc will help us find a plane," Colonel Tinh had assured Clicker.

The next morning, Clicker headed to Tan Son Nhut. He wore his flight suit to avoid extra questions as he scurried around the air base to locate the sergeant. He threw a pair of shorts, a tropical shirt, and sandals into the back seat to wear to meet Rick Guerri. Clicker hoped to spend the morning locating a plane. The new pilot was arriving at two in the afternoon on a commercial flight.

Clicker found the maintenance hangar to meet Sergeant Khắc. The sergeant was on the flight line, working on his aircraft. Clicker parked his car at the nose of the C-123. The Provider, the Air Force's name for the model, was not a large transport. But it was large enough for the F-5 maintenance team. It was a twin-engine, piston-powered airplane from the early 1950s. Yet, the small jet engines next to the large reciprocating engines surprised Clicker.

As Clicker stepped out of his car, a Vietnamese Air Force sergeant walked over.

"Sergeant Khắc?" Clicker inquired.

"Yes," the sergeant replied.

"Did Colonel Tinh explain our problem to you?"

"He did," Sergeant Khắc replied in fluent English.

"Colonel Tinh thought you could help."

The sergeant shrugged. He looked around, then led Clicker on the side of the car away from the airplane.

"Our generals keep transports in reserve for their special missions."

"Special missions?"

"High priority cargo. For the generals."

Clicker's brow furrowed. He gave Sergeant Khắc a questioning look.

"Special cargo," the sergeant clarified.

Clicker guessed what this was. He had heard rumors. Colonel Tinh had even hinted at it. Clicker was tired of innuendos. The sergeant needed to be explicit.

"What special cargo?" he pressed.

The sergeant hesitated. Clicker waited. Sergeant Khắc looked around.

"Heroin," he finally muttered.

Clicker nodded. His shoulders sagged. Clicker finally admitted to himself something he had suspected for months. He was fighting a losing battle in South Vietnam. Clicker could no longer hide from reality. He understood.

Screw them, then, Clicker concluded. *It's their damn war.*

The F-5 could stay in Pleiku; looters could have it in pieces.

———•———

MR. RICK ARRIVES

W hen Rick informed his new boss that Sue and David would go with him to Saigon, he initially met some resistance. But when he told him he wouldn't take the job otherwise, the company quickly relented. Besides, he could stay in Saigon for the entire year of his contract. The company would save the cost of round-trip tickets to the States for the duration of Rick's contract.

Rick breezed through his training. The company's instructors, who were experienced fighter pilots and combat veterans, trained Rick. They had a few tricks up their sleeves, which surprised Rick when they first pulled one. Their favorite one was repeating an instruction Rick gave when they played the role of a South Vietnamese student. Then, they would exaggerate doing the opposite.

"Tôi sẽ lái máy bay," Rick learned to say. "I'll fly the aircraft." He'd correct the mistake, repeat the instruction, then say, "You try it now."

Getting the feel of the F-5 took no time. It wasn't as complex as the F-105, and Rick had flown a version of the jet in pilot training. While advertised as a supersonic fighter, it didn't have the speed of the Thud. That would be less critical in the missions the Vietnamese flew.

None of them flew against the intense air defenses around Hanoi. The South Vietnamese Air Force flew primarily close air support missions for the army. Precision low-level bombing and strafing were the principal skills required. Occasionally, the South Vietnamese Air Force would attack a convoy on the Ho Chi Minh Trail. The intensity of anti-aircraft fire, though, dissuaded the generals from using their precious planes on the Trail.

After a month of training, his instructors deemed Rick ready for the real South Vietnamese students. Sue reluctantly agreed to follow Rick to Saigon after two weeks. He convinced her he needed to find a place to live before she and David arrived.

As the World Airways airliner approached Tan Son Nhut Air Base, Rick gazed at the midday haze over Saigon. Rick had flown into the air base twice during his tours in Southeast Asia. Both had been quick trips for conferences at Seventh Air Force Headquarters. As the jet turned to final approach, Rick noticed anti-aircraft batteries around the airport. He wondered whether they were still active.

Stepping out of the plane's door onto the stairway, the heat and humidity enveloped his body. By the time he reached the bottom of the stairs, his short-sleeved tropical shirt was damp from perspiration.

At least I'm not wearing starched fatigues, he thought.

He had forgotten how oppressive the Southeast Asian heat could be. By the end of his two tours in Thailand, he had adapted to the heat, even though he remembered he never stopped perspiring. He wondered if Sue would rethink her insistence on being here with him.

Rick was relieved when the last official pounded the last stamp on his passport and waved him on. He walked through the door into the arrival hall, scanning the crowd for someone with his name on a card. Dragon Air Associates, the company that employed him, promised another pilot would meet him.

To his right, Rick spotted a lanky, tanned man waving a paper with "Rick" printed in block letters. As he approached Rick, the man extended his right hand.

"Rick, glad to meet you. I'm Gene Cruthers. Everyone calls me Clicker, though."

Rick put his B-4 bag down and shifted his leather briefcase to his left hand to shake Clicker's outstretched hand.

"Clicker, glad to meet you."

"Let me get that," Clicker replied as he reached for the heavy bag. "Didn't have any trouble finding you. Your company picture looks like you."

Rick sized up his fellow pilot. The handshake was firm, but not crushing. Clicker was clearly a civilian. His hair was well outside military grooming standards. His sideburns were full, down to the bottom of his ear. The hair hung over his ears by at least an inch and extended over his collar as well. He wasn't quite what Rick had expected. He looked older than Rick by ten years. Crow's feet spread from his eyes, which looked slightly bloodshot. One eye seemed to float as Clicker shifted his gaze. As Clicker turned to lead the way, Rick noticed a bald spot on the top of his head. Clicker wore loose, lightweight shorts. Leather sandals were on his feet. The shirt was loose-fitting, and while it appeared clean, it had a heavily worn look.

Outside the terminal, Clicker led Rick through the throng along the street to an old Citroen at the curb. The car had seen better days. Faded green paint and several dents marred the car's sides and rear. Clicker put a key into the trunk lock, raised it, and tossed in the B-4 bag. He slammed it down and jiggled it to ensure it locked.

"I'd hold the briefcase on your lap," he suggested as he went to the driver's side.

Clicker steered the car into the moving traffic. Its roar on acceleration revealed it needed a new muffler. Exiting the main gate to Tan Son Nhut, they maneuvered around the cars, oxcarts, and people in the street. Rick noticed Clicker used the horn more often than the brakes. Gone was the smell of jet fuel at the airport. Now, exhaust fumes competed with the odor of humanity and stifling humidity. As they passed an open-air market, aging vegetables and unrefrigerated meat added their aromas.

Rick tried to remember the traffic on his two other trips to Saigon. Riding in a car was different. On his other visits, he had been in a military bus with wire mesh covering the open windows. Some Viet Cong sympathizer couldn't lob a grenade into the bus through the mesh. The biggest change, though, was the composition of the traffic. He saw no olive-drab military vehicles on the streets now. Before, military jeeps and trucks had been everywhere. Military uniforms on the street were rare now, as well. Today the street teemed with motor scooters, taxis, bikes, and rickshaws.

Well, Rick thought, *maybe the Peace Agreement meant something to the suffering Vietnamese.*

As Clicker maneuvered the Citroen around a couple of corners, Rick tried to pay attention. He looked for street signs; a couple hung on poles. They were faded and hard to read at a glance. The heavy traffic and pedestrians did not give the driver time to study them. He'd have to rely on visual cues to learn his way around.

"Been here before?" Clicker asked as he noticed Rick studying the surrounding throngs.

"Twice. Once in '68 and once in late '72. Both quick in-and-out trips from Thailand."

"So you didn't have much chance to enjoy the nightlife?"

"Not really."

"Well, we can do that before your wife and kid get here. When do they arrive?"

"In a couple of weeks."

Clicker chuckled as Rick shifted his gaze toward two young, pretty Vietnamese women in their colorful long dresses.

"Enough time to sample the local massage parlors."

He took his hand off the stick shift to make quotation marks around the word "massage."

"Not my style," Rick replied.

"To each his own," Clicker rejoined. For the first time, Rick heard his companion's tongue click. "But Saigon can be a bachelor's dream place."

When Rick said nothing, Clicker added, "Well, your wife ... Sharon is it? Must be a special gal. Gutsy, too, to come here."

"Sue is her name. Why gutsy?"

"Well, few of the military bring their wives or families. More of the diplomatic and civilian government employees do. The war is only on pause, sort of."

"Well, maybe neither of us understood the actual situation here."

Clicker laughed. "Shit, no one does. Least of all those politicians or the 'fourth estate' that are always trying to pump you for a scoop."

"My first time in Thailand," Rick answered, "we had a couple of pilots whose wives lived in town outside the base. No kids, though."

"Well, the Thais didn't take any shit from the Commies. When I was TDY in Thailand in '66, one wife was there. Kind of cramped a lot of our styles, though."

"Do you have a wife in the States?" Rick had noticed Clicker had no rings on either hand. But he felt he needed to ask.

"Just two ex-wives."

"Remote tours and cruises on carriers are hard on a marriage," Rick conceded.

"Yeah," Clicker agreed. "But coming home and giving the little lady the clap didn't help, either." Clicker chuckled.

"Well, I guess my first order of business, other than getting checked out, is to find a house or apartment."

"As your official sponsor," Clicker responded, clicking his tongue again, "I have a viable solution."

"That would help."

"Two of us can live in an old Frenchman's large house close to the base in Bien Hoa. The company bought it and divided it into apartments. There is a two-bedroom available. Kitchen and eating area, small living room, and one bathroom with a shower."

"Sounds adequate."

"It's ten minutes from our office on base," Clicker said as he wheeled the car around a bicycle taxi.

"How far from here?" Rick inquired

"The house is about an hour from Tan Son Nhut."

"I'm not sure how I'll adjust to the tropics again," Rick stated as he wiped the perspiration off his eyebrows. "Might be the biggest adjustment for Sue. Living in the summer humidity of south Texas is different."

"Well, we have window air conditioning units at our villa," Clicker announced. "When the electricity doesn't go out, that is. And we have plastic to cover the windows to keep the AC inside. Velcro holds them in place, so we can roll them up when the electricity goes out."

The drive to the house went by fast. Rick realized that learning the sights to navigate anywhere would take a few trips.

Clicker swung the car into a narrow driveway with an open metal gate. The driveway widened as Clicker pulled around the back of a large, two-story frame house.

"Have to talk to Binh about keeping the gate closed," Clicker stated.

"Why's that?"

"To slow down the curious with sticky fingers. We lock it at night."

"And Binh is?" Rick asked.

"He keeps the grounds mowed and the plants healthy. He is a combination yard boy and light security." Clicker's tongue clicked. "He's still learning the security part."

Rick looked over the small yard. It was well maintained. The house stood a couple of feet off the ground on rock pillars. A broad, screened-in porch wrapped around the front and sides. The house had a recent paint job of bright yellow.

"Home sweet home," Clicker announced.

Rick grabbed his B-4 bag from the trunk and followed Clicker through the back door.

A short Vietnamese woman in a small parlor at the rear greeted them as they walked in.

"Welcome," she said in accented English, as she gave a slight bow.

"Mai," Clicker said. "This is Mr. Rick. He will stay with us for a while, or maybe permanently."

Unsure of the Vietnamese custom for an introduction, Rick smiled.

"It's a pleasure to meet you, Mai," Rick responded, bowing slightly.

"I am honored to meet you, Mr. Rick." Mai returned Rick's bow.

"Please, call me Rick."

"Mai is our house girl," Clicker explained. "She keeps our house clean and in tip-top shape. Give her an hour's warning, and she can do marvels with Vietnamese cuisine. She can also fix a mean gin and tonic or whiskey and soda." He motioned to a wet bar next to a door that led to the side porch. "We can drop your stuff in the apartment, then kick back while I give you your first in-briefing over drinks. Or you can take a nap to work off the jet lag."

"A nap sounds good," Rick replied. He looked at his watch. "I figure I've been traveling about thirty hours or so. What's the local time?"

"Ten minutes to three ... on February fifth. I'll show you upstairs to the apartment."

Clicker led Rick down a short hall and up a staircase in the middle of the first floor. The stairs had a landing that reversed direction. It opened onto a hall that led to the front and back of the house.

"Your apartment is at the back of the house," Clicker explained. "Better to give some buffer from the street noise."

Rick dropped his bag and briefcase inside the door to the small living room.

"I don't figure you need a tour," Clicker offered, again with a click of his tongue. "My apartment is the front one." He motioned back up the hall. "Just knock if you wake up for cocktails or some food. We have a full kitchen on the first floor. Mai can fix you some fried rice or something quick. She has a room off the kitchen that she shares with her seven-year-old son."

After Clicker left, Rick surveyed the apartment. It seemed a little smaller than the one in College Station. And that was with sparse furniture. The living room had one rattan couch and a small rattan rocking chair. A painted crate was the coffee table. The eat-in kitchen had a round wooden table and four cane chairs. The kitchen was a basic L-design. Small counters and cabinets flanked a sink with a window above. A cooktop was on the right wall with an oven below. Around the corner of the counter, a small refrigerator stood.

The bathroom with its shower stood at the end of the short hall. Rick turned on the hot water on the vanity. Cold water flowed. He left it running while he checked out the bedrooms.

Two bedrooms flanked the bathroom, each with a small closet. One bedroom had a double bed and a small dresser, while the other one had a single bed and another small dresser. Rick assumed Mai had made the beds with light floral blankets. He sat on the double bed and took off his shoes. The mattress felt okay. Rick returned to check on the hot water. It had turned warm but not hot. He'd have to ask Clicker about it.

Returning to the bedroom, he sat on the bed, then stretched out his legs and turned to his side. The place would do fine for him, he decided. He knew Sue would find the space disappointing. She had often said how she looked forward to living in their own house again.

Finding a place to live had been his biggest concern. He had to think about how to make it more attractive before Sue and David arrived. But how? Clicker did not impress him as having any talent in interior decorating. Maybe fresh paint, a couple of pictures, and an upgraded coffee table in the small living room would improve the apartment for Sue.

He would have to scramble to prepare the small apartment for their arrival. Clicker and Mai could help him locate a few pieces of furniture to augment its austere decor. American workers returning to the States should be eager to sell items at reasonable prices.

Just before Sue and David arrived, he would ask Mai to go to the market and buy items for their meals. Even with Mai preparing most of the meals, Sue would want to learn Vietnamese cooking. It would give her one project to keep her hours occupied. He wondered how she would fill the rest of her time. The Defense Attaché Office and the American Embassy offered the only employment opportunities for Americans. But they were too far away in Saigon.

He also needed to buy a used car. He hadn't decided how much he wanted to drive in Bien Hoa, but having a car would give them the option. He'd have to ask Clicker how to go about that.

As the fatigue from the long trip overtook him, he doubted his decision to accept this job. Maybe he hadn't thought through what it would be like to live on the economy in Vietnam. He had spent little time off base during his two tours in Thailand. Saigon was not a tour to which military people brought their families. A large military base with a base exchange and a commissary for groceries was absent. His information packet said Tan Son Nhut had a small commissary and a small BX.

What have I signed up for? Rick wondered as he fell asleep. *Was I hasty in jumping at the first job with good pay?*

Rick slept for two hours. When he opened his eyes, he could feel the beads of perspiration on his forehead. The room was hot. He slid off the bed on the side with the air conditioner mounted into the wall. He turned it cooler.

Rather than try to go back to sleep, he checked his watch. Since it was nearly five o'clock, he decided to stay awake until his usual bedtime.

Might as well start figuring out this job here, Rick decided.

He walked down the hall to Clicker's apartment and tapped on the door. When he received no response, he headed down the stairs. He found Clicker on a side porch reviewing some paperwork.

"Winning the battle against jet lag?" Clicker inquired.

"Some. I thought if you had time, we could start the in-briefing you mentioned."

"Sure. It's completely informal. No paperwork to fill out like in the military."

Clicker looked at his watch. "It's time for cocktails. Mai will start fixing dinner too, if you're up for some food."

"Both sound good."

"Help yourself to your beverage of choice while I let Mai know."

After Rick poured a whiskey, he sat in a comfortable rattan rocking chair on the porch. Clicker returned with his drink.

"As I recall from the info I received," Rick began, "we will work mainly with Lieutenant Colonel Ngo. At least, from the info, that was his last name."

"That is correct. But the Vietnamese custom is to refer to people by their given names, even with their titles."

"So we call him Colonel Tinh, then?" Rick asked.

"Correct. In the Vietnamese convention of putting the last name first, he is Lieutenant Colonel Ngo Tinh."

Rick nodded.

"Might need a little getting used to. What's your impression of him?"

"A thoroughly professional officer," Clicker answered. "And an excellent pilot. He insists we tolerate no slackness from his pilots."

"Good to hear."

"We train his instructor pilots, so they can train the line pilots. But we have to take care not to use our usual brash American approach with them. Like all of Asia, 'losing face' is a big deal."

Both sipped their drinks.

"Tomorrow," Clicker continues, "I'll take you to meet Colonel Tinh and show you around his squadron. We'll get your flight equipment, as well as a tour of our small office. We have a company maintenance rep that we share space with. I also serve as the Technical Rep for the company. We'll take a couple of familiarization flights in the following days."

A PLANE TO PLEIKU

Early the next morning, Rick walked down the stairs to Clicker eating breakfast on the side porch. Mai came from the kitchen.

"Would you like eggs and bacon, Mr. Rick?" she asked.

"Yes, Mai, I would," Rick replied. He eyed some sliced fruit on Clicker's plate. "What is the sliced fruit?"

"Mango," Clicker replied. "Mai, introduce Rick to mango."

"I tried it in Thailand," Rick answered. "Yes, Mai, some mango, too."

"How do you like eggs?" Mai asked.

"Scrambled, please. I'll come get coffee," he added.

Mai bowed and tiptoed back to the kitchen with Rick following her.

"How did you sleep?" Clicker asked when he returned with his coffee.

"Okay, but I definitely feel the jet lag."

"We'll be at the base just for the morning. We can plan your first flight in a couple of days."

An hour later, Clicker parked the Citroen in front of a small Bien Hoa Air Base building.

"We'll stop to see if Colonel Tinh is in," Clicker announced.

They found the Vietnamese Air Force commander in his cramped office. Clicker introduced Rick.

"Rick flew two tours flying the Thud up north," he finished his introduction. "That makes him an expert at dive-bombing."

The colonel nodded. Rick tried to study him without staring. The colonel stood several inches shorter than Rick's six feet one inch. He was lean, but he appeared wiry. His eyes did not lock onto Rick's when he spoke. Rick could tell, though, that the colonel was studying Rick in return.

"Excellent," the colonel replied to Clicker's last comment in excellent English.

The guy's probably been to training in the States, Rick concluded.

"Have you had the chance to visit the United States?" Rick inquired.

"Yes. I was fortunate to have my training in the F-5 in Arizona," Tinh replied. "Hotter than Saigon, even," he added.

"We always call it a dry heat," Rick offered.

"Hence, you only bake, but don't boil," Clicker added.

The colonel smiled. He turned to Clicker.

"What did you learn from Sergeant Khắc?"

"Not much, I'm afraid. It seems the general keeps transport on a short leash for his purposes."

"Heroin," Tinh replied.

The answer surprised Clicker. Such directness was not a characteristic he had noticed in Colonel Tinh before. Clicker nodded.

"Sergeant Khắc said the same thing."

Lieutenant Colonel Tinh sagged into his worn chair behind his desk.

"Greed by our generals will lose us this war," he said quietly, more to himself than to the two Americans. He looked up at Rick.

"I'm sorry you have to learn what we face here on your first day. But I hope it will not discourage you. My pilots need to learn to dive-bomb better. I hope you can help Clicker instill that in them. We are fortunate to have pilots like Clicker and you to help us."

Clicker sat in a chair, so Rick pulled a third chair over.

"Do you have any ideas on how to get to Pleiku to repair that plane?" the colonel asked Clicker.

"Sergeant Khắc promised to spread the word to all the crew chiefs of our need for an airplane. Unfortunately, he said notice for flights close to the border is very short. Like last minute," Clicker added.

"We need a couple of hours to get the equipment together, as well as the mechanics and their tools," Colonel Tinh mused. "Other than an engine, we don't have extra to set aside."

"Can we pre-position any of it at Pleiku?" Rick asked.

Colonel Tinh shook his head.

"We are lucky that the Army Rangers can protect the plane itself. But an attack can pull them out at any time. We would risk losing any other equipment we sent ahead of time if they have to leave."

"No Chinook helicopters are available to send the engine and equipment?" Rick posed.

Again, the colonel shook his head.

"We have the same problem with them as with the cargo aircraft."

"We'll have to hope we have time to get the engine, tools, and mechanics ready if an aircraft becomes available," Clicker concluded.

A Vietnamese airman walked briskly into the office. He and Colonel Tinh exchanged a few sentences in Vietnamese. The colonel punched a button on his phone and picked up the handset. He held a brief conversation and hung up. Tinh then issued instructions to the airman, who rushed out.

"Sergeant Khắc says a C-123 is leaving for Pleiku in two hours. If we can get two mechanics ready with their tools and equipment to Tan Son Nhut, they can hitch a ride to Pleiku."

Colonel Tinh stood and walked into the next room. Clicker followed with Rick behind them.

"What can we do to help?" Clicker asked.

"If your maintenance rep can help our mechanics get the engine on a truck ASAP, that would help."

"Let's go," Clicker told Rick as he headed to the door.

Clicker led Rick to the next building and into one of two adjoining offices. Another American sat at a desk with paperwork spread in front of him.

"George, meet our new pilot, Rick," Clicker said.

George stood and extended his hand to Rick.

"We have a shot at getting an engine to Pleiku." Clicker quickly explained the challenge to George.

The trio dashed out a door leading to a worn jeep. George raced across the tarmac to a nearby hangar and screeched to a halt. They sprinted into the hangar. Two Vietnamese airmen rolled a jet engine toward the hangar door.

The maintenance rep held a quick conversation in Vietnamese with the airman. Clicker seemed to follow their exchange. Rick wondered whether he should have taken a crash course in Vietnamese before flying here. Finishing his conversation, George turned to Rick and Clicker.

Rick's first thought was, *How will we get that heavy engine into the truck bed?*

As if reading his mind, George turned to Clicker and Rick.

"We need your help to load it."

George led them to the side of the hangar. Rick noticed a set of tracks stacked together.

"We borrowed these from the aerial port guys at Tan Son Nhut a couple of days ago. We need your muscle power to help roll that engine into the truck bed."

"Borrowed?" Clicker asked.

"Kind of on a long-term basis," George replied.

Rick and Clicker looked at each other.

"You think we can push that engine up to the truck bed using these?" Clicker posed.

"Maybe with five of us pushing."

"Does the truck have a winch?" Clicker asked.

"No," George conceded.

"I'd suggest finding an aircraft tug," Clicker answered.

George issued instructions to the Vietnamese mechanic who had followed them. The airman ran off.

By the time the three Americans had dragged the tracks over to the back of the truck, an aircraft tug pulled up. The group lined up the tracks to the engine's trailer wheels and secured the tracks to the truck's bed.

Twenty minutes later, the engine was secured on the truck bed. The team quickly loaded a few other pieces of equipment and toolboxes into the truck.

"Ready for a ride to Tan Son Nhut?" George asked.

"Do you think you'll need us?" Clicker asked.

"Hard to know."

"We'll follow you in my car," Clicker answered.

The traffic from Bien Hoa to Tan Son Nhut was unusually heavy. Instead of the usual hour, the drive took an extra thirty minutes. An accident between a bus and a pair of motor scooters clogged the usual route. Clicker followed the truck through backstreets around the traffic jam.

As they crossed the Saigon River, Rick looked at his watch.

"How much time do we have?" Clicker asked.

"It's nearly two hours since Colonel Tinh received the call."

"Hope the plane waits a few minutes. We're still ten minutes away."

As the truck turned onto the street approaching the Tan Son Nhut gate, Clicker dug his wallet out of his back pocket.

"Better get out your passport for the guard to check. Wish they had issued you your Department of Defense ID card before they sent you here."

The guard at the gate waved the truck through. As Clicker pulled beside the guard, he flashed his ID.

"We're with the truck. They have a jet engine we are loading onto an airplane."

The Vietnamese guard looked at the ID, then at Clicker.

"He's with me. He just arrived yesterday," Clicker stated as the guard's gaze shifted to Rick's passport. The guard waved them through.

Clicker floored the accelerator to catch up with the truck. The truck halted on the tarmac beside a hangar. Only one C-123 stood near the hangar, and it did not look like it was going anywhere.

"Shit!" Clicker exclaimed.

The Vietnamese mechanics and George climbed out of the truck. They searched the ramp, hoping to spot another C-123. None were in sight. While the group stood wondering about their next step, a jeep drove out of a nearby hangar. The driver spoke with George, who turned to Clicker.

"The assholes left already."

As the group turned toward the runway, the roar of reciprocating engines reached them. A C-123 lifted off the runway and headed north.

George gestured to the jeep driver.

"Meet Sergeant Khắc," George introduced the jeep driver to Rick.

"The pilot tried to wait longer," Sergeant Khắc explained. "But their commander ordered him to take off immediately."

Shaking his head, Clicker turned to Rick.

"Welcome to your new world."

"The same thing will happen anytime we hear of a plane going to Pleiku," George stated. He turned to Sergeant Khắc. "Do you know any Chinook crew chiefs at Bien Hoa?"

Sergeant Khắc thought for a few seconds.

"One," he finally replied.

"Would you write his name down for me?" George requested, digging a paper and pen out of his pocket. "Maybe between him and Colonel Tinh's friend, we'll find a Chinook to get our mechanics to Pleiku."

———•———

WHY A RING?

———•———

Dobie crouched in a dark corner of the lobby bar in Saigon's Caravelle Hotel. His position gave him a good view of the wooden bar, the entrance, and the hall with the restrooms. Dobie had selected the bar and hotel because of its usual clientele. It had been a favorite place of the press during the war. Thus, Americans and Europeans were the typical customers. Since Dobie had scrupulously avoided the press his entire career, none of them knew him. Jeff Nickerson had a similar aversion to reporters. Therefore, a meeting between a Special Forces veteran and an intelligence officer would not attract any press interest. Dobie had called Jeff to ask if he knew any pilots who were in Saigon.

"A fighter pilot friend has just arrived in Saigon," Jeff had responded. "Why do you ask?"

Dobie merely said it might shed a little light on some information. Talking about the mysterious ring on the telephone did not seem prudent. The secret police of any Southeast Asian country could listen to any call, especially with the American Defense Attaché. Jeff had promised to bring the pilot.

Dobie nursed his cheap Scotch whiskey. He had arrived early for their appointment. His practice was to study those who came into the bar around his meeting time. He did not expect that he had aroused any interest among the secret services running rampant in Saigon. But Dobie had learned to assume nothing.

Five minutes before their agreed-upon time, Jeff Nickerson walked in the door to the bar. Dobie studied the man with him. Both were in jeans and lightweight shirts. The companion was taller than Jeff. The friend's hair and sideburns were outside US military standards, which made him a civilian. As they came toward him, Dobie studied how this stranger walked. He walked with a purpose. The guy glanced around, just as Jeff did.

The two men sat across from Dobie at the table. A waitress immediately walked up.

"What do you have?" Jeff asked Dobie.

"The finest Scotch in the house," Dobie winked.

"That's what I'll have," Jeff told the waitress.

"Do you have any bourbon?" the friend asked.

"Yeah, we got," the waitress assured him.

"Straight up."

"You're looking good," Jeff commented to Dobie. "Retirement seems to agree with you."

"Still need a purpose to get up," Dobie responded. He turned his attention to the companion.

"Call me Dobie."

"Rick Guerri," Jeff's companion said, extending his hand across the table.

Rick sized up this retired Green Beret. He had the look of an adventurer. His attire would be at home in the jungle and suitable for the streets of Saigon. He agreed with Jeff's description. His face had the angles of a Doberman. His short hair was black. Even his ears looked alert. Rick now understood the nickname. Sitting in the corner with a glass of Scotch, he watched.

"Rick flew F-105s out of Thailand during two tours," Jeff noted. "We taught together at Kent State when all hell broke out."

Dobie nodded. "That must have been very interesting."

"It started interesting," Jeff added. "Then it got crazy."

He turned to Rick.

"Tell him about your conversation with your two lady acquaintances."

"My uniform offended two young ladies," Rick explained. "They confused me with a baby killer. So, I corrected their misperception."

"Then, their 'advisor'," Jeff made quotation marks with his fingers, "showed up at the big riot."

"I knew guys who were spit on when they went through San Francisco on the way home," Dobie reported.

The waitress walked over with two drinks and set them on the table.

"Put it on my tab," Dobie instructed.

The waitress left.

"You said you wanted to run something by a pilot," Jeff continued.

Dobie kept his voice low.

"I've heard something very curious that I wanted a pilot's perspective on," Dobie began. "When you flew over Indian Country, did you sanitize yourselves?"

"You mean our flight suits, personal possessions?" Rick inquired.

Dobie nodded.

"Most carried only our military ID cards, a worthless Geneva Convention card, and dog tags," Rick replied. "Some guys wore their black and olive drab name tags and wings. But I never did. No sense in giving the Gooks any more personal information than necessary."

"What about wedding rings?" Dobie inquired.

"Those too," Rick answered. "One guy left a wedding band on. He couldn't get it off. His finger had swollen in the tropical heat. I suggested he get the ring cut off and resized."

"Fraternity rings? Class rings?" Dobie pressed.

"It would be highly irregular for a guy to have one of those on him on a mission."

"What have you heard?" Jeff asked his former Green Beret partner. "Has a ring turned up?"

"I've heard that a military academy class ring has shown up in the possession of an NVA deserter."

Jeff gave a low whistle.

"In Laos?"

Dobie nodded.

"The ring has a name engraved on the inside."

"And?" Jeff pushed.

"Something like Catuin Rooso. Spelling and pronunciation are unclear."

"No shit," Rick joined in.

"When you write it out," Dobie explained, "the first name could be something like Calvin. The last name could be Rose or Reese."

It was Rick's turn to whistle.

"A guy from my squadron named Cal Reese went down in 1968," he explained. "He was a Zoomie."

"An Air Force Academy grad," Dobie added. "The deserter didn't give a specific place or time of the ring owner's shoot-down. When and where in '68 did Reese go down?"

Rick answered immediately.

"April, near Channel 97 in Laos. I remember because I flew ResCap over him."

"Any confirmation that he bailed out?" Dobie inquired.

"We talked to him on the ground," Rick responded. "He was on the move. An enemy patrol was pursuing him. We didn't get a good fix on his position. On his last transmission, we heard gunshots. I thought I heard a whistle. Like a referee's whistle. Then we lost contact."

"The NVA and Pathet Lao use whistles to communicate," Dobie added.

"The guy argued he wouldn't get captured. He would fight." Rick stopped.

"You were forced to leave someone behind," Dobie acknowledged. "Toughest thing to do. You second-guess yourself, thinking you could have done more. Even when you couldn't have."

Rick nodded in agreement.

"It was rough not getting this guy out. He had ninety-nine missions with just one left before going home."

"So, he went down on his last mission?" Dobie inquired.

"Not exactly," Rick explained. "The ticket home required one hundred over North Vietnam. But planners usually didn't send you to Hanoi on your last couple of missions. Were the North Vietnamese involved in the attack on the navigation site? I thought it was just Pathet Lao."

"The North regulars helped the Pathet Lao," Jeff responded. "They exercised some influence or even control over their Lao allies."

"The Air Force used the navigation station flying to North Vietnam," Rick noted. "It makes sense the Vietnamese would want it taken out. It also had a radar site."

The group stayed silent for a minute. They sipped their drinks.

"So, how did this deserter get the ring?" Rick asked.

"Claims he took it from the owner when captured."

"What does he want now?" Jeff asked.

"What do you think?" Dobie responded. "Money for the ring and information."

"It would be highly unusual for a pilot to have his class ring with him," Rick mused. "Why would he carry a ring? Guys I know left their rings in their hooch."

Dobie thought for a minute.

"Would someone have brought a class ring with him to Vietnam?"

"This guy did," Rick answered quickly.

Dobie and Jeff looked, awaiting further explanation.

"He was a ring knocker," Rick explained. "Always had it on at the Stag Bar. Always reminded everyone he was an Academy grad."

"Ring knockers," Jeff responded. "We knew our share of those, didn't we?" he stated to Dobie.

"One West Point guy made me want to cut his damn finger off with the ring," Dobie confessed.

"Your general friend," Jeff countered.

"The asshole," Dobie scoffed.

"Just so you know, Rick, you are in the rare company of a Green Beret who refused a Silver Star," Jeff reported.

"How do you refuse such an esteemed medal?" Rick inquired.

"By not showing up when the asshole wants to pin it on you," Dobie explained.

Rick waited for a more complete explanation. None came. They sipped their drinks in silence.

"Did Calvin Reese show up on the POW lists?" Dobie finally asked Jeff.

"I'll have to check."

"He didn't," Rick stated. "I looked for it among the names the North Vietnamese released. His name would still appear as MIA."

"Then the ring would confirm that the Commies captured him and have denied it," Dobie offered.

"Maybe our MIA team can ask about him specifically," Rick suggested.

"Not likely," Jeff noted, shaking his head. "We have demanded information on specific cases with evidence that they captured him. It has shaken no info loose."

"Then it would be better not to ask," Dobie responded. "I need to think about how to approach this."

"Would we pay for the ring and information?" Rick asked Jeff.

"So far, the policy is not to pay. The Commies are demanding reparations for information. The official US position is to demand adherence to the Peace Agreement, which requires us to exchange information."

"What about a private citizen offering to buy the ring?" Dobie asked.

"Not encouraged," Jeff informed him. "At least officially."

"But if the family, or say a charitable citizen, wanted to pay …" Dobie pressed.

"I guess that would be their right," Jeff conceded.

"But you would prefer not to know about it," Dobie offered.

"Technically, I don't see that I'm obligated to volunteer any rumor I may hear. But if I'm asked a specific question, not knowing would make it easier to answer."

Dobie looked at Rick.

"What happened to a guy's personal items after he was shot down?"

"Somebody packed it up and sent it home to a wife or parents. The purpose was to clear out any embarrassing stuff."

"Cal Reese's stuff would have gone home then."

"It went to his wife," Rick stated. "A friend of mine sent it."

"Would the friend know if the guy's class ring was among his stuff?"

"If he remembered. If not, the wife should know."

"Can we contact the packer and ask him?"

"I remember who it was. I know where he is. But if we don't want to talk about a ring on an open line, I would need a secure military line."

Jeff turned to Dobie. "How tightly do you prefer keeping this info?"

Dobie thought for several seconds.

"Once info gets into the rumor mill, there's no controlling it," he said. "I don't see any purpose in asking about a ring at this point. If word gets back to this deserter about his army looking for the ring, we'll lose him."

Jeff nodded. He turned to Rick.

"If you give me the name of the guy who packed the box, I can call him or send an encrypted message."

"I could call him to tell him to be on the lookout for it," Rick offered.

They sipped their drinks.

"If I hear about the ring, how do I get in touch with you?" Jeff questioned Dobie.

"I'll call you," Dobie answered. He held up his glass. "In chit-chat, I'll ask how the whiskey supplies are holding up. If you have heard nothing about the ring, say something like, it's okay. If the ring was in his stuff, then the deserter is making the ring up. Tell me the last whiskey shipment took too long to get here. Or we can meet the next time I'm in Saigon."

Jeff nodded. Then he repeated Dobie's instructions back to him.

"If the ring went home with his items," Rick posed, "how would the deserter know the pilot's name and place of his shoot-down?"

"I'd assume that this guy's unit captured the pilot, and the deserter heard his name. He could have learned some details about the pilot from the initial interrogations. Then he made up the ring to add some incentive for us to pay him for information. The ring could also be counterfeit." Dobie thought a second before continuing. "Before anyone pays this deserter a dime, someone needs to interrogate him."

Rick turned to Jeff.

"Now that it's been two years since the Peace Agreement, do you think we'll ever learn much about the MIAs?"

"The Commies need some incentive to give us something. But with their flagrant violations of the Peace Agreement, any foreign aid is unthinkable. Getting any useful info is a long shot."

"Is there any chance that some prisoners remain, and the Commies will offer them for ransom?" Rick asked.

Jeff shrugged. He looked at Dobie.

"Have you been snooping around that question?"

Dobie hesitated.

"I've heard some very indefinite things. The problem is that the CIA doesn't seem to be at all interested in chasing down any reports."

"Well," Jeff interjected, "they will have to be the ones to do it. Defense is highly unlikely to get any Congressional funding or authorization to send in any special ops teams to investigate."

"Not even in the black part of the budget?" Dobie questioned.

"The problem is that senior leadership doesn't want to spend political capital on it," Jeff noted.

"It strikes me," Rick added, "that any prisoners left behind would most likely be in Laos. Of the pilots I know who remain MIA, most went down there. There is little doubt in my mind that MIAs died during capture or from torture. The North Vietnamese will never own up to that."

The conversation stopped for a minute.

Jeff downed the rest of his Scotch.

"What are you going to do while we wait to clarify the ring question?" he posed to Dobie.

Dobie leaned back in his chair.

"I have other information to check out."

Rick finished his drink. He reached into his pocket and put a few piastres on the table.

"I should be going."

"Me too," Jeff agreed. He put money on the table and looked at Dobie. "I hope we answered your question."

"Yes, you did. Good to see you again, Jeff." He turned to Rick. "And glad to meet you."

Rick and Jeff headed for the door. Dobie watched if anyone noticed the two Americans leaving. No one seemed to care. He sat for a while, thinking.

He had long ago concluded that the CIA would not go looking for remaining prisoners. They had their priorities, and recovering any POWs was not among them. The military needed money and Congress to tell them to look for remaining POWs. Congress was unlikely to do so. They had already cut aid to South Vietnam in half.

No, Dobie realized, *any POW rescue had to be a private affair.* But the big question remained. Were there POWs to rescue?

If POWs existed, any rescue operation had to be a small, focused, quiet group. A large team crashing through the jungle would do one of two things. The captors would move the POWs deeper into the forest or quickly kill them.

My next step is a talk with Mr. Ashley Peabody, Dobie concluded. Mr. Peabody, the publisher of *Direct Action* magazine, had stated that he was interested in bringing any MIA home. His only price for financing such a venture was exclusive rights to the story.

———•———

PEABODY

———◆———

Dobie nursed his Scotch at the Manila Hilton. The hotel was a classic Hilton, definitely above Dobie's budget. Mr. Peabody, though, stayed here and was paying for Dobie's room. Being a Hilton, the price of Scotch was above Dobie's usual budget, too.

As with all meetings when Dobie wanted to remain unobserved, he had arrived early. He sat in his usual dark corner facing the entrance. Mr. Peabody had never met Dobie. He said, though, that he had a picture. Dobie knew what Mr. Peabody looked like. In the shadows of the corner, Dobie knew that he would have to walk over when the publisher walked in. He could delay a minute to see if anyone else in the bar noticed the magazine publisher.

Waiting in the bar, Dobie reviewed what he knew about the publisher. His biography stated he had been with the Office of Strategic Services, the OSS, during World War II. It reported that he had worked in Southeast Asia toward the close of the war. Rumors claimed he had not only met Ho Chi Minh; he had helped save his life.

Dobie couldn't miss him when Ashley Peabody walked into the bar.

Jeez, the guy couldn't stick out more if he wore a neon sign, Dobie thought. The discreet Dobie wondered how this guy could have worked for the CIA's forerunner.

Peabody wore a polo barong, the short-sleeved version of the formal Philippine barong shirt. Peabody left the shirt unbuttoned, and a large gold Thai baht chain adorned his tanned neck. A large ring glistened on his right ring finger. Dobie could see the thick tonic in his black hair, which he combed straight back. It looked dyed. He had a slight paunch, but he walked with a brisk stride, which suggested some routine exercise. Still, Peabody wasn't completely out of place in the bar full of businesspeople.

Dobie scanned the room twice. No one in the late afternoon crowd seemed to care about Ashley Peabody. Dobie rose, and Mr. Peabody looked his way.

Dobie just nodded, then sat down. Mr. Peabody strode to the table. His walk said that he was used to getting his way. Dobie resolved to be firm in his needs from Mr. Peabody.

As Ashley Peabody reached the table, Dobie rose and extended his right hand.

"Colonel Bill Starbuckle." Dobie decided to remain on a formal business basis with the publisher.

"Colonel, Ashley Peabody. I'm honored to meet you, sir." Peabody shook Dobie's hand in a firm grip. He sat down.

A waitress quickly walked over.

Mr. Peabody looked at her and smiled.

"Lovely lady, bring me the best Scotch in the house. A double, please, straight up." He looked at Dobie. "Need a refill, sir?"

"I'm good, thank you." Dobie wanted to keep a clear head. He had been slowly nursing his drink, and the melted ice ensured it would not cloud his thinking.

"I always forget how hot the tropics get," Mr. Peabody stated. "As often as I've been to them, though, I should remember."

"It does take a few days to adjust," Dobie reflected.

"How many times have you found yourself in Southeast Asia?" Mr. Peabody probed.

"I've been in the region five times in twelve years. Three tours in Vietnam and two personal visits."

"Including this one?"

Dobie nodded. "Including this one."

"Did your Nam tours comprise a full year?"

"They did," Dobie responded. "During one I extended a couple of extra months."

Mr. Peabody arched his thick eyebrows. "For what purpose?"

Dobie realized that behind the small talk, Mr. Peabody was interviewing him.

This guy gets down to business quickly, he thought. Dobie's hope for a beneficial meeting increased.

"One item of interest needed a little extra time," Dobie replied, deciding to see how curious Mr. Peabody was.

"Regarding ...?" Peabody probed.

"We needed to corroborate some gossip."

"Gossip? From whom?"

Mr. Peabody seemed curious.

"An uninvited guest at our camp mentioned a few things we needed to confirm."

"Did you find the information?"

"We did," Dobie admitted.

"Do you speak Vietnamese?"

"Reasonably well," Dobie answered.

"When you interrogated these guests, was it in Vietnamese?"

Dobie nodded.

"But we started in English to achieve a slight tactical advantage when the subject said he didn't understand."

The waitress returned with the drink. Mr. Peabody pulled a clip of Philippine pesos from his pocket.

"Keep the change," he said as he handed a few to the waitress.

She beamed.

"Thank you, thank you."

Peabody waited until she had left.

"Did you spend any time in Laos or Cambodia during your official visits to the area?"

"I'm not at liberty to say," Dobie replied.

Mr. Peabody nodded. "I understand."

Dobie decided it was his time to ask questions.

"Our mutual friend mentioned your interest in any Americans still living in Southeast Asia, not by their own choice."

Mr. Peabody nodded.

"Before we get on that topic, I'd just like to say that my pleasure in meeting you is genuine. Special Forces veterans I know regard you highly."

Dobie tried not to show his surprise. That Mr. Peabody may have already done some inquiring about him was unexpected. Dobie had hoped that the publisher would be thorough enough to do that. He had just assumed it might be after they had met.

"May I suggest," Peabody continued, "that to discuss that topic, we retire to my suite. We can better carry on a conversation without being overheard."

"That is an excellent idea," Dobie replied. "I'll follow you a few minutes after you leave."

"My suite is number 820." Mr. Peabody picked up his drink as he stood and extended his right hand. "I'll see you in a few minutes."

The publisher turned and headed for the door. Dobie looked around as Mr. Peabody walked through the bar. He then glanced at his watch.

While he waited the few minutes, Dobie finished his watered-down drink. So far, this meeting was exceeding his expectations.

Dobie left the bar and rode the elevator to the eighth floor. He found the suite easily and gently knocked on the door. Ashley Peabody opened it immediately and ushered Dobie into a spacious sitting area. Mr. Peabody was not alone in the suite. A tall, square-jawed man rose from a couch as Dobie entered. The stranger appeared to be in his thirties. He had a close-cropped military haircut.

Dobie also noticed the stocked bar along the wall to the right. Besides the hotel miniature liquor bottles, a bottle of fine single-malt Scotch was on it.

"May I refresh your drink?" Ashley Peabody offered.

Dobie nodded. "On the rocks," he requested.

As Mr. Peabody stepped to the bar, he gestured to the other man.

"Charles Lautin, meet Colonel Bill Starbuckle."

Charles walked with a noticeable limp to Dobie and shook his hand firmly.

"Pleasure to meet you, Colonel."

"Charles also served in the Special Forces," Ashley Peabody offered. "I've retained him as my in-house expert. His job is to fact-check stories written by our reporters. Not all of our writers have the widest experience in military matters."

"Where were you stationed?" Dobie immediately inquired.

"Phu Bai, Quang Tri," Charles answered

"I know both areas," Dobie admitted. "Who was your platoon commander?"

"Jeff Nickerson."

"I know Jeff well," Dobie responded. "Served with him in another place." *Good,* Dobie thought, *I can check on this guy.* "How were you wounded?" Dobie inquired, shifting his gaze to the ailing leg.

"Poisoned punji stick near the DMZ," Charles offered. "We couldn't get extracted for a day, and the darn thing got a nasty infection."

Dobie noted Charles did not specify which side of the DMZ. Peabody handed Dobie his drink and motioned to a chair.

"Have a seat, and we can discuss MIAs," he stated before continuing. "I've heard a report, Colonel, that you once refused a Silver Star medal."

"That is correct," Dobie confirmed.

"Why would you do that?" Peabody pressed.

"I did not want to be part of a general's attempt to cover up his blunder," Dobie stated.

"What kind of cover-up?" Peabody pressed.

"After the Son Tay POW rescue attempt, a general wanted a similar feather in his cap," Dobie replied. "I did not wish recognition for rescuing my men, whom the misguided general put in danger. I lost a few good men because of the general's search for glory."

Peabody nodded.

"Charles believes that the sleazy politicians have abandoned some of our boys in Southeast Asia," he started. "He believes a properly organized mission could rectify their situation. I'm interested in two related questions, Colonel. One, is Charles correct; and two, if so, can anyone do anything about it?"

Before answering, Dobie sipped his drink. The Scotch was definitely above his pay grade. He turned to Charles.

"Have you come across any evidence of POWs left behind?"

Charles cleared his throat.

"Nothing specific," he admitted. "Only rumors."

"Rumors of?" Dobie pressed.

"Sightings, camps, messages stamped out on the ground."

"But nothing solid," Dobie stated.

"No, sir."

"And what about you, Colonel?" Peabody asked.

"The same, I'm afraid," Dobie confessed. "We know of specific cases of prisoners that the Commies have denied knowing anything about. Keeping a few as hostages for aid is entirely credible."

"Do you know of any military or intelligence efforts to confirm sightings or to investigate reports?" Peabody continued.

"I do not," Dobie responded. He turned to Charles. "Lieutenant Colonel Nickerson is now an intelligence officer with the DAO in Saigon. He admits that the CIA and the DIA have little interest."

"Meaning," Peabody added, "that any serious investigation has to be a private venture."

"That is my conclusion, sir," Dobie responded to the publisher.

"Do you know anyone with the skills and interest to investigate sightings or prison locations?"

"Given the right circumstances, Mr. Peabody," Dobie replied, "I would consider it a matter of duty and honor to investigate."

"What's your motivation?" Peabody pressed.

"Sir, as Charles can confirm, all special forces are committed to leave no one behind. I know the pilots who flew over Vietnam felt a similar obligation. It is part of the American warrior's ethos. When a soldier requires help, I can give but one reply."

"And what financial reward would you feel would be warranted?" Peabody insisted.

"Well, sir, I have skills I can use to earn some money to supplement my military retirement income. I feel that reasonable compensation to help me pay my bills is all that is necessary."

Peabody turned to Charles.

"Charles, I think we have found our man."

Charles nodded.

"Subject to completing satisfactory details," Peabody added, looking at Dobie.

"Mr. Peabody, I would consider it an honor to investigate credible reports," Dobie stated.

"This calls for another drink," Ashley Peabody stated as he stood and turned to the bar. "Charles? Do you need a refresher, Colonel?"

Charles limped to the bar.

"I'll do the honors, sir," he stated. "Colonel?"

Dobie walked to the bar.

"Just a slight topping off, no ice." Dobie decided not to dilute Mr. Peabody's fine Scotch.

"Are you available to have dinner with us, Colonel?" Peabody inquired. "We can order room service and begin discussing how to accomplish our mission."

"I'm available."

"Good. We need to flesh out the details of our venture. And you can relate any relevant info you haven't yet told us about."

Dobie's opinion of this magazine publisher inched higher.

"I have heard of two developments which would interest our partnership," Dobie stated.

"Outstanding!" Peabody exclaimed, clapping his hands.

The group ordered dinner from room service. It arrived quickly. During the wait, Peabody quizzed Dobie about a couple of his interesting missions. As the three men sat down to dinner, Peabody returned to the meeting's purpose.

"You mentioned interesting developments. Tell us about them."

Dobie explained the mysterious ring along with the questions surrounding the curious deserter. He also described Marcel's investigation of the cave with prisoners.

"What course of action would you suggest?" Peabody inquired.

"A recon mission to converse with this deserter," Dobie replied. "Since it has a known MIA name associated with it, that makes it the most promising. The deserter probably knows more about the ring's owner than he is revealing. If possible, the same trip could check out the cave. But my gut says the cave holds local prisoners. And it carries significant danger."

Peabody looked at Charles.

"What do you think?"

"Limiting ourselves to the ring makes the most sense to me."

Peabody nodded.

"About the ring," Dobie started. "Lieutenant Colonel Nickerson reported we do not know if a ring was in the MIA's effects that were shipped home. The pilot who packed his items couldn't remember. It would be useful to know before we talk with this deserter."

"Could the military ask the wife?" Peabody wondered.

"They probably won't," Charles responded. "It would suggest that they know something. The wife would naturally ask questions. The Pentagon doesn't like to answer MIA questions."

"So, a private inquiry from a concerned citizen?" Peabody asked.

"Would be the only way to find out," Charles answered.

"As long as the wife does not blab it around," Dobie added. "A talkative wife would compromise the secrecy of a mission."

Peabody nodded. "We'll have to think about it." He turned to Dobie.

"What would you need for a trip to investigate the ring?"

Dobie's spirits continued to rise.

Peabody has a definite bias for action, he realized.

"Weapons, ammo, a small amount of travel rations, and, importantly, a good radio. Up to now, I've had to beg the spooks to contact Marcel for me. Marcel relies on others in Laos. It won't do for them to know anything about us. They'll run across us in due time. But the farther away we stay from them, the better."

"What kind of radio?" Peabody pressed.

"A durable one," Dobie noted. "One small enough to carry in the jungle."

"We know a source for the comm gear," Peabody explained. "Other supplies are easily available. Charles will be your contact point with me and serve as a command post. He can operate out of Manila. Unless you think you need him in Thailand."

Charles spoke uninvited for the first time.

"Despite its risks, any radio to carry into the jungle will have a limited range. We will have to have a base in Thailand close to the Laotian border. The Thais are nervous about groups operating with sophisticated gear in their backyard. They realize the traffic on the Trail means only one thing. The North is prepping for an invasion. They don't want to create any reason for the Commies to look across the Mekong River at them. They also want to protect their revenue source out of the Golden Triangle."

"We'll have to manage the risk of having a comm base in Thailand," Dobie interjected. "I would suggest Nakhon Phanom. There is still a large American presence there, so a few more of us won't stand out. With the Air Force moving its Seventh Air Force HQ there, we can use Air Force shuttle flights."

"With your retiree ID cards?" Peabody inquired.

"Yes," Dobie replied. "My potential partner will be a retiree, as well." Doble looked at Charles. "What is your military status?"

"Medically retired," he answered.

"Well, then, having you near a US base will be useful, too. Before we decide to purchase the ring, I will need to ensure it is authentic. I can find an Academy ring to study the crest and basic design. But we'll want to test it to ensure it is gold and not a fake. The Thais are excellent forgers."

Peabody rubbed his chin.

"We can get a simple testing kit. The kind a smuggler might use to test for genuine gold. Deciding to purchase the ring is a decision you will have to make in the field." Peabody paused before continuing. "What about other personnel?"

"One more would suffice," Dobie offered. "I know two potential recruits, one still in South Vietnam. My first choice, though, is in the States. I'll have to find him and discover his interest. We will need Marcel and Keej as guides. A team of four will be enough. Any more would create too many opportunities to be noticed. Security risks rise exponentially as team size increases. A key requirement is stealth. A noisy group slashing through the jungle is a recipe for disaster."

Peabody again looked toward Charles, who nodded. Mr. Peabody turned back to Dobie.

"We need to draw up some paperwork for our joint venture. It's best to have a clear understanding from the beginning. Write your ops plan for this recon trip. I'll write my requirements for financing the venture. You can stay here to do that. When you finish, I'll pay for your ticket to Saigon to locate your additional team member. If the ring mission provides intel to proceed to the cave, we'll discuss that as information develops."

He paused. When Dobie nodded, he continued.

"Charles will remain here to answer any questions that emerge. Does a week sound reasonable for you to write your ops plan, recruit another team member, and communicate with your guides?"

"Ten days would be preferable," Dobie countered.

"Then we will meet here in ten days to finalize our arrangement."

When everyone had finished their meal, Peabody rose.

"Colonel, this has been a most productive meeting. I can see you are a man of action. It's been a pleasure." Peabody shook Dobie's hand. Dobie recognized that the meeting was over. He had work to do, so he shook the offered hand.

"Mr. Peabody, the pleasure has been mine."

Walking down the hall to the elevators, Dobie felt like cheering. But he could not afford any celebration to call attention to himself, even in the empty hall or elevator.

The game is afoot, he told himself, quoting his favorite fictional detective.

———•———

WHERE ARE THE HOUSES?

———•———

Sue's anxiety grew as she planned to move to Vietnam. She looked for tourist books on Vietnam to help her plan. None were available in the local bookstores. The only recommendation by the university bookstore was a fictional book. It was about the CIA's early work in Vietnam by a British author. Sue had no idea how realistic it was. The encyclopedia in the library did not give her any insight into living in Vietnam.

Reading about Vietnam's hot and humid climate, she knew to buy new wash-and-wear clothes for David and her. The airline baggage limitations forced her to decide what to ship or what to carry. Rick had been specific in his directions to check only three suitcases.

Sue hoped her anxiety would ease once she and David were on their way. She quickly discovered it didn't. Ushering David through the airports while changing planes required constant vigilance. They changed planes twice. First, the small puddle-jumper had flown them to the new Dallas-Fort Worth Regional Airport. It was a massive airport on the open prairie north of the two cities.

They easily made the connecting flight to Los Angeles International Airport. The chaos at that major airport had overwhelmed her. She wished she had a leash for David to keep him from wandering away. The flight from Dallas-Fort Worth arrived late. Their international flight had finished boarding when they finally reached the gate. She hoped that their three checked bags had made the connection.

Approaching Saigon, Sue heard the jumbo jet's engines power up and the plane level off. She put the Vietnam book on her lap. Sue's ears popped from the change in pressure. She looked at David sitting in the middle seat next to her. He was doing fine. She had given him a piece of gum when the flight attendants had announced their descent into Saigon.

She looked left out the window. The plane descended below the layer of scattered clouds. Between the clouds, the pretty South China Sea gleamed in the sunlight. Alternating bright blue and blue-gray patches of the ocean mesmerized her. The plane leveled off, taking David and her to their waiting adventure. She did not know what to expect or how big the adventure would become.

David poked her to ask a question.

"Are we there yet?"

It was the tenth time he had asked on the thirty-hour trip. Thankfully, he had no trouble sleeping on the trip through Honolulu, Guam, and Manila.

"Almost, dear," she answered.

The plane entered some bumpy air. Sue looked out the window and saw a massive river with green jungle on both sides. The sun found spaces between the white clouds, gleaming off the water in irregular shapes.

"See," she pointed out the window, "we have crossed the coast of Vietnam. Don't the river and the jungle look pretty? It won't be long now."

"Will Daddy be there?"

"Yes, he will meet us at the airport."

As the plane resumed its descent, Sue spotted small boats on the river. No wakes followed them, though, as was common on the rivers and lakes in Texas. Sue wondered if water skiing on the river was a popular sport. Maybe they could rent a boat and try it. The owners of the boats, she guessed, were fishing. The clear air over the ocean gave way to a haze.

As the plane flew toward the airport, the haze became thicker. The flight attendant asked for the attention of the passengers. She issued a list of directions. They included completing their customs declarations, keeping their passports handy, stowing their carry-on bags, and fastening their seat belts.

"We will land at Tan Son Nhut International Airport in several minutes."

Then, the flight attendant repeated the instructions in another language. Sue guessed it was Vietnamese. She looked at the book on her lap.

Is the idea of learning a little Vietnamese going to work? she wondered as she listened to the strange accent and intonations. *Yes,* she reassured herself. Once Rick accepted her coming to Saigon, Sue became determined not to be another "ugly American."

Sue looked out the window. The green of a jungle gave way to the outskirts of a city. The landscape changed from a hazy view of a pretty river and lush tropical forest to the brown smog of a city. Los Angeles's smog had surprised her, but this smog was thicker.

The plane slowed further. Then a slight bump followed a low whine. A minute later the plane shuddered.

"We are ready to land," Sue told David. Her excitement and apprehension inched a little higher.

Remember, this will be a fun adventure, she told herself.

Finding their luggage and navigating David through customs and immigration were confusing. The airport terminal was smaller than she expected. It direly needed a facelift. Sue felt the stillness of the muggy air.

Don't they even have air conditioning? she wondered.

The commotion and unfamiliar sights fascinated David. He constantly wandered toward the next new distraction. Locating their luggage took a long time. One bag failed to appear. The short Vietnamese airline official patiently explained to Sue that it would arrive "tomorrow." His English was very good, even with his Vietnamese accent. When the customs official asked the purpose of her visit, he seemed pleased by her answer.

"I'm joining my husband, who works with the Vietnamese Air Force."

He stamped their passports with no further questions.

Spotting Rick as she exited the door to the meeting area, Sue felt all her tension release. David spotted him first.

"Daddy!" the youngster shouted and ran ahead before Sue could react.

Rick scooped up his son. He walked to Sue and the suitcases and pulled her close with his free arm.

"Glad to see you, babe!"

He hugged them both tightly. Seconds passed. He released Sue and placed David on the floor.

"Only two bags?"

"The airlines lost one," she explained.

"Not surprising."

Rick grabbed the bags and led them out the door. As Sue followed him, the wet velvet blanket of Saigon's humidity enveloped her. Initially, it felt soothing. By the time Rick had stopped by a beat-up Japanese car, the humidity became oppressive. She looked at David beside her. He shifted from one foot to the other. His eyes darted around. When Rick opened the car's trunk, Sue eyed him quizzically.

"This is our car?" she asked.

"Don't worry. You won't need to drive it. It's better if you don't drive here."

Her look demanded further explanation.

"Taxis are cheap," Rick explained. "But keep the windows open. And you don't have to navigate."

"Windows open?" Sue immediately reacted.

"They don't have air conditioning, and most need new exhaust systems."

"But you are driving here."

"Remember, I fly jets."

Sue rolled her eyes. She was glad to be here with Rick. She had missed his quips.

Rick strapped David into the back seat of the car. Sue noticed that Rick had improvised a car seat. The battered car did not come equipped with seat belts.

As Rick maneuvered the car into the deluge of oncoming vehicles, Sue looked around. It reminded her of a trip they had taken to a border town on the Texas-Mexico border.

Well, she thought, *I've done this before.*

"How far to our apartment?" she quizzed Rick.

He shrugged.

"Fifty minutes."

"I thought you said we lived close to the air base."

"Not this base," he replied. "Another one northeast of Saigon."

Sue observed the strange sights, sounds, and smells. Every conceivable means of transportation clogged the street. Blue taxis with cream-colored tops darted everywhere. A few green ones with red tops appeared among them. Old, battered compact cars honked at each other. Only a few models looked familiar, twenty-year-old models of Chevies and Fords. A blue Ford pickup passed them on the right, honking its horn. It reminded her of the old pickup on her friend's farm in Kansas. The bed of this one overflowed with young men, women, and kids.

Motorbikes appeared popular, all with a passenger hanging on to the driver. One had a small child precariously perched on the gas tank. She saw rickshaws pulled by men, and bicycle rickshaws with the passenger on a seat in front of the driver. They met small buses with open sides, teeming with passengers. Straw baskets teetered on the roofs.

Her biggest surprise, though, was the noise. Every car blared its horn constantly. Mufflers seemed in short supply. The motorbikes made high, shrill shrieks. Over the din, she heard shouting along the sides of the streets. Individuals hawked every conceivable type of merchandise, including food, clothing, baskets, and hats.

While sections of the street had faded white lane markers down the center, the myriad vehicles disregarded them. Cars, bikes, and rickshaws maneuvered into any gap, cutting off anything in the way. Rick was correct; she had no desire to drive here.

Sue studied the women's clothing. Many women wore black or white pants with a long white covering. A few pretty ladies with long jet-black hair wore colorful, form-fitting dresses. And she spotted several wearing tight miniskirts. Others, though, wore loose, pajama-like pants and tops. These were common among the women squatting by large straw baskets of fruits and vegetables against the cramped buildings. Nearly all of them had conical straw hats shading their faces.

Sue studied the buildings. The block seemed to be a shopping district. She spotted a few signs above weathered awnings. A rare one was in English, but the name was unfamiliar. Groups of squatting merchants haggled with customers under large umbrellas on the sidewalk.

A side street teemed with trash and splintered wood. A building seemed on the brink of collapse. Pedestrians jostled with the motorbikes on the street. No sidewalk gave them a safe place to walk. When Rick screeched to a stop, a child appeared at Sue's open window. He held a flower in one hand, his other hand open in front of Sue's face. Interspersed with Vietnamese, Sue heard "flower" and "pretty lady." She shook her head and looked forward. Rick floored the accelerator, rushing into an opening.

Rick steered the car across a bridge over a narrow river. She looked at the muddy water with floating trash. Small boats maneuvered in both directions. Could this dirty river be the pretty one she had seen from the airplane? It looked too small. Sue twisted in her seat to look at David. His wide eyes and open mouth showed his amazement at the surrounding scenes as well. His tiny hands gripped the sides of the small car seat Rick had fashioned for him. She glanced at Rick. He wore an intense look, his eyes shifting right and left. He alternated between shifting gears to speed into any opening or braking as another vehicle swerved into their path. The motorbikes enjoyed playing "chicken" with any vehicle of any size for any crease in the traffic.

Several blocks past the river, the shopping district gave way to other commercial shops. Cars with hoods up or doors open surrounded a gas pump at the curb. One man tinkered with the engine while three watched. A stack of old tires leaned against a shack.

"I'm hot," David whined from the backseat.

Sue turned to look. The boy was dripping with sweat. Sue rummaged through her purse for a handkerchief to wipe his face. She found a used tissue.

"Can you pull over so I can wipe David's face?"

"If I do, we'll never get back into traffic."

Rick pulled a handkerchief from his back pocket.

"Give this to David," he instructed Sue.

Sue reached behind and wiped David's face. She could not do a decent job, even though the car was small.

She turned to examine the dashboard.

"There's no air conditioning," Rick advised.

"It looks like it has it."

"It's broken. No parts to fix it." Rick angled his head slightly, but he kept his eyes on the traffic. "You'll get used to the heat, son."

This will be a fun adventure, Sue reminded herself again. She began to question whether this job was a good idea.

Eventually, traffic thinned out, and Sue noticed they had left the commercial stretch. She could see more of the side streets off the highway. The buildings were a mix of two-story frames and sheds. They looked like the run-down buildings on old farms off the Texas highways.

Where are the houses people live in? she wondered.

For a short time, buildings gave way to green fields with standing water. A farmer trailed a water buffalo. She saw straight rows of green plants.

Then the road became crowded again, and another string of low buildings lined both sides of the street. Rick continued to honk and shift gears, braking, then speeding into any gap.

The smelly exhaust fumes from the cars, trucks, and motorbikes filled the air. Sue also detected the aroma of a landfill.

Was one in the city? Why don't they put them in the country?

They crossed another bridge across a wide river. The smell of dirty water and dead fish permeated the air. Sue quickly dispelled any thought of water skiing.

"Ew! What's that icky smell?" David shouted.

"It's the smell of the city here," Rick responded. "You'll get used to it."

"Yuck!"

I hope so, Sue thought as David responded. Aloud, she asked, "How much farther to the house?"

"Not far."

Looking down the side streets, Sue felt compelled to ask.

"Is our street nice?"

Rick glanced over, seeing where she was looking.

"Yes, better than here. We live near some Vietnamese Air Force officers. It's a pleasant neighborhood, away from the busy streets. Our house is an old colonial mansion that my company bought and converted into two apartments. It also has a common kitchen, dining room, and sitting area. Each apartment has a kitchen and a sitting room. The house has a nice big porch that wraps around the front and a side."

"You mentioned a house girl in your letter. Does she live with us?"

"Mai has a room next to the kitchen for her and her son Lei. She'll do all the cooking if you want."

"How old is Lei?"

"He is seven. His father was a Marine who died before he was born."

"Poor woman. How old is Mai?"

Rick thought for a second. He had never asked Clicker if he knew Mai's age.

"I guess she is about twenty-five."

"I'm assuming her Marine did not marry her."

"That's correct."

Typical American soldier, Sue thought.

"I think you will like Mai. She is soft-spoken and eager to please. And she works very hard."

Rick turned off the main road. After a couple of blocks, Sue noticed the buildings had changed. From small, crowded shanties, the buildings became larger with two or three floors. Yet, they were all in need of repair.

Then it struck Sue. She had seen clothes hanging on lines outside a few small shacks and on porches of two-story buildings. The implication finally registered in her mind. Those small shacks and battered buildings were the homes of the average Vietnamese.

I'm already the "ugly American," she realized to her dismay. She resolved to become a quiet American.

———•———

JIMBO

M aster Sergeant Jimbo Atkins, retired US Special Forces, nursed his second double of Tennessee whiskey. He drank it on ice, allowing the melt to dilute it as he sipped. The elixir began to relax him. His six-foot frame dwarfed the flimsy bar stool. Jimbo had crossed the county line to avoid the military crowd in the bars and strip clubs near Fort Bragg, North Carolina.

The Post hosted the 82nd Airborne and Special Operations units. US Special Forces. Army Rangers, Marine Recon, and Navy SEALs trained in the nearby forests. These groups fought each other not only on the mock battlefields. They carried their fierce unit pride into the Fort Bragg NCO Club and the nearby bars. The Air Force, which flew the soldiers to adjacent drop zones, put the NCO Club and many bars off limits to its personnel. The service did not want its flight crews involved in the many brawls.

Jimbo had routinely defended the reputation of the US Special Forces, known to most citizens as the famed Green Berets. Tonight, he just wanted a place to drink quietly. Meeting some short-term female companionship would be a bonus.

His retirement from the Army had not been smooth. Jimbo had no expectations when he took off the uniform. He had imagined something more productive. The Army had informed Sergeant Atkins a year ago that his services were no longer needed. Jimbo had been part of a wild brawl at the Fort Bragg NCO Club.

A Navy SEAL had been unaware of Jimbo's penchant for unconstrained violence. The sailor made a snide remark about the Green Berets. Before the melee concluded, two other SEALs hit the floor. A wet-behind-the-ears Military Police lieutenant ordered Jimbo to "stand down." The lieutenant joined the SEALs on the floor. Rather than court-martial a decorated Green Beret for punching an officer, an Army Judge Advocate advised Jimbo to retire.

Jimbo had not fared well as a civilian. He had tried owning a piece of a small business. Army friends asked him to invest in a bar outside Fort Bragg with them. He also worked as a bartender to earn some "sweat equity" in the enterprise. Jimbo's partners soon noticed that Jimbo drank more than his share of the bar's profits while working. The drinks he poured for friends also contained unprofitable amounts of alcohol. Hence, his business partners forced him to sell his minority stake back to them.

That move had happened earlier on this day. He didn't understand his partners' view on enjoying the bar's liquor. After all, what was the point of owning a bar if you couldn't drink? He accepted their decision, though, with no anger. Hanging around Fort Bragg was boring. Jimbo needed some excitement after a dull year as a civilian.

He finished his drink and waved to the bartender for a refill. Jimbo surveyed the patrons. Only one table near the front held a single prospect for companionship. She had a weathered face, the result, Jimbo guessed, from hard living. She met the basic requirements. The cleavage displayed from a partially buttoned blouse was her best feature. Studying her face, though, convinced Jimbo that he needed another drink. Her appearance needed to improve. Her female companion fell below Jimbo's low standards.

His experience in seeking such companionship taught him one lesson. Waiting for the drinks to improve a prospect was a risky gambit. Competitors with similar tastes could sweep in. Hence, Jimbo scanned the bar. He saw no competition.

Good, he thought. *I can enjoy another drink before sweet-talking her.*

Jimbo reviewed his options for the next phase of retirement. His modest Army pension offered enough for his simple needs of food and shelter. Entertainment funds, though, would be scarce. He had invested his modest savings in the bar to help provide for those. Now he needed another source of income. Wisely, he had deposited the cashier's check for the ownership stake his partners had paid him.

While visiting the familiar bars around Fort Bragg, Jimbo heard a former commanding officer was looking for him. Colonel Starbuckle had a potential project in Southeast Asia. No one knew what it was. Jimbo knew one thing about Lieutenant Colonel Dobie Starbuckle. Colonel Dobie did not go chasing after windmills. Jimbo decided to look up the colonel. Dobie, the rumor mill reported, was in Saigon.

He downed his drink and looked at the woman.

Damn, Jimbo realized, *she isn't getting better.*

Time to settle his bar tab and head back to his motel, Jimbo decided. He motioned to the bartender. Reaching into his pocket, he pulled out bills to cover it.

The door of the bar crashed open, and three young men stormed in. They marched straight to the center of the bar. While they sported short beards and short hair, their neat appearance gave them away.

Shit, Jimbo thought. *Swabbies. What the hell are they doing this far from the Post?*

Jimbo knew they were Navy SEALs. Since it was Friday night, their week in the forests playing war games was over. Jimbo guessed it had been a successful week for them in their mock battles. Their superior attitude was unmistakable.

"Three beers and three shots," the nearest one yelled to the bartender. His wavering voice left no doubt. This wasn't their first bar of the evening.

Jimbo recognized the North Carolina accent. Having grown up in eastern Tennessee, he recognized the regional variations in southern accents. This SEAL was a local boy who had made it through the grueling training. That meant he had access to a car to wander this far from the Post.

While they waited for drinks, the trio turned their backs to the bar to study the room. One eyed the two women at the table. He nudged the guy next to him and muttered something. They both laughed. The local one turned toward Jimbo. He nodded.

"How's it hanging, pops?" He tilted his head to the women. In a low voice, he muttered, "Looks like your kind of gals," he snickered.

Their drinks arrived.

"Depth charges!" the one farthest from Jimbo yelled.

The three picked up the shot glasses of whiskey and dropped the shot glasses into the beer. Beer sloshed onto the bar.

"Dive, dive, dive!" the local guy ordered.

The trio guzzled the glasses of beer and whiskey. One let out a loud belch.

Jimbo shook his head. Other patrons watched the antics of the SEALs.

The bartender made change for Jimbo, who reached to gather the coins. Jimbo's short sleeve slid up to reveal his Green Beret tattoo on his right bicep.

"Whoa," the local SEAL yelled. He turned to his friends. "It appears we have a member of the green beanies among us," he announced. "Hey, bartender, a boilermaker for our green beanie friend. On me!"

The bartender looked at Jimbo.

"Thanks, I'm good."

"Come on, don't be a candy ass! Someone has to redeem your special service after we kicked their butts this week." He made quotes in the air around "special."

"Special Forces," exclaimed the one at the end. "More like special education forces."

They laughed.

Tired of their baiting, Jimbo slid off the bar stool to start for the door. The nearest SEAL stepped in front, blocking Jimbo's way. He stood a head shorter than Jimbo.

"You aren't very friendly," he taunted.

Little pipsqueak, Jimbo thought.

Jimbo moved right to go around the SEAL. Perhaps the SEAL did not notice the two scars on Jimbo's face in the dim light. Maybe the alcohol in his bloodstream clouded his judgment. The SEAL slid to block Jimbo's path, reaching out his right arm to stop Jimbo.

In a blur, Jimbo grasped the wrist with his right hand, twisted it, and locked the arm under his left armpit. He pulled the wrist toward him. A loud snap permeated the bar as the fibula snapped. The SEAL howled in surprise. Jimbo dropped the wrist. The next SEAL advanced on Jimbo. Jimbo shot a straight punch from his shoulder into the proboscis of the advancing SEAL.

A target that large makes it too easy, Jimbo thought as the SEAL's legs buckled.

The third SEAL was slow to react to Jimbo's fierce and swift violence. By the time he moved, Jimbo was two steps toward the door.

"Hey!" the sailor yelled, moving toward Jimbo.

Sliding to his right, Jimbo put a table between the last SEAL and himself. They danced around it for several seconds. Jimbo countered each move the sailor made to get around the table. The bartender began yelling into a telephone behind the bar.

"You'd better calm down," Jimbo advised the SEAL. "Your pals need your help. You need to call an ambulance for them."

In response, the SEAL grabbed a chair and hurled it at Jimbo. Before he could get much muscle into it, though, Jimbo rammed the corner of the table into his groin. It slowed down the attack.

"You son of a bitch, I'll kill you!" the sailor yelled.

Jimbo backed to the door. Before he could shove it open, two deputy sheriffs charged in, nightsticks ready. Jimbo stepped to the side and held up his hands, palms facing the deputies. The SEAL stumbled toward Jimbo. Holding his nightstick with both hands, the lead deputy shoved the sailor down.

The deputies surveyed the bar. The last SEAL stumbled, trying to stand.

"I strongly recommend you remain on the floor," the deputy growled.

The sailor remained on his knees.

"Now what the hell is going on here?" the second deputy demanded.

"I was leaving peaceably," Jimbo started, "when that one ..." he pointed to the SEAL cradling his broken arm, "attacked me with no provocation. That one ..." Jimbo pointed to the one holding his shirttail to his bloody nose, "continued to attack me."

The deputy examined the two casualties.

"As you can see, I defended myself," Jimbo concluded.

"He's a damned liar!" screamed the one on his knees. "We were just joking with him when he assaulted us for no reason! He is a menace to society and needs to be locked away."

The deputy turned to Jimbo.

"I see you have graced us with your presence again, Sergeant Atkins," he snarled.

"I was enjoying a peaceful evening, Deputy Ferguson, when these assholes attacked me," Jimbo stated.

"Really," Deputy Ferguson retorted. He turned toward the few people in the bar. "What did you see?" he asked the women.

"Officer, we were minding our own business. We didn't see a thing."

Deputy Ferguson walked to the bar.

"You?" he asked the bartender.

"I didn't see how it started. I heard a scream and saw that guy holding his arm. Then he ..." pointing to Jimbo, "flattened that one."

"I was just going to my friend's side," Bloody Nose stated, "when he punched me for no reason."

Deputy Ferguson looked to the few other patrons.

"Anybody?" he asked.

"Arrest his ass!" the kneeling SEAL demanded, pointing at Jimbo.

All the other customers remained quiet.

"You," Deputy Ferguson demanded, pointing at one.

"Sorry, Deputy, I didn't see a thing."

The deputy shook his head.

"You better call an ambulance," he ordered the bartender. He pulled a handheld radio from his belt and spoke into it. Then he looked at Jimbo. "We're taking a quick ride to the office to sort this out."

Jimbo held out both fists together.

"You want to cuff me?"

"Only if you resist."

Jimbo shrugged.

——◆——

As Jimbo awoke from his recurring nightmare, the sinister, sneering face surprised him. Jimbo's bad dream changed little. Details shifted, but the essential elements remained consistent. The point man had tripped a booby trap in the thick jungle. He didn't die immediately. But he cried for help. Jimbo tried to reach him. He had failed to notice the sinkhole obscured by vines and vegetation on the jungle floor. Jimbo slid into it. He took two minutes to crawl out of it, hampered by the slippery growth and entangling vines. He reached his man and pulled the tourniquet from his combat kit. It was too late. The soldier bled out before Jimbo could tighten the strap. If Jimbo had reached him immediately, he could have stopped the spurting artery. The soldier would be alive today.

Varying details were the weather or the time of day. Some versions of the nightmare occurred on a pitch-black night. Others during a steamy, sunny day. This version was in a monsoon downpour.

Jimbo crawled out of the sinkhole, drenched, and charged forward. He coughed, shaking his head, hoping to dislodge the water and clear it. Rather than spotting his bleeding point man, Jimbo stared into the shocked face of a fat deputy sheriff. The deputy stood in an open cell door, holding an empty bucket. The fat deputy enjoyed waking up the drunks in his cell with a bucket of water. Deputy Warden thought he was a sheriff in a Western movie.

Jimbo stopped his charge. He remembered where he was, in a jail cell in the county next to Fort Bragg. The three beaten SEALs had all sworn that Jimbo had started the ruckus the night before. The deputies arrested Jimbo. A deputy interviewed two of the SEALs in the local hospital emergency room.

"Time to wake your sorry ass up," the deputy smirked. "Your sleazy lawyer is here."

Deputy Warden was a clone of Fatso Judson from the movie *From Here to Eternity*. The deputy was a sadistic, fat, slovenly police officer. His mission was to torment anyone whom he didn't think respected his badge. Jimbo had failed to show the proper respect to Deputy Warden on previous occasions.

"You've got three minutes to wash your face before I come back for you."

Deputy Warden waved to the sink and a thin towel in the corner of the dirty cell.

Jimbo staggered over to the sink. He rubbed some lather from the coarse bar of soap and washed the sleep out of his eyes. He stared at his face in the dirty mirror. It contained no fresh scars. A bruise and scratches, though, adorned his right knuckle. When the deputy returned in four minutes, Jimbo was ready.

The deputy led Jimbo to a small, stuffy room reserved for lawyers and their clients. Ike Anderson sat in the worn chair by the table. Jimbo sat opposite him as Deputy Warden left, locking the door.

"You'll see the magistrate at ten o'clock," his lawyer stated.

"What time is it now?"

"Nine."

"What's my best defense?" Jimbo quizzed his legal counsel. "Defending my honor and the honor of the Green Berets against piss-ant swabbies?"

Ike smiled.

"Just throw yourself on the mercy of the court. The DA here knows your reputation too well. I'll emphasize your superb record of defending the world against the evils of Communism to attest to your moral character. Keep your mouth shut except to say, 'Your honor,' occasionally. The judge should release you if you pledge to appear on your court date."

Jimbo shook his head.

"Can't I just pay a fine now and leave?"

"Not likely. They know this isn't the first time you've graced their county with your presence."

Two hours later, Jimbo walked out of the courthouse with Ike Anderson.

"See you in two months for your court date."

"Right," Jimbo replied. "Send me my bill."

Ike chuckled. "Show up for your court date. Otherwise, these assholes will issue a warrant for your arrest. Anyway, those SEALs won't be here to testify. They will be too embarrassed that a single old Green Beret whipped them. You'll be free as a bird."

Ike dropped Jimbo by the bar to reclaim his beat-up car. Back at the motel, Jimbo grabbed the duffel bag and paid his bill. It was time to leave North Carolina. He vowed it was the last time he would set foot in the state. Jimbo had seen enough of it during his Army career. He had no intention of coming back for his court date. The assholes could come looking for him. But he'd be out of the country.

The judge made one mistake in ordering Jimbo to appear before him in two months. He had not asked Jimbo for his passport. Catching military hops from nearby Pope Air Force Base through California to Southeast Asia would be easy. With activity heating up again, the Air Force flew plenty of cargo planes that way. Jimbo had told the friend to send word to his old commander that retired Master Sergeant Atkins was on his way. Selling his old car would only take Jimbo a day. In four days, Jimbo figured he could be in Saigon.

DOBIE'S MISSION

---·---

D obie checked his watch. It showed 0629 Zulu, 1329 local time in Nakhon Phanom, Thailand. In ten minutes, he would call Marcel on the new radio.

The last two weeks had been a flurry of activity for Dobie. He had written his operational plan to locate and interrogate the North Vietnamese deserter with the ring. Mr. Peabody had written an agreement to fund the mission. They had negotiated and settled on the terms and payments. Importantly, they had agreed on the highest price they would pay for the ring. Dobie would decide on its authenticity or usefulness in identifying an MIA.

Dobie had flown to Saigon and recruited Jimbo Atkins. Master Sergeant Atkins had one major characteristic that Dobie needed for this mission. Sergeant Atkins responded to any real, imminent physical threat with maximum over-whelming force. Dobie credited his continued breathing on planet Earth to this characteristic.

During one firefight, Dobie had noticed Jimbo grinning as he fired his M-16 on automatic. After the firing stopped, Dobie had crawled over to him.

"What was the grin about?"

"Grin?" Jimbo had asked.

"Yea, you had this big-ass grin in the middle of the fight."

Jimbo had shrugged.

"Guess I was only enjoying my favorite pastime."

"Your favorite pastime?"

"Yes, sir. Killing Commies."

Thus, Jimbo had left for Southeast Asia certain that whatever Dobie had in mind would involve Jimbo's favorite pastime. Sergeant Atkins had also worked extensively with Hmong guerrillas in the "secret war" in Laos. He spoke passable Lao, a little Thai, and a dialect of the Hmong.

That Jimbo was available did not surprise Dobie. He had been sure that the retired NCO would accept the job. Yet, Master Sergeant Jimbo Atkins had surprised Dobie by showing up in Saigon so quickly. He had heard that Jimbo was a part-owner of a bar near Fort Bragg.

Dobie had also asked Jeff Nickerson about Charles, Mr. Peabody's lieutenant. Jeff reported that former Captain Charles Lautin was an exemplary Special Forces warrior. Charles's description of his wound had understated the situation. The incident had earned a Silver Star medal for Charles.

Dobie sat next to Charles in a room at Nakhon Phanom's best hotel. At 1339 local, Dobie keyed the mike on the new radio.

"Hook, this is Pan. Over."

Static came back through Dobie's headphones. Then ...

"Pan, go ahead."

"Let's talk," Dobie answered.

"Roger."

Dobie switched off the radio.

"What now?" Charles asked.

"We talk again in twenty-four hours."

Dobie had noticed that Charles was a man of few words. He was curious about the speed with which Ashley Peabody had agreed to back the mission. He decided it was an opportune time to ask.

"One thing has intrigued me about getting this mission organized," he began.

Charles volunteered nothing. He waited for Dobie to continue.

"Mr. Peabody surprised me with how quickly we met in Manila," Dobie added. When Charles offered no response, Dobie concluded he would have to be specific. "Mr. Peabody accepted my suggestions immediately. From what I had read, he is not prone to rash decisions."

Charles only nodded. "He isn't, I agree."

"How much background checking on me had he done?"

"He spoke with one former CO of yours when your name came to his attention. He had me talk with Jeff Nickerson."

"Which former CO?" Dobie pressed.

"I don't feel I'm at liberty to say."

"So, based on two references for one applicant, he decided?"

"We had looked into another possibility, who had contacted Mr. Peabody."

"Who?"

Charles's answer didn't surprise him.

"I'm not at liberty to say."

"But you passed on him because ..." Dobie prodded.

Charles cleared his throat before responding.

"Mr. Peabody wasn't sure of his motivation or his information. He immediately began talking about the amount of money it would take. He also demanded equal rights to the story."

Dobie was aware of one other Special Forces veteran who was trying to finance a POW rescue mission.

"Does this other gentleman seem to enjoy a TV interview or to engage the help of a psychic?" Dobie pressed.

Charles unsuccessfully suppressed a smile.

"Yes, he enjoys the TV camera. I don't know about a psychic."

"I have a guess who it might be. It's better to steer clear of him."

"Mr. Peabody thought so, too."

"During our conversation, Mr. Peabody mentioned you held the opinion that American POWs were abandoned. Is your opinion based on any intel you have seen?"

Charles hesitated.

"Well, I planned one rescue mission in Laos before the Christmas bombing of Hanoi. But we couldn't verify the info to the satisfaction of the civilian leadership. The team wanted to go anyway. The intel was the best anyone involved had ever seen. No released POW reported being in that camp. So, we left anyone there behind."

"Or none were there," Dobie noted. "But you still hold the opinion that they exist."

Charles suppressed a smile.

"In our conversation, Mr. Peabody slightly exaggerated my views. He was trying to bait you. That led to an animated monologue in our conversation with the other candidate. Mr. Peabody, though, was less than impressed by the details that he volunteered."

"Mr. Peabody concluded that this other gentleman was full of BS," Dobie suggested.

"Yes."

Dobie now suppressed a smile. *Charles answers questions and provides information like a politician.* Dobie concluded that he could have worn stars one day in the Army.

"Is it true that Mr. Peabody worked with Ho Chi Minh in World War II?" Dobie asked.

"Yes, as far as I know."

"I heard he saved the Commie's ass," Dobie added.

"I don't know about that," Charles replied.

"How did you get to work for Peabody?"

Charles seemed to squirm from Dobie's question. He cleared his throat.

"A gentleman I worked with in Laos knew Mr. Peabody."

Charles spoke as someone choosing his words carefully.

"A spook …" Dobie paused to see if Charles would elaborate.

"They had worked together in Vietnam during the World War with a group led by General Giap."

"Really?" This piece of information surprised Dobie.

"So, Mr. Peabody has the acquaintance of both Ho Chi Minh and his general," Dobie commented. "Has Mr. Peabody ventured an opinion of the North's recent incursion into Phuoc Long, South Vietnam?"

Charles shifted noticeably in his chair.

"Only to say that General Giap will not stop until he wins the ultimate victory."

"Then we had better get in and out of Laos quickly," Dobie concluded.

Twenty-four hours later, Dobie and Charles were in the same hotel room. Dobie keyed the microphone again.

"Hook, this is Pan. Over."

Static was louder than the previous day. Yet Marcel's voice came through.

"Pan, go ahead, Hook."

"Let's meet to check on Tinkerbell. Usual spot in two weeks. Over."

"Roger," was Marcel's terse reply.

"I will have some new items, over," Dobie added.

"Do I need additional assets, over?"

"Negative. I will have one. Let's stand by in one plus two if there are contingencies. Over."

"Copy that, over."

"Roger and out," Dobie finished.

"Out," Marcel concluded.

To Charles's inquiring look, Dobie explained.

"We listen on frequency in one week plus two hours. If either of us has to change our rendezvous, he initiates the call. Otherwise, neither says anything."

Charles nodded.

"We also need to ship another radio to be here," Charles stated.

"I've contacted a former partner who works with Air America," Dobie explained. "We duplicate how we got this one here. We pack it in a Japanese stereo receiver box. I catch a hop out of Clark to U-Tapao, then on to our jump-off point. My new team member will meet me in U-Tapao."

———

THE MARKET

———•———

S ue had been in Bien Hoa for nearly two weeks. She hadn't acclimated to the tropical heat and humidity. David was miserable.

"I'm hot," was his refrain. "I'm uncomfortable! Can we go swimming?"

David was used to the south Texas heat and humidity, but it was nothing compared to South Vietnam's climate. Their apartment's two window air conditioning units kept the rooms manageable for Sue. So far, the electricity had only gone out twice. Yet, it was still technically winter. She worried about what the summer heat would bring. Sue remembered Rick complaining about boils due to the summer heat during his tours in Thailand.

Besides the heat, other features of this poor country required acclimation. Sue had never seen such enormous rats. Some rivaled the size of a house cat. They came out in the evening and scampered through the yard when she and Rick sat on the porch. Mai's constant attention to the lid on their outside trash can encouraged the rats to look elsewhere for food. Yet, the garbage rotting in the Vietnamese heat attracted them. Sue's greatest fear became encountering a rodent inside the house. Geckos in the kitchen also took getting used to. Mai assured Sue that they kept the bug population under control. The small variety quickly became normal. One morning, a large one on the outside stairs startled her. Its call sounded similar to an angry insult.

While their house had indoor plumbing, boiling all the water became a habit after only two weeks. Keeping a pitcher of cold water in the refrigerator was mandatory. Sue constantly had to stop David from drinking from the faucet. She also asked Rick to look for a larger refrigerator. Sue learned to store rice, flour, sugar, and cereal in the refrigerator. Otherwise, the bugs, geckos, and rats would enjoy them.

Rick worked an erratic schedule. Some days he put in long hours at the base. On other days, he didn't go in. It depended, he said, on the funds available to train

South Vietnamese instructor pilots. How could those funds vary in such a short time? He assured her that his flying was not dangerous. He trained experienced pilots to become instructors. It involved no flying close to combat. The rules of his company's contract forbade combat flying by Rick or Clicker.

With no Americans for her to meet, Sue became desperate for a friend. Mai proved to be an efficient housekeeper and cook, so domestic duties were absent from Sue's responsibilities. Mai cooked dinner for them each evening. She would also fix a tasty lunch if asked. Although he first hesitated at the unfamiliar food, David learned to like Mai's cooking. Watching Lei enthusiastically eat his mom's cooking encouraged David.

Initially, Mai and Lei ate separately. Sue's insistence soon had them eating together. Mai also kept the house spotless, including the upstairs apartments. Thus, Sue found unfilled time on her hands.

Since she expected to be in Vietnam for a year, Sue decided to learn some Vietnamese and to cook a few Vietnamese dishes. She woke up one morning with a new resolve. As she walked down the hall with David to the stairs, she heard a woman giggling in Clicker's apartment.

Sue stopped for a second. Clicker had been out the previous evening. He hadn't returned by the time she had put David to bed. With David in bed, Sue remained in their apartment. Had Clicker brought a guest home? Sue remained uncomfortable sharing the house with Mai and Clicker. She and Rick were newcomers to the house. It seemed to be Clicker's house more than theirs. She would have to get used to it. David was young enough that awkward questions about Clicker's overnight guests were unlikely.

She was fixing a glass of iced tea when a young Vietnamese woman walked in. Clicker followed.

"Sue, this is my friend, Huyền," he stated.

Huyền bowed slightly. Sue returned the gesture.

Is that the correct response? Sue's next thought was, *She looks young.*

"I am honored to …" Huyền stumbled over the last words.

Sue noticed a heavy accent.

Well, it's better than my Vietnamese, Sue acknowledged. Greeting people would be her first lesson in the language, which Mai would teach her.

"I am pleased to meet you, Huyên," Sue replied. She thought Huyên's mascara looked overdone. *Why so many gold chains around her neck?*

"Sue is my fellow pilot's wife," Clicker explained.

"I am pleased to meet Mr. Rick's wife," Huyên added.

"You've met Rick?" Sue clarified.

"Oh, yes. Mr. Rick is very handsome man."

"And what am I?" Clicker retorted with a smile.

"You are most handsome man," Huyên clarified.

Clicker pulled her close and kissed her. Huyên blushed.

"You'll learn, Sue," Clicker explained, "that a public display of affection makes the Vietnamese uncomfortable."

Mai walked in. She and Huyên engaged in a quick conversation in Vietnamese. They seemed to know each other more than casually. Glancing at Sue, Huyên commented to Mai and giggled like a schoolgirl. Sue felt that she was the subject of the comment.

Several thoughts whirled through Sue's mind. That Huyên and Mai seemed to know each other suggested Huyên was a frequent guest. No girlfriend of Clicker's had come up in conversation, though, in the two weeks she had been in Bien Hoa. Sue found that curious, especially since Rick had not mentioned it. But Clicker having a girlfriend relieved a nagging concern. Sue had noticed Clicker looking at her. The glances had not seemed natural in the context at the times. Sue almost sensed that Clicker had been sizing her up. She had felt uncomfortable when she had noticed it.

The presence of Huyên made Sue think she had been overly sensitive. Sue gave Huyên a few glances, trying to observe her discreetly. She looked slightly younger than Mai, but Sue had already found judging ages in Vietnam difficult. Huyên was prettier than Mai. She was more gregarious than Mai, who often seemed to want to blend into the background.

Mai's reticence, though, felt very reassuring for Sue. In this new culture, Sue knew that a forceful personality would make her adjustment more difficult. Sue was normally the leader in friendships. Of her two friends from Rick's Air Force training time, Sue had been the leader. Not being in charge of a group of women was new to Sue. In her new environment, having Huyền in a group would make Sue uncomfortable.

"I'm going now," Huyền stated to Clicker.

Clicker walked her toward the front door. Sue looked at Mai.

"Mai, when you go to the market next, I'd like to go with you. I want to learn some Vietnamese recipes. Will you teach me what to buy and how to cook a couple?"

"Yes, ma'am," Mai replied, some hesitation evident.

"Don't worry, I don't mean to take your job. I enjoy cooking new things."

"Yes, ma'am."

"Please, you don't have to call me 'ma'am,'" Sue explained. "Please call me Sue!"

"Yes, ma'am," Mai instinctively said. "Oh, sorry."

"It's okay," Sue assured her. "Can we go to the market this afternoon?"

"The afternoon is not a good time to go," Mai explained.

"It's not? Why?"

"Food has sat in the hot sun all morning. Not good. The best food is gone."

"I hadn't thought of that," Sue replied.

"We will go early tomorrow morning."

"Do you bargain for the price you pay?" Sue inquired.

"Oh, yes. You never pay the first price."

"Will you teach me some Vietnamese? I want to learn the names of the food and how to count. Then you won't have to do all the shopping for me."

Mai seemed unsure when she answered.

"Yes, if you'd like. I can teach." She hesitated.

"But ..." Sue prompted.

"You will pay a higher price because you are not Vietnamese. They know you have more money than me."

"Well, that is okay," Sue conceded.

"If I help you buy food, too, they will know I buy for you. Then I'll have to pay a higher price."

"Well, I will go with you at first. Maybe next time I can buy fruit at a different place than you buy other food."

The following morning, Sue and Mai prepared for their trip to the market. Mai called to Lei, who was playing by himself on the porch. Sue had noticed that Mai took Lei with her whenever she went out.

"Mai, Lei can stay here with David and Rick if he wants to. Rick is not going to the base today."

Mai hesitated.

"I'll run upstairs and get them. The boys can play on the porch."

"Mr. Rick does not mind?"

"Rick will be fine watching them while we go," Sue assured her.

Mai spoke with Lei as Sue ran upstairs. She returned, followed by Rick and David. David had a set of bricks he enjoyed building with. He also had three toy cars.

"David doesn't mind playing with Lei?" Mai inquired.

"You would like to play with Lei, wouldn't you, David?" Sue asked her son.

David nodded enthusiastically. Mai spoke with Lei, who nodded in response. David handed Lei two of the cars, and David led them to the side porch. Rick poured some iced tea.

"Have fun at the markets," he told Sue.

"You ready to go, then?" Sue asked Mai.

They caught a pedicab in front. As Mai directed the driver, Sue looked around. It was her first real outing since arriving. She had stayed comfortably around the house, only venturing short distances with Rick. The maze of crossing streets and different angles made it easy to become lost.

Crowds along the street increased as they traveled from the house. The number of half-dressed and naked toddlers shocked Sue. Garbage, with its accompanying odor, littered the streets. Sue had crossed the Texas-Mexico border a few times to buy unique gifts or souvenirs. The streets were crowded, and she didn't remember garbage or naked kids. She understood, though, that she had stayed in the tourist district.

The pedicab stopped at a corner, and Mai paid the driver. Sue studied the market. She assumed grocery stores as she knew them did not exist. Stalls selling different food items crowded the walkway. People jammed the streets. The smell of the open-air markets in Vietnam's heat greeted her. It contrasted with the clean, air-conditioned grocery stores in the States. Sue could not imagine how the market would smell by the afternoon.

Whole plucked chickens hung from racks, with the vendor occasionally shooing flies away. He did not chase them away often enough. Unfamiliar meat hung in a different stall. Many strange vegetables spilled over the rims of round, shallow baskets on the walk. Customers and sellers haggled over prices. Sue saw customers turn and walk away, only for the vendor to call them back. Sometimes, the customer ignored the vendor's latest offer. Sue understood none of the words.

Mai found one vegetable on her list and stopped. She began a rapid exchange of words with the seller. The vendor glanced at Sue once during the exchange, which drew an immediate response from Mai. The woman's black teeth shocked Sue. Finally, Mai and the seller agreed on the price. Mai's aggressive interaction with the vendor surprised Sue. Mai pulled a small bag from her larger tote bag. She placed her purchase in it.

Sue wanted to ask Mai the names of the unfamiliar fruits. But she didn't want to interrupt Mai's shopping. One stall displayed fruit with red skin. At least Sue assumed it was a fruit. The inside was white with black specks. Mai asked a question and then sampled one cube from a stained bowl. She took another piece and handed it to Sue.

"Try this," she encouraged.

Sue nibbled it. The sweet taste surprised her. It was nothing like anything Sue had tried. Its soft texture reminded her of a banana.

"What is it?" she asked Mai.

"Thanh long," Mai replied.

Sue repeated it, taking a couple of tries before saying it correctly.

"Dragon fruit," Mai added.

After some quick haggling, Mai bought two.

Sue could not get used to the smells of the market. Once, Mai waded deep inside a shop for an item on her list. Sue focused on breathing through her mouth to suppress a gag. The last item Mai found was a chicken hanging on the rack. She inspected three before she pronounced one satisfactory. The customary negotiation over the price followed.

As Mai led them to a corner to hail a cab, Sue reassessed the advisability of shopping for herself. It would be some time before Sue would learn enough Vietnamese to try it. The array of unfamiliar fruits and vegetables overwhelmed her. Mai's negotiating skills impressed Sue.

When they arrived back at the house, Rick looked up from paperwork on his lap. The boys were laughing on the porch. Lei delighted in crashing a toy car into a building he had constructed.

"How was shopping?" Rick inquired.

"Whew!" Sue exclaimed. "Mai, you were ruthless! You should have seen her, Rick."

Mai blushed.

"Mai, why were some people's teeth so black?" Sue inquired.

"From chewing betel nuts," Mai answered.

"But why do they do it if it turns their teeth black?" Sue pressed.

"They like how it makes them feel," Mai responded. "And some think it is a sign of beauty."

Sue shivered.

———•———

The morning after her trip to the market, Sue sat with Lei and David on the front porch looking at a picture book. Lei was showing them the pictures and telling them the Vietnamese words. Three older Vietnamese boys spotted them from the walk and came through the gate to the porch. The oldest one said something in Vietnamese. The other two repeated a Vietnamese phrase. Sue tried to focus on understanding it. But the sound of Vietnamese was strange to her, and she could not catch the phrase. Then the three began chanting it together.

From the tone, Sue surmised it was an insult. She watched Lei. He said nothing in response. He lowered his head. Sue noticed a tear form in his right eye. The chant changed to something else. Lei lowered his head further.

"Lei," Sue interrupted the boys. "Could you help me inside with something?"

Lei looked up, and Sue motioned for David and him to follow her inside.

"Bring your book. I have another to read."

Lei wiped his eyes with the back of his hand and sniffled.

Later, Sue asked Mai about it. She tried to repeat the phrase, but Mai could not understand her pronunciation. Yet, she learned her guess was correct.

"Other Vietnamese children do not want to associate with Lei," Mai confessed. "They call him names."

"Why are the children so mean?" Sue asked Mai.

Mai lowered her head.

"It is because Lei's father is American." She paused. "Are American children nice to other children who are different?"

"American children can be mean to each other," Sue admitted. "Every playground has its bully who feels compelled to pick on any different child."

Lei had one friend, Mai told Sue. He lived at the nearby Hoa Sen Orphanage. Quý had an American father, too. His mother had died in fighting near Da Nang. Catholic nuns had found Quý on the streets of Da Nang as a baby in 1968. They had arranged for him to find a home at Hoa Sen in Bien Hoa.

———•———

CROSSING THE MEKONG

Dobie stepped off a C-130 at U-Tapao Royal Thai Air Base. He stood by the crew door, looking across the tarmac in the haze. Transient services parked the plane on a remote side of the base between two old hangars. Two minutes later, a panel truck pulled up. A group wearing civilian clothes emerged. The Air Force flight crew from Clark Air Base climbed into the van. One of the arriving group wearing black cowboy boots walked up to Dobie.

"I see you are still in the game," he greeted Dobie as he held out his hand.

Dobie shook the offered hand.

"Not ready to just fade away, Cowboy," Dobie answered. "Thanks for offering my partner and me a ride."

Jimbo Atkins stepped off the van wearing a large rucksack and carrying two duffel bags.

"Any problems with the gear?" Dobie asked.

Jimbo shook his head.

"None."

"The radio is in the box inside." Dobie motioned to the crew door. "Repack it while I review our destination with the pilot."

Jimbo climbed up the crew steps into the airplane.

"Let me check with our crew chief," Cowboy said. "Need to make sure all the markings are off."

Dobie watched the crew chief in civilian clothes scamper up a maintenance stand. He loosened the screws on the black US decal on the side of the fuselage. In a few minutes, the Air Force plane became a ghost plane, devoid of any national markings.

The pilot pulled an air chart from his tattered flight bag. He unfolded it, then refolded it. He pointed to an airfield symbol along the Thailand-Laos border.

"Here is the best place to drop you. It's as close to the border as we get. Will that work for you?"

Dobie held a topographical map, which he unfolded. He checked the pilot's chart, then his own.

"That's perfect," he exclaimed. "It's a short hike to a place to cross the river."

"Should take us about one hour and fifty minutes. We will stay low and not fly a direct route. It'll be a bumpy ride with the thermals. A few thunderstorms are along the way. We leave as soon as we load two pallets."

The flight north took five minutes longer than expected. Dobie and Jimbo were the only passengers. The cargo consisted of small container delivery system pallets with parachutes. Dobie did not ask the pilot where the cargo was going, and the pilot did not inquire about what Dobie was doing in Thailand.

During the bumpy flight, Dobie and Jimbo repacked their rucksacks and checked their equipment. Jimbo had purchased weapons and ammo from funds provided by Charles. He also bought a few food items and various sizes of Thai gold baht chains. Gold remained a popular currency in Southeast Asia. Dobie and Jimbo split the gold chains between them. The weapons and ammo remained in the duffel bags, out of sight. Jimbo stuffed the radio into a waterproof pack made for it.

They planned to meet Marcel and Keej across the border in Laos in two days. Marcel would have a few other food items and another form of currency they would need: small packs of raw opium.

Keeping a low profile for two days troubled Dobie. But they had to build flexibility into their schedule with Marcel, who had to travel through territory hostile to the Hmong. Jimbo hoped that the message he had sent to one of his old Hmong contacts had gotten through. This individual's village was further south than Marcel's. Jimbo had asked if two Hmong were available to help him and Dobie move their supplies to a safe hiding place.

The two soldiers discussed what to carry on their jungle trek looking for the deserter. The radio was too large and too important to take with them. They decided to leave it at Marcel's hut in his village. Traveling light for speed and stealth was a priority.

Dobie had barely closed his eyes for a quick nap when the loadmaster tapped him.

"Twenty minutes out," he shouted over the din of the engines and rattling tie-down chains.

Dobie nodded, then passed the message to Jimbo.

Fifteen minutes later, the loadmaster made a belting signal. It was time to tighten their lap belts on the troop seats. The airfield was packed dirt, and the pilot wasn't sure of its condition. He would have to make a low pass to inspect it. If he thought it could handle the sixty-ton airplane, he would land. If it wasn't, Dobie and Jimbo would have to attach parachutes hanging in the cargo compartment to their equipment. Then they would don chutes themselves.

The loadmaster put on a restraining harness and secured himself near the cargo ramp. He then raised the rear cargo door. He picked up an M-16 and lay down to look out the back.

The plane entered a steep left turn. Dobie realized the pilot was approaching the airport from directly overhead, spiraling down in a tight turn. After a few minutes in the turn, Dobie felt the airplane level off. He heard the power increase as he twisted his head to look out a small window. He saw the tops of trees barely below them. Then, the airplane climbed steeply. It entered a sharp left turn.

The loadmaster stood and lowered the cargo door. A rumbling of the landing gear and the whine of the flap motors told Dobie the pilot judged the runway to be in good condition. The loadmaster strapped himself into a troop seat in front of the two cargo pallets. After another tight left turn, Dobie felt the plane drop toward the runway. He turned to see foliage outside go by in a blur. The big aircraft slammed onto the rough runway, bounced once, then stayed firmly on the ground. The propellers roared into reverse. Dobie and Jimbo lurched forward as the pilot slammed on the brakes.

The loadmaster signaled to Dobie and Jimbo. They unbuckled their seatbelts. As the airplane turned around on the runway and taxied, the two soldiers gathered their gear and shuffled to the ramp. Dobie stumbled as the plane lurched left. The plane jerked to a stop. The loadmaster opened the cargo door and lowered the ramp under it.

Dragging their gear, Dobie and Jimbo hustled down the ramp into the heat and haze of the nearby jungle. They had walked only a few feet before the pilot added power and the hot exhaust and dust swirled around them. Minimum ground time was essential for the plane to arrive at a drop zone in the jungle.

They placed their rucksacks, the duffle bag, and the radio pack at the edge of the taxiway next to the brush. Dobie gazed around, looked at the sun, then pulled his map out of his pack. They planned to hike the few miles to a river crossing. They needed to entice a fisherman with a boat to ferry them across. The area was remote, so they hoped not to encounter any official demanding a bribe to allow them to cross.

Dobie and Jimbo slipped their arms through the shoulder straps of their heavy packs. They picked up the duffel bags and the radio pack and hiked into the jungle on a narrow path. After an hour of slogging, they heard the faint sound of a rushing river. Another hour passed before the sound increased.

"At ten o'clock," Jimbo said softly.

Dobie looked to his left front. A glimmer of water appeared between the heavy vegetation. The path widened and turned toward the river. After a slight left turn, the vegetation cleared, and Dobie and Jimbo faced the mighty Mekong River. It was running high and fast. The rainy season in Laos had ended two months before. However, all the Mekong's tributaries still poured the rains into the large river. Two other paths through the jungle emptied into the clearing. Two large canoes stood near one path.

The men lowered the duffel bags and the radio, then slid their packs off. Dobie checked his watch. They stored their rucksacks and duffel bags in the brush out of sight.

"We have a few hours before the sun drops lower," he told Jimbo. "I'll stay awake if you want to get a few winks."

"I'll nap for an hour," Jimbo responded. "Then wake me so you get a few winks."

An hour before dusk, Dobie tapped Jimbo. Jimbo's eyes popped open.

"Company's coming," Dobie told him.

Minutes later, four Thais carrying fishing nets stepped into the clearing from the path close to the canoes. They stopped near the canoes when they spotted the Americans.

Jimbo rose and called a greeting to them in Thai. One responded, and the group inched forward. Jimbo pointed to the canoes and asked a question. The Thais spoke among themselves. Jimbo pulled a small baht chain from a pocket in his combat vest. He unsnapped a few links. Holding three up, he asked another question.

One Thai shook his head. Jimbo added another link.

The Thai looked at his partners, then turned and nodded his head.

"We have transportation across the river," Jimbo declared.

The two soldiers retrieved their gear and plodded to the canoes. The Thais gathered their nets and carried the canoes to the edge of the river. Twenty minutes later, Dobie and Jimbo stood on the Laotian side of the Mekong River.

———•———

HOA SEN ORPHANAGE

———•———

Sue and David had been in Saigon for three weeks. With Mai's guidance, Sue had learned her way around their Bien Hoa neighborhood. She had bought a few food items at the nearby market. The market carried a few snack items David learned to like. But shopping at the large markets would take a long time.

Rick and Clicker returned from the base early on a Wednesday afternoon. As he placed his flight bag near the stairs, Rick heard clicking on the side porch. He walked onto the porch. Lei and David played with blocks on the floor. Sue and Mai sat at a card table with rows of colorful bamboo tiles arranged on the table.

"This is a khàn?" Sue asked, pointing to three tiles.

"No. It is a phỗng," Mai answered. "A khàn is four tiles together."

Sue leaned back and laughed.

"This will take some time to learn!"

"What's going on?" Rick inquired.

"Mai is teaching me to play Mạt chược," Sue responded, struggling to pronounce the last word.

"Vietnamese Mahjong," Mai clarified.

"We have been at it since before lunch," Sue explained. "Mai must think I'm the slowest learner."

"You learn very well," Mai responded. "Vietnamese Mahjong is not easy. I learned over many years watching my grandfather and uncles play during Tet."

Clicker walked in.

"Uh oh," he stated. "Be careful playing mahjong with Mai."

Sue looked at him.

"Why?"

"Because she is an expert."

"She is teaching me," Sue explained.

"Well, you have an excellent teacher then."

Sue slid her chair back.

"My brain is exhausted. Let's quit for now. Let's resume my lessons tomorrow."

"Will some tea or a cocktail help your brain recover?" Rick asked Sue.

"Iced tea," Sue replied.

"What would you like, Mai?" Rick asked.

"I can get it," Mai said as she stood.

"Rick doesn't mind getting it, do you, dear?" Sue interjected.

Mai glanced at Rick.

"Not at all," Rick assured her.

"Lemonade, please."

Minutes later, Rick returned with a wicker tray of drinks. He handed Sue and Mai their drinks. He sat in a wicker chair with his bourbon.

As she sipped her iced tea, Sue glanced at Mai. As she had with her Air Force friends, Sue felt a bond growing with Mai. Although Mai and Lei's father had never married, she regarded Mai as a soldier's widow. Sue looked at Rick.

"Do you think I could find a job at Jeff's office? I'll go stir-crazy sitting around here in this heat and humidity. Mai has agreed to look after David. For pay, of course. You could ask Jeff."

"The Defense Attaché Office is a long ride from here," Rick observed.

"Yes," Sue conceded. "I guess that wouldn't make sense."

"We always need help at the orphanage," Mai volunteered. "But it cannot pay."

"That sounds like a worthwhile way to be helpful," Rick suggested.

"Tomorrow we start a big cleaning," Mai continued. "It will be a big job. We need more help."

"What will I do with David?" Sue asked.

"I always take Lei there with me. He plays with his friend and other young children while I work."

"If Lei does it," Sue replied, "David will think it is a fun game. I'll come with you."

———·———

Following breakfast the next morning, Mai hailed a pedicab in front of their house. David and Lei sat on their mothers' laps. Sue clutched David as the driver zipped through the streets to Hoa Sen Orphanage.

Sue had no reference on what to expect at the Vietnamese orphanage. She had never visited an orphanage in the States. But she knew Oliver Twist, Huckleberry Finn, and Little Orphan Annie were fictional orphans.

The decrepit house shocked Sue when the cab pulled up to it. It stood on a dingy back street off Highway 1 to Saigon. Mai's comment that it needed cleaning was a massive understatement. The building needed to be razed and rebuilt. She could not imagine how it remained standing.

She felt discouraged that she could make any noticeable dent to improve its condition. Sue felt she was adjusting to the culture shock. Looking at the Hoa Sen Orphanage brought back the shock when she had first left Tan Son Nhut Air Base.

Her first thought was, *What have I signed up for?*

As Mai led Sue and David through the open front door, Sue watched David. His eyes were wide with surprise. Nothing in the four-year-old's life in America had prepared him for this. Lei, however, took the interior of the orphanage in stride. He waved to another Amerasian boy his age and led David by the hand over to him.

Sue could not tell if they were in some kind of common room or in a room that housed children. She saw no beds or cribs. Mats were on the floor. The large room contained low tables scattered around. Three adolescent girls scrubbed three of the tables with sponges.

"This is the dining room and living room," Mai explained, reading Sue's confused look. "The bedrooms are down the hall and upstairs. Each room has children of varying ages. That way, the older children help with their younger brothers and sisters."

Sue only nodded.

"Come, let me introduce you to Sister Helene, the Mother Superior."

"How many nuns are here?"

"Sister Helene has two other nuns to help, Sister Francis and Sister Barbara. Sister Helene is from France, and the other nuns are Vietnamese."

"How many children?"

"I'm not sure. Maybe seventy-five to eighty."

Mai led Sue down a short hallway into the kitchen. A nun stood at a sink washing dishes, talking to three other girls. She looked up when Mai and Sue entered. She finished quick instructions to the girls and walked over.

The nun wore a traditional black habit with a veil covering her white head-piece. Beads of perspiration dotted her forehead. She had rolled up the long sleeves to the elbows.

"Sister Helene, this is my friend, Sue," Mai introduced her. "She wants to help."

Sister Helene wiped her wet hands on her tunic and held out her right hand.

"I am so glad to meet you," the Mother Superior said. "We are always in need of help from generous friends."

Sue detected a French accent in her English.

"Sue brought her son, David, too," Mai added. "Lei is introducing David to Quý in the dining room."

"Excellent!" Sister Helene responded. She looked at Mai. "Would you and Sue mind cleaning the nursery upstairs?"

"Not at all," Sue responded.

"Mai knows where all our cleaning supplies are. I'm afraid I don't have time to sit and chat with you right now. We have so much to do. We can get acquainted at tea this afternoon."

The nun's eyes sparkled as she spoke. Sue guessed that Sister Helene was about fifty years old. She shifted her gaze from Mai and Sue back to her helpers at the kitchen sink.

"I see my helpers need a little more guidance. If you will excuse me."

She turned back to the sink and issued instructions in Vietnamese to the girls.

"Follow me," Mai instructed Sue. "As you can see, Sister Helene is all work. We have a hard time getting her to relax."

Sue followed Mai through the back door to a porch with tall cabinets. Mai opened one and removed two pails and several rags. She poured powdered soap into the pails and led Sue to a pump just down the back steps. After they filled their pails with water, Mai walked back into the house. They walked up creaking stairs, down a short hall, and into a room.

The nursery had a dozen cribs in varying degrees of disrepair along the walls.

"The babies sleep here, right next to the nuns' rooms," Mai informed Sue. "They stay in the nursery until they are about two and have learned to follow the instructions of the oldest children."

The scene broke Sue's heart. Diapers were fashioned from rags. The room smelled of soiled diapers. Two young girls changed diapers. Two boys stripped torn, dirty sheets from some cribs and put on clean ones. They simply rolled the babies from one side of the crib to the other while they accomplished the feat.

"We need to wipe down and clean the cribs," Mai revealed. "Sister Helene is insistent on keeping the cribs and sheets clean. The boys take the dirty sheets downstairs and wash them in tubs out back."

"Sister Helene seems to have the children well organized," Sue observed.

"She believes that taking care of their home and their brothers and sisters gives them a noble purpose. Sister Helene does not tolerate sloth or sitting around feeling sorry for oneself. She teaches the children that idle hands are the devil's workshop."

Sue peeked into the nearest crib with the tiniest baby she had ever seen. The umbilical cord looked like a newborn's. A handwritten label on the wooden crib said, "Thi."

Sue nudged Mai.

"Look at this little sweetheart."

Mai stepped over and peered at the baby.

"She is new!" she exclaimed.

Mai turned to one girl and asked a question in Vietnamese. Sue waited while the girl explained something.

"Hồng says that Sister Barbara found her on the doorstep in a box two mornings ago," Mai explained. "Sister Barbara named her."

The baby let out a healthy cry. Sue reached in and gently picked her up. Her heart melted as she gazed at the unfocused look of a newborn. Sue lifted the loose-fitting diaper.

"She needs changing. Where is a clean diaper?"

Hồng understood, and she retrieved a clean rag from a pile. Sue took it and laid Thi down in the crib.

"She has a terrible diaper rash," Sue said. "Do they have anything for it?"

Mai quizzed Hồng again, who shook her head in response.

"What about some gentle soap?" Sue asked.

Mai retrieved a coarse bar of soap and handed it to Sue.

"This is all we have."

Sue took it and wet a small rag in a basin of clean water. She rubbed it on the bar of soap, then dabbed the baby's bottom. After she dabbed the baby dry with another rag, Sue folded a new rag into a diaper. Thi continued crying.

"She must be hungry," Sue said, looking at Mai.

Mai asked another question, and Hồng rushed into the hall.

"Hồng will get a bottle of formula from the icebox."

Minutes later, Hồng returned with a small bottle. She handed it to Sue.

"Thank you, Hồng. You are very helpful."

Mai translated for Sue. Hồng's face broke into a broad smile. Sue sat in a worn wicker chair and fed Thi. As the baby gulped the formula, Sue watched the four children in the room continue their chores. They were incredibly thin. The children wore tattered clothes. Yet, the children and their clothes were clean. And while the children were not whistling like Snow White's Dwarfs, they went about their chores without whining or stalling. Their attitudes were unlike most American children Sue had observed when work was to be done.

Any idea about finding a job vanished from Sue's mind. This was where she needed to be during her time in Vietnam. Ruth, Karen, Maggie, and all her American friends would hear about the Hoa Sen Orphanage. Sue knew her friends would send needed items. She also made one decision to tell Rick.

When Rick returned from the base late that afternoon, he found Sue on the porch writing a letter at the table. Two other letters in addressed envelopes sat in front of her.

"Who are you writing to?" he inquired.

Sue paused and looked at him.

"I'm writing to Maggie Sorensen."

"Who are those letters to?" he asked, gesturing to the two envelopes.

"Ruth and Karen."

Sue finished her letter and reached for an envelope.

"What about?"

Sue stopped and looked at Rick.

"Oh, Rick," she began, her voice quivering. "You should see the orphanage. It will make you cry. The children are so thin. They wear rags for clothes. Diapers for the babies are just rags."

She stopped. Rick could see tears forming in her eyes.

"And there is this cutest, most precious baby. She can't be over four days old. A nun found her on their porch steps two mornings ago."

Sue stopped and took a tissue from the box on the table. Rick noticed other crumpled tissues in the basket next to the table. Sue wiped her eyes and blew her nose.

"We have to adopt her. I want to bring her to live with us. Tomorrow. Her name is Thi."

Rick sat in the chair opposite his wife. He looked at her. She was not asking what he thought about this idea. She was merely informing him. He nodded.

"If that's what you want. But we'll have to find out how to do that."

"Sister Helene, the Mother Superior, will know. She will help us."

"Is that what you are telling everyone about?"

"No. I'm asking them to send things the orphanage needs. I wish I had taken our camera so I could have pictures of the children. But I want to mail these right away. The orphanage needs diapers, children's clothing, soap, sponges, and diaper rash ointment. I'm asking them to convince their churches and book clubs to donate. And for Maggie and Karen to ask their Officers' Wives Clubs."

Rather than leave for the base the next morning, Rick asked Mai for directions to the orphanage. He and Sue drove there to meet with Sister Helene. The Mother Superior immediately agreed to begin the paperwork for Rick and Sue to adopt Thi. They rushed to the small Base Exchange and Commissary at Tan Son Nhut to buy the available baby supplies and formula. They found diapers, three changes of clothes that were too big, and some formula.

On the way to their house, they stopped at Hoa Sen to pick up Thi. Sister

Helene gave them the small crib that Thi had been using. The Mother Superior thought it would take two to three weeks for the adoption approval.

Setting Thi's crib in their small bedroom, Rick watched his wife. For the first time since she had arrived in Vietnam, she looked cheerful.

———◆———

DOWN INTO THE WEEDS

——•——

March 1975 did not start well for the Army of the Republic of Vietnam (ARVN). The People's Army of Vietnam (PAVN) launched an assault on Hue. The historic city, the site of pitched battles during the Tet Offensive in 1968, stood about fifty miles south of the Demilitarized Zone. Fortunately, the ARVN fought off the attack.

Thursday afternoon, Clicker walked into the small office.

"Colonel Tinh wants to talk to us."

"About?" Rick asked.

"A problem with his pilots was all he said."

Rick stood to follow Clicker into the hall.

"He wants to meet here," Clicker advised Rick. "He's on his way over."

"Any guess what his problem is?"

"I have a couple. But let's let him tell us."

The colonel arrived in a few minutes. Both Americans stood when the Vietnamese officer walked into the office.

"How can we help you?" Clicker began.

Colonel Tinh unfolded an aeronautical chart on the desk.

"Tomorrow we are to bomb a North Vietnamese base our Rangers have discovered."

The colonel pointed to a large red circle on the chart. Smaller circles ringed the location.

"Southwest of Ban Me Thuot," Clicker noted.

"And north of Bình Phuoc," Rick added, "where the NVA remains entrenched after their January victory."

"The target is near the Trail from Cambodia," Colonel Tinh explained. "Intel thinks a buildup is occurring to attack Ban Me Thuot. But Army commanders in the area think that Pleiku would be the target."

"Making Hue only a diversion?" Rick asked.

"The ultimate target of an attack isn't my problem," the colonel responded. "My challenge is to convince my pilots to drop their bombs from a lower altitude to increase their accuracy."

"Still dropping them too high?" Clicker asked.

"Yes. They are leery of waiting to get low."

"What altitude are they dropping from usually?" Rick inquired.

"Nine thousand feet," the colonel admitted.

"You can't hit squat from that high," Rick noted. "They need to get down into the weeds. No higher than six thousand."

"With the anti-aircraft guns around this part of the trail, that will be hard to convince them to do," Clicker noted.

"Maybe rolling in from a lower altitude will help them wait," Rick suggested.

"I am leading an attack tomorrow morning. I intend to drop my bombs from six thousand to show them the improved accuracy."

"But you still need to convince the rest to follow your lead, right?" Clicker concluded.

"Do you have a good flight leader who will follow your example?" Rick asked.

"One or two, I hope."

"Do they understand they are wasting valuable bombs by dropping too high? And that they will have to go back to the target again?"

Colonel Tinh shrugged his shoulders. "I have emphasized that frequently."

"What you need," Rick started, "is a good wingman to follow you down. Two good hits on the target right away would encourage them."

"How many flights are hitting the target tomorrow?" Clicker asked.

"Only three," the colonel responded. "The ARVN Rangers will launch an assault on the site after artillery continues to pound it after we hit. Another wing will provide close air support for them. A third wing will be on alert if the Rangers need more support."

"Do you have a forward air controller to mark the target?" Rick asked.

"No FAC," Colonel Tinh admitted. "Strelas are everywhere now. A slow FAC plane is an easy target for the missile. But a Ranger team will be close to call in artillery for an hour before our time-on-target. Another Ranger team is at our initial point. They will call for artillery to stop before we pop up. The last few artillery rounds will be Willy Pete to mark the target. The white smoke should give us a clear aim point."

"You'll need your two best flight leaders behind you," Rick added. "What about a strong wingman following you?"

"I'm afraid I don't have one I can count on," the colonel admitted.

"I wish we had a good answer for you," Clicker stated.

When Colonel Tinh stood to leave, Rick followed him out the door.

"Let me grab my flight manual," he told the colonel. "I'll help plan the route and pull-up point. If we roll in from ten thousand coming straight in, it will limit the time in the flak."

"We?" The colonel raised his eyebrows.

"I'll fly on your wing. We'll show your pilots how to dive bomb accurately."

"How will you get permission to fly?"

"I'll beg for forgiveness rather than ask permission. Schedule one of your junior lieutenants on your wing. When he gets to his plane, give him the day off. If you don't tell anyone, I won't."

Colonel Tinh considered Rick's offer. Then he nodded.

———·———

Rick woke the next morning before Sue for the dawn mission briefing. He was glad he didn't have to explain why he wore his flight suit, especially since he had "sanitized" it. Black Velcro patches adorned the olive green jumpsuit where his name tag and company patch went.

During the mission briefing, Rick sat quietly in the back, jotting down notes on the pad on his kneeboard. Colonel Tinh had a copy of the mission flight plan for Rick. Riding out to the planes with the colonel in his jeep avoided any obvious question from any curious pilot. The colonel ensured their jets were parked together. When the young lieutenant arrived on the crew bus, Colonel Tinh took him aside. Then he handed the jeep keys to him. Rick received a glance from the lieutenant as Rick walked around the F-5 during his preflight.

At the planned takeoff time, Colonel Tinh released the brakes of his F-5 and lit the afterburners. Twenty seconds later, Rick popped his brakes, lit his burners, and roared down the runway after him. Butterflies churned in his stomach.

Getting reprimanded for this flight was the least of his worries. While this mission was far simpler and less dangerous than he had flown over North Vietnam, it was no milk run. Half of the artillery rounds that rained down aimed at the guns protecting the target. But hitting guns with other guns required an artillery spotter up close. The South Vietnamese Rangers directing the artillery, though, were not that close.

Rick quickly joined on Colonel Tinh's jet, slipping into an extended fingertip formation. Rather than the loose trail formation of Rick's fighter units, the colonel liked his pilots closer. He had told Rick that he wanted his wingmen up close, where he could watch and lead them effectively.

Like most of his combat missions, the navigation checkpoints flashed beneath them. Staying in position and navigating left little time to ponder the welcome that awaited them. Rick hoped his instincts would take over once the flak started exploding around him. Yet, it had been over two years since his last combat mission. Like any skill, proficient combat flying demanded recent experience and the ever-essential luck.

Past the initial point, the last checkpoint leading to the target, Colonel Tinh spread the formation into close trail in a climb. As he climbed, Rick looked to the east at the "softening-up" artillery. He noticed a few muzzle flashes.

Shit, he thought, *hope they got the word.*

He knew, however, that the chances of getting hit by one of their inbound rounds were minuscule compared to the AAA ahead. As Rick scanned the terrain ahead in his climb, white smoke began appearing on the hill ahead.

The marker rounds were landing in a tight cluster.

The South Vietnamese Rangers must be damn close, Rick thought.

Colonel Tinh rolled his F-5 inverted and pulled into his dive. Two seconds later, Rick followed him down. No AAA rounds were visible. Instinctively, Rick glanced from his bomb site to above the glare shield, where the F-105 had its radar warning panel. The F-5 did not have it. The space was empty, but his instincts proved difficult to ignore. South Vietnamese pilots flew blind, unaware of enemy radar tracking them. Maybe it was better the F-5 didn't have the warning system. It would make the Vietnamese pilots more nervous. Rick had known F-105 pilots who had turned the system off before they reached a target.

The artillery has kept the bastard's heads down, at least, Rick concluded.

As Rick saw the Colonel's bombs fall, all hell broke loose around them. Flak exploded everywhere. Checking his altitude, Rick saw that the colonel had waited until the last second to drop his bombs. Rick punched the "pickle" button for his bomb load.

As he rolled left to follow the colonel, his jet shuddered violently. Instinctively, Rick checked the Master Caution light below the glare shield. It was dark. Yet, the fighter seemed to respond sluggishly to his inputs to weave away from the target. Rick spotted the colonel ahead and lit his afterburners to close the distance. The jet buffeted.

He checked the Master Caution again. One light flickered. Rick scanned the engine instruments. Was his fuel flow on the right engine fluctuating? Rick held the jet steady for a second.

Damn, he noticed. *A definite wobble in the fuel flow.* Nothing else looked abnormal.

Colonel Tinh banked into a tight right turn. The colonel planned to set up an orbit out of AAA range, to watch the rest of the F-5s diving on the target. He wanted to know which pilots dropped their bombs too high. Rick slid to the outside of the colonel's turn. He needed to have the colonel check him over.

Rick needed to say something more than a quick response in Vietnamese on the radio. Now, everyone on frequency, including the North Vietnamese, would know an American was in the formation.

"Lead, check me," he broadcast quickly.

Two clicks acknowledged his call. The colonel turned away from the target. Rick watched the colonel slide to his right wing, then under him, reappearing on Rick's left side.

"Head zero niner zero," came the brief call in English. "Go Winchester."

The colonel wanted to talk to him off the strike frequency, on UHF frequency "thirty-thirty," 303.0, a frequency often used by Air Force pilots.

Rick dialed it in. His Master Caution came on, followed by the engine fire light on the right engine. Rick immediately pulled the right throttle to idle. The light stayed on. Rick pulled the throttle to the OFF position, shutting down the burning engine.

"Fire on number two," Rick radioed.

"You have a large hole where the right wing joins the fuselage," the colonel said. "You are streaming fuel. Looks like there are holes in both fuel tanks. Your right flap also has damage. How's the fire?"

"Light still on," Rick informed him. Rick shut off the fuel switch on the right engine.

"Let's get to the coast," the colonel responded. "Turn ten right."

Rick glanced ahead where he saw the nearest blue of the ocean in the distance. He eased the fighter into a shallow right turn. The engine fire light went out.

An emergency locator beacon started wailing on the emergency frequency. Two seconds later, a frantic Vietnamese voice shouted on the "guard" frequency. Rick understood the call.

"TWO, EJECT, EJECT!"

It sounded like two other planes were in trouble. But a second beacon didn't sound. Rick keyed his mike.

"Lead, coast in sight. Fire light is out. Head back if you need to."

"I'll stay with you," the colonel responded. "Fuel stream has increased. Go to cross-feed."

Rick checked his fuel. He could see it had decreased.

The emergency frequency became busy. Rick gathered that a rescue helicopter was being requested behind them.

"Nha Trang is at twelve o'clock at four one," Colonel Tinh advised. Rick looked at his tactical aeronautical chart for the navigation station frequency. He dialed it into his navigation radio. The needle pointed straight ahead. The distance counter showed forty nautical miles.

Suddenly, Rick's plane banked right and yawed. Rick countered the roll with the control stick and a slight tap on the left rudder.

"Your right flap is loose on the inboard side," Colonel Tinh advised. "Throttle back."

Rick nudged the left engine throttle back. His airspeed slowed.

"Your right flap looks like it will tear loose," the colonel warned. "If it does, I recommend you bail out. I'm sliding further out."

The colonel's plane slid out of view off Rick's right shoulder.

"I'll be off frequency for a minute," the colonel advised.

Rick clicked his mike button to acknowledge.

A minute later, the colonel was back on the Winchester frequency.

"I've called for a helicopter to pick you up after you land. Wait at base ops. They'll tow the plane from the overrun if you end up there. I suggest a no-flap landing. Even with a short runway, I don't think you should move your flaps."

"Understand," Rick answered. "I want to do a controllability check."

Rick nudged his power back, allowing the aircraft to slow to final approach speed. He maintained his altitude. It was better to find out if he was going to have control problems with extra altitude. The jet slowed to the no-flap approach speed. Rick needed nearly full left aileron to keep the wings level and an unusual amount of left rudder. The loose aileron was creating drag that pulled his plane to the right.

"Do you see any damage near the gear doors?" Rick asked.

"Negative."

"Gear's coming down."

Rick lowered the landing gear handle, adding power. The rumbling created some turbulence to overcome. Three green lights came on, showing the gear was down and locked.

"I'm leaving the gear down," Rick advised.

"Change to Nha Trang tower," the colonel ordered, reciting the frequency for Rick.

The colonel spoke to the tower in Vietnamese, explaining Rick's need for an emergency landing.

"You're cleared for a straight-in to runway one-two," Colonel Tinh radioed. "Plant it on the threshold, hold the nose off to aero-brake, then stand on the brakes."

"Copy that," Rick agreed.

Rick's respect for the Colonel increased. He was providing excellent help to a wingman in trouble.

He's as good as any Thud pilot, Rick recognized.

Keeping the nose elevated after landing would create drag to slow the aircraft. He needed to save the brakes as long as he could. They would be dangerously hot by the time he stopped in the overrun. Normally, the F-5 had a drag chute to use on landing. The South Vietnamese Air Force, though, did not have any chutes.

As the runway threshold approached, Rick saw a fire truck on a taxiway halfway down the runway. He expected it would be right behind him as he stopped.

The main wheels touched the runway threshold stripe. Rick held the stick back to keep the nose up. Once the stick was full aft, he gently eased it forward to allow the nose wheel to touch down. Better to do it with control than it slamming down on its own. Rick knew he was still going too fast for the short runway. He aggressively applied pressure to the tops of the rudder pedals for full brakes. The runway markers slowed as he raced past them.

The fighter stopped at the end of the overrun of the runway. Rick shut down the left engine and quickly finished the emergency engine shutdown. The fire truck swung around to the nose of the airplane. Two firemen dragged hoses toward the main landing gear. Rick opened the canopy and reached out to open the steps on the side of the aircraft. He unhooked his seat belt and connections, then stepped over the side of the plane.

After the firemen determined that no danger remained, Rick walked to inspect the damage. The size of the holes shocked him. Colonel Tinh had understated the damage. A hole the size of a basketball sat at the junction of the right flap and the wing. A similar hole bored into the fuselage at the wing root. The right flap dangled by one piece of twisted aluminum on its outboard side. Rick could not understand how it had remained attached to the wing. The hole in the fuselage showed a charred engine, with fuel, hydraulic, and electrical lines burned through. He had never landed with such battle damage to his jet.

"Nice landing, sir," the Vietnamese fire chief complimented Rick in English. "I hope Charley paid a dear price for this," he finished, touching the twisted metal.

The chief studied Rick as if he wanted to ask a question. Instead, he reached to shake Rick's hand.

The fire chief offered a ride to Base Operations. Rick walked up to the operations desk.

"I'm expecting a helicopter from Bien Hoa," he advised the Vietnamese airman, who only nodded. Rick wished he knew more Vietnamese.

An officer came from an office behind the desk.

"Your base called. There isn't a helicopter available to come pick you up. They will send one in the morning."

Shit, Rick thought. "Is there a phone I can use to call my office?" Rick asked. The operations officer pointed to the end of the counter. Rick dialed his office number, hoping Clicker was there. Clicker picked up immediately.

"Can you tell Sue I'm staying here?" he requested. "Just say I had to fly here to check on a plane and that my plane then broke."

"Gotcha," Clicker answered. "But I'll send a messenger over since I'm stuck here trying to get maintenance set up for the other plane that was shot up. He ended up at Tan Son Nhut."

"I heard a third plane took a hit. Any word on it or the pilot?"

"His wingman didn't see him bail out, and the plane augured in."

"Tough day for the Colonel," Rick noted.

"Yep. I was especially glad when the Colonel called to say you'd landed okay." Silence ensued.

"Listen, Rick. No more of this shit. I don't want to be the one to tell Sue you are MIA or worse."

"Yeah, you're right. I wonder if my $10K GI life insurance would cover this."

"Well, even if it did, no other life insurance would. The small print excludes acts of war."

"Make sure Sue gets the word I'm here for the night and everything is okay."

"I'll send a messenger. When I get back to the house, I'll make sure."

"Thank you."

———•———

NOT GOOD

———

Three days after Rick's near shoot-down, Sue walked into their small kitchen to fix David's breakfast. Rick was putting his breakfast dishes into the sink.

"Clicker and I are leaving for the base," he announced.

Sue checked her watch.

"It's earlier than you usually go."

"Things are happening," he replied without elaboration.

He kissed her and rushed out the door. She heard him talking to Clicker as they walked down the stairs.

As David played with his breakfast, Sue turned on the radio. The Armed Forces station from Saigon started its news reports. Sue listened intently, trying to remember the names of places the news referenced.

A major city had fallen to the invading Communists. The South Vietnamese president ordered his army to withdraw from the Central Highlands. Sue did not know where that was, nor where the city was. She had been in Vietnam for less than a month, and the news alarmed her. She ran to her bedroom to find the tourist map of Vietnam.

David watched as Sue spread the map on the table. She found the city, Ban Me Thuot, north-northeast of Bien Hoa. She placed her finger on the map's scale and tried to measure. The scale was in kilometers. Her rough measurement looked to be over 200 kilometers. She thought that equaled about 120 miles, less than a two-hour drive in Texas. That sounded close to her. A knot formed in her stomach. She would have to ask Mai about the Central Highlands.

David finished his cereal.

"Let's go down and find Lei," she suggested. "Bring some toys."

David could skip brushing his teeth this once. Sue picked up Thi and carried her downstairs. David found Lei on the side porch with Mai. After putting a babbling Thi in her playpen, Sue made a glass of iced tea and grabbed a slice of

Mai's pastry. Sue spread her map on the coffee table.

"Where are the Central Highlands?" she asked.

Mai came over to the table. She circled an extensive region on the map.

"Here."

"That is a large area!" Sue exclaimed.

Sue checked the map's scale again.

"It is a few hundred kilometers long. I heard on the American radio that your president has ordered the army to retreat from there," Sue reported. "The North has conquered this city."

She pointed to Ban Me Thuot. The women looked at the map in silence for a minute.

"If he has ordered the Army to retreat, what does that mean?" Sue asked.

"It means the news is not good," Mai conceded. "People will run away."

"Where will they go?"

"Toward the coast," Mai answered.

Sue looked for the place Rick had stayed overnight less than a week ago. She pointed to it.

"Will they go here?" she asked.

"Yes, and all along here." Mai swept her finger to the north.

Sue studied the towns along the coast. She did not recognize any until she came to Da Nang. That city made the news frequently. She remembered it had been a major US air base when Rick had been in Thailand years before.

Sue looked at Mai.

"Does this frighten you?" she asked.

Mai nodded rapidly several times.

"Very frightened." Mai looked toward Lei.

Sue put her hand on Mai's hand. She detected a quiver.

"Are you afraid of what will happen to you and Lei if the Communists win?"

Mai only nodded.

"Mai, I promise we will not leave here without you and Lei."

"But I have no papers to leave Vietnam."

"We'll talk to Rick's friend in Saigon. There has to be a way."

That afternoon, Rick brought home a one-day-old copy of *Stars and Stripes.* The issue contained the story of the South Vietnamese Army's defeats. As Sue looked at the pictures of refugees fleeing the battle zones, her worry increased.

"What are those columns of smoke around the refugees?" Sue asked.

"Explosions," Rick replied. "They are shelling the refugees."

"We have to help Mai escape with us!" she implored him. "When should we leave?"

"Mai will need a Vietnamese passport first," he advised. "She should apply for one immediately. However, I hear the Vietnamese have very long delays."

"We have to try something!" Sue begged. "Can't Jeff help?"

"I'll talk with Clicker. Maybe Colonel Tinh can help."

"I promised her we will do everything to help them escape with us."

"Any day now," Rick predicted, "the US Embassy will start to evacuate American citizens. Jeff has told me the desire to help Vietnamese who have worked for Americans is widespread."

———•———

The next morning, Sue listened to the news on the radio again. People fled the Central Highlands and headed for the coast. Why had Rick taken this job? What were they doing here in the middle of a war? It was those damn fast jets again.

Sue needed something to stay busy. She would go to the orphanage. Helping the overworked nuns gave her a purpose. While her friends had not had time to send supplies, Sue had bought items at the Tan Son Nhut Base Exchange. The store contained limited children's clothing. It carried some needed cleaning supplies. Mai went with her to the orphanage so the boys could play with Quý.

As they cleaned the nursery, another project occurred to Sue.

"Mai," she began, "I want you to teach me to cook two Vietnamese dishes."

"Yes, ma'am," Mai replied. Sue had insisted that Mai drop the "ma'am." But Mai still used it occasionally.

"Let's cook tonight. I'll finish here so you can go to the market."

Realizing that their time in Vietnam was bound to be short, Sue knew that learning to speak any Vietnamese and to shop was pointless. But she wanted to learn at least two Vietnamese recipes before they fled.

When Rick and Clicker returned from work that afternoon, Mai and Sue were busy in the kitchen.

"What's going on?" Rick asked.

"Mai is teaching me Vietnamese cooking," Sue responded with enthusiasm.

"What's that wonderful smell?" Clicker inquired as he came in.

"Mai is holding a cooking class for Sue," Rick replied.

"I may have to cancel my date tonight to eat here, then," Clicker announced.

"Why don't you just invite Huyền to dinner?" Sue inquired.

Clicker paused.

"Well, my date is with Linh tonight," he admitted.

Sue raised an eyebrow. *A different girlfriend,* she noted.

"Well, bring her to dinner," Sue announced. "We'll have enough, right, Mai?"

"Yes, plenty to eat."

"What's on the menu?" Rick asked, eyeing a red broth.

"Bún Bò Huế." Sue struggled to pronounce it correctly. Mai helped her.

"It's a dish from Mai's hometown, Hue," Sue added.

Rick was glad to see Sue's smiling face. Cooking something new always invigorated her. The recent news had given her a stressed look.

When Linh arrived, Clicker brought her into the kitchen.

"Sue, this is Linh."

Linh gave a slight bow.

"I am pleased to meet you," Linh said.

Sue returned the gesture.

She's young, too, leaped into Sue's thoughts. *What is it with these young women?*

"Sue is our chef this evening," Clicker explained.

"Under Mai's excellent instruction," Sue explained. "But I take responsibility for any mistakes."

Linh did not seem to understand.

Sue glanced from Linh to Clicker.

Is he watching me? Sue wondered.

SMOKE

———•———

Jimbo and Dobie had been in Laos for two weeks. The North Vietnamese deserter who claimed to have the Air Force Academy ring was hard to locate. Marcel and Keej returned from a trip to several Hmong villages.

Dobie and Marcel studied the topographical map of a section of central Laos. Marcel pointed to the contours on the edge of a mountain.

"My Hmong contact says the deserter will meet us here," Marcel explained. "He'll be there for a week starting the day after tomorrow. The guy has become very skittish in the last month. Thousands of North Vietnamese Army troops have flooded into Laos. He is afraid of running into someone who would recognize him."

"Is there a village there?" Dobie asked. No dot on the map suggested one.

"Only a few huts of Hmong who have moved away from all the activity. As you can tell, it sits on a plateau below these peaks." Marcel pointed to two mountaintops north of the location of the huts. "The soil around there is good for poppies."

Dobie studied the terrain to the southwest of the location.

"Pretty rugged getting there from here." He unfolded another grid map, laying it below the lower left corner of the other.

"Do you know any trails through here?" Jimbo asked. He pointed to contours that depicted a valley through one section of peaks.

"None we know of," Keej answered. "It is a dense jungle."

"An easier route is to swing around to the north of it."

Marcel moved a finger over points on the map.

"What about swinging east through this valley?" Jimbo posed.

Marcel pointed to the contours to the right of Jimbo's fingers.

"Pathet Lao troops have moved into this next valley across these ridges. It makes it too risky."

"Are they massing there or going through?" Jimbo queried.

"It doesn't matter," Marcel replied. "Their pattern has been to create supply caches and leave a squad to guard them."

"Suggests that some operation is in the wind," Dobie suggested. "Are the Royal Lao forces getting concerned?"

Marcel shrugged.

"The Laotian generals worry more about protecting the opium revenue from Burma than fighting the Communists."

Jimbo grunted.

"Like too many of the fucking South Vietnamese generals."

"With the Commies on the move, is the northern route any safer?"

"As far as Keej and I can guess. We hooked a little north on our last trip to talk to people up here," he said as he pointed to dots on the map. "Life seems normal."

"Okay, then," Dobie concluded. "We hike north and swing around. We leave before daylight tomorrow." He checked his watch. "It's coming up on our window to talk to Charles. Mr. Peabody, he reports, is getting edgy about the delay."

"Screw him," Jimbo muttered. Keej smiled.

For two days, the trails north were easy and well-used. Dobie took two nights to get used to sleeping in the jungle again. Night in the jungle was always an intense time. It took some acclimation. The blackness of the jungle night was total sensory deprivation. The thick canopy overhead blocked all starlight and any moonlight.

During the night, blood-sucking critters would descend on any warm, sleeping body. Natural bug repellent used by the locals worked better than the smelly Army bug juice. Eating the local diet helped slightly, too. But any defense was only partial. Dobie pulled out his head net and rolled into his poncho liner to fight off the bugs. He buttoned all his pockets on his shirt, pants, and pack. Finding a tarantula or a small poisonous snake in a pocket in the morning was best avoided. Dobie forgot how many venomous snakes inhabited the forests of Southeast Asia.

Am I getting too old for trekking through the jungle? Dobie wondered.

On the first morning, Dobie awoke to find a large bug bite on the side of his neck. An insect had found the one crack of exposed skin. Jimbo appeared to need some adjustment, too. His eyes looked bloodshot from lack of sleep on the first morning. Besides the myriad of flying insects, the ever-present leeches required constant vigilance. Following any water crossing came the required quick inspection. Leeches also clung to leaves, so one could hitch a ride from any vegetation.

After one section of thick brush, Dobie tapped Jimbo.

"You picked up a blood-sucking passenger," he noted.

Dobie opened a shirt pocket for the small salt and pepper shaker he kept handy. He sprinkled salt on two leeches on the back of Jimbo's neck. The insects immediately curled up and died. Dobie brushed them off. A quick inspection revealed that leeches had attached themselves to Keej and Marcel.

On the third day, they swung around a mountain to hook back toward the meeting place. The trail became rougher. They took turns with the machete clearing the path through the brush on the trail. Vines entangled their feet.

"Sure hope no Gooks are nearby to hear this racket," Jimbo muttered as he swung the large knife.

Before dusk settled, Keej called a halt. The four men dropped their packs to the ground. Keej pointed off the trail to their right.

"That bamboo grove looks like a good place to spend the night."

He picked his way carefully toward it. He disappeared for several minutes. When he reappeared a few minutes later, he waved the others over.

"Be careful to leave as little trail as possible," he instructed.

They followed Keej through a small gap in the bamboo, up a small ridge, and into a small clearing surrounded by bamboo. Jimbo looked around.

"Where's the back door?"

Keej pointed behind where Jimbo stood.

"The bamboo thins as it goes up another ridge before it opens to thick brush."

Jimbo grunted his approval.

Keej walked around the small clearing.

"From here, we can crawl to see part of the trail. Any trouble will most likely come from there. We should hear it well before it reaches us."

Dobie turned to Marcel.

"How far are we from any known Commies?" he inquired.

"As far as I know, twenty klicks and a few mountain ridges."

"Then we should not expect any trouble," Dobie concluded. He undid a couple of folds of a grid map. "How far are we to our rendezvous with the deserter?"

"A day and a half," Marcel replied. He studied the map, then pointed to a spot. "We're here." He unfolded part of another map, laying it next to the other. "The meeting point is here."

Dobie counted grid squares; then he studied the contour lines.

"We'll have to really hump it," he remarked.

"By the end of tomorrow, the trail should get easy. We'll be on trails more in use."

"What about a fire to cook some rice?" Jimbo asked.

Dobie had decided against carrying US Army food on the mission. Cans of C-rations were far too heavy. Freeze-dried meals used for long-range recon patrols were tasty and easy to carry. But both screamed that Americans were around. Dobie did not want his and Jimbo's presence shouted around the region.

Marcel looked into the trees outside the bamboo. Then he looked at Keej.

"The breeze is blowing back the way we came," Keej replied. "We can have a hot meal. As long as we put the fire out as soon as we're done."

"I'll get some wood," Jimbo replied. "I also spotted some wild sweet potatoes to enhance our meal." He disappeared through the small opening.

"I'll get cooking water and refill our canteens," Keej offered. "We have a stream close by."

Ten minutes later, Jimbo returned carrying a bundle of sticks. After he set them in the middle of the clearing, he opened a bag he had carried.

"Also found these delicacies to enhance our menu," he beamed. From the bag, he retrieved four frogs and two large sweet potatoes.

"Excellent work, Sergeant," Dobie commented.

Jimbo gathered his firewood and produced a flint and steel with some tinder. He quickly had a small fire burning. Keej produced a small pot from his pack. Marcel pulled out a small bag of rice. Keej accepted the role of cook, and the foursome enjoyed a wholesome jungle meal. As dusk settled into the blackness of night in the jungle, Keej extinguished the fire.

"Since we are creeping close to unknown territory, do two-hour watches sound reasonable?" Dobie inquired. "I'll do three hours at 2100 hours to start. Then,

I'll wake Marcel, followed by Jimbo, then Keej," he offered.

Since darkness came early in the tropics, the group did not settle down for a few hours. Quietly, they discussed their plan for the next few days.

"The deserter will dash into the jungle if all four of us show up together," Marcel explained. "Just Dobie and I should meet him to negotiate for the ring."

"Okay," Dobie replied. "Keej and Jimbo will hide nearby. Will he be alone?"

"Kaus, my Hmong contact, will be with him. I insisted that he be the only one."

"Keej and I will cover your flanks," Jimbo stated. Keej nodded his agreement.

"Do we know this deserter's name?" Dobie asked.

"He goes by Ngai," Marcel answered.

They settled down for a quiet night. By the time that the dawn had cleared away the murky shadows of the forest, the group was ready. Marcel studied the maps.

"Once we move out of this next valley," he started, pointing to the map, "we have to be quiet until the trail becomes easier."

Dobie looked at the area Marcel pointed to.

"Do less hacking with the machete?" he asked.

Marcel nodded.

"See this valley from the north that snakes into the one we will follow?"

Dobie nodded.

"It comes from the northeast," he explained. "It connects to a valley with trails that the Pathet Lao use to move supplies and troops. We don't want to assume they aren't checking their flanks. Past this intersection, we can pick up cutting our way if there aren't any signs of them."

Three hours later, the team had crossed a stream when Keej, who was cutting the brush, halted.

"Break time," he suggested. "Let's refill our canteens."

Marcel studied the map, then looked around. Heavy vegetation limited the visibility.

"We are at the point we want to become quieter," he announced. "The intersecting valley is a couple of klicks away. For now, we stop slashing and shove the branches to the side. Follow each other closely and hold the brush back for the one behind you."

After a ten-minute break, Marcel slid his arms through his shoulder straps and stood. He picked up the machete and started down the overgrown trail. Rather than the noisy slashing of the vegetation, he pushed branches and vines aside until Jimbo behind him held it back. Dobie followed Jimbo, allowing the sergeant's larger frame open space in the brush for him. The pace became very slow. While some branches snapped, the sound seemed quiet compared to the noisy machete.

The group proceeded for another hour before Keej tapped Dobie in front of him. Rather than say anything, he held his hand in a fist, facing Dobie. He immediately passed the message to Jimbo, who tapped Marcel.

Marcel looked to Keej, who touched his nose with an index finger. Marcel sniffed the air, slowly moving his head sideways. He looked again at Keej, still a question on his face. Keej moved both hands from near the ground up to shoulder level, wiggling them.

Dobie immediately understood. Keej smelled smoke. Marcel sniffed around again, then nodded twice. Dobie sniffed the air. He could only detect the damp forest and its mixture of floral, musty scents. But he did not doubt that Keej was right.

Marcel and Keej held a whispered conversation. Keej then took off his pack and snuck up the trail, taking his M16 and one of his canteens.

"Keej will inspect the source of the smoke," Marcel whispered. "We are within a klick of where the other valley intersects this one. Smoke could be friendly or hostile."

The trio waited, leaning against their packs. Dobie checked his watch. Every several minutes, Dobie sniffed the air. He noticed Jimbo doing it as well. Jimbo shrugged his shoulders slightly when Dobie looked quizzically at him. Neither of the Americans could detect the odor of burned wood.

Over two hours passed before a slight rustle announced Keej's return.

"We are about a klick from the intersection of the valleys," he murmured. "Our trail becomes an easy walk past it. It doesn't show any signs of recent use. The trail from the other valley does. Not by Hmong or mountain people. Someone has cut the brush within the last two days. The smoke is drifting out of that side valley. I'm not sure if it's fresh from this morning. Maybe from last night."

"Pathet Lao?" Dobie inquired.

"Most likely," Keej answered. "It looks to me they came from the valley to check the trails for activity. They didn't clear the trail today. It was yesterday, most likely. Seeing little use, they left. They probably camped a klick or two away from the intersection and sent a patrol to look at it."

"If we had been here a day or two earlier, we might have run into them," Jimbo suggested.

"Or left signs we had been by," Dobie added.

"We proceed slowly, then, leaving as small a trace as possible," Marcel stated.

"Good thinking," Dobie agreed. *Marcel and Keej are earning their pay*, he concluded.

The group hoisted their packs. Keej led the way, with Marcel bringing up the rear. The Americans worked hard not to snap any branches or leave footprints in any soft soil. After they forded a stream, Keej stopped.

"We should refill our canteens," he suggested.

Their packs came off. Everyone drained one canteen. Then they refilled them from the trickling stream.

"Where does this stream flow from?" Dobie quizzed Keej.

"It comes out of the valley that we will follow to the meeting place."

"Does some livestock shit and piss into it?" he queried.

"Most likely," Keej admitted.

"Then it's time to get out the iodine tablets," Dobie commented, reaching into a pocket on his pack. He opened a small bottle and dropped a tablet into each of his canteens.

Jimbo dug into his pack as well.

"How far to the intersection?" Dobie asked.

"About half a klick," Keej answered.

Dobie glanced at his watch.

"Once we hit the used trail, any chance we can get to the village before dark?"

Keej thought for a second.

"If we move fast," he announced.

"Then let's move," Dobie ordered.

They lifted their packs. As he slung his pack onto his shoulders, Jimbo did not notice his small iodine bottle drop from the unzipped pocket of his pack.

———•———

THE DESERTER

Dobie and Marcel sat together in the small hut in the mountains of central Laos. Two weathered faces sat opposite them. Kaus, the leader of the two, was Hmong from the mountains near the northern Vietnamese border, across from Dien Bien Phu. The other man, Ngai, was the reason for the meeting. Formerly a soldier in the People's Army of Vietnam, he had the Air Force Academy ring.

Setting up the gathering had taken two preliminary meetings between Marcel and Kaus. While Ngai was in the market to sell the ring to Americans, he was skittish. Marcel had to mislead Ngai about the number of Americans. As far as Ngai and Kaus knew, only Marcel and Dobie were here. Jimbo and Keej hid in the jungle outside. They waited in case reinforcements were needed during the negotiations. The skittishness of the Vietnamese deserter made Dobie wary. Marcel and Dobie carried their sidearms. They had left their M-16s with Jimbo and Keej.

Dobie and Marcel planned to negotiate the price of the ring in Vietnamese, hoping to make the deserter at ease. The $600 price Ngai demanded for the ring was above the price Peabody and Dobie had decided to pay. Dobie was sure he would have to pay less. More importantly, Dobie wanted to clarify the circumstances under which Ngai had obtained the ring.

"Is the price acceptable?" Ngai pressed.

"You overestimate its worth," Dobie replied calmly. "We need to verify its validity."

"Do you have the ring here?" Marcel pressed.

Ngai's eyes darted between Marcel and Dobie. He shifted his hands on the table. He did not answer.

"It's a simple question," Dobie commented.

"It is close by."

"We will need to inspect it," Dobie informed him. "I also need to understand how you acquired it. Tell us about it."

"I took it from the prisoner when we captured him," Ngai stated.

"Describe that to me," Dobie pressed.

The deserter hesitated.

"We were waiting for him when he landed." He stopped.

"And then …" Dobie cued him to expand his explanation.

"We took his parachute off him, stripped him out of his clothes and boots."

Dobie nodded when Ngai stopped.

"And?" Dobie prompted.

"I found the ring in a pocket of his uniform."

Dobie avoided looking at Marcel. He wanted to avoid giving anything away. With his peripheral vision, Dobie could tell Marcel was studying the Vietnamese.

"He landed in his parachute, and you immediately captured him," Dobie confirmed.

Ngai nodded.

"Did he resist capture?" Marcel asked. "Did you have to shoot to get him to surrender?"

"No," came the quick answer. "He raised his hands to surrender right away."

If the ring belonged to Cal Reese, Dobie knew this deserter was lying. This story contradicted the one Rick Guerri told about Cal Reese's shoot-down.

"I am interested in where the People's Army shot down the American, and where you captured him," Dobie continued. He tried to make his demands seem like normal curiosity.

"We were attacking a mountain. The fighting was fierce. The prisoner was bombing us. Some in our group wanted to kill him."

"Did you?" Dobie asked.

Ngai looked unsure of the question. Marcel repeated it using different words.

"No! It was not allowed!" came the excited answer. The Vietnamese fidgeted. His eyes darted from Dobie to Marcel. He wiped his sweating hands on his clothes. The air in the hut was stifling. Yet, no one else sweated like this North Vietnamese deserter. He was getting very agitated. Did he sense Dobie knew something? Not wanting to spook him, Dobie thought he needed a break.

"You said the ring is close by. We need to examine it before we can buy it.

Can you bring it to us quickly?"

Ngai seemed reassured by Dobie's question.

"Yes!" came the excited answer.

"How long to get it?" Marcel asked.

"Ten minutes," Ngai answered.

"We will sit outside," Dobie stated.

"Better you wait in here," Kaus said.

"Ngai may leave, then we will wait outside," Dobie informed him. Kaus nodded.

A minute after the deserter left, Dobie stood and exited through the door. Marcel followed a few paces behind. Dobie angled left toward Jimbo's hiding position. Marcel angled right toward Keej. Both kept their hands on their sidearms. They ambled toward the bush, trying to act nonchalant.

At the perimeter of the clearing, both paused, scanning the jungle. The jungle remained quiet. Dobie and Marcel turned and sauntered toward each other. It was the signal to assure Jimbo and Keej that all seemed well. Otherwise, they would have slipped into the jungle. They met at a spot close to the hut. Two large trees towered over them as they sat at an angle facing each other.

"His story doesn't jibe," Marcel noted.

"It's BS," Dobie agreed.

"Any bets the ring is a forgery?" Marcel asked.

Dobie shook his head. He dug into his shoulder satchel and removed a small bag.

"This will tell us."

Marcel moved his head, surveying the jungle. The pair sat in silence, allowing the sounds of the forest to return. A few birds began chirping. Fifteen minutes passed before the jungle went silent. Ngai emerged on a trail beside the hut. His head jerked from side to side.

"The guy is spooked," Marcel observed.

They stood and walked back to the hut. Dobie opened the small bag and took out two small bottles, a jeweler's magnifying eyepiece, and a small pick. He looked at Ngai.

"The ring, please," he requested.

Ngai removed a small bag from a string around his neck, opened it, and removed a ring. He slid it across the small table. Dobie picked it up, turning it over slowly. The ring appeared to be white gold. It was dirty, with grime in the tiny recesses of its engraving. From his small bag, Dobie retrieved an old toothbrush. He poured drops of water from his canteen on it. Dobie gave the face and the inside a quick cleaning.

The Air Force Academy crest was on one side. On the other was the crest for the class of 1963. Dobie had studied pictures of both. He examined the ring through the magnifying lens. Marcel held a flashlight to fully illuminate the ring as Dobie studied it. A jeweler he had consulted had pointed out places where a forger might make a slight mistake. Both crests looked authentic. He studied the blue sapphire setting. No scratches were evident. Dobie did not know which stone the ring should have.

He turned the ring over to look behind the setting. Seeing an engraving, Dobie picked up the jeweler's glass and studied the inscription. Grime still obscured it, so he brushed it cleaner. He examined the engraving, positioning the ring to get the best light.

"Calvin L Reese" was discernible through the magnifying lens. Dobie's guess about the ring's authenticity changed. Why would a forger bother to engrave a name? And how would he get the name of an MIA, including the middle initial?

On one side, he saw the "14K" label. Dobie passed the ring and glass to Marcel. While Dobie unscrewed the cap on one of the small bottles, Marcel looked at the inscription. He handed the ring back to Dobie.

Dobie turned it over to find an inconspicuous place on the inside. He put a small drop of the acid from the bottle labeled "14K" on the spot.

The deserter reached for the ring. Dobie moved it out of his reach.

"What are you doing?" Ngai shouted. "You will ruin it!"

"Calm down," Dobie stated. "I won't damage the ring. We have to test to see if it is gold."

Dobie looked at the spot of acid. Nothing changed.

Well, the surface is 14-karat gold, he concluded.

Dobie took the small pick. At a different point, he put pressure on the pick so it would penetrate any plating. He twisted the pick back and forth several times. He then etched marks beside the pinhole to penetrate any plating.

Dobie placed another drop of the acid on the scratches and the pinhole. The acid did not change color.

He looked at Marcel, who had been watching closely. Marcel raised his eyebrows.

Dobie brushed the acid away with the toothbrush. He then opened the small bottle with the "18K" label. He put another small drop on the scratches. The liquid changed color.

"Well, this isn't 18-karat," Dobie muttered. He knew his marks were deep enough to get an accurate reading.

Dobie looked at Ngai.

"Well, the ring is authentic 14-karat gold," he declared.

The relief in Ngai's eyes was evident.

"So, you will pay the price," he exclaimed.

"The ring may be genuine, but your story of how you acquired it is not," Dobie stated. "We need the true story."

"What … what do you mean?" Ngai stuttered.

"We know that the People's Army did not capture Captain Calvin Reese as soon as he landed in his parachute," Dobie answered. "Following his shoot-down, a pilot contacted him by radio."

Ngai's mouth opened slightly.

"That pilot, he is lying," came the feeble response.

"If you don't tell us the true story, we will not buy the ring," Dobie replied. Dobie held the ring away from Ngai. "We are not concerned about how you gained the ring. But we need the truth."

Kaus whispered something to Ngai.

"If I tell you the truth, you will pay for the ring?" Ngai pressed.

"If I believe you," Dobie stated.

Ngai's shoulders slumped.

"You have no one else to sell the ring to," Dobie pointed out. "No other Americans will come. I'm the only one. While your price is too high, I will pay you much more than the gold is worth."

Dobie placed the ring on the table. Ngai picked it up. He looked inside at the pinhole and the scratches. He put it back on the table.

"I stole the ring at Takhli Base," he confessed.

Dobie's eyebrows raised.

"You stole it at Takhli?" he repeated.

"Yes. I spied at the base, cleaning in the Officer's Club. I also listened when I cleaned tables in the bar and cafe. The ring was in the latrine late one night. I took it."

"What were you spying for?" Dobie asked.

"During the day, I sat outside the fence and counted the airplanes when they took off. I gave the number to my comrade, who radioed the number to his superiors."

"Why did you keep the ring so long?" Dobie asked in English. "Why did you not sell it quickly?"

"A big fuss ... missing ring happened," Ngai answered in broken English. "Thai military police asked questions. Other workers afraid of losing jobs. I could trust no one. Two days later, pilots talked in the bar at night. They said the ring's owner was shot down while attacking a mountain. I asked the woman who cleaned his bedroom. She said he was missing. Another pilot had sent his things to the US."

"So, you were afraid to ask about selling it," Dobie confirmed, switching back to Vietnamese.

"Yes. With his name on the ring, I became afraid. I kept the ring."

"And you carried it with you all the time? Even into battles afterward?" Dobie inquired.

"I did not go into battle. When I was told I was being sent to Laos to fight after working at Takhli, I ran away. I did not go to my unit as ordered. I've hidden from the People's Army since then."

Marcel did a quick calculation.

"For six and a half years, you've been hiding in Laos?"

"Yes."

"Doing what? Hiding where?" Dobie added.

"Ngai has lived in many villages all over the mountains," Kaus answered for Ngai. "After living in my village for a year, he left for a couple. He has been back and forth since then. When he was in my village, he worked in the fields."

From his pocket, Dobie pulled a gold Thai baht chain and laid it next to the ring.

"This gold chain is worth five hundred US dollars. That is far more than the small amount of gold in the ring. I will pay you that much for the ring."

Ngai picked up the chain. He fingered it. He bit one link.

"You can test it with these," Dobie suggested, gesturing to the bottles. "It is 18-karat gold."

Ngai looked from the chain to Dobie. He seemed to weigh his alternatives. "Okay."

He placed the chain in the small bag and secured its string around his neck. Dobie put the ring into his small bag. He tightened the lids on the bottles and returned them to the bag. After he placed the pick and the eyepiece into the bag and closed its drawstring, he stood. He and Marcel marched out the door and onto a path leading into the jungle.

After walking for an hour, the pair turned off the narrow path. They threaded their way through thick brush to a small clearing. They were out of sight of the trail. Ten minutes later, they could hear the rustle of branches along the way they had come. A clear, descending whistle of a babbler called twice. Marcel answered in a slightly different tone. Seconds later, Keej and Jimbo emerged from the brush.

"Your tail is clear," Jimbo reported. "No curious followers."

He sat down.

"Well, did you get it?" Jimbo asked.

"Yes, we did."

"But the deserter's first story was bull," Marcel added. "We got what we think was the true story."

"And …?" Jimbo prompted.

"He did not get the ring from the prisoner. He simply stole it from the O'Club at Takhli."

"What?" Jimbo prodded.

Dobie repeated the story that Ngai had relayed.

"Being a spy sounded credible," Marcel noted. "He speaks English well enough."

"I guess that's believable," Jimbo concurred. "But we know nothing more about the fate of Calvin Reese."

"Welcome to the murky world of MIAs," Dobie concluded. "I'm not sure Mr. Peabody will enjoy having no story to publish."

"You aren't considering poking our noses into prison camps, are you?" Jimbo quizzed.

Dobie hesitated.

"For the record," Marcel interjected, "activity in the north and along the Trail has reached a frenzy. The Commies will capture any curious adventurer approaching the area."

"That settles it, then," Dobie assured Jimbo. "Mr. Peabody will have to make do with what we have."

———•———

FOLLOWED

———·———

Dobie's team exited the clearing and returned to the trail. On the well-used path, leaving their footprints was not a concern. When Marcel had quizzed Kaus about Ngai's skittishness, his response was a warning. The Communist forces were on the move everywhere in northern Laos and encroaching further south and west. Dobie had decided a stroll back to Marcel's village was not an option.

They approached the intersection of the valleys and trails in short order. At a stream near the intersection, Keej ventured ahead to scout. The rest used the opportunity to refill their canteens. Jimbo reached into the pocket for his iodine tablets. They weren't there. He rummaged through other pockets. Finally, he gave up.

"Boss, I fucked up," he announced to Dobie.

"How so?"

"My iodine tablets are missing. The pocket was unzipped. They must have fallen out somewhere on the trail."

"I have enough to share," Dobie said. He handed a tablet to Jimbo.

"I'm more concerned with them being found by the wrong guy," Jimbo admitted.

"We'll have to be a little extra vigilant," Dobie concluded.

Keej returned after twenty minutes.

"The side trail has had additional traffic," he announced.

"Bad guys?" Dobie inquired.

"I assume so," Keej replied. "They didn't hide their presence."

"Is it clear now?" Marcel asked.

"Looks clear. But I suggest we hurry past the intersection. We need to be careful for the first klick once beyond it. We don't want to arouse any curiosity."

"Let's move, then," Dobie ordered.

Dobie studied the path heading north at the trail intersection. Broken branches and footprints proved its recent use. Their progress slowed as they became careful to leave no trace. Keej brought up the rear, looking to smooth over any tracks that the less nimble Americans might leave.

Marcel kept them at a slow pace for several kilometers. He knew the Communists sent out scouting pairs ahead of a patrol. The balance between stealth and speed in unfriendly terrain always remained a precarious edge.

Evidence of the traffic on that side trail proved that the country had become less friendly. Marcel picked up the pace. They took minimal breaks to refill canteens. Keej often lingered behind, watching the forest and ridges.

An hour before sunset, Marcel stopped.

"We need to scout a place to camp tonight. Off the trail."

"No fires tonight," Dobie added. "Let's watch for a suitable place."

Twenty minutes passed before Marcel halted again after they crossed a stream. He pulled one canteen from its pouch on his belt and leaned over to fill it. The others copied him.

"Up that ridge," he pointed. "We can follow the stream to eliminate leaving a trail."

As they started up the stream, Keej stayed behind. Rather than follow them immediately, he went back down the trail. He branched off into the forest in the opposite direction the group had taken. Minutes later, he rejoined the group on top of a ridge above the stream. Marcel had located a bamboo thicket with an obscured way into it. He also located a back door in case they needed it.

"Claymores," Dobie instructed. "Let's use four to cover the way from the stream. Put one out ahead with a trip wire."

Jimbo nodded. He pulled one of the fragmentation mines from his pack. Everyone else offered one from their packs. Jimbo carried the mines into the forest. He returned as darkness enveloped the jungle. He pointed to the locations of the Claymores and the area they covered. Dobie nodded with satisfaction. He hoped they wouldn't be needed.

The group nibbled on pemmican and cereal bars from their packs. While not a very satisfying cuisine, the dinner fulfilled the need for calories. The group stayed within touching distance of each other, alternating watches.

As the black night receded, Keej tapped Marcel, then pointed with a couple of other gestures. Marcel nodded as Keej crept off into the jungle.

As the gray of dawn approached, Dobie held a brief conference with Marcel.

"I say we head out ASAP," he suggested.

"Keej will be back soon. He crawled away a short distance to sit, watch, and listen. He wanted to confirm there aren't any strangers near."

Minutes later, Keej crept back, carrying one Claymore.

"We are clear," he announced.

"I'll get the Claymore with the tripwire," Jimbo announced. "Give me a three-minute start."

Dobie and Marcel retrieved the other two mines. The three met Jimbo at the point near the stream. They retraced their steps to the trail and started down it. Marcel took the point, while Keej again brought up the rear. They walked at a brisk pace, stopping rarely and only for brief breaks.

Shortly after noon, they stopped on a ridge that gave a vista of the valley they had crossed. A haze clung to the treetops across the valley. The group munched some snacks and drank from their canteens. After a few minutes, Dobie stood.

"Time to move," he announced.

Three of them stood and hoisted the packs. Keej kept staring across the valley. Suddenly, a flock of birds took to the air near the top of the far ridge. Keej studied it. Marcel edged over to him.

"We are being followed," Keej stated.

Dobie knelt next to them. He retrieved a pair of binoculars from his pack. Adjusting the focus knob, he stepped into the shade of a tree. He scanned the opposite hills below the birds. At first, he saw only the jungle. A faint glint of sunlight flashed.

"Somebody is using binoculars below the top of that far hill," he announced. He looked at Keej, who nodded.

"That's where our trail came through that saddle."

Marcel turned and started walking. The others fell in behind. Dobie started playing through scenarios in his mind as he trudged forward. Two hours passed before Marcel stopped.

"What are the odds that those followers are not hostile?" he inquired.

"Pretty low."

"Do they know for certain we are here? Or are they sweeping for recon?"

"No way to know," Marcel answered. "They could be surveying that valley to check for any signs of habitation or cultivation. Patrols have forced us out of many available valleys."

By this time, Keej had joined them. He put his hand into the dirt and tasted it.

"This is good soil for poppies," he reported.

"They might know that and are doing some recon," Dobie suggested.

"Without my missing iodine, I'd go with that idea," Jimbo added. "But if the Gooks found it, this ain't no casual recon."

"Distance is our best friend," Marcel noted.

"We could increase that," Jimbo suggested, "if I stay here along with a couple of Claymores for calling cards. If they are unfriendly, I could set them off and give them a reason to pause and continue slower."

"We aren't at the point of needing suicide stands," Dobie rejoined. "Let's get hoofing."

The group marched for the rest of the afternoon without breaks. Marcel slowed the pace twice to allow their tiring muscles some rest. They sipped from their canteens while walking. Perspiration soaked their clothes. After the sun had settled well below the treetops, Marcel paused at a stream.

"We have about an hour before sunset," he said. "We can follow this uphill to find a place, or continue to the next one."

"How far to the next one?" Dobie inquired.

"A little over an hour."

"Let's pick up the pace to it," Dobie decided.

As dusk settled, they arrived at the next stream. Marcel immediately stepped into the shallow water on the near side and started uphill. A hundred yards later, he branched off it and led the team up a rocky ledge. Again, Keej backtracked and made a subtle trail leading in the opposite direction.

Jimbo set up a defensive perimeter again with Claymores. He waited until Keej returned before stretching the trip wire across the base of the ledge. They spent another restless night with a cold supper.

The danger of being hunted now added to the usual concerns of the jungle night. So far, their trip had seemed like a training exercise in the forests around Fort Bragg. Now, it had transitioned into a mission out of Dobie's past in Southeast Asia. But it held one major difference. Special Forces teams in the wild had maintained contact with a mother ship orbiting high above. If trouble arose, a quick call could mobilize help. A team always had the expectation of Army helicopters for a quick extraction. In addition, helicopter gunships and Air Force fighters stood ready to help. But not now. The team was on its own.

Hence, no one slept soundly. Those not on watch only caught catnaps. As the black night surrendered to dawn, Keej awoke suddenly. He lay still, listening for what had stirred his light sleep. Silence for several minutes did not reassure him. When all was well, Keej's sleep slowly gave way to the approaching day. When he awoke with his senses alerted, his sleeping brain had detected something unwanted. Had a distant monkey's warning shriek disturbed him?

Through the murky light, Keej looked at Marcel, who had the watch before dawn. Marcel cupped his right hand near his ear and pointed to the trail. Keej nodded and crept away, avoiding the wired Claymore. Thirty minutes passed before Jimbo and Dobie stirred in the approaching dawn. Dobie looked at Marcel.

"Keej and I heard a monkey shriek," Marcel murmured.

Dobie's mouth became dry. His nervousness gave way to real fear. Quietly, slowly, he opened his canteen for a drink. On Dobie's right, Jimbo rolled over and studied the jungle past the drop in the terrain toward the trail. Jimbo sipped from his canteen quietly. His throat was dry, too. Marcel's gaze studied the forest, a section at a time. All three lay still, looking and listening for several minutes.

Instead of the initial chattering of the birds after dawn, the forest remained quiet. The jungle veterans knew this meant something was moving out there. It was unlikely to be Keej. He would be still before the birds started their morning songs. Something or somebody else was moving. It could be a tiger, but the battles of recent years had forced them to move to isolated mountains.

Then, Jimbo touched Dobie's shoulder. When Dobie looked at him, Jimbo pointed straight out over the ledge. Dobie studied the forest, straining to listen.

Dobie heard a low bump, like the stock of a rifle hitting a tree trunk. A swish of a bush followed it. It came from the base of the rock ledge, near the trip wire. Dobie detected the low sound of the safety of Jimbo's M16 flicking off. Dobie slowly thumbed his safety off. Jimbo stared intently in the direction he had pointed.

Dobie glanced at Marcel, who was looking off to the side of Jimbo's stare.

BAM!

The flash of a Claymore mine lit up the jungle at the base of the ledge. Jimbo quickly lit up the adjacent area with an entire clip of his M16. Leaves and branches exploded. Dobie and Marcel held off firing. They searched the jungle in different directions. Nothing moved for minutes.

Keej crawled from Jimbo's right.

"Three scouts," he reported. "Claymore and Jimbo got them. Main force looks to be half a klick away down the trail."

"They'll be here soon enough," Dobie said. He dug into his pack for another Claymore. Jimbo reached into his pack and brought out his remaining mine. He scrambled off to his right. It took him a minute to return, trailing the cord to trigger it.

"Should cover the way to our back door," he stated.

Dobie crept forward toward the ledge. He placed his mine pointing down the ledge before crawling back.

A hasty retreat to their escape hatch at this point made little sense to Dobie. Better to stand and fight here behind their Claymores. Those would slow down and reduce the size of any pursuing force.

Minutes later, activity rustled on the trail. Commands spoken in Laotian sounded below.

"Should only take them a minute to decide which way to come," Dobie whispered.

"Look for a few at first to make us show our position," Marcel added. "Only the first one to spot them shoots first."

Jimbo crawled further to his right, as Keej moved further left.

Several minutes ticked by.

"Past the Claymore area," Jimbo hissed.

Dobie saw branches moving in the jungle. No one fired. Then the bushes to the right of the area started moving. A head appeared between the bushes. A single shot rang out from Jimbo. The head dropped, and Jimbo scrambled to his right.

AK-47s started firing from below. The dirt and brush flew where Jimbo had been. Dobie fired a series of single shots at the muzzle flashes. Then he moved right. The brush exploded where he had been. Marcel destroyed the brush around those muzzle flashes.

More scurrying came from the brush below. It fanned out right and left. Then a whistle blew. Bushes parted, and figures emerged, firing as they came. The four on the ledge opened fire, shooting short bursts on automatic at any moving figure or bush. The exchange lasted less than a minute. When the shooting stopped, leaves, dust, and smoke floated in the air on the ledge and in the jungle below.

"Everyone okay?" Dobie asked. Three "goods" were the answers.

Dobie knew the attack had only begun. His team had limited options to repel it. Noises of movement drifted from below. Another blow of a whistle. The brush came alive again. Larger numbers rushed from below.

Figures appeared in the clearing created by the tripwire mine. Dobie pulled the clacker for the one on the ridge as he shouted, "Claymores!"

Two Claymore mines below exploded simultaneously.

"Move!" Dobie commanded. He and Marcel scrambled back toward the narrow opening in the brush and rocks behind them. They moved to the side of it, whirled, and knelt on one knee. Marcel and Keej scrambled back as Dobie and Marcel fired. Jimbo squeezed the clacker in his hand to set off the last Claymore.

Suddenly, M16s cracked from their left near the trail. A volley of them! The AK-47s shooting in front of them paused. Sporadic shots rang out, but the bullets were not coming their way. Some group was firing at the Pathet Lao from behind them!

Dobie, Marcel, Jimbo, and Keej fired in unison. Their attackers retreated laterally, away from the M16s firing from below them. Dobie rammed another magazine into his rifle. He switched his M16 to single-shot and started selecting visible targets, squeezing off two shots per target. Figures fell consistently. Marcel was following the same routine. Jimbo remained on automatic, chewing up moving brush and figures. The AK-47s moved farther away and back up the trail. M16 bursts followed them.

After three minutes, a lifetime to the group on the upper ledge, the firing ceased. A few sporadic single cracks of an M16 rang out. From down below, a voice called in the Hmong dialect.

"Marcel! Keej! Is that you? Daj!"

"Mee!" Keej yelled back.

Dobie looked at Marcel.

"It's Keej's nephew!" Marcel exclaimed. "That is their authentication code. Names of their youngest daughters."

A brown rag waved from the brush below. Keej stood up. A figure emerged below the brown rag.

"Glad you came along!" Keej yelled.

"Just out for a walk."

The two figures scrambled toward each other and embraced in a hug.

Dobie stood and worked his way down the ledge. Keej introduced him.

"Meet Luj, my brother's youngest son."

Dobie bowed to the young man facing him.

"You came in the nick of time," he said. "Thank you."

"We received word that the Communists were moving toward the trails you had planned to take. So we thought you might need a few extra guns. Luckily, we were two klicks up the trail when our scouts reported they had spotted this patrol. Then your first Claymore exploded."

A Hmong approached the group and exchanged a few words with Luj, who turned back to Keej and Dobie.

"We have a couple of prisoners to question," he reported. "Please excuse me."

Dobie looked at Marcel.

"I think Mr. Peabody will find it in his heart to offer a little bonus to this group."

"Shit, yes!" Jimbo agreed. "And I'd say more than a little."

———•———

CHAOS

————

S ue was not happy. It was a Saturday morning, and she had spent a hectic week at the Hoa Sen Orphanage. Ten more children had arrived on its doorstep. It remained a mystery who had left them there. Sister Helene concluded they had come with the waves of refugees fleeing the highland provinces of South Vietnam. Sue anxiously awaited the needed items from her friends in the States. The struggle to find diapers and clothes had drained her emotionally. Sue had looked forward to a weekend with Rick looking after David and Thi.

The hectic work at Hoa Sen was a tiny part of the confusion and fear sweeping the country. Sue was just getting over Rick's unauthorized mission three weeks before. When he and Clicker had not returned home that night, she recognized the curfew could have trapped them on base. Yet, she raced to their office the following morning. Driving their battered Toyota had been a rare occasion for her. But with no telephone, she could think of no other way to find out where Rick was.

On the way, she made two wrong turns. Fortunately, she recognized her mistakes quickly. She met a haggard Clicker in their small office, talking on the phone. He looked like he had slept little.

"Where is Rick?" she had demanded.

Clicker told whomever he was talking to that he would call him back.

"You didn't get the note I sent last night?" he asked.

"No!"

"Damn it," was his reply. "I sent a note with one of our employees."

"No one delivered it. Where is Rick?" she demanded again. The urgency in her voice was becoming irritation. Sue took some comfort in understanding Clicker would not have sent only a note if something bad had happened to Rick.

"He spent the night at Nha Trang."

"Why? Where is that?"

"His plane had a malfunction, so he landed there as a precaution," Clicker replied. He walked over to a map on the wall. "It's here, about 180 miles north-east, on the coast."

"What kind of malfunction did he have?"

"I'm not sure," Clicker had answered. Technically, it was the truth. He did not know the extent of the damage to the airplane.

Sue eyed him suspiciously.

"What was he doing flying up there with all the fighting going on everywhere?"

Clicker's hesitation did nothing to placate Sue's growing suspicion.

"He was helping Colonel Tinh."

"So how badly damaged was Rick's plane?"

"I'm not ..." Clicker stopped. He had fallen for Sue's trick question.

"Why the hell was he flying a damaged airplane!"

Clicker had never encountered this version of Sue. Her petite frame held a formidable will.

"I'm sorry, Sue. I know very little. A helicopter is on its way there to pick him up. Why don't you go home? I'll drive him home as soon as he gets here."

When Rick arrived home a couple of hours later, Sue was dismayed to learn that Rick had come close to being shot down. He promised he would not fly any more combat.

But today, she was suspicious again. She had been reading the *Stars and Stripes*, which chronicled the fighting in the northern provinces of South Vietnam. The war was not going well for the fragile Republic of Vietnam.

"So explain why you need to go to the base today!" Sue demanded at breakfast.

"Clicker and I are giving Colonel Tinh a hand," came Rick's vague reply.

"Doing what?" Sue demanded.

Rick sighed. He would have to tell her.

"The colonel wants help to retrieve some F-5s from Da Nang," he began. "He has asked if Clicker and I will fly him and another pilot up there so they can save two of the jets."

"Why can't South Vietnamese pilots do that?"

"Four other pilots are going up there in a C-119 to get other planes."

"Why don't all the pilots go in the C-119?"

"I'm not sure. There are probably only four seats available on the C-119. Colonel Tinh would not ask if he wasn't desperate."

"Why don't the pilots from Da Nang fly the planes here?"

"A few are. But they don't have enough pilots available."

"I don't understand," Sue pressed. "Why not?"

Rick hated her constant questioning. For the last three weeks, whenever he left for the base, she had demanded to know what he was doing that day.

"The South's military is having a problem with soldiers leaving their units to take their families to safety."

"Well, at least somebody puts their families ahead of a lost cause. When will you be back?"

"Should be later this afternoon."

Rick did not want to give her a precise time frame because he did not know. No one was sure what they would find at Da Nang. The People's Army was likely closer to the city than this morning's news suggested.

Rick stood as a knock sounded on their door.

"I have to go. The colonel wants to get there ASAP."

Rick grabbed his helmet bag and flight bag by the front door. He opened the door to a waiting Clicker.

"Let's go," he told Clicker.

"Sue's not happy?" Clicker asked as they drove to the base.

"Nope."

"Sorry to hear that. Look, today, we take the colonel and his other pilot up to Da Nang, gas up quickly if we have to, and get the hell out of Dodge. I'm afraid the shit's gonna hit the fan soon up there. No sense in waiting around for it."

"I agree," Rick replied. "Hopefully, the few commercial flights going in mean the shit hasn't hit the fan yet."

"I'll fly lead," Clicker instructed.

"If you insist."

"I do."

Lieutenant Colonel Tinh waited for them in his office. As soon as they walked in, he grabbed his helmet bag.

"We need to go now," he ordered, hastening toward the door. Another Vietnamese pilot met them. The colonel briefed the pilots as they dashed to their planes.

"Things are getting hectic in Da Nang. The city has been shelled. So far, the shelling has spared the air base. But panic has spread through the streets. Clicker and I will lead. We will climb to flight level two eight zero for fuel efficiency."

He stopped walking momentarily.

"Fly loose trail behind us," he advised Rick. "Don't worry about precise positioning. Conserve your fuel. You and Clicker will not want to refuel on the ground. As soon as we hop out, leave immediately."

He resumed walking briskly.

"If your fuel runs low returning, Phan Rang is your only alternative for fuel. They should have some."

Seven minutes later, Rick advanced the throttles into afterburner to follow Clicker down Bien Họa's runway. He cut Clicker off in the northerly turn and settled in eight hundred feet behind him.

Forty-five minutes later, he followed Clicker in a steep descent toward Da Nang Air Base. Clicker had delayed their descent until the last possible moment. Rick checked his fuel as he ran the approach checklist.

Looks good, he concluded.

"Da Nang Approach, Tudo flight of two F-5s is thirty miles north," Colonel Tinh called.

No one replied. He called again in English and Vietnamese. Finally, he directed Rick to the control tower frequency. Several calls went unanswered. Finally, a shaken voice responded.

"Tudo flight, a straight-in approach approved. Stand by for landing clearance. You are number one behind World Airways taking off!"

The fear in the controller's voice was palpable.

Rick's initial reaction was, *What the …?*

Even in the sky around Hanoi during his two combat tours, he had never heard such panic in a radio call!

"Two, close it up!"

Colonel Tinh's call carried urgency. Rick inched the throttles up to close his distance on Clicker and the colonel.

Does he want a tight formation for landing? Rick wondered.

"Close trail," Clicker called, reading Rick's question.

Rick closed the distance on Clicker, but he stayed far enough back so he could scan past him. Something was happening on the ground that he wanted to see.

"World Airways Five One, taxi to Runway Three Five Left; you are not cleared for takeoff. We have a flight of F-5s on a straight-in approach."

The tower controller pleaded with the World Airways airplane.

"Five One has people in our way. Request security clear the runway of those trucks," the World Airways pilot responded. "We are having trouble closing our rear door. People are climbing in it."

Rick looked past Clicker's jet, trying to make out the air base ahead. They were still too far away to see what was happening. He wondered if Clicker would get them down in time to slow for landing.

"Idle, boards!" Clicker announced curtly. Rick pulled his throttles to idle and clicked the speed brakes. The jet shuddered. Rick could tell Clicker aimed short of the runway overrun, giving them space to slow.

Rick's crosscheck jumped from his airspeed to Clicker to the approaching runway. A smoky haze enveloped the base. Small pillars of smoke rose from the runways.

Is it being shelled? Rick wondered.

"Two, a helicopter is orbiting over the airport," Clicker advised.

"World Airways, you are cleared for an immediate takeoff. If unable, hold short for F-5s!"

The tower controller pleaded with the airliner. It was not the usual crisp instruction.

"Gear!" Clicker called.

Rick slapped his landing gear handle down.

"Flaps!"

Rick pushed the lever to the full-flap position. He jockeyed the throttles to keep his position behind Clicker.

"World Airways is rolling from the taxiway!" called the airliner.

"From the taxiway?" yelled the pilot behind Rick.

"World Airways, take off from taxiway not approved!" shouted the tower.

Behind the airliner on the parallel taxiway, Rick spotted throngs of people. As the airliner accelerated, explosions on its left side threw debris into the air. The airliner would not get off the ground ahead of the speeding fighters. Vehicles blocked the runway. Clicker noticed them, too.

"Tudo flight is going around!" Clicker yelled.

Clicker's speed brakes snapped up as the landing gear started to retract. The spacing between them lengthened. In a blur of movement, Rick shoved his throttles full forward, thumbed up his speed brakes, and raised the gear handle. As the jet leveled off, Clicker banked right to fly alongside the runway. Both fighters quickly overtook World Airways, which sped down the taxiway.

Rick raised his flaps as the F-5s closed on the struggling World Airways airliner. The big jet barely cleared the rocks at the edge of the taxiway. Rick noticed the open rear door. A body jammed it open.

As Rick pulled alongside the airliner, he nearly lost control of his jet in shock. He watched one body, then another, fall from the left landing gear! Another figure clung to the right landing gear!

"Đụ má!" the Vietnamese pilot behind Rick swore. Rick quickly refocused on flying his airplane and looked ahead for Clicker. He eased the control stick back as he sped past the struggling airliner and climbed to rejoin Clicker. Had he seen what he thought he had seen?

"Did you see that?" the pilot behind him asked.

"I'm not sure," Rick replied.

"People fell off that airplane. They were holding on to the wheels!"

"Two, are you with me?" Clicker called.

"Roger, at your six," Rick replied.

"We're aborting the mission," Colonel Tinh called. "Romeo Tango Bravo."

Tinh's "return to base" order released a mountain of tension from Rick's body. With the mob on the air base, they would never have gotten off the ground if they had landed.

Clicker pulled into a steep climb and turned right for the coast. As the coast slid below the jets, Clicker rolled out, heading south. Pulling behind Clicker, Rick glanced below at the docks of Da Nang. Millions of ants scurried along the docks to clamber aboard the ships. Except Rick knew they weren't ants. Panic gripped Da Nang.

After leveling off at twenty-nine thousand feet, Rick settled into position behind his leader.

"How's your fuel?" Clicker called.

Rick checked his fuel gauges and his fuel flow indicators. He did a quick calculation.

"Looks good," he answered.

The pair of F-5s flew in silence for several minutes. Then Colonel Tinh directed them to a new radio frequency. He called the C-119 carrying the other pilots on its way to Da Nang.

"Da Nang Air Base is overrun with people trying to escape. Abort the mission," the colonel ordered.

Rick looked east at the blues and greens of the South China Sea. The view made an ideal postcard picture. He then shifted his gaze west to the picturesque green forest. On the horizon, white puffs of clouds climbed from the mountains of the Central Highlands. Rick found it impossible to comprehend this beauty with the chaos he had just witnessed. Turmoil was destroying this beautiful country. He had never felt such helplessness.

BABYLIFT

—·—

Rick asked Sue to sit down.

"What?" Sue demanded. She recognized that look. She had seen the set jaw and look twice before. Both times, he had news that she did not like.

Rick hesitated. How could he convince Sue to leave without him?

"Okay, you've got something to say. Spit it out, bub!" Sue ordered.

"You need to leave with David and Thi."

"Why?"

Sue listened to the Armed Forces Radio Network and read the day-old *Stars and Stripes*. She grasped that the war was going badly for the South Vietnamese. *But he has to tell me*, she thought.

"Saigon will not last much over thirty days," Rick answered.

"So, what about you?"

Rick accepted he had to answer that question. He had not thought of a suitable answer. Sue sensed his delay.

"If it is too dangerous for David, Thi, and me, why not for you!"

It wasn't said as a question. Explain yourself, Sue was demanding.

"It is getting dangerous," Rick admitted. "Very dangerous."

He struggled to articulate what he felt in his gut. He could tell Sue was giving him time to explain himself.

"When I took this job and agreed that you and David could come, I never imagined we would be in this situation. At least, not before my year here was up."

Rick stood and went to the window facing the side yard of the house. His mouth was dry. He heard David and Lei playing in David's bedroom. Thi napped in their room. He turned and sat next to Sue.

"Honey, something in me won't let me leave yet. Besides, the company needs to release me from my contract. That could take a week."

"Why? If Saigon is going to fall, what can you do to stop that? What work do you need to do?"

"None," he admitted. "But we are about to abandon the Vietnamese who trusted us. I can't cut and run."

"You are not cutting and running!" Sue shouted. "You've come over here twice to fight this fucking war!"

It was only the second time that Rick had heard Sue use that word.

"Do you know how I worried every day you were over here? Every time we read that a plane had been shot down, Karen, Ruth, and I worried ourselves sick. There were days when one of us found it hard to get our butts up and go to work. We took turns having days paralyzed by fear. But we did it with each other's help. When that blue car showed up in front of Ruth's place after Zack went down, our worst fears stared us in the face. There was a lot you guys never told us. But we never told you a lot, too!"

Sue's eyes filled with tears.

Her shouting brought David and Lei into the living room. David was not used to his mother's loud voice, at least not being directed at him. Both boys stopped when Sue and Rick turned to them. Sue walked over.

"It's okay, sweetie. Daddy and I are just talking." She led them to the small kitchen. "How about some coconut crackers? You can take them to your room."

The boys scampered back to David's room with their treats. Sue sat down on the couch. A silence ensued. Rick searched his mind for some explanation.

"When we leave, we have to take Mai and Lei with us," Sue stated.

"We won't abandon them. You heard about World Airways flying orphans out, right?"

"Yes."

"Well, the Air Force brass can't let a corporate CEO upstage them. Jeff says that a C-5 is inbound to carry orphans out. He expects President Ford to announce the orphan airlift in a day or so."

"That's the big airplane, right?"

"Yes, the giant cargo plane."

"How many kids do they plan on carrying?"

"I'm not sure. But hundreds. The mission is named Operation Babylift."

"Will they let civilian dependents and a Vietnamese woman and kid on it?"

"They need volunteers to help with the kids on the flight," Rick continued. "Jeff says he can get you and David on it. Especially since you've been working with the orphanage. Many wives and children of Jeff's coworkers have orders to leave on the flight."

"What about Mai and Lei?"

"Well, since she has worked for Americans for years, she is in the 'threatened group', according to Jeff. Also, Lei's dad was an American GI. So, they qualify as refugees. And if we volunteer to sponsor them, it'll cinch it, according to Jeff."

Rick hoped Sue had forgotten about his staying. Sue was not so easily distracted.

"Why don't you come along?"

"I don't fit the profile of an escort for orphans."

While Rick knew this was true, he also recognized that Sue would not buy it.

"So, we just buy airline tickets for the four of us and for Mai and Lei, too."

Rick sat next to Sue.

"I love you. I love David and Thi. You are my life. I can't stop this country from falling to the Communists. But I can't run out on people I might help. People who have depended on me. It just isn't in me." He paused. "Colonel Tinh still needs my help. Yesterday, he looked me in the eye and asked, 'When will you flee?' He turned around and walked away so I wouldn't have to answer."

Rick struggled to explain his reason for staying.

"I can't escape when I might help Colonel Tinh and his family."

"What can you do?" Sue pressed.

"I'm not sure. Maybe help him get his family out. As an Air Force officer, they will face imprisonment and worse."

Rick stopped. He held Sue's hand. Finally, he said, "How can I cut and run on him?"

He shrugged his shoulders and slouched.

Seconds passed, a minute.

"I left a guy once when I could have done more. I can't do it again."

"When was that?"

"A pilot ejected over Laos. We flew cover over him for a while. Then we lost contact. Our fuel ran low. So we left him." Rick stopped.

"What more could you have done?"

"Hit the tankers, refueled, and returned." Rick paused again for several seconds. "But we didn't. The guy never came home. The Air Force still lists him as MIA." Rick cleared his throat. "Two weeks ago, a team recovered his Academy class ring from a North Vietnamese deserter in Laos. But they learned nothing about him. He probably died in the jungle."

Sue sighed. Several seconds passed in silence again. She watched Rick, who stared at his hands.

"How long do you think the South Vietnamese can hold out?" she finally asked.

Rick shrugged.

"Six weeks, eight weeks, if aid arrives tomorrow."

"In three weeks, I expect you to be on a plane out of here."

Sue squeezed Rick's hands as hard as she could. Then she reached across and wrapped her arms around Rick's broad shoulders. "Otherwise, I'll never talk to you again."

"Okay, in three weeks, I'll be on a plane out of here, even if I have to steal one."

Sue did not doubt that Rick would steal an airplane if he had to. He had given his word. It was enough for her.

The morning following their discussion, she approached Mai downstairs.

"You need to get ready to leave with David, Thi, and me."

Mai looked at her quizzically.

"A big Air Force airplane is coming to carry orphans out," Sue explained. "I will be on it with David and Thi to help with the orphans. Since you have been volunteering at the orphanage, you can come too, with Lei. Rick says he can arrange it."

Mai did not react immediately.

"Can it be true?" she finally asked timidly. "But I have no papers to leave."

"Rick says his friend can arrange it. You go to the orphanage and start getting the kids ready. Rick and I are going to see his friend to get any paperwork you need."

Sue and Rick then raced to Jeff Nickerson's office at Tan Son Nhut Air Base.

"How many children does the orphanage have under the age of ten?" Jeff asked her.

"Why the ones under the age of ten?"

"The South Vietnamese will only allow children under ten years old to leave. So keep that in mind when you fill out the forms."

Sue did some quick figuring.

"I'd guess we have about thirty or forty."

Jeff had gathered most of the forms she needed to fill out to get the orphans on the C-5. The biggest challenge: birth certificates for all the children. Few of the children had one. Jeff reassured her.

"Here is an office to visit. Ask for Mr. Nguyễn. He will give you blank birth certificates. Fill them out for each child and bring all the forms back to me."

"But we don't know details about many children," Sue protested.

"Do they have names you use at the orphanage?"

"Yes."

"Okay, use those."

"But we aren't sure of both parents or even where they were born."

"Do you have any idea?" Jeff pressed.

"For some."

"Okay, use those. For the ones you aren't sure about, make your best guess. An American father would help."

"Ask Mr. Nguyễn what to do about the children with unknown parents. It can't be uncommon here for the orphanages. We won't have time to get an exit visa for Mai. We'll have to sneak her past the Vietnamese at the base. I doubt she has a passport, so hopefully she has a birth certificate. Mr. Nguyễn can help with that if she doesn't."

Jeff paused to think.

"You'll also need any paperwork the orphanage has for each child. Especially important are forms or letters signed by a family member releasing custody to the orphanage. And the names of any American families waiting to adopt them."

The following morning, Rick and Sue returned the paperwork to Jeff.

"Mai has a birth certificate and an old passport," Sue informed Jeff. "She got it when she was pregnant with Lei. Lei's father promised to take her home when he finished his tour. But he died in a battle."

Jeff looked over the forms. He kept some of them. Others, including the birth certificates, he returned to Sue.

"Bring the children with these forms to the gate tomorrow morning," he instructed. "Bring your passport, David's, and papers for Mai and Lei. The C-5 is due in mid-morning. You are allowed one small bag each."

He thought for a minute.

"We'll have to smuggle Mai on board. Dress her in a set of your clothes so she is less conspicuous. Sister Helene might have an idea."

"How do we get a bus or a van to bring the kids to the airport?" Sue inquired.

Jeff opened a desk drawer and pulled out a tattered business card.

"Go see this guy. He does some transport for us. Tell him I sent you. His office is a small building down the street from the air base gate. Tell him how many children you have. Be sure to bargain about the price he gives you."

———+———

The next morning, the blue- and cream-colored taxi with Sue, Rick, Thi, Mai, and the boys pulled up to the Hoa Sen Orphanage. Sister Helene, Sister Barbara, and Sister Frances had the children organized. The babies lay in boxes of every kind, with extra diapers and bedding. The toddlers sat in larger boxes. Each had some sort of old toy, doll, or stuffed animal. The older children waited on the orphanage veranda. Rick noticed how quietly they all sat. Each of the older children had a younger one in tow. The children over ten watched from inside through the open windows.

Rick informed Sister Helene about their problem with Mai's missing exit visa.

"I have an idea."

She rushed into the orphanage. Three minutes later, she returned carrying a habit. She walked to Mai.

"Put this on. We are all coming to help load the children. You'll be one of us. But when you get on the plane, take it off and hide it. Then hide among the children. We'll keep any curious official busy."

Three battered vans arrived as Mai pulled on the habit. Sister Helene led one small group toward one of the battered vans. The driver stopped them.

"Now what?" Sue asked pensively.

The driver chattered to Rick, who had hastened over to him. Rick could not understand the words, but he had a good guess. Mai rushed over and answered the driver. She exchanged several sentences with him, then she turned to Rick.

"He wants more money. He says the price of gasoline has shot higher again."

Rick's guess had been right. "How much?"

He was prepared for this, as he had pocketed extra wads of piastres with him. Rick had divided the money into four wads, one for each pocket.

"The driver demands double the amount he agreed to yesterday."

"Bullshit," Rick snapped back to the driver. "Tell him I'll give him half of that increase."

The extra amount roughly amounted to one of the extra wads. Rick pulled out the original amount agreed to, then added the extra wad to it.

"If he doesn't like that, tell him we'll get someone else." Mai translated Rick's message. The driver screamed his reply.

"He doesn't believe you," Mai explained.

Since Rick had expected delays of any kind, he knew they still had time.

"Fine," Rick responded. *The jerk is bluffing*, Rick told himself.

He turned to Sue. David stood next to her, his eyes wide.

"Start walking back," he muttered to her. Rick stepped toward Sister Helene. "Have the children wait in the shade while I find another ride," he instructed.

Sue turned, and the nun started shooing the older children back to the orphanage. The driver started talking to Mai again. Rick turned, feigning only mild interest in what the man was saying. Mai turned to Rick, barely suppressing a smile.

"He says okay. He'll do it for your price."

Rick nodded.

"Okay." He turned to Sue and the nuns. "Let's get the children loaded before he changes his mind."

Sister Helene motioned to the nuns, who gathered the children. Each older child held one box with an infant in her lap as they crowded into the vans. Sister Helene handed the envelope of forms to Sue.

Sister Helene, Sister Francis, and Sister Barbara squeezed into the vans with the children.

Rick hustled Sue, David, and Lei into their waiting taxi. Sue still held Thi close.

"I'll ride in the first van," Mai told Rick.

Just before the taxi pulled away, Sister Helene ran back to the steps for a box.

"You'll need this for Thi," she said to Sue, placing the box on her lap in the crowded taxi.

The little parade snaked through the traffic toward Tan Son Nhut. Mai urged the van driver in front to stay right on the taxi's tail. Rick tried looking straight ahead at the traffic, but his eyes wandered to the stares from the people they passed.

Am I seeing the beginnings of panic on their faces? he worried.

A taxi with Americans followed by two vans full of children was not a common sight on the streets of the tense city. The crowds needed little imagination to understand the purpose of this procession.

As the sun reached its peak in the sky, they pulled up to the main gate of Tan Son Nhut. Rick showed his passport to the guard and his defense contractor ID card. He also showed a letter from Jeff on embassy stationery. Sue handed the guard the envelope of paperwork. The guard quickly inspected the passport and the sheaf of papers. He stepped aside and raised the barrier. Rick directed the taxi to the curb at the passenger terminal. The vans pulled behind it. Throngs of people milled around the doors.

"We have to get out here," he told Mai as he walked to the lead van. "Other help should be here. Let's get the children into the shade of the building." Rick paid his taxi driver, then walked over to the vans. He gave each driver their share of the agreed price, adding a small tip.

By the time the older children had helped their younger ones into the little shade, Jeff walked up to them.

"Take the children into the terminal. Then you, Sue, and Sister Helene come with me to the customs and passport desk."

It took more than an hour for the Vietnamese officials to go through the paperwork. They asked many questions. Sister Helene answered all the questions calmly. She pointed to different forms for each child as the officials quizzed her.

This nun is a battle-hardened veteran, Rick recognized.

Finally, the information satisfied the officials.

"Bring the children through one by one with their paperwork," the senior bureaucrat instructed.

"The sisters and I need to help take the children to the airplane," Sister Helene informed him.

He looked at her and the nuns.

"Okay."

Sister Helene stood by the official as each child walked past. She murmured a Hail Mary as the children went through the customs gate. Sister Barbara, Sister Francis, and Mai ushered groups of children toward the flight line.

"Come on," Jeff said to Rick. "We can walk them to the aircraft."

As the group walked out of the terminal onto the tarmac, the sight shocked Sue. Children were everywhere. There were too few volunteers to help them all. Some were crying, but most sat quietly on the hot tarmac in the bright sun. Behind the throng of children stood the largest airplane Sue had ever seen. She saw a large crowd around the rear ramp. The T-shaped tail rose high above them. Ground crew scurried around the landing gear and reached up to the massive engines. One walked along the top of the nearest wing.

Jeff led the orphanage group to an Air Force officer.

"Sue, this is Lieutenant Ann Jagger," he said to Sue.

"I'm the chief flight nurse on the plane," Ann replied. "I understand you will help us with the children."

"My friend, Mai, is coming along too, to help," Sue responded as she motioned to Mai.

"Mai couldn't get an exit visa in time," Jeff explained quietly. "Can you help her find a place to ditch the habit after she gets on board?"

Ann Jagger nodded.

"We have all kinds of nooks and crannies to hide the habit. The babies and infants will go to the upper passenger deck. We'll get her up there. We need all the help we can get."

Ann turned to Sue.

"Do you have your children traveling with us?"

"I have my son, David, and Mai has her son, Lei," Sue informed the nurse. "We are adopting little Thi." Sue had not let go of the infant.

The flight nurse surveyed the group.

"You can be in the upper troop compartment. It has airline seats for seventy-five, but we have to fit at least twice that number up there. I'm afraid we won't have any seats for the adults to sit in. But I expect we will be busy the whole flight caring for the children. We'll carry each child to the bottom of the ladder. Then, crew members will move the children up the steep stairs to the compartment. Mai, just climb up with them. I'll have another nun climb up, too, so it doesn't look odd."

Sue studied Lieutenant Jagger for a second.

Lieutenant Ann Jagger looks younger than me, Sue thought. But her attitude comforted Sue.

"Let's load the babies first, then the toddlers," Ann instructed. "The toddlers will share the seats with the babies in your boxes. It would have been nice if the planners for this had thought of infant seats for the babies."

Ann picked up the nearest baby.

"Let's get started, one baby at a time." Lieutenant Ann turned and walked toward the ramp of the giant plane.

"David, stay here with Daddy while I help load the babies," Sue instructed her son.

Rick took David's small hand and reached for Lei's hand. "We'll wait here."

Carrying Thi, Sue followed Ann Jagger, and Mai picked up a baby and followed. When her eyes adjusted to the dim interior, it shocked Sue. No seats were in the cargo compartment for the children. The cargo floor was a flat metal surface with straps strung across it.

"Where are the seats?" she quizzed Ann.

"We are doing a combat load. Everyone down here slides under one of these straps for their seatbelt. Using seats would cut our load capacity by more than half."

"But … if…?" Sue began.

"If the pilot expects a bumpy landing, we tell everyone to face forward and wrap their arms under their legs," Ann explained.

After many trips up the ramp, the Hoa Sen babies were on the airplane. Lieutenant Ann Jagger then took the hand of an older child.

"Come along, sweetheart. It's your turn now."

Sue took another child by the hand and followed the flight nurse. Sue helped the child up the ramp toward the main cargo deck. When the last of their orphans were on board, Sister Helene turned to Sue and Rick.

"Bless you for doing this. We will pray for a quick and safe journey."

The elderly nun's eyes filled with tears as she hugged Sue. Sue hugged Sister Helene for several seconds.

"Tell Mai goodbye for me," Sister Helene said.

"We will stay with the children and see that they get to America," Sue promised.

Sue turned to Rick. She looked him in the eyes and tried to smile. But tears filled her eyes. She wrapped her arms around him in a clinch.

"Promise me again," she demanded. "You will get on a plane in less than three weeks and get out of here. David and I won't leave until you promise."

"I will," he replied.

"Say the whole thing," she ordered.

"I promise I will get on an airplane and leave," he repeated.

"In three weeks," Sue continued.

"In three weeks," Rick promised. He knew he had to keep that promise.

Sue clung to him, burying her face in his shoulder. Her tears added to the moisture of her and Rick's perspiration. When she lifted her head back, his shirt was wet. He kissed her, not wanting to let go.

This is the third time I've had to say goodbye because of this poor country, he realized. *Never again,* he vowed to himself. When he let Sue go, Rick leaned over to pick up David.

"You help Mommy. I know you can be a big boy and a big help. I love you."

He squeezed and kissed his son, then put him down. He hugged Sue again. "I love you."

Sue took David's hand while Ann took Lei's hand.

With Lieutenant Ann Jagger leading the way, Sue and the boys walked to the waiting giant airplane. Sue held her small bag in her left hand and squeezed David's with her right hand.

As they walked away, Jeff moved beside Rick.

"Looks like they have about everyone on board," he observed. "I hope this hastily organized mission goes off with no hiccups."

"No shit."

Jeff turned and spotted Sister Helene in a tense conversation with a Vietnamese official. As he walked over, he heard Sister Helene say in Vietnamese, "You must have miscounted. You know we all look alike."

She turned to Jeff.

"He insists he counted four of us. He wants to know where the fourth nun is."

"I saw only three nuns," he assured the official.

Rick walked up.

"How many nuns did you see helping load the orphans?" Jeff asked.

"I saw three."

The official looked from Jeff to Rick, then back to Sister Helene. He shrugged and walked away.

"We can wait in my office until after takeoff," Jeff commented to Rick.

"Thank you, Sister," Rick told the nun.

"We shall pray for a safe trip for them," Sister Helene stated, looking at the large airplane. She crossed herself. "May God forgive me for the little lies I had to tell today."

———•———

SWIRLING SNOW

S ue stood at the base of the tall stairs leading to the troop deck high above. She glanced into the cargo compartment, which teemed with children. The few crew members and escorting adults moved among the children. They struggled to explain how to slide under the cargo straps.

We need more adults, Sue thought. *God help us.*

She looked up the steep stairs in front of her. She couldn't make a good guess of how high they were. But they went up higher than the stairs in their house.

These aren't stairs, she realized. They were steps of a ladder with a flimsy handrail. Sue wondered whether an airline flight might have been a better idea. She sighed and lifted David onto the second rung. But the children from Hoa Sen needed her help.

"Hold on to the railing and climb up. It's like a playground. Mommy is right behind you. I won't let you fall."

David's short legs climbed the stairs, one rung at a time. Sue nestled against him, two steps below. She clutched the thin railing with an iron grip. Ann Jagger helped Lei follow Sue up the ladder.

Finally, David scampered into the troop compartment. Sue stepped onto the floor, blocking the opening to the abyss below.

"Move on," she instructed David. "Let's find Thi so you can sit with her."

Sue quickly surveyed the scene. At least there were airline seats here. But they faced the wrong way. The seats faced backward.

Count on the Air Force to put the seats in backward, she thought.

Ann Jagger appeared behind her. She saw Sue's quizzical look.

"Right, they face the wrong way," she commented. "But not really. Facing backward is much safer. The airlines put their seats in the wrong way."

Sue nodded. Maybe the Air Force did know something.

"Thi is across the way," Lieutenant Ann continued. "I've saved a place next to her for David. There is a space for Lei, too."

Sue placed David in the seat with the box with Thi. She wasn't sure how to fasten the seat belt around both of them. Ann came over.

"Put it around David and over the top of the box," she advised. "It's the best we can do."

Mai came from the front.

"Here is a place for Lei on the other side of Thi," Ann instructed. A baby in a box already sat in the seat. Mai loosened the seatbelt around the box and slid Lei under it.

Thi started to cry.

"It's time to feed her," Sue commented.

"We have bottles in the galley fridge and coolers," Ann noted. "I hope we have enough. I think there is one for each baby, at least. It'll be about three hours to Clark." Ann pointed past the stairs to the rear of the compartment.

Sue retrieved three bottles. She gave one each to two babies in boxes in the row, and she knelt on the floor to hold the bottle for Thi. Mai went for more bottles, returning with two juice boxes and crackers for David and Lei.

Air Force crew members filtered through the compartment. Some fed and others changed diapers. Boxes of paper diapers sat stacked in the back corner of the compartment. When Sue finished feeding Thi, she checked on the other two bottles. The lights flickered, then Sue heard the whine of jet engines starting. Soon, she felt the airplane move.

Minutes later, a male voice made an announcement.

"Ladies, gentlemen, and children. The tower has cleared us for takeoff. Please sit down. Those in the main cargo compartment, please slide under the nearest strap and face forward."

Almost immediately, Sue heard the engines whine louder, and the plane accelerated. She knelt on the floor in front of David and Thi and tried to grasp the edge of their seat cushion. In a minute, the rumbling of the runway ceased, and the ride became smoother. She could feel the huge jet claw its way into the humid Saigon air.

They were off! Sue looked at her watch. 4:00 p.m.

Sue turned to Mai, kneeling next to her on the floor. Tears formed in Mai's eyes as they felt the airplane climb. The enormity of the journey for Mai and Lei hit Sue. This small woman with her child was leaving the only home she had ever known for an uncertain future. America would be a strange land where she would struggle to learn the customs. But at the end of this trip, there would not be a prison camp called a "reeducation center." Mai and Lei could expect to have happier and more comfortable lives.

How would I feel if our roles were reversed? Sue wondered. *Scared stiff.*

Sue reached for Mai's hand, gave it a gentle squeeze, and smiled at her friend.

The air cooled as the pressurization system pumped in air-conditioned air. Sue felt her ears pop as the plane climbed to the heavens.

Flight nurse Ann Jagger knelt behind Sue and Mai.

"If we lose pressurization for some reason," she began, "oxygen masks will drop from the overhead. Remember to put one on yourself first, then take turns holding one to the children. We won't need them long, though. The pilot will dive to a lower altitude where we won't need them."

When Sue and Mai nodded, Ann stood and moved to another couple of escorts to talk to them.

Sue checked Thi's diaper, discovering it needed changing. She retrieved a few diapers from one box in the corner. *No doubt,* she assumed, *other babies needed changing too.*

Finished with checking diapers all across her row, Sue knelt in front of David. The young boy had remained unusually quiet for the entire journey from the house. She felt grateful that he had not needed constant attention.

"Are you nervous, honey?" she asked. David nodded.

"When will Daddy come?"

"Soon, honey," she reassured the boy. *Dear Lord, make it soon.*

Sue began standing to check on other children when *BAM!*

It was a loud explosion!

An unseen force knocked Sue backward. Swirling snow enveloped the compartment! A blast of cold air created goosebumps on Sue's arms. A blur swept through Sue's peripheral vision on her right. Dirty diapers, plastic bottles, and pieces of paper flew through the compartment. Loud, rushing air filled the surrounding space. The oxygen masks dropped from above! The plane lurched from side to side. Then it nosed over. Babies, toddlers, and adults screamed! The dive steepened. The aircraft bounced up and down. Events around Sue evolved in slow motion.

We've lost pressure! Sue realized.

Sue reached up for an oxygen mask, teetering to reach it. She strapped it to her face, then grabbed the one next to it. As she leaned over, the aircraft lurched again. She fell on David and Thi. As she struggled to hold the mask to David's face, she saw to her right. Against the rear bulkhead by the gate and the ladder, Ann Jagger's crumpled body lay. Sue quickly shifted the mask to Thi for two seconds, then strapped it to David.

Sue rushed to Ann, tearing off her mask and bumping shoulders with Mai.

"I'll see to Ann," she told Mai. Mai nodded, then turned back to the children in the row.

Sue's ears popped. She took a deep breath and pinched her nose to clear them. She got to Ann as she stirred. Ann's eyes popped open.

"Explosive decompression!" she yelled. "We've had an explosive decompression. Get an oxygen mask!"

Rather than leave the nurse, though, Sue helped Ann sit up. Ann shook her head slightly, like a boxer trying to clear his head after a hard blow. A crew member in a flight suit and oxygen mask appeared beside them. He carried another mask with a small tank attached to it. Fastening the mask to Ann, he hung a strap holding the bottle around her neck. Sue felt him nudge her, and he pointed to a swinging mask nearby. Sue understood. He wanted her to put on that mask.

As Sue strapped the soft mask to her face, Ann struggled to her feet. She leaned against the rear bulkhead. The crewman moved her away from the gate and motioned to Sue to move back, too.

As Ann shifted over, Sue saw through a grate to the cargo compartment below. Past the mass of bodies, Sue saw the beautiful blue ocean.

"Dear God in heaven!" Sue exclaimed into her mask. "The back of the airplane is missing!"

The crewman disappeared down the steps into the void beneath.

David! she thought. *How was he?*

Sue turned to check on David and her row of children. They sat there. David's eyes were wide with fear. She removed the mask from David and held it to Thi. Then she grabbed another mask on her right and held it to another infant's face for several seconds. Mai was doing the same at the other end of the row. Lieutenant Ann limped forward and out of view. She was gone for less than a minute. As she came back to Sue's row, the crewman scampered up the ladder. He removed his oxygen mask and held a quick conversation with Ann. He explained something to her, and she nodded.

As he rushed down the ladder again, Ann removed her mask and stumbled to Sue and Mai.

"We don't need the masks. We've descended low enough." Her voice was raised, and it sounded hoarse.

"Where did the back of the plane go?" Sue inquired. "How are we still flying?"

Sue had heard Rick talk enough about flying that she knew the plane could not fly without a tail. Yet, they were not tumbling out of the sky.

"The rear cargo doors blew off," Ann explained. "That caused the rapid decompression."

"How much trouble are we in?" Sue pleaded.

Ann hesitated.

"We have turned back to Saigon. We will make an emergency landing there. We have to get ready for it!"

While still flying, Sue could feel the cargo jet lurch and yaw. She heard the engines get louder for a while; then they would power back. She was sure she heard different levels of engine noise from one side of the plane to the other.

"Let's check on all the kids," Ann shouted over the din in the compartment. "Make sure the belts are tight."

Sue and Mai nodded and started along the row. When they finished in their row, they moved to the next one forward.

When they returned to their row, Lieutenant Ann produced a long piece of cloth.

"Here," she instructed. "The landing could get rough. Hold Thi in front close to you. I'll wrap her to you with this." Sue picked Thi out of her box and clutched her. Flight Nurse Ann wrapped the scarf around Sue and Thi with the moves of an expert bandager.

"It can't be too tight, but she must stay with you no matter …"

Sue jiggled Thi. She didn't move. Yet, she could tell the baby wasn't smothered against her. She nodded to Ann. *What aren't you telling us?*

"Okay, now kneel against the seat here, putting Thi's butt on the seat. You too, Mai."

Sue complied. From somewhere, Ann produced a white tie-down strap.

"I'm going to wrap this behind you and Mai and around the seats. David and Lei will be fine here in front of you, strapped in their seats. You'll stay together, no matter …"

There was that "no matter" again.

No matter what? Sue worried.

Sue and Mai both nodded, thinking they understood. Ann ran the strap behind Sue and Mai and pushed one end forward between the cabin wall and a seat ahead. Then she disappeared into the row in front. She reappeared, attached the strap's hooks together, and cinched the strap tight. Then she limped into the aisle to check on another row of children.

While Sue lost all sense of time, she knew the plane was descending again. The cool air warmed, and the humidity rose. The engines continued to get loud, then quiet, only to power up again. As a pilot's wife, Sue guessed the pilot was manipulating the power to control the airplane. The large jet yawed and buffeted as it raced through the air pockets at the lower altitude of the tropics.

Sue and Mai tried to cling to the seat cushions in front of them, the white strap securing them in place. Suddenly, Mai squirmed. Sue looked at her. She reached to a child across the aisle, who was wriggling out of his seatbelt.

Mai spoke to the child in Vietnamese, but the toddler kept wiggling out of his seatbelt. Mai slid out of the white strap to reach the child. Sue looked back to check on David and Lei. Both boys sat still, eyes wide, looking at Sue and Mai. Sue tried to give them a reassuring smile.

Then, the engines ramped higher and higher. Out of the corner of her eye, Sue saw Mai secure the escaping child into its seatbelt.

THUD!

A blur appeared where Mai had been. The sharp jolt threw Sue forward. Her body twisted sideways, and her head slammed against David's legs. The jolt pinned Thi's little legs between Sue and the seat.

Then Sue was floating.

But only momentarily.

THUD! … THUD! Again and again.

Sue twisted on her knees, the white strap slipping off behind her. She heard the screech of bending metal. The lights in the compartment went out. Sue tried to cling to Thi, strapped against her, while reaching for David. She thought they were tumbling!

Where had Mai gone? Sue worried.

Debris bounced off Sue's arms and legs. She lurched from side to side, up and down, powerless to control her body. The impact loosened her grip on Thi. In the dark, she moved her left arm, searching for David. She merely waved at the air.

Then the tumbling stopped. Sue lay on her side. Something crushed against her face. She had trouble drawing a breath. She smelled smoke. It was acrid smoke, not the comforting scent of a warm campfire. Minor explosions popped around her.

Are they close? Are they far away? Sue could not tell.

Deep inside her, some unknown sense urged her. *Move! Find David! Find Lei! Find Mai! GET OUT!*

In panic, Sue reached to her breast. *Is Thi still here?*

Her hand felt a warm, tiny head with soft hair. She felt a warm, damp breath above her right breast.

Clinging to the small body strapped to her with her right hand, Sue shoved up with her left hand. She had to move whatever was holding her down. It felt like a seat cushion.

Fear shot through Sue. If the cushion was on top of her, where was David? Where was Lei? And again, where had Mai gone?

As Sue shoved the cushion away, she saw shafts of light shining around her. Light smoke and dust wafted through the air. She struggled to sit up, careful not to crush Thi against the surrounding wreckage. She heard a soft cough near her feet.

"David!" she shouted.

A small cry.

"Lei!"

Another small cry.

Sue pushed against another cushion to her left. Underneath it, in the shadows, Sue saw David and Lei sitting, still strapped into their seats. But the seats were no longer attached to the floor.

Sue got to her knees. Letting go of her grip on Thi, she used both hands to find the seat buckles and release both boys. A baby's cry reminded her that another infant was with Lei. She reached across and felt the cardboard box that had been that baby's cradle. Crying reassured her that the baby was alive, at least for now.

Around her, Sue heard thrashing and junk being ripped away. Then she saw Ann Jagger's face. Blood oozed from a gash on her forehead, but the nurse frantically tossed debris out of the way.

"Sue," she called. "We need to get out! Do you have David and Lei?"

"Yes, and there is another baby here too!"

"Can you hand it to me?"

"I think so!"

Sue scooted to the cardboard box, reached in, and lifted the crying baby. She held it against Thi as she moved debris with her left hand. She crawled to Ann.

"Here he is."

Ann took the baby and then looked at David.

"David, you need to hang on to my pants leg real tight and crawl after me. Lei, you follow David. Sue, follow us all. I know the way out!"

Ann led the group toward what Sue guessed was the front of the passenger compartment to an open door. Bright light from the afternoon tropical sun shone through the opening. The glare made it impossible to see what lay beyond the door. At the door, Ann halted until they were all together.

"We have to crawl down a rope ladder a little way to the ground. It's wet and muddy down there."

Ann turned around and backed out of the hatch, then stopped.

"David, come here. Get right next to me and grab the rope. We are going to crawl down together. Like a playground."

David hesitated as he looked through the door into the haze.

"Go on, honey," Sue urged. "Nurse Ann won't let you fall. I'll be right after you with Lei."

David got on his hands and knees and inched to the opening.

"Now turn around and step onto the ladder. Climb down with me," Ann urged.

When Ann's head disappeared below the bottom of the door, Sue crawled to it. She peered out and saw Ann gather David under a free arm and limp away into the haze. Sue turned around and motioned to Lei.

"Come on, honey. We go next."

Lei followed David's example and scampered down the rope ladder. Sue followed him, holding Thi against her with one hand. At the bottom, she scooped Lei up like Ann had done and stumbled through thick mud and water into the haze.

Stumbling for what seemed like forever, Sue finally came upon Ann, David, and a small group of other survivors. Sue collapsed into the mud.

Ann crawled next to her.

"Do you think you can keep the children together here while I go back to bring more out?"

"Go back?" Sue was incredulous. After surviving a plane crash and climbing out of it, Ann was going back.

"Yes, there are still people trapped in there."

"But you're bleeding," Sue protested, reaching for the cut on Ann's forehead.

Ann wiped her head.

"It's just a scratch."

Then Sue noticed a cut on Ann's left thigh.

"And your leg has a cut."

"Keep the kids safe here," Ann ordered. Then she headed back to the crash.

Sue looked to her right. Wreckage littered the muddy field. Far to the right, a small fire blazed. She could see no one moving near any of the large field of wreckage or the fire. Ann disappeared into the haze near the hulk of the aircraft from which they had just escaped. It appeared to be the top part of the fuselage where their compartment had been. It looked reasonably intact, though it tilted to one side.

Sue looked around at the few people near them.

Where is Mai? she wondered again, scrutinizing each person's face.

At first, Sue did not hear them, but a pulsing became a *whoop, whoop,* WHOOP, WHOOP. Then a wind hit her. She turned to her left and saw a hulk settle into the field. Then, more noise and more shapes. Her reeling mind took a minute to realize.

Helicopters! Men scrambled out of the first one carrying stretchers and ran to a group near the helicopter. Then a familiar form plodded through thick mud in her direction. It stopped to check a couple of shadows on the ground, then resumed its slog toward her.

A muffled voice sounded over the din of the helicopters. She heard it clearly.

"Sue!" it called. "Sue!"

"Rick!" Sue stood and waved. Her handsome husband scampered to her and swept her up in his arms.

"Sue, Sue, Sue," was all he said. He clung to her for seconds, then set her down.

"Thank God you're okay. I thought I'd lost you." Rick gulped a lungful of air. "David?" he asked. "Where's David?" A tremble in his voice betrayed his worry.

"Daddy!"

Rick picked up the muddy child and kissed the mud off his cheek.

"Ouch."

"Sorry, son, I'm squeezing you too hard." Rick relaxed his grip and shifted David to a hip. He quickly surveyed the small group. He looked at another small, muddy form. "Lei?" he asked tentatively.

"Yes," Sue answered. "Lei's here too."

"And Mai?"

Sue burst into tears.

"I don't know where Mai is. She was helping one child back into his seatbelt. Then we hit. I fell forward. When I looked again, she was gone. Where could she have gone? She was there. Then, in a flash, she just disappeared." The torrent of words came out in sobs. "Then we hit again, and I heard the airplane coming apart all around." Sue gasped for breath.

"I'll go look for her," Rick yelled over the continuing *whoop-whoop* and wind noise of the helicopters. He carefully placed David next to Sue. He took one step toward the wreckage when a shape carrying a bundle stumbled out of the haze.

Lieutenant Ann Jagger carried two babies as she stooped to hand them to Sue.

"Mai?" Sue begged. "Did you see Mai?"

Ann's shoulders slumped. "I found her," Ann whispered hoarsely.

"Did you get her out?" Sue pleaded.

Ann shook her head.

"She died in the impact. I found her crumpled against the front bulkhead. The crash must have thrown her the entire length of the compartment."

"Ooohh!" Sue cried. "NO!"

Ann's shoulders heaved as she reached for Sue.

"I'm so sorry. I couldn't save her. She had no pulse." Ann paused, then wiped her cheek with the back of a muddy hand. "I need to go back. I think there are still others." She struggled to stand, but her legs buckled under her.

"Catch your breath," Rick said. "Rest a minute. I'll go."

He stumbled through the mounds of mud and water toward the crash. In his ten years of flying jets, Rick had never been to the scene of a crash. He could have told no one what he would have expected to find. But even the confusion and disorientation of flak over North Vietnam had not prepared him for the experience. The wind was blowing the smoke from the burning wreckage toward the hulk in front of him. Fortunately, there was no fire nearby. But over ten yards to his left, a puddle suddenly burst into flames.

Burning embers must be landing in pooled fuel, he concluded.

Taking in the scene was not an option. The smell of jet fuel was strong, so he knew other pools of fuel must be all around. A flying ember could ignite any of them. Rick pulled himself up the rope ladder leading to the compartment with two leaps.

Damn, he thought. *I should have grabbed a flashlight off the helicopter.*

He did not have the luxury of waiting for his eyes to adjust from the glare outside to the dim interior of the turmoil inside.

Rick stumbled to the first row of crunched seats. He righted one tilted seat to search the mass of trash on the floor. Seeing nothing, he worked his way across the row, shoving clumps aside with his foot before shifting his weight to it. A muffled cry sounded. Moving cushions, diapers, and bottle remains, he found a bundle on the floor. He gently lifted it. Wide eyes stared back at him in the dim cabin. The baby opened its mouth to howl.

"It's okay," Rick whispered. "I have you now. It's going to be okay."

Rather than turn around, he clutched the baby close with his left arm and used his right hand to steady himself. He reached the end of the row, finding no one else. As he turned to his left to work back to the exit, he spotted the crumpled figure against the bulkhead. His heart sank.

It was Mai. Without thinking, he placed his right index finger along her neck, searching for a pulse. He knew that Lieutenant Ann would have found one. Rick looked at Mai's still face. Her eyes were closed. He wondered if Ann had closed them.

Can I carry her out and still hold the baby?

He didn't know. But he also knew that he could not leave Mai lying there. "Leave no one behind" leaped into his thoughts. Low fuel had forced him to leave a downed pilot alone in the jungle. Only when he had no other choice. That decision still haunted him. He would not leave Mai.

Rick gently laid the baby on a nearby seat cushion. He shifted Mai so he could hoist her over his right shoulder. The slight woman was not heavy for his tall frame. As he squatted with her over his shoulder, he picked up the baby and worked his way to the door. He was trying to figure out how to get down the rope ladder when another figure scampered up. It reached the top and saw Rick's problem.

"Hand me the baby," it requested. Rick quickly complied, and the figure disappeared. Rick turned and climbed down the ladder with Mai. When Rick approached the group, Sue was wrapping a bandage around Ann's thigh. A helicopter crewman stopped with a stretcher. He knelt on the other side of Ann.

"Ma'am, I can take over," he told Sue.

He inspected the wound, put a combat pressure bandage on it, and tightly wrapped the cloth Sue had been using. He took another bandage and wiped the blood away from the cut on Ann's forehead.

"You're going to need several stitches for both wounds, ma'am," he noted. Then he noticed the flight nurse's wings on her uniform. "But I'm probably not telling you anything you haven't figured out."

Ann struggled with a weak smile.

"Thank you, corpsman."

"Let's get you into a helicopter and to the hospital."

"There are more people to rescue," Ann protested.

"Ma'am," the medic responded. "You have done more than your fair share. More help is inbound."

Sue turned as Rick lowered Mai's body to the mud. She gasped and cried.

"Oh, Mai, Mai, Mai," she cried as she collapsed next to the lifeless form. "I am so sorry we got you into this. Please forgive us."

Lei, who had quietly watched Rick set Mai down, crawled over to his mother, sobbing. Sue wrapped her arms around the boy. He mumbled in his language as he reached for Mai's hand.

Another stretcher and bearers arrived. They lowered it next to Mai. After several seconds, one spoke.

"Ma'am, let's get you and your friend to the helicopter, too." Sue gently took Lei's hand from Mai's and scooted back.

"These men will take care of your mom now," she assured him in a gentle voice.

The corpsmen lifted Mai onto the stretcher and placed a poncho over her. Then they strapped her down. Sue led Lei to the helicopter. Rick took David's hand and followed.

As the Huey lifted off the muddy field of the crash, Rick looked the scene over in the late afternoon light. He had heard the report just before dashing to the helicopter. The pilot reported that he had lost all flight controls to maneuver the giant transport. He was using only the throttles to shift power to turn the airplane and to control its descent.

An amazing feat of airmanship, Rick recognized. He hoped the pilots had survived. While all who had died would haunt the pilots, Rick wanted to shake their hands and say thank you.

Thank you for bringing my wife, son, and daughter back to me.

———·———

LEI AND THI

Doctor Phúc at the hospital examined Sue and the children for concussions and broken bones. He found no serious injuries. Sue, David, and Lei only needed Band-Aids to patch up scratches. Sue had bruises on her left arm and leg. Bundled in Lieutenant Ann's swaddle, Thi survived with a slight bruise on her forehead. The hospital needed beds for the seriously injured.

When he had finished checking them, Doctor Phúc pulled Rick aside.

"Bad thing," Doctor Phúc noted. He paused, then glanced around quickly. "Will there be more flights? Many more?"

"I would think so," Rick replied a little warily.

"Vietnamese who help the Americans can get on them?"

"I think the President will want to help as many as possible." Rick could guess what the doctor's real question was.

The doctor reached into his pocket and pulled out a tattered card.

"I want my family to leave and go to America." He handed the card to Rick.

"I am a citizen of the state of Texas," he stated. "I think it will help me and my family."

Rick looked at the frayed card. It simply stated, "Doctor Phúc Ông is an Honorary Citizen of the Great State of Texas, USA. He is therefore entitled to all privileges and rights associated therewith." The signature line stated, "John B. Connally, Jr., Governor." The Governor had scrawled his signature above the name.

"Governor Connally gave that to me at Brooks Army Hospital in 1965 when I finished my training there." Doctor Phúc then pulled out his business card and shoved it into Rick's hand. "He said to call him if I ever needed help. Can you get a message to the Governor for me?"

"Yes, I'll see what I can do," Rick promised. *How the hell do I call the ex-Governor?* But Doctor Phúc had just treated his family and many others from the crash. He could not refuse to try.

The sun had long set as they crowded into a taxi to ride to their house. The group was silent. Sue leaned against Rick, clutching his arm. She clung to Thi with her other arm.

When they walked through the front door, Clicker was there. He surveyed the group.

"Where is Mai?"

Sue's tears gave Clicker the answer he feared.

"She didn't make it," was as much as Rick could say. Lei stood inside the door, looking lost. Rick walked to him. He took the boy's hand and led him to the couch.

"I am so sorry about your mom," he started. Rick hugged the boy as Lei sobbed. After a few minutes, Rick continued. "We will look out for you, Lei. We will not leave you."

David sat next to Rick and took Lei's hand.

"Sister Helene needs to be told," Sue mumbled. "We need to find all the children from Hoa Sen."

"I'm sure she has heard already," Clicker stated. "The news of the crash has spread like wildfire."

Sue looked at Lei and then at little Thi in her arms.

"I'll run over to the orphanage to check on Sister Helene," Clicker announced as he stood.

As Rick stood up, Clicker pointed at him.

"You stay here, bub. I'll be back in a jiffy. Then we figure out what's next."

"Thi needs some formula," Sue said.

She looked helplessly from Thi to Rick.

"I'll get some from upstairs," Rick stated.

Sue wandered to the side porch. She clutched Thi and stared into the yard. Rick quickly brought the bottle of formula.

"Why can't I think of what else to do?" she pleaded.

"It's shock," Rick answered as he stood next to her. "It's a natural reaction."

"We have to keep Lei and Thi with us," Sue told Rick. "No matter what comes next. We have to take them home with us."

"We will," Rick assured her. "Don't worry about anything. I'll get David and

Lei into the bathtub to wash off all the mud. Then I'll fix some food for them. Come up when you finish feeding Thi."

Sue nodded.

As David and Lei munched on snacks, Sue came into the apartment. She stood in the small living room, a lost look on her face.

"You go take a bath," Rick instructed her. "You'll feel better. When you finish, I'll shower."

"Thi needs a bath, too," Sue said. "I'll take her in with me. I'll call when she is clean."

Sue took only a few minutes to bathe the baby. Rick put a diaper and clothes on Thi. Minutes later, he heard Clicker come in and run up the stairs. He knocked on their door.

"What did you find out?" Rick asked.

"Sister Helene had already left for the hospital. The other nuns at the orphanage are in shock."

"Well, Sister Helene will find all her children. She is a determined and resourceful force."

Sue joined them.

"I should put Thi to bed. While she doesn't understand what has happened to her, I think she is exhausted."

Sue sat next to Rick when she returned. After a minute, she looked at Rick, then at Clicker.

"What do we do now?"

"I'm guessing that another plane will leave ASAP with as many children as it can carry. But it won't be a C-5. The Air Force will ground all those planes until it figures out what happened. This is a huge embarrassment to the President and the Embassy."

"Embarrassment?" Sue shouted. Her mouth opened to say more, but she could think of nothing else.

"I wonder what happened," Rick mused. He looked at Clicker. "Do the Gooks have SA-2s between Saigon and the coast? Could one of them have shot the plane down?"

Clicker shook his head.

"I have seen nothing to suggest that. But then, we aren't told much in the way of intel."

"Could someone have smuggled a bomb of some kind on board?"

"Well," Clicker replied. "The anti-hijacking inspection didn't seem rigorous. But with only one small bag allowed, I doubt it."

Rick turned to Sue.

"Can you talk about it? Can you tell us what happened?"

Sue shrugged.

"We were caring for the children when suddenly, bang! I heard an explosion of some kind. Things flew everywhere. It even snowed."

"Explosive decompression," Clicker responded.

"That's what Ann said," Sue stated. "When she regained consciousness."

"It knocked Ann unconscious?" Rick confirmed.

"Yes, she was on the floor against the rear bulkhead, by the ladder down to the cargo hold. But I don't remember her being anywhere near there when the explosion happened. I could see down into the cargo area through a grate. Out the back of the plane, I could see the ocean."

"The cargo doors blew off," Clicker immediately stated. "A lock probably failed. The building pressurization in the cabin blew them open."

"The doors must have knocked out the flight controls," Rick concluded. "Someone ran in when I was about to leave Jeff's office. 'The plane's in trouble,' he yelled. We rushed out. Jeff's boss was there. We asked what he knew, and he said the pilot reported having trouble controlling the jet. They were on their way back to Tan Son Nhut."

"That damned C-5," Clicker responded. "That jet's been nothing but trouble since they dreamed it up. The Air Force has two squadrons of Herks nearby in the Philippines and another one in Japan. But the generals had to use the cursed C-5!"

Silence reigned for a minute. Sue sat slumped over.

"Why don't you go lie down next to Thi?" Rick suggested.

Sue shook her head.

"I couldn't sleep." She squeezed Rick's hand. "What do we do now?"

She turned to Clicker.

"Do you know any of Mai's family? Does she have any nearby? I never heard her talk about any, even when we talked about her coming with us."

"I don't know if she has any left," Clicker confessed.

"No one?" Sue persisted.

Clicker shrugged.

"I never heard her mention any. All I know is she is from Hue. She fled there in 1968 from the fighting. I met her at Chu Lai. She worked as a maid at the BOQ. Lei had just been born. His father died in action before Lei was born."

"Does anyone know his name? Maybe his family would want to adopt Lei," Rick posed.

Clicker shrugged. "I don't know it."

"What about Lei's birth certificate?" Rick inquired. "Would it have his name?"

"All the paperwork was on the airplane," Sue noted. "I'm sure it's all lost. Even my passport and David's were left on the plane."

"Mai always used her surname for Lei's," Clicker stated. He shrugged again.

"It doesn't matter," Sue murmured.

Rick looked at his wife's ashen face.

"We will adopt Lei," she stated.

"How can we do that in the middle of this turmoil?" Rick asked her.

"I don't know, but we will."

Sue's lost look momentarily changed to one of absolute determination. Rick pulled her close to him.

"Okay. It is the best we can do for Lei," Rick responded. "Trying to talk to the embassy now will be a waste of time. I'll talk to Jeff to see what ideas he has."

"I'll run to his office and find him." Clicker walked to the door. "Besides, C-141s have to be inbound with no return cargo. The Defense Attaché Office will get its people on them. They must have lost several on the C-5. The office must be in shock."

Rick stood. "I'll come too."

Before Rick could walk out, though, Clicker put his hand on Rick's shoulder.

"You need to stay here. Your family has survived a plane crash. Sue needs you here."

Rick gazed at his wife. Sue sat on the couch, staring into space. He had never seen her like this. He nodded to Clicker.

"You're right. Thanks."

Clicker raced the Citroen from Bien Hoa to the Defense Attaché building on Tan Son Nhut. Walking in the door, he recognized that the place was in distress. While it was well past office hours, people sat at desks, staring into space through tearful eyes. A couple talked on the telephone. Others milled around in muddy clothes.

Clicker found Jeff in his office.

"How are Sue and David?" he asked immediately.

"Doing fine, though, in shock. Mai, our house girl, died in the crash. Lei, her son, though, is with Rick and Sue. Sue is determined to adopt Lei."

Jeff shook his head.

"I can't stop thinking I dodged a bullet," he muttered. "If my wife and kids had come here with me, they would have been on that plane. Over half of the family members from the office didn't survive. A few are missing."

"Any plan for the next flight?"

"We are working on it. A C-141 will arrive around 0400 tomorrow. We are rounding up survivors to get on it. As many dependents as we can fit into it will leave, too. The plane leaves at 0800 in the morning for Clark."

"Sue, David, Lei, and Thi need to be on it then," Clicker responded. "But how do we get paperwork replaced for Lei and Thi in such a short time? Sue and David's passports went down with the plane."

Jeff nodded.

"It doesn't matter."

"Rick needs to be on that plane tomorrow, too," Clicker pressed.

"Will he leave?"

"I think I can help Sue convince him to get out. If the guy has any sense, he'll take his wife and the children. She isn't in any shape to handle all three alone. She looks shell-shocked."

"Get them here right after curfew in the morning," Jeff ordered as he stood.

"Nobody has any paperwork from the crash. But our CO has assumed responsibility for loading them on planes to Clark."

"What about your Vietnamese staff? Any plans to start their evacuation?"

"None at the moment," Jeff replied. "The Ambassador refuses to consider any evacuation." Jeff looked around the room. Seeing no one close to them, he lowered his voice. "I would bet on an unofficial evacuation."

Thirty minutes elapsed before Clicker ran through the front door of the house in Bien Hoa. He beat the midnight curfew by minutes. He took two steps at a time up the stairs. Stopping in front of the Guerris' door, he wondered. Should he knock and peek his head into the apartment? He was debating when Rick came up the stairs.

"What did you learn?" he asked Clicker.

Clicker's tongue clicked.

"Jeff says a C-141 will leave early in the morning."

"Great."

"He said for you to get out there ASAP after curfew. You need to leave with them," Clicker pressed. "Sue really needs you now. The Commies are marching toward Xuân Lộc, just forty-five miles east of us. They've been sealing off the highways to keep the South Vietnamese from reinforcing it. It's the road to Saigon."

Rick looked at his friend. He nodded.

"It's dawned on my thick head that you are correct. Our job here is done. There aren't any Vietnamese pilots left for us to train."

He held some papers in his hand. "I looked in Mai's room for something she might have left to help us with Lei."

He handed the papers to Clicker, who glanced through the few letters and a couple of photos. The pictures were not in focus, but one showed Mai and a Marine lance corporal under a tree. The corporal wore his jungle fatigues. Clicker squinted at the young man, studying his uniform.

"Looks like he has a black and green name tag on his uniform," he noticed. "With a magnifying glass, you might make out his name."

"That's what I thought," Rick responded. "But how can we stop the bureaucrats from taking Lei from us wherever we land?"

"When I asked Jeff, he said the missing paperwork didn't matter. He didn't elaborate. You need to pack one small bag each for you and Sue, along with food and diapers for Thi. I can get those together. Put Mai's papers in with your stuff. Arriving at the base early in the morning is mandatory."

"What was the scene at the Defense Office?"

"Turmoil and shock. Jeff said all dependents are leaving."

"Any word about their Vietnamese help?"

"None. Jeff said, though, that an unofficial evacuation might be in the wind."

"Do you think there is anything we can do for Colonel Tinh and his family? I'm afraid once we are both gone, they'll be forgotten."

"I'll keep in touch with Jeff. The Colonel, though, will not leave quickly. The guy has a strong sense of honor and duty."

"What about your girlfriends?"

Clicker shook his head.

"I have no desire to get involved with their families. Huyẽn's family doesn't like Americans. I met a brother briefly once. It wouldn't surprise me if he was a Viet Cong!"

"It still feels like I'm deserting Colonel Tinh," Rick mused.

"Let me convince him to go. You take care of your family."

Rick took Mai's papers to the bedroom. He let Sue sleep. Stripping off his muddy clothes, he stepped into the shower. When he finished, he set the alarm clock for four o'clock the next morning. He lay down next to Sue.

He only dozed through the night. Sue cried in a fitful sleep. Once, when he could recognize her calling Mai's name, he gently patted her shoulder.

"It's okay, sweetheart," he whispered. "It's okay."

When the alarm went off, he didn't feel rested. But he gently shook Sue.

"Honey, we need to get the children and get to the base. A flight is leaving this morning."

Sue woke with a start.

"Where's David?" she shouted.

"In his room with Lei and Thi," he reassured her.

She looked at him and began to cry.

"I had the most awful nightmare."

"I know. We can talk about it later. But now we have to hurry to the base. We are leaving this morning."

"You too?" she whimpered.

"Yes, we are all going."

Sue threw her arms around him.

Twenty minutes later, a gentle knock sounded on their front door. Rick opened the door to Clicker.

"We're ready," Rick said.

Clicker stepped into the apartment.

"Dear God, forgive me!" Sue blurted. Rick turned to her. "We haven't even thought of Mai! We need to stay to give her a respectful burial. I've been so selfish that I forgot about her."

At a loss for how to reply, Rick looked at Clicker.

"You need to leave now," Clicker insisted. "I will see to Mai. I'll find where they took the bodies from the crash and get her."

Sue stood in silence for several seconds. Clicker walked to her.

"I promise. She was a little sister to me. After Lei's father died, I helped her when she didn't know what had happened to him. I'll see to her."

Sue walked to the couch and sat.

"We can't leave without taking care of Mai," she stated, looking at the floor.

Rick sat next to her.

"We have to leave to get on the airplane this morning."

"We can leave after we bury Mai."

"I'll get Sister Helene to help me," Clicker added.

Sue looked at Rick.

"Mai was my only friend here. I cannot leave without seeing to her. Just like you find it hard to leave without helping Colonel Tinh."

Sue looked from Rick to Clicker. She remained on the couch.

"Okay," Rick resigned. He was at a loss about what to do.

After a minute, Clicker cleared his throat.

"I'll go to the orphanage to see what Sister Helene suggests. We know she will track down her children."

Rick followed Clicker out the front door to the hall.

"You stay here and take care of your family," Clicker advised. "I'll check back after I have found Sister Helene."

Rick returned to their apartment. Sue remained on the couch.

"Why don't you take Thi and get some rest?" he suggested. "I'll take care of David and Lei."

Sue nodded. She picked up Thi and walked to the bedroom.

"I'm hungry," David complained.

"Come on. We'll get some breakfast."

Rick led the boys to the table.

Sue napped off and on until early afternoon. When Clicker knocked on the door near two o'clock, she came from the bedroom. Clicker looked hot. His face had lost its usual tanned coloring.

"How about some iced tea?" Rick offered.

"Thanks."

He sat, saying nothing. Rick put a glass of tea in front of him. He drank it all.

"What did you find out?" Rick asked. He took Clicker's glass to refill it.

"I've been with Sister Helene."

Rick handed him the refilled glass. Clicker took another drink.

"That nun is a strong trooper," he began. He took another drink and stared at his glass. "We spent hours at the hospital's morgue."

Sue and Rick waited. They both sat down. Clicker looked up and glanced around the apartment.

"The children are in the back?" he asked.

"Yes," Sue answered.

"The morgue was rough?" Rick inquired.

"You don't want to know."

Clicker looked at Sue.

"We found Mai and some of the children." He took another drink. "Most of the children are missing."

Sue's hand went to her mouth.

"Dear God," she prayed.

"The infants who were upstairs survived." Clicker stopped. He looked from Rick to Sue.

"Sister Helene says she wants you to get on a plane as soon as you can. She and I will see to Mai. Sister Helene said we will bury Mai in a plot with the children they find. But she insisted that you and Rick take Lei and Thi and escape."

"Lei's friend, Quý?" Sue whispered.

Clicker shrugged.

"She looked and looked for him."

"Oh, Mai," she sobbed. "Quý! We should have taken him upstairs with us. What have we done?"

———◆———

Early the next morning, Clicker stood inside the front door of the Guerri's apartment again. He looked at Rick and Sue. Their bloodshot eyes told him that neither had slept well.

"Ready?" he asked. Sue nodded, clutching Thi. She held her hand out to Lei. Rick took David's hand.

"Let's go," Rick answered.

Clicker picked up three small bags inside the door. The group walked down the stairs and climbed into Clicker's Citroen. Clicker raced to the base, employing the horn constantly. Sue shuddered at every honk. A line of taxis and people clogged the main gate. Another tense twenty minutes elapsed before Clicker edged to the gate. The Marine guard recognized Rick and Clicker and waved them through. Clicker turned to the DAO compound.

People streamed out of the building onto a bus near the flight line side of the building.

"You stay here," Clicker suggested. "Get a place in that line just to make sure. I bet the bus is going to the plane. I'll check with Jeff."

Rick agreed and led Sue and the children toward the line.

"What's up?" Rick asked a young woman in line in front.

"We are riding the bus to a plane to leave," she replied.

"Is it the 141?"

She shrugged. Rick noticed her muddy clothes.

Clicker ran out of the building to Rick.

"This is the bus. Jeff says you are on the manifest. Get on it."

Sue looked from Clicker to Rick.

"That's it? Where are the other children?"

"They are coming from the passenger terminal on another bus. Jeff says there are about one hundred of them. They want this bus there first to help with the children."

Rick grasped Clicker's hand and shook it heartily.

"Thanks for all your help," he said. "It's been a privilege flying with you. Now, you get your ass on a plane out. Don't worry about any of the stuff we've left."

"Sure thing."

Sue stepped to Clicker and hugged him.

"Thanks, Clicker," she said, not fighting the tears. "Listen to Rick. You come to see us. Somehow, we'll get in touch."

His tongue clicking, Clicker returned Sue's hug. Then he knelt to hug Lei.

"Rick and Sue will take good care of you. Don't you worry. You will find that America is a great country."

The ride to the C-141 was quick. The bus stopped behind the large jet's ramp. As Rick took Sue's hand to help her out of her seat, he felt it tremble. She stared at the airplane. She stood without moving. Her hands clutched Thi.

"Come on," he encouraged.

"Can we wait to leave tomorrow?" she asked.

"I don't know whether another plane will be here."

People on the bus waited in the aisle behind her. A man behind Sue stared at the plane, too. Rick placed his hand on her back and nudged her forward. Sue took a hesitant step.

"Come on, David," Rick encouraged his son into the aisle behind Sue.

Sue stumbled forward and out of the bus door. Rick took Lei's hand to lead him to the front of the bus. On the tarmac, Sue stopped. She reached for Rick's arm as he stepped off the bus.

"I'm afraid to get on the plane," she whispered.

"It will be okay," he assured her. "I'm right here with you."

Sue swallowed hard and inched toward the plane. A crewman in a flight suit motioned them to the ramp and into the cargo compartment.

"Move all the way in," he instructed.

Sue crept up the ramp, brushing past a soldier with a rifle at the base of the cargo ramp. His eyes shifted from side to side. He looked nervous.

Sue saw that web seats lined the walls and the center of the cargo compartment. All the seats faced sideways. From the dim cargo compartment, Rick heard a voice call him.

"Splainin, is that you?"

Rick had not heard his pilot training nickname in years. Who here would even know it? A figure walked out of the dimness into the bright sunlight.

"Gear Check!" Rick replied. It was a friend from his pilot training class whom he had not seen in nine years. "I'll be damned."

The pilot grasped Rick's hand.

"What in the hell are you doing here?" Gear Check asked.

"I've been teaching F-5s," Rick replied. He turned to Sue.

"You probably don't remember Gear Check, do you?"

Sue shook her head.

"Sue, I remember you," Gear Check replied. He gently took Sue's free hand. "Dan Price, to most people," he said with a twinkle in his eye. "But I remember the foxiest-looking wife in our class."

Sue's subdued response made Rick realize his wife's uncharacteristic silence needed an explanation.

"Sue was on the C-5 with our son David, and these two children we are adopting."

Dan's face dropped.

"Oh, that was rough," was the most he could say.

"I think nearly all your passengers are survivors," Rick informed Dan.

"So we've heard. We will fly especially smoothly for you. The takeoff and climb might feel a little steep, though."

Dan looked around, then motioned to Rick and Sue.

"Come up near the crew door. I'll sit you right up front behind the cockpit. I'd put you up there, but we have a full house with a couple of flight nurses and their bags up there."

As they walked, Rick asked the pilot.

"I was sure you'd be flying for the airlines by now. Who else would take a copilot's slot out of pilot training if you had other options?"

"Well, things change," Dan answered.

Another armed soldier stood inside the crew door. Before they arrived at the front, Jeff Nickerson called Rick's name from behind. He scampered forward, waving a manila envelope.

"You'll want these papers," he said as he handed the envelope to Rick. "Keep them safe. Sister Helene gave them to me."

"What are they?" Rick inquired.

"Adoption papers for Lei and Thi. Before I even asked her, that canny nun had convinced a Vietnamese mandarin to sign them. You'll need them in the confusion when you get to Clark. It will be a real zoo there about paperwork."

Sue looked at Jeff.

"You mean we've adopted them? Already?"

"According to the government of South Vietnam, they are your children now."

Sue's frown eased slightly.

"Give Sister Helene a big hug from us," Sue responded.

Jeff grasped Rick's hand.

"Good luck."

"Let's get this bird in the air before anyone changes their mind," Dan stated. He ushered the group up the crew door steps into the front of the cargo compartment. Rick looked at the soldier.

"To protect the plane from a mob," Dan explained.

"Good," Rick replied. "I witnessed Da Nang."

Sue laid Thi gently on a web seat and helped David and Lei settle next to her. As she placed their three bags under the seat, a flight nurse hobbled over. Sue looked up in surprise.

"Ann!"

Lieutenant Ann Jagger limped over. She wore a cast on her left ankle and calf. A small Band-Aid covered her forehead wound.

"Sue, David! I'm glad you are on the plane with us."

"How are you?" Sue inquired, pointing to the cast. Sue's demeanor improved.

"Only a slight break in my foot," Ann smiled meekly.

"For heaven's sake," Sue pleaded. "Sit down. Take your weight off it."

"I've got work to do."

Rick stepped over with Dan Price.

"Ann saved our lives in the crash," Sue informed the pilot. "You have a genuine hero to take care of on this trip."

"Take a seat for a minute, please, Lieutenant," Dan told Ann.

"Sorry, sir, but I'm on duty." To Sue, she said. "I'll get a box for Thi. After takeoff, I'll come back. I promise I'll sit down for a while."

Behind the rear ramp, two buses stopped.

"That will be the children," Ann stated. After handing Sue a box for Thi, she limped through the cargo compartment to the rear.

"That trooper doesn't quit," Rick said to the pilot. "You're going to have to give her a direct order."

"She is my senior flight nurse," he stated. "I don't think she'll listen. We'll be starting engines as soon as the children are inside." He patted Rick on the back and whispered something to him. Then he turned to climb into the cockpit.

Sue and Rick sat along the sides, facing David and Lei. The box with Thi sat between them. Minutes later, Rick and Sue noticed the cargo ramp rise and the clamshell cargo doors close. Yet, two shafts of light sliced in through open doors in the rear, one on each side of the compartment. Rick noticed white tie-down straps stretched across the doors. The engines started, and in minutes, the plane moved. They stopped briefly, then moved again.

"Tower has cleared us for takeoff," a voice announced over the PA.

Sue looked to the back. She saw the light from the open doors. A crewman stood next to each door, looking out. She nudged Rick.

"Does the pilot know those doors are open?" she asked, pointing to the back.

"They will leave them open while we climb out," he answered.

"Why?"

"The guys looking out are scanners," he replied.

"What are they looking for?"

Rick didn't answer. Sue arched her eyebrows.

"They are watching for something. What?"

Rick sighed.

"They are watching for missiles."

"Coming at us?" Sue pressed.

Rick nodded. "Yes."

"What good can they do?"

Rick knew a partial answer wouldn't satisfy Sue.

"They each hold a flare pistol. Any missile coming will be a heat-seeking missile, homing on the engine exhaust. They fire a flare at it to divert the missile away from the airplane."

"Does that work?"

"It has in the past. The pilot will also turn toward the missile to point the exhaust away from it."

Sue reached across Thi to clutch Rick's arm. She put her other hand on Thi in her box. The airplane accelerated and started a steep climb.

Dear Lord, Sue prayed. *Give us a safe flight today.*

The climb felt steep to Sue. After ten minutes, the climb became much shallower. Sue looked toward the rear. The light from the open doors was gone.

Three hours later, the C-141 Starlifter touched down at Clark Air Base, the Philippines. Rick, Sue, David, Lei, and Thi had completed the first leg of their trip home as a family.

MRS. REESE

———•———

Dobie Starbuckle fidgeted in the back seat of the sedan. He wasn't sure why he had agreed to come along on this trip. Mr. Peabody had insisted. Yet, nagging senior officers had rarely convinced Dobie to do something he didn't want to do. But his contract with Ashley Peabody on the ring's recovery contained a requirement for Dobie to help with the story. This trip was an essential part of the story.

With no information on the fate of Major Reese, returning the Academy class ring became important. It brought some closure to the story. Mr. Peabody had located Mrs. Reese and spoken to her on the phone.

She had been a challenge to find. The Air Force gave no information to Mr. Peabody. The service had no interest in a magazine that did not feature many stories about it. A network of contacts provided by Rick Guerri led to finding the North Dakota town where she lived. Arriving there required that the trio fly on Regional Air, a small carrier serving small towns. The trio then rented a car for an eighty-mile drive from the small airport to her house.

In his conversation with Mrs. Reese, Mr. Peabody had been upfront about the purpose of the visit. His primary aim was to return the ring. He also wanted to see if he could use her name and something about her life in the article. An MIA wife living in limbo would add some drama. It would add a poignant touch to an otherwise less-than-satisfying story.

Ashley Peabody's original hope in financing the mission was to discover some piece of the puzzle about Calvin Reese's fate. After returning to Marcel's village, Dobie radioed the news to Charles in Nakhon Phanom. The lying deserter with no information on Cal Reese had bitterly disappointed Ashley Peabody.

Ashley Peabody turned in the passenger seat toward Dobie.

"We should prepare to answer a tough question or two," he warned. "In my two conversations with Mrs. Reese, I have concluded that answers interest her."

"She may not like them," Dobie commented.

"We owe her honest answers."

"But we should try to be gentle," Charles added. "I don't think we need to add to her anguish."

Dobie decided to inform Mrs. Reese what Rick Guerri had said about his shoot-down. Dobie assumed that the Air Force had told her nothing about the location. Pilots talking to Cal Reese on the ground would also be news to her. Dobie had looked for insight into how much to say to Mrs. Reese. Rick Guerri had been unsure, but Sue Guerri had a firm opinion.

"She will most likely want to know everything!" Sue had insisted. Sue knew one other pilot's wife in a similar circumstance.

How did I get myself into this part? Dobie asked himself.

The car stopped in front of the house. Ashley Peabody led the trio up the walk and rang the doorbell. A middle-aged man wearing a dark sports coat and a clerical collar answered the door.

"I'm Ashley Peabody. I've arranged to speak with Mrs. Reese."

"Yes, please come in," the greeter replied, shaking Ashley's hand. "I'm Reverend Daniel Crocker."

Ashley offered his hand to the gentleman. A thirty-something woman with black hair approached the group at the door.

"I'm Rachel Reese," she introduced herself. "I'm glad to meet you, Mr. Peabody."

Ashley shook the offered hand; then, he introduced Charles and Dobie. A middle-aged woman stood by the couch.

"This is Lois, my wife," Reverend Crocker explained.

"Please come in and sit down," Rachel Reese offered, motioning to chairs and the couch. As she sat, Dobie noticed she folded and unfolded her trembling hands. Ashley Peabody seemed to notice her nervousness as well. He got right to the point.

"We appreciate your willingness to see us, ma'am," he began. "I cannot imagine how difficult your life has been these past seven years."

He paused.

"We appreciate your time in coming to see us, Mr. Peabody," Reverend

Crocker responded.

Dobie removed a small cloth bag from his inside sports coat pocket. He handed it to Mrs. Reese.

"As I told you on the telephone, Colonel Starbuckle successfully recovered Major Reese's Air Force class ring," Ashley explained. He cleared his throat. "I am so sorry we don't have any definitive information about your husband."

Rachel held the bag on her lap for a few seconds. Then she opened the bag. Her hand trembled as she looked at it. She turned it over to look at the back of the setting. Tears welled up in her eyes. She wiped them with the back of her hand. Then she held the ring to the minister.

"Reverend Crocker, can you please check the inscription?"

The minister took the ring and looked at it. He nodded.

"It has Cal's name on it," he confirmed.

Rachel composed herself.

"The Reverend married Cal and me," she explained. "I am interested in how you found the ring and recovered it. I didn't have the desire to go through Cal's things from Thailand for years. He had written that he had lost his ring. He planned to have a replacement made in Thailand. But then ..." Her voice trailed off.

"Colonel Starbuckle can share the story with you," Ashley Peabody offered. He turned to Dobie, who cleared his throat.

"First, ma'am," Dobie began. "Has the Air Force or anyone told you about Major Reese's shoot-down?"

"Almost nothing," she admitted. "Only the date and the fact that the Air Force listed Cal as missing in action. I've asked where he was shot down, but I have received no information."

Dobie nodded.

"I am afraid that is all too common. In trying to gather information to assess the veracity of the ring, I learned a little." Dobie paused, trying to tell if he should continue.

Mrs. Reese took a deep breath.

"Colonel," she responded. "I have clung to hope and prayers all these years.

But my hopes of ever seeing Cal again have given way to wanting to know the truth." She paused. "I've asked Reverend and Mrs. Crocker here to help me bear any truth you can offer. Praying with them all these years has comforted me. I need to hear anything you know."

Dobie cleared his throat.

"Colonel, would you care for a glass of water?" Lois Crocker inquired.

"Yes, ma'am, I would," Dobie admitted.

"I'll get it for you while you start," she said. "Would anyone else like one?"

Ashley and Charles shook their heads.

Rachel looked expectantly at Dobie, so he began. Dobie told the story of Cal Reese's shoot-down that Rick Guerri had described. He left out the part about Rick hearing gunfire. Then he described Marcel hearing of a North Vietnamese deserter with a ring to sell. He explained the information correlated best with Cal Reese's shoot-down. The description of the name was an important piece of the puzzle. Dobie omitted the claim that the deserter had taken part in Cal Reese's capture.

"We had hoped that the deserter would have information on Major Reese," he explained. "After contradictory information in the deserter's story, we convinced him to tell us the truth. He had gained the ring by finding it in the Officer's Club at Takhli."

As Dobie relayed the story, Rachel listened intently. She continued to fold and unfold her hands on her lap. As Dobie concluded, he could tell she fought back tears.

"I cannot express adequately my disappointment in learning nothing about Major Reese," he finished.

Silence enveloped the room. Mrs. Crocker scooted closer to Rachel.

Finally, Reverend Crocker spoke.

"Why did it fall to you to tell Rachel about Cal's ... " he stammered, "incident?"

"The military no doubt considers it classified information," Dobie suggested. "The 'secret' war in Laos was one of the worst-kept secrets of the Vietnam War."

"While it provides no more hope for Cal," Rachel interjected, "it is a comfort to know how the pilots supported each other." She dabbed her eyes with a tissue.

"I also greatly appreciate the dangers you endured to bring the ring to me. I don't know how to thank you, Colonel. Laos must be a very dangerous place for an American."

"It was my duty to a fellow warrior, ma'am," Dobie replied.

"As I mentioned in my phone call," Ashley Peabody said, "my magazine, *Direct Action*, will publish the ring's story. While we could use a pseudonym for Major Reese's name, his real name would add credibility. My readers will also find the information vacuum for families of MIAs interesting."

He stopped, trying to read Rachel's reaction. When she only nodded, he continued.

"If you would like that to be part of the story, my writer can visit you to talk about what you would like to share."

Charles spoke for the first time.

"There is a good reason to use a pseudonym," he added. "Our lawyers have not given us an opinion on the risks of disclosing classified information about Major Reese. Using a pseudonym would enable us to protect our sources, which include you."

"I'll have to think about being part of the story," Rachel responded.

"We can talk in a week or two," Ashley replied.

Rachel looked at Dobie.

"Colonel Starbuckle, I have a question I feel compelled to ask."

"Ma'am?" Dobie responded.

"Do you believe that our government has abandoned live prisoners of war in Vietnam?"

Dobie cleared his throat.

"Mrs. Reese, I do not know. The Communists are capable of retaining some prisoners as a bargaining chip. Whether our government knows that to be true is another question. However, I continue to probe my contacts in Vietnam and Laos on that subject."

Dobie paused. He had to choose his next words carefully.

"To date, I have heard no confirmed information suggesting live POWs remain. I have heard speculation and hearsay. Some are reckless and only cause additional grief to families like yours."

After a brief pause, Ashley Peabody spoke.

"Mrs. Reese, it has been our privilege to bring your husband's ring to you. If you have no further questions, we will not take up more of your time."

The minister looked at Rachel. When she shook her head, he stood.

"Gentlemen, Rachel deeply appreciates your efforts. Thank you again."

Reverend Crocker walked them to the door.

As the car pulled away, Charles looked in the rearview mirror toward Dobie.

"Colonel, you relayed the story of Major Reese with great compassion."

"Yes," Ashley echoed. "You relayed the delicate information expertly."

"Thank you. I would also like to make a strong recommendation. I think the story needs to use pseudonyms for Major and Mrs. Reese. Other reporters will certainly bother her after the story comes out. We cannot expect them to have any sensitivity to her position. Others are likely to come out of the woodwork, some with malevolent motivations. I have no objection to my name being used. I can handle any asshole who wants to make an issue of the story. But the MIA families have endured years of uncertainty and sorrow. We should have no part in adding to that."

"You make an excellent argument, Colonel," Ashley agreed. "We can even make that point in the article as to our reason for the pseudonyms."

With the decisions made on the article, Ashley Peabody turned in his seat.

"I wonder if we can pick up a local radio station," he mused aloud. He looked at his watch. "It should be about time for a noon news show. Maybe we can find out what's happening in the wider world."

He fiddled with the car radio until a station came in clearly. Confirming Mr. Peabody's expectation, the noon news update was beginning.

"Tragedy in Saigon: Officials remain unsure what caused the crash of a large Air Force transport shortly after takeoff from Saigon. The plane left Tan Son Nhut Air Base early this morning local time. Speculation continues that the C-5, carrying over 200 orphans from the embattled city, sustained damage from enemy fire. We continue to await word of any survivors."

The trio waited silently for additional details. None came. The news quickly turned to local events.

"That's it?" Ashley Peabody asked the radio.

"Fucking generals," Dobie muttered in the back seat.

When Ashley Peabody turned to him, Dobie felt compelled to elaborate.

"They couldn't stand the commercial airlines getting all the publicity saving orphans. They had to jump into the fray with their problem-riddled Fat Albert."

"You don't think the Commies could have shot it down?" Peabody quired.

"More likely, it had a malfunction and crashed on its own," Dobie stated. He stared out the window at the small farmhouses off the state highway.

"Let me pose a question to you two warriors," Ashley Peabody stated. "How long can South Vietnam survive? Congress will give no further aid. The ARVN can't seem to mount an effective resistance."

Charles glanced in the rearview mirror at Dobie.

"I don't see them lasting much past the end of this month," Dobie stated. Peabody shifted his gaze to Charles.

"If I were optimistic, I'd give them six weeks."

"Meaning," Peabody continued, "that to rescue vulnerable Vietnamese, the brass better get their asses in gear."

"And soon," Charles added.

"My source at the Defense Attaché Office," Dobie stated, "fears the Ambassador refuses to admit the war is lost. He is delusional."

"Or he knows that acknowledging it and starting an official evacuation will cause a panic," Peabody concluded.

"He is between a rock and a hard place," Dobie agreed.

"What about Laos and Cambodia?" Peabody pressed.

"Phnom Penh is under siege," Dobie answered. "Cambodia has less time than Vietnam."

"Laos?" Peabody pressed.

Dobie shrugged.

"Anytime the North Vietnamese want to push their allies to finish Laos, it will be quick. Our Hmong friends are hanging by a thread."

"So, nearly all the dominoes are falling," Ashley Peabody concluded.

"And some experts say the domino theory was invalid," Charles noted.

"Any official rumors of evacuating our Laotian allies?" Peabody asked.

Dobie scoffed.

"I'm sure the Hmong general will get himself and his close associates out. One rumor reports he has a large Swiss bank account."

"What about our friends?" Charles asked.

Dobie shook his head.

"They cut ties to the general a while ago. They ran out of young boys to feed into his army," Dobie concluded, catching Peabody's eyes.

"Since they saved your team, we must help them," Peabody stated. "How do we do that?"

Dobie checked his watch.

"I'll try to give Jimbo a call in Thailand from the airport. Jimbo needs to get a status update from Marcel. We've maintained contact every few days. Let's see what Marcel thinks. It'll take helicopters or short-field transports, though."

Charles slowed the car and turned off the highway to the small airport. The trio had two hours before their small airplane left. While Charles turned in the rental car at the single counter, Dobie headed for the pay phones. He pulled his long-distance calling card from his wallet.

——·——

CLARK AIR BASE

The C-141 stopped; the engines shut down; and the rear cargo door opened. Rick stood. Sue struggled to stand. The Spartan troop seats contained no padding. Her entire body ached. Rick gave her his hand and lifted gently. She clung to Thi. Lei and David jumped up. Both had slept much of the flight. Rick envied their ability to sleep in any position.

He wasn't sure what to do. Should they follow the Vietnamese, who made up most of the passengers?

Dan Price came down the steps from the cockpit.

"Is there a bus for Americans?" Rick asked him.

"There should be. The Command Post said they sent buses for the refugees and Americans. The refugees are going to the gymnasium for temporary housing. I guess the Americans are on their own."

"Will there be flights to the States from here?" Rick asked.

"I'm sure there will be. But this airplane is being refueled and cleaned to fly back to Saigon. My crew is going into crew rest before we fly back into Saigon."

Two airmen walked up the ramp and led the passengers off the airplane. Rick, Sue, and the children followed the crowd to the back of the airplane. An airman directed the few Americans in a different direction from the Vietnamese. Rick motioned Sue toward the bus for Americans. When they approached the door, another airman noticed Lei and Thi.

"The Vietnamese children go on the other bus," he ordered.

"They are our children," Rick retorted. "They'll stay with us."

The airman paused. Sue clutched Thi, and Rick took Lei's hand. The airman motioned them to the bus.

Inside the passenger terminal, a line formed at a counter. When they reached it, an officious sergeant demanded their passports. Rick handed his passport across the counter.

"My wife and children lost their passports in the C-5 crash," he informed the sergeant. The sergeant eyed Lei and Thi, whom Sue held to her breast.

"They are your children?" he inquired.

Rick pulled out the adoption papers from the envelope that Jeff had given him.

"Here are the adoption papers."

The sergeant looked at them, checked Rick's passport again, and then handed it back.

"As soon as you can, go to the Personnel Office and fill out the paperwork to replace the lost passports," he instructed. He grabbed other forms from a drawer. "What is your full name, ma'am?"

"Susan Maria Guerri," Sue replied.

The sergeant wrote the name on one form. He scrawled a signature at the bottom. He grabbed three other copies of the form and quickly scribbled a signature at the bottom of each one.

"Fill in your children's names on these before you take them to Personnel," he instructed. "You will also want to replace Mrs. Guerri's dependent ID card at personnel."

He then stamped Rick's passport and the forms.

"Where do I catch a taxi to the BX?" Rick asked. "We could not bring any clothes with us."

"In front of the terminal," he answered, motioning them to move on.

Rick grabbed the forms and shoved them into the envelope with the adoption papers. He led them away from the counter and into the terminal building.

Thi began crying.

"I'm sure she needs her diaper changed," Rick noted. "Why don't you go to the restroom and change it? I'll take the boys to the bathroom, too. Let's meet at those chairs over there. We have to figure out our next steps."

Ten minutes later, they sat on chairs in the terminal. Rick looked at Sue. She looked exhausted. Having not slept well the night before, he felt the need to rest as well. But there were too many things to do. And he had no playbook.

What does one do after fleeing a war?

He felt sympathy for the Vietnamese. At least his destination was his home country. Everything there would be familiar. He was only a little disoriented here at Clark Air Base. He had been here before, and Clark and the town outside the gates were a small island of America. Hundreds of others would not share his hotel room.

Rick decided. He turned to Sue.

"Let me go find a snack bar and get some food. Wait here. I think there is a snack bar in the terminal or nearby."

Sue merely nodded. Rick looked at Lei and David.

"You boys stay here with Mom," he instructed. "Take a nap if you need to. I'll be right back with something to eat and drink."

Lei's wide eyes darted around the terminal. David grabbed Sue's arm and sat still. Rick reconsidered. He might need help to carry food and drinks.

"Lei, would you like to come with me to help?"

He remembered how Mai would put Lei to work doing small things to help at their house.

Maybe that would help him, Rick considered.

Lei continued to look around the terminal, then at Rick. He nodded.

Rick held out his hand for Lei to take.

"We'll be right back," Rick promised.

Rick led Lei toward the center of the terminal and looked around. He spotted the snack bar and headed toward it.

In line, Rick studied the small menu.

"Have you ever had a hamburger?" he asked Lei. Rick pointed to a picture on a placard. The boy looked unsure. "No time like the present to try one."

To hedge against Lei's uncertainty, Rick ordered some fried rice he saw on the menu as well. He also ordered French fries. Rick remembered Clark reconstituted its milk from powder. He grabbed three small cartons. Lei helped Rick carry the trays of food back into the terminal to Sue, David, and Thi.

"I thought Thi could probably handle some milk here if we only have a little formula left," he told Sue. "It's reconstituted, so it should not be too creamy for her."

Rick handed Lei a hamburger. He helped him hold it in his small hands.

"Try this. See how you like it."

Lei nibbled on the sandwich.

"How is it?" Rick asked.

Lei took another bite. Rick was sure he saw the hint of a smile as the boy chewed his first hamburger.

"Pretty good, huh?" David asked him as he took a bite of another hamburger. "Here, try a French fry."

Lei carefully took the fry.

"Try a little ketchup," Sue suggested. She opened a small pack and squeezed some on a few fries. Lie took one to eat.

This time, Rick knew he saw a smile. Sue reached over and patted Lei's back.

"You are going to like America, Lei, I promise."

Sue took the last bottle of formula to feed Thi.

"Let me feed Thi," Rick offered. "You eat. Do you want the last hamburger or the fried rice?"

A hint of a smile showed on Sue's face.

"If you don't mind, I'll have the hamburger."

As they ate, Rick formed a plan.

"The first thing is to find a hotel room. I don't know how crowded the hotels are, but I'd feel more comfortable getting checked into one fast."

Sue nodded as she chewed.

"We can go to it," Rick continued, "and you and the children can rest. I'll come back to the BX and Commissary on base to get basic items. A couple of suitcases, a change of clothes for everyone, diapers, toiletries, and formula. We'll work on the passports tomorrow."

"Thi and the boys need beds for a good rest," Sue agreed. "Me too. But I feel a lot better with some good American food in my stomach." She looked at her boys. "I bet you guys do, too."

After eating the fried rice, Rick stood up.

"I'm going to phone around for a hotel. Will you be okay here?"

Sue nodded.

"Please don't get a cheap one."

"A good one is right outside the main gate. It might even have suites."

Rick thumbed through the telephone directory in the pay phone booth. He found the number for the Oasis Hotel and dialed. Unfortunately, they had no rooms available. He asked about comparable hotels. The clerk gave him two names and their phone numbers.

He dialed the number for the Angeles Hotel. They had one-bedroom suites available with a sleeper sofa in a small living area. The rooms were air-conditioned when the electricity was on. Each suite also had a small refrigerator and a hot plate. It was farther from the base than he wanted, but the suite was a necessity. Jeepneys, colorful refurbished Army jeeps, served as inexpensive taxis in the Philippines. A change to a base taxi at the gate would be necessary, but Rick remembered taxis lined up inside the Clark main gate.

Perfect, he thought.

He booked a suite for a week, guessing it could take that long to get passports.

When Sue walked into the suite an hour later, he could see the tension ease out of her body. She quickly determined that the boys and Thi could share the bedroom. Rick helped her bathe the children and put them down for a nap. He let her shower first, then he took one. While their travel time from Bien Hoa to Clark had only been about eight hours, it had been a tense trip. Rick felt refreshed, even putting on the same clothes he had been wearing.

By mid-afternoon, Rick arrived at the Clark BX looking for the basic clothing they needed. He thought Sue could bring the children in the following days to expand on the basic underwear, shorts, and t-shirts he purchased. Never having bought clothes for David, he had to guess at sizes for the boys. He figured getting clothes a size too large was better than too small. Sue had told him her size for shorts, a blouse, and underwear. He had bought Sue a negligee or two over the years, but never a bra or panties.

The first night in the hotel suite was rough. Lei had trouble sleeping. He cried, napped, and woke up after only an hour to cry some more. Holding him close, Sue tried to comfort him. It broke her heart to see him so distressed. They cried together.

Thi developed a severe case of diarrhea and nausea. While Rick played with the boys at the hotel pool, Sue jumped into a jeepney to take Thi to the Clark hospital. When she walked up to the pedestrian entry to Clark Air Base, she realized she didn't have an ID card to show.

"I need to get my baby to the hospital," she began explaining to the security policeman at the gate. "I lost my ID card in the C-5 crash." Sue looked hopefully at the airman.

He seemed unsure of how to respond. Then he turned and called a staff sergeant over.

"This lady wants to go to the hospital, but she lost her ID card," he explained.

"On the C-5 crash," Sue added.

"Are you a dependent?" the sergeant inquired. He noticed the bruises on Sue's arm.

"Department of Defense dependent," Sue replied.

"Is your husband traveling with you?"

"He is at the hotel with our boys," Sue explained.

The sergeant thought for several seconds.

"We'll let you on base," he finally began, "but you'll have trouble seeing a doctor at the hospital without an ID."

Sue's shoulders sagged. She felt like crying. *Why is everything getting so difficult?*

"What hotel are you at?" the sergeant inquired.

"The Angeles."

"You can use our phone to call it."

The sergeant led Sue to a telephone. He consulted a sheet next to it and dialed. He handed the phone to her. She asked for their room, but no one answered. The reception desk did not pick up the line again, so she hung up. Sue looked at the sheet to find a list of nearby hotels. She dialed the hotel again.

"Could someone page Mr. Guerri at the swimming pool, please?" she requested when the reception desk answered. "This is his wife, and I need to speak with him."

Minutes passed before Rick came on the line. She could hear David complaining about having to leave the pool.

"What's wrong?" Rick answered.

"I'll need you at the hospital to get any service without my ID card," she explained.

"Damn," Rick swore. "I should have known that. I'm sorry. Are you at the hospital?"

"I'm at the base gate."

"Will they let you on base?"

"I think so."

"If they will, take a taxi to the hospital and see what you can do. I'll grab my ID and meet you there. Otherwise, wait at the gate."

Sue hung up and walked back over to the airman.

"Mr. Guerri will meet me at the hospital," she explained.

The airman waved her through the gate.

"Taxis are over there," he pointed to where a couple stood.

Sue walked through and waved to the front taxi driver. He pulled up.

"To the hospital, please."

The drive was quick. Sue asked for the outpatient clinic and soon found herself in a long line. The line was to get a number to wait longer for it to be called. While she waited, Sue looked around the waiting room. A mix of Americans, Filipinos, and other Asians filled the room. The hospital looked like a modern facility. She sat next to another woman with a preschool child. The woman smiled.

"Is it usually this busy?" Sue asked.

"Not usually. Is this your first time here?"

"I arrived yesterday," Sue answered, glad to see a friendly face.

"Wow. You picked an exciting time to transfer here."

"I know. I arrived on a flight from Saigon."

The woman's eyes widened.

"You poor dear! Is your baby sick?"

"Terrible diarrhea," Sue answered quietly. "We just adopted her from an orphanage near Saigon."

"You came in on a Babylift flight?"

Sue nodded.

"That was horrible about the C-5!" the friendly face exclaimed.

Sue just nodded. *Everyone seemed to know about the C-5*, Sue realized.

"Did you know anyone on it?" the woman asked softly, with a hint of sympathy.

Sue could only nod. Then the woman quickly glanced at Sue's bruised arm and leg.

"I'm sorry ..." she hesitated, "but were ..." She stopped.

Sue nodded.

"You poor dear!" she exclaimed. "Your baby, too?"

Sue only nodded as tears formed in her eyes.

The woman gently patted Sue's hand. She held out the small card with her number.

"You take my number. You need to see the doctor more than I do."

Sue shook her head. She wiped an eye with the back of her hand.

"Thank you, but I'm waiting for my husband to get here. I don't have any ID left, so I have to wait until he arrives before they'll let me see a doctor."

"If he gets here before they call my number, you take it," the woman insisted. "Medical teams have flown in from across the Pacific to augment the Clark hospital staff."

Sue nodded. "Thank you."

A receptionist called the woman's number before Rick arrived. The woman pulled a piece of paper and a pen from her purse to jot down her telephone number and name.

"If you have any trouble here or need someone to talk to, please call me. We live on base, so we have a phone."

Sue thanked her again.

Rick finally arrived before Sue heard her number. Upon hearing the reason for her visit and missing ID, Sue and Thi saw a doctor immediately. Sue had thought to bring a recent stool sample for Thi. Hearing that they had survived the C-5 crash, he examined her as well. Within an hour, the nurse came out.

"Mrs. Guerri, here are two prescriptions to fill at our pharmacy for the baby," she said, handing Sue three prescription slips. "There is one for you when you have pain or swelling."

"What is wrong with Thi?"

"Thi has intestinal worms," the nurse responded. "Most likely from water that wasn't boiled sufficiently to mix her formula."

The news distressed Sue. She had not taken good care of her baby girl. The nurse, reading Sue's thoughts, assured her.

"We have seen it in many of the infants who are arriving. It was probably the formula they gave you on the flight. Processing babies on these flights is a new experience for the crews we've sent to Tan Son Nhut. We have emphasized the importance of boiling the water adequately to prepare bottles for the babies."

"Thank you," Sue replied. Sue looked at the prescriptions. "Are both for worms?"

"The second one is a high-potency nutrient supplement. Because Thi is tiny for her age, the doctor wants to make sure she is getting enough nutrition to grow. When you arrive home, you should get her a full examination with your family doctor."

The nurse paused, and Sue nodded.

"Do you have other children with you?" the nurse asked.

"Yes, two boys, seven and five." Sue pointed to where Rick was walking the boys around.

"Wait. I'll get another prescription for the worms from the doctor to have filled. Worms can infect a child by touching contaminated surfaces. If either develops symptoms, you can give them some of the medicine, too. If it doesn't help within a day, though, get them to a doctor. Make sure they wash their hands often."

"I think we'll be here for several days. My son and I lost our passports in the crash."

"One of our head flight nurses was on that flight," the nurse replied.

"Ann Jagger?" Sue asked.

"Yes. Do you know her?"

"Ann led my children and me out of the crash. She saved our lives! Is she here now?"

"No, she is still flying into Saigon."

"With a broken foot, no less," Sue added.

"That's our Ann. The flight surgeon here tried to ground her. But she put up a fight."

Sue filled the prescriptions at the hospital pharmacy. Immediately, she gave

Thi a dose. She didn't have a measuring spoon, so she just used the cap from the prescription bottle.

The family climbed into a taxi to return to their hotel. Sue sat in the back with the children, while Rick rode in front. As the taxi drove through the base, Sue clutched Thi and gazed out the window.

She wrapped her free arm around Lei, hugging him close. She lost her battle against tears.

Oh, Mai, she thought. *I so wish you were with us. But we will take extra care of Lei.*

Sue realized that fifteen weeks had passed since Rick had come home to say he would go back to Vietnam. When Rick resigned from the Air Force for graduate school, she had thought they were through with that awful war.

Now, she realized, *we are finally through with that f…ing war. But at what cost? Why had fate or God sent us to the Vietnam War again? And why, when we they had to flee, couldn't Mai come away with us?*

Hugging Lei, Sue knew one thing: leaving Mai behind would haunt her for the rest of her life.

———•———

THE BUREAUCRAT

When they returned to the hotel, Sue put Thi down for a nap and chased the boys out of the bedroom.

Rick called the Clark personnel office to replace the missing passports. During his phone conversation, Rick scribbled notes and asked a few questions.

"What is the embassy address?" He jotted down the answer.

"What is the best way to get there from Angeles City?"

He wrote another note.

"What should we bring?"

He scribbled more notes.

"How long should it take to get the passports?"

When he hung up, he looked at his notes. Then he looked at Sue.

"Tomorrow morning, we need to go to the BX to have passport pictures made for you and the children. Then, we have to catch a bus to the US Embassy in Manila. The personnel office will take longer to process them. They suggested we go to Manila."

"How long will it take to get the passports?"

Rick shrugged. "It's hard to guess. I need to call the embassy to get an appointment for tomorrow afternoon."

He picked up the telephone. After several transfers, he appeared to have reached the correct office. He explained the situation, jotting more notes during the call. He objected to some answers to his question.

"We have official adoption papers signed by Vietnamese government officials!" he insisted. Frustration showed on his face when he finished the call.

"I don't think this will be easy to get Lei and Thi's passports. The jerk insisted they should get on a plane with other orphans being flown to the States."

"No, they shouldn't!" Sue shouted. "They stay with us."

"I know," Rick assured her.

"Well, when we get there tomorrow, we'll have to stay calm. You catch more flies with honey than with vinegar."

"In theory," Rick responded. "We have a two o'clock appointment. I wonder if there is a place near here to get the photos before morning. Two buses leave the passenger terminal in the morning. The embassy is one of its three stops."

They had passport photos taken at a small store near the hotel. At nine o'clock the next morning, the family boarded the bus for Manila. Rick wanted to sit up front so he could see the way to Manila. He tried noting the corners where the bus made turns. When they got on what seemed to be the main highway, he saw no highway signs to identify it. Signs for Manila were conspicuously absent as well.

Their bus was a luxury ride compared to the local Philippine Rabbit Buses he saw on the road. Driving practices in the Philippines mirrored those in Saigon; the road belonged to the most fearless or careless driver. The Rabbit Buses routinely passed ox-driven carts and Jeepneys with little regard for opposite-direction traffic. Their bus driver was only slightly more cautious. Rick could not hazard a guess as to the frequency of deadly accidents.

After three hours of nonstop traffic, the bus stopped at the American Embassy. Since it was two hours before their appointment, Sue asked that they find a place to eat. David had started complaining during the rough bus ride. Sue guessed he was getting hungry and would only get grumpier. At a local stall on the street, they found food for sale. To avoid any fresh vegetables, Rick advised that the safest option would be the rice dish. With Thi's worm problem still unresolved, Rick opted for bottled American soft drinks. While the bottles looked familiar to Lei, he had never had one. Soft drinks were a rare treat for David as well, so both boys enjoyed the sodas.

"Maybe the sugar will keep their energy level up for the afternoon," Sue hoped.

The family arrived back at the Embassy an hour before their appointment. Anticipating the necessary paperwork, Rick asked the receptionist for forms to replace passports. He also asked for forms for new passports.

Rick looked around the crowded room. He assumed some of the Americans had fled Saigon and needed new passports. Several young women looked Filipino to him, accompanied by young men. Rick speculated they were new wives of young servicemen, preparing for their first trip to the States.

Their appointment time passed. At fifteen past the hour, Rick asked for an update on their appointment.

"Mr. Goodwall is running a little late," she informed Rick. "We have been swamped for the last two days."

The room grew stuffy. Rick's shirt became soaked with perspiration. The embassy's air conditioning struggled to run effectively. Sue's face became flushed, as did Thi's face. Rick and Sue alternated taking David and Lei into the hall when the boys became agitated.

Finally, an hour after their appointed time, the receptionist called Rick's name. She led them into a small office down a narrow hall. Mr. Goodwall stood as they entered.

"I understand you need lost passports replaced," he began. "Do you have the required forms?"

Rick passed the forms across the desk.

"We also need new passports for our two adopted children," he informed Mr. Goodwall. Rick placed the passport application forms on the desk.

Mr. Goodwall raised his eyebrows.

"Let's work on the lost passports first," he declared.

He scrutinized the forms. Rick watched him nervously, dreading difficulties he could not predict.

"I see your passport," he began, addressing himself to Sue, "was lost on the C-5, as well as David's. Do you have a driver's license for identification? Or birth certificates?"

"I lost everything in the crash," Sue replied. "All our IDs. We were lucky to get out of the crash with our lives."

"Yes, I suppose so," Mr. Goodwall replied. "Then we will need another form, an affidavit, to fill out."

He dug into a desk drawer and pulled another form out. He passed it across the desk. Rick handed Sue his pen.

"About your," Mr. Goodwall hesitated, "… adopted children. Do you have the adoption papers?"

"Yes," Rick immediately replied. He pulled the forms out of the envelope that Jeff had given him in Saigon.

Mr. Goodwall studied them. He pursed his lips. His brow wrinkled. He angled the forms to study the official stamps at the bottom of the forms below the signatures.

"Who prepared these forms?" he inquired.

"Sister Helene of the Hoa Sen Orphanage in Bien Hoa," Sue quickly answered. "She is the Mother Superior of the orphanage." Sue pointed to Sister Helene's signature. "She filed them with the local mandarin for children's affairs in Bien Hoa. That is his signature and seal."

Sue pointed to the bottom of the form.

"I am not familiar with Vietnamese requirements for adoption," Mr. Goodwall answered. "It would have been preferable to have applied for the passports at the Saigon Embassy."

Rick felt his neck getting warm.

"As you can appreciate," he began, trying to remain calm, "the situation is stretching the Saigon Embassy thin right now, with the country imploding. Have you read about what happened in Da Nang?"

"It looked horrible," Mr. Goodwall conceded.

"I saw it firsthand," Rick informed him. "It was worse than you can imagine. We applied for the adoptions over a month ago, but only received the paperwork on the day we left on an emergency evacuation flight. The Embassy and the Vietnamese government officials cleared the exit of Lei and Thi. They advised us to leave and apply for passports at the first opportunity."

Rick figured there would be no way for Mr. Goodwall to verify such a statement in the chaos at the embassy in Saigon. He also pulled out the Vietnamese exit visas for Lei and Thi. He allowed Mr. Goodwall to look at them before taking them back.

"Still …" Mr. Goodwall continued, "I will have to keep these and verify their authenticity with the Saigon Embassy before processing any passport application for the Vietnamese children."

"I can't let you keep the originals," Rick advised him. "Please make any official copies you require. As they are the only copy, we will not let go of them."

Mr. Goodwall appeared to think for a few seconds.

Rick's anger began to seethe. *Come on, you bastard, get off your fat ass and do your job,* he fumed.

"I can give you a notarized copy," Mr. Goodwall offered.

"If you don't have the authority to make a notarized copy for your use, perhaps we need to speak with your supervisor," Rick countered.

"Give me a few minutes to confer with a colleague," Mr. Goodwall replied. Rick grabbed the adoption papers before Mr. Goodwall could take them.

"We'll wait," Rick answered.

"I'll be back in a few minutes," the bureaucrat stated as he opened the office door.

When Mr. Goodwall left, Rick looked at Sue. Her face was red. He could not tell whether the warm office or anger caused it. He opened the office door, hoping for a little more circulation.

David, who had watched the exchange with no interest, squirmed.

"I'm hot," he moaned. "Can we leave?"

Lei sat in silence, unable to follow the conversation or have any idea what the meeting was about.

"Let's go into the hall for a few minutes," Rick offered, extending his hand to David. "You can come too, Lei."

He led the boys into the narrow hall.

"I have to pee," David complained.

"Okay, we'll find a restroom."

Rick peeked into the office to tell Sue.

"I heard," she assured him.

Five minutes later, Rick returned with the boys.

"No Mr. Goodwall?" he asked Sue.

She shook her head.

"I was afraid we might run into some bureaucrat on this," he stated. "But I was hoping some common sense and a little compassion would win the day."

"What will we do if we can't get passports?" Sue asked.

"I'm not sure," Rick answered. "Let's cross that bridge when we have to."

"I need to check Thi's diaper," Sue said as she stood. "Where are the restrooms?"

Rick pointed down the hall.

"Around to the left."

When Sue returned, she rustled in her new bag and pulled out a bottle for Thi.

"I'm afraid Thi isn't feeling too well," she started. "Her diarrhea is better. But she seems to sleep more than normal."

"Well, her little body needs to rest to heal," Rick assured her.

Another ten minutes passed before Mr. Goodwall returned.

"We can make official copies for our use," he informed them.

Before the official could take the adoption papers off the desk, Rick grabbed them. He took the exit visas as well.

"I'll sign as a witness," Rick offered, keeping his eyes fixed on Mr. Goodwall.

The official quickly understood that Rick would not let the papers out of his sight.

"Follow me, then."

When they returned, Mr. Goodwall reviewed all the paperwork.

"I need your address in the Philippines where I can reach you."

Rick pulled out the card from the hotel, jotted down their room number, and handed it to Mr. Goodwall.

"Your replacement passports should take twenty-four to forty-eight hours. We'll call you when they are ready. They will be valid for one year. I don't know about the passports for the Vietnamese children."

Rick grabbed Mr. Goodwall's business card from a holder on the desk.

"Well, thank you for your help," Sue said, trying to sound friendly and appreciative.

Rick offered his hand.

"Yes, Mr. Goodwall, thank you. I'll call if we don't hear in a couple of days."

When they reached the front of the embassy, they learned that the last bus to Clark had left.

"Now what do we do?" Sue cried.

Rick put his arm around her. He hailed a pink and blue Jeepney. "Take us to the Hilton Hotel," he requested.

———•———

SAVE YOUR FAMILY

———•———

Clicker's advisory job as an instructor pilot was over. Could he still help as the tech representative for Northrop, the F-5 manufacturer? He counted two other Vietnamese air bases still in the fight. The rest had fallen to the Commies along with countless airplanes and bombs. The North's air force had never had an offensive capability until now. The collapsing South Vietnamese had left F-5s and A-37s at their disposal.

Everyone in the South Vietnamese Air Force knew the North already had a couple of pilots who could fly them. They had been wearing South Vietnamese uniforms for years, though. That had been proven just a week ago. A South Vietnamese F-5 pilot had lagged his formation, then turned around to bomb the Presidential Palace in Saigon. Then, he had flown to a captured air base west of the city. His undercover work for years earned him a heroic welcome. The only saving grace was that he was not a competent pilot. His bombs had missed their target. Nobody believed that he was the only one.

Two weeks had passed since Clicker had convinced Rick to take Sue and their children to safety. He had heard that the Guerris were still in the Philippines, fighting for passports for Lei and Thi.

Worthless bastard REMFs in the State Department, he fumed silently.

But at least Rick and Sue were now safe. Clicker realized it was his time to escape. When he called his company to tell them Rick had left, the executive gave him permission to leave. They would figure out how Clicker and Rick could fulfill their contracts later. Clicker had only three months left in his contract. Rick had most of his one-year commitment to complete.

Before Clicker could think further, a high-pitched whine interrupted his thoughts. He cocked his head.

Shit! Incoming!

Clicker hadn't heard the whine of artillery overhead in over seven years. He hit the floor beside his desk, away from the window. If he heard it, it was flying over him. But instincts were hard to resist.

A second later, CRUMP!

The explosion rattled the glass. His coffee mug bounced off the desk and shattered.

That was close!

Another whine, then a third. *CRUMP! CRUMP!*

All too close.

They are aiming for the runway! Clicker realized.

Seconds later, another series arrived, slightly farther away.

They're finding their range, Clicker realized. *But how close are the artillery spotters?*

Clicker grabbed his helmet bag and ran out the door. He dashed down to Colonel Tinh's building.

Colonel Tinh stood on the flight line by his building, rushing two pilots toward the nearby F-5s. Clicker saw ground crews pulling start carts to the planes. The colonel was directing the evacuation of the precious jets.

"Which one do you want me to take?" Clicker asked as he ran to the Tinh's side.

Tinh looked at Clicker.

"Grab a parachute and take the first one you can get started. I'll be following in a minute."

As Clicker emerged from the squadron building lugging a parachute, a crew chief plugged a start cart into a nearby jet. Clicker headed to it, scampered up to the cockpit, threw the parachute in, and climbed in. He didn't bother to strap himself in or strap on the parachute. That could come later. He did pull on his helmet to get it out of the way.

Clicker looked outside at the crew chief. The chief raised a single finger and twirled it. Clicker turned on the jet's battery switch, fuel switches, and hit the start button for the left engine. As it spooled up, he looked back out to the crew chief. The chief twirled two fingers over his head. Clicker punched the start button for the right engine.

As the left engine stabilized at idle power, Clicker gave the crew chief two hand signals: unplug the cart and pull the chocks. In seconds, the crew chief was back in front, motioning Clicker forward.

An experienced crew chief, Clicker thought. He released the brakes, advanced his throttles, and saluted the crew chief as the plane sped past.

By now, the explosions were walking down the runway.

Bastards have their artillery spotter inside the wire!

Two F-5s raced down the parallel taxiway in close succession. Clicker turned behind them, shoved his throttles full forward to the afterburner stop. He waited a second and then slammed both into afterburner. The jolt forward told him both burners lit; no need to check his engine instruments. He was airborne in a minute. Clicker pulled the jet into a steep climb. As fast as he could, he wanted to get above four thousand feet, away from any rifle or machine gun that might want to bag an F-5. And from the incoming artillery rounds. Only then did Clicker think to look at his fuel gauges. Relief flowed through him when he saw full tanks. Somebody had the foresight to keep the jets fueled.

Probably Colonel Tinh, Clicker figured.

Passing four thousand feet, Clicker pulled the throttles out of afterburner and turned southwest toward Tan Son Nhut. He plugged in his mike cord and turned on his radio. He loosely buckled his parachute harness and his seat belt. The shoulder harnesses dangled across his shoulders. The F-5s in front of him had disappeared. When he dialed in the Tan Son Nhut tower frequency, he heard them talking. Tower knew of the shelling of Bien Hoa Air Base and was clearing airplanes to land.

Clicker spotted the air base in the haze, waited for a break in the radio traffic, then made a call to the tower. The tower instructed him to follow the F-5 five miles in front of him. After a minute of searching, Clicker spotted two in front.

Now, the South's air force only has two air bases in operation. It doesn't look good for the home team.

Tan Son Nhut tower cleared one F-5 to enter a right downwind for runway two-five right. He knew he would receive the same landing instructions. Lieutenant Colonel Tinh's voice called the tower next. He reported that the runway at Bien Hoa was no longer usable.

How many other jets will take off? Clicker wondered.

The artillery spotter would quickly direct fire to the taxiways. The tower called Clicker's aircraft number. By now, Clicker was nearing the downwind leg of the traffic pattern parallel to Tan Son Nhut's two runways. The tower told Clicker to follow the F-5 in front of him.

As Clicker rolled to the end of the runway after landing, the tower told him to keep following the F-5 in front. The first two jets to arrive had stopped next to the boneyard of wrecked planes. Minutes later, Colonel Tinh pulled up beside Clicker.

"I don't like being lined up," the colonel complained as soon as he climbed down from his cockpit. "Too easy to take them all out."

He looked around, seeking a better solution. As the other pilots gathered, the colonel issued an order.

"Nobody leaves. We'll be moving these planes."

The colonel hailed a jeep that approached the group, spoke to the driver, and then sped off.

Fifteen minutes later, the jeep returned with an aircraft tow bar sticking out of the back.

"I found a better place to park. Two covered hardstands are available across the runway from us. We'll taxi the planes over to them, then use the jeep to push two into each spot. Follow me across the runway."

The four F-5s quickly taxied to parking spots under sheet metal roofs that gave some protection. Satisfied, the colonel called his pilots together.

"We'll take this jeep back to Bien Hoa. Gather your families and move them as close to the base here as you can find. It's only a matter of days before Bien Hoa faces a full attack. This spot here is now our squadron location until I find a better one. We meet here in two days at 0900 for further orders."

With that, the colonel drove the pilots back to Bien Hoa, who scattered to gather their families. When his pilots had left, he turned to Clicker.

"Thank you for saving one of our planes. You have no more work to do here now. I think it is time for you to follow Rick. I appreciate the work you have done. My pilots are much better now."

The colonel extended his hand to shake Clicker's hand.

Clicker took the offered hand. "Colonel, with all due respect, it is time for you to save your family. If you won't go with them, then at least get them away to safety. You know what will happen to you and them when this is all over."

Clicker could see Colonel Tinh's normally squared shoulders sag slightly. He looked at the smoke billowing from the flight line behind the squadron building. The smell of burning aviation fuel and rubber permeated the air. The pair walked around the building to survey the damage. Several airplanes burned on the ramp, and rubble littered the taxiway where the four jets had escaped.

"I know my country is lost," Colonel Tinh conceded. "But my duty is not finished. I know what you say about my family is true. But how can I send them away when the families of my men face the same fate?"

Suddenly, a gigantic explosion east of them rocked the ground. Both dove to the ground, although no cover was near them. A large column of smoke billowed up east of them.

"They have hit the ammo dump!" the colonel shouted.

Clicker could only read Colonel Tinh's lips as his ears rang from the concussion of the explosion. Additional explosions thundered. When the thunderous explosions paused, both men stood and ran for the wall of the building. Smaller explosions rippled through the air.

Clicker opened his mouth wide, trying to clear his ears. After minutes, his hearing partially recovered.

"Colonel," Clicker shouted, "leaving your family here will change nothing for your men. But as a commander in the Air Force, you and your family are in greater peril. If I could find a way to get all the families out, I'd do it. But I'll work on a way for your family first."

Colonel Tinh remained silent for minutes as he studied the destruction before them.

"That explosion was a saboteur who snuck in during the artillery attack," he finally admitted. "The battle of Xuan Loc has turned against us. It won't be long before they are here."

Clicker saw a look of sadness he had never seen in this warrior. It seemed close to a look of resignation. But not quite. The colonel squared his shoulders and turned to Clicker.

"I would not refuse any help for my family that you can offer."

Clicker's tongue clicked. He took a step back and saluted Colonel Tinh. The colonel returned the salute. Clicker did an about-face and jogged toward his building. He knew it was time to grab his stuff, race to the house, get two changes of clothes, and return to Tan Son Nhut. He could find a room at a nearby hotel.

The following day, he would meet Rick's friend, Jeff Nickerson. Jeff would know how to get the Ngo family on an Air Force plane.

———•———

EXIT VISAS

————•————

Clicker pondered how to help the Ngos escape Vietnam. Officially, the US Embassy was evacuating no one. The only Vietnamese authorized to leave the country were orphans. But the Air Force had halted orphan flights on the same day as the shelling of Bien Hoa. Orphans in the States were being united with their American parents. As far as Clicker heard, Rick and Sue continued to battle the Manila Embassy for passports for their adopted children.

The US Ambassador to the Republic of Vietnam refused to admit that South Vietnam was lost. He hoped President Ford and Congress would again fly to the aid of the beleaguered country. Nearly three months had elapsed since the President had requested Congress for an aid package. A fact-finding Congressional delegation had come and left. Leaders in the US Senate held up the request. The Ambassador also feared that if any evacuation of Embassy staff or "at-risk" Vietnamese citizens began, a general panic would ensue. The lessons of Da Nang remained foremost in everyone's mind.

Yet, news of events in South Vietnam had to rely on the rumor mill and *Stars and Stripes* newspapers smuggled from the Philippines. Local Saigon papers faced a blackout on reporting any war news. The authorities banned all English news-papers. A few copies of the *Stars and Stripes* remained in the Defense Attaché compound. Nobody knew the penalty for possessing one.

Two days passed before Clicker caught Jeff Nickerson at the Defense Attaché compound. As he entered his office, a group passed a *Stars and Stripes* around. Jeff came over and shook Clicker's hand.

"I was sure you would have been smart enough to get out by now," Jeff began.

"Marines have a hard time leaving a fight," Clicker replied. He motioned to the group reading the paper. "What's the news?"

"Phnom Penh has fallen," Jeff reported. "The Khmer Rouge has entered the city. All evacuation flights have stopped."

"So, Cambodia is lost," Clicker concluded.

Jeff nodded.

"The first of three, maybe four, dominoes," he said.

"Any word about what's happening in Laos?"

"Hard to tell," Jeff responded. "But the North Vietnamese have had no trouble driving material and troops down the Trail for months. It's a paved highway now. Intel reports reinforcements are streaming into the country. Draw your own conclusions."

"Any word about evacuating your Vietnamese employees?"

"Still no evacuation of Vietnamese or US staff here or at the Embassy. We have gotten dependents and nonessential staff out, though. So, we have quietly started Option Two in our general plan."

"Option Two?" Clicker asked.

Jeff pulled Clicker aside from the group discussing the newspaper.

"Military aircraft," Jeff responded. "Option One was commercial aircraft, which is moot."

"How many options are there?"

"Option Three is sealift. But we saw what happened at Da Nang, so no one believes that is viable. Option Two only works if we can secure the airport and protect the airplanes."

"If not, then what?"

"Option Four," Jeff answered. "Helicopters from the ships offshore pick up people here and at the Embassy."

"Are you suggesting that we contractors leave?"

"Unless you have a compelling reason to remain, I'd recommend getting out ASAP."

"The Ambassador is still hoping for a miracle from Washington?" Clicker pressed.

Jeff nodded.

"Seems so."

"Delusional bastard," Clicker retorted. "How long do you give Saigon?"

"Best judge of the future of Saigon is the black-market exchange rate for the piastre."

"I've noticed my local newsstand gave me a thousand this morning, more than yesterday."

"And well above the official 755," Jeff noted.

"What is the unofficial word on evacuations?"

"So far, the South Vietnamese government is not allowing any draft-age male to leave. Swift punishment will fall on any who attempts." Jeff made a pistol with his right hand. "Exit visas for others are required. And don't expect quick action on those. Do you have any Vietnamese employees you want to get out?"

"I want to help Lieutenant Colonel Tinh's family to escape."

"How many?"

Clicker shrugged.

"You know Vietnamese families. Four immediate family, including a fourteen-year-old son. Maybe two sets of parents."

Jeff frowned.

"The son is a challenge."

"But you suggest they get exit visas ASAP?" Clicker prompted.

Jeff nodded.

"Don't let the lack of an official position on evacuating at-risk Vietnamese discourage you," Jeff advised. "We have serious concerns here about our employees. There is no stomach to leave them here."

"How can I keep informed of developments here?" Clicker asked.

"Do you plan to leave before them?"

Clicker had thought of this chain of events. He had reached a decision.

"No," he answered. "I want to make sure the Ngos escape. I'll leave with them."

Jeff thought for a minute. Without telephones in every hotel room and with him on the move solving problems, timely communication was a challenge.

"Keep checking with me here." Jeff picked up a card from a nearby desk. "If you can't find me, ask for this guy, Tech Sergeant Davis. I'll tell him to help. If you can't find either of us, leave word with anyone here that you are looking for me."

Clicker recognized he had learned all he could for now. He would need to check in daily. Or when the exchange rate for the piastre signaled panic. Not knowing what rate that would be, he hoped to recognize it.

Clicker headed for the revetments with Colonel Tinh's F-5s. Only two pilots had shown up for the scheduled meeting that morning. Either the others had deserted, or, as Colonel Tinh hoped, relocating their families took longer than expected.

Colonel Tinh sat on a crate in one revetment. He was talking to one pilot whom Clicker recognized. The pair finished their conversation, and the pilot left. Clicker walked over to Tinh. Rather than trade idle conversation, Clicker came right to the point.

"I've been asking around," he began. He had Tinh's attention. "Your family needs exit visas. But you will have trouble getting one for your son."

"That's been on my mind. I know a solution."

Clicker raised his eyebrows.

"I'll swear him into the Air Force, and he will be my driver. Once he gets on base here, he'll never leave."

Clicker asked no further questions about the son.

"Officially, no evacuations other than US dependents are occurring," Clicker reported. "But the Defense Attaché does not intend to abandon its Vietnamese employees. If we can stay in their information loop, I'm hopeful we can get your family out with them."

"I know a couple of their employees," he continued. "I'll ask them to keep me informed of developments."

For the next two days, Clicker shuttled from his hotel to the Defense Attaché Office to Colonel Tinh's new office near his jets. The colonel had found another Air Force squadron commander who shared his space. On his way to the DAO on day three, Clicker picked up a copy of the *Saigon Post* to see a rare story about the war. But it wasn't about South Vietnam. It reported that the Khmer Rouge in Cambodia were savagely executing their opponents. News had leaked that beheadings were ongoing in Phnom Penh. Clicker rushed to the DAO with increased urgency.

Jeff's office was buzzing with hushed conversations as he entered the section. He found Jeff in a conversation with several people. He motioned Clicker over.

When Jeff finished speaking with his colleagues, he motioned Clicker off to the side.

"The People's Army has captured Xuan Loc. The South Vietnamese Army has fallen back to Trang Bom."

Clicker remembered it was about ten miles east of Bien Hoa.

"Not good," Clicker commented.

"But the other big news," Jeff continued. "President Ford has authorized the evacuation of at-risk Vietnamese."

"Great!" Clicker nearly shouted.

"Just one catch."

Clicker's enthusiasm quickly evaporated as he waited for the "but."

"The Ambassador hasn't authorized any evacuation."

"What … how?" Clicker stammered.

Jeff shrugged.

"We are working on it." He looked around as if fearful someone might hear him. "An Embassy guy, a reasonable one, is setting up a processing center here at the theater."

Clicker's confusion showed.

"Have your people gotten their exit visas?" Jeff probed.

"Not that I've heard."

"Well, keep working on them." Jeff paused. "Write down your hotel and room for me. If you get a message that says 'snow is forecast', get your ass here ASAP. It means I have important info for you."

"Snow is forecast?" Clicker wrinkled his brow.

"Ever listen to Armed Forces Radio?" Jeff asked.

"I forgot my radio in Bien Hoa."

"You might find a radio and listen a few times daily."

Clicker's head tilted with his furrowed eyebrows.

"If you hear any strange weather forecast or unseasonal music, get your ass here ASAP," Jeff advised.

"What have you heard about the executions in Cambodia?"

"Just what the Saigon paper and the *Stars and Stripes* have reported. But intelligence reports people are streaming out of the cities into the countryside."

"Fleeing the Khmer Rouge?"

"Unclear. Reports say the Khmer Rouge troops escort them."

A stir among those across the room caught Jeff's attention. An Army captain rushed over to Jeff.

"Thieu has resigned!"

Clicker recognized the name of South Vietnam's President.

"Means he will soon be here wanting a ride out," Jeff predicted. He turned to Clicker. "Gotta go. Check back in the morning."

Clicker noticed a *Stars and Stripes* on a desk. He skimmed the article about the executions. On the front page, he also read that the North Vietnamese had attacked Highway 13 in Laos between Vientiane and Luang Prabang. He didn't remember how far apart the cities were. On the wall, he spotted a map. It covered Vietnam, Cambodia, and Laos. He found the Laotian capital on the Mekong River and traced the highway north. Luang Prabang was about 200 miles north, by his estimate. Quite a distance away in this war. He wished the article was more specific. US allies in Laos were feeling the pressure as well. All of French Indochina was falling to Communism.

Damn French, he thought. *If they had developed native leaders and given independence, we wouldn't be fighting these wars.*

Clicker resolved to call French fries by their British name, chips.

With nothing more to learn, he went to find Tinh. He would have insight into President Thieu's resignation. He found the squadron commander in his temporary office, staring out the window.

"What's the meaning of the President resigning?" he asked immediately.

Colonel Tinh shook his head.

"I'm not sure it means much at this point. Most likely, the generals forced him out. I hear one general angling to replace him thinks he can negotiate with the Communists." Tinh shook his head. "Why would they negotiate?"

Clicker told him about the US President's authorization for evacuation. Tinh's mood seemed to improve perceptibly.

"We need to get exit visas soon. Before the Americans change their minds."

"The Ambassador has authorized no evacuation yet," Clicker informed Tinh. "But I got the sense from Lieutenant Colonel Nickerson that the Attaché Office will not wait for one. We need to stay in their loop of information."

"I've spoken to my friends there."

"We need to keep checking," Clicker concluded.

Early the next morning in his damp hotel room, something woke Clicker up. He sat up. Was it the result of the struggling air conditioner in the room? He felt clammy. It was still dark outside. Clicker walked to his window and raised the blinds. The cord broke. He peered through the partially open blinds. Although his window faced the nearby base, Clicker could only see the usual lights. He cocked his head to listen. No telltale whine of incoming artillery rounds sounded.

Fiddling with the air conditioner temperature, he set it to full cold. He straightened his sheets and lay back on the bed. Holding the alarm clock at an angle, he read four in the morning. He had an alarm set for six. Arriving at the DAO early every morning seemed essential. Anything and everything could change overnight.

Clicker had just dozed off when a sound woke him again. This sound he recognized. It was the distinct sound of a C-130 when the propellers went into reverse on landing. Had that noise awakened him earlier? Clicker had learned to recognize the sound of a C-130 landing years earlier at Chu Lai Marine Corps Air Base. It meant that two important morale items had arrived: the mail and the beer. Everyone on base anxiously awaited the sound of those Herk props. Everybody checked their watches. They had learned how long before the mail would be in their mailboxes and the beer would be cold at the Club.

He checked the clock. The hands told him twenty minutes before six. He looked out his window. Dawn was not perceptible yet. He had noticed C-130s before at Tan Son Nhut, but the larger C-141s had done the heavy cargo lifting. Frequent C-130s meant something had changed. He got up to go to the base as soon as curfew was over. He showered quickly.

Clicker was finishing his third cup of coffee in the small hotel restaurant when he heard it again. Another C-130 had landed. He checked his watch. It said 7:35. Three Hercules landing within four hours was new. Were the desperately needed military supplies finally flowing into Saigon?

Too little, too late, he thought.

Now he heard the distinct sound of a C-130 taking off. He had to see Jeff to find out what this meant.

On his way to Jeff's office, Clicker remembered what Jeff had said about the theater. He swung by it. A short line of Vietnamese with an occasional American snaked out the door. Three buses stood at the curb.

Damn, they've started the evacuation!

Clicker found Jeff in the hall outside his office. As soon as Jeff paused for a fraction of a second in his conversation, Clicker interrupted.

"What's the line at the theater for?"

"People with exit visas," Jeff answered. "If your group has their visas, get them in line."

Jeff nodded. He raced to Colonel Tinh's office. No one was there. Why had he never asked where the Ngos were staying? How could he find them? Should he leave a note?

Clicker searched for paper. He pulled a pen from his pants pocket. But what should he say? If he was explicit, someone could use the information for themselves. Seats on a US Air Force plane would be precious. Every seat used by one Vietnamese meant another Vietnamese would not escape. He dared to leave only an innocuous note.

Finally, he wrote.

"Dropped by to chat. So sorry I missed you. Let me know when you'll be in."

Clicker hoped the colonel would understand a note signaled urgency. He checked the telephone. It had a number in the middle of its dial. Clicker wrote it down.

In his rush to the base, Clicker hadn't bought the useless newspaper to check on the exchange rate. He drove back to his hotel to repack his "bug out" bag again. Whatever he took out of the country had to fit into his small knapsack. It had to be with him all the time. His traveling money and passport stayed in a money belt inside his shirt. He had closed his bank account and transferred what remained to a stateside bank.

Clicker bought the English Saigon paper, with blank spots instead of stories. He bought several dollars in piastres. The exchange rate was 1,600 to the dollar, much higher than three days earlier.

Should I buy more piastres in case he needed to bribe a Tan Son Nhut guard to get the Ngos on the base? No, he realized, dollars would be more valuable for bribes. *If only I had thought to buy some gold chains a few months ago!*

Clicker walked into the lobby of his hotel. He was unsure of what to do. Should he wait in his room for Tinh's message? If he went back to the base to wait in the office, what if Tinh never came in? As he stood trying to decide, the desk clerk called to him.

"I have a message for you, Mr. Clicker," he said, waving a paper.

Clicker grabbed the note.

It was only an address from Tinh. Clicker asked the clerk if he knew where it was.

"Close to the hotel," he reported.

Clicker wrote the directions down, not wanting to rely on his memory. Five minutes later, Clicker drove up to a small store. He checked the number of the address on the note. It matched the faded sign above the door. He guessed the Ngos were staying above the store with a relative. One, no doubt, who would want a ride out of Vietnam on an American plane, too.

Clicker stepped into the small shop. His eyes took a minute to adjust. He saw a variety of religious objects neatly arranged on clean shelves. One section held various sizes of statues of a meditating Buddha. Another held statues of saints. Hanging on the wall were crosses and crucifixes. Clicker realized how little he knew of Tinh's life or family away from an air base. He had never met Mrs. Ngo.

Colonel Tinh emerged through a doorway of beads at the back of the shop.

"I'm glad you understood my message," he said.

"Did you receive the message I left at your office?"

"Sergeant Khắc called with it," Tinh replied. When Clicker didn't show any sign of remembering the name, Tinh added, "The C-123 crew chief."

"The Americans are processing people for evacuation," Clicker reported. "Those with exit visas."

"Sergeant Khắc reports that C-130s are expected regularly to fly refugees out," Tinh reported.

"Any word on your family's exit visas?"

Tinh shook his head. "The price to receive them just went up."

"Of course," Clicker noted. "How much?"

"Fifteen hundred US dollars. More than a poor Air Force lieutenant colonel can afford, I'm afraid."

"Is there any way to get the family on base?" Clicker asked.

Tinh shook his head.

"The South Vietnamese military police are checking papers at a checkpoint before the main gate. They understand why people are arriving there with exit visas. Some are demanding a fee as well."

Clicker bit his lip. His tongue clicked. He did a quick calculation. At this morning's black market rate, an exit visa would cost the colonel over two million piastres. Clicker had no idea how to help.

———•———

DESPERATE!

A fter the meeting with Mrs. Reese, Dobie spent ten days catching Air Force planes to Bangkok. Charles flew there as well. The pair met in a respectable Bangkok hotel. Charles had stashed the radio in Bangkok with a contact of Mr. Peabody's. They tried calling Marcel at their usual time on three consecutive days with no success.

Dobie recognized they were operating the radios at the limit of their range. If he couldn't make contact after one more try, they would have to move north to Nakhon Phanom. Dobie preferred to remain in Bangkok, though. Coordinating assets for a rescue would be easier there. More military flights transited the city, as well as the U-Tapao base south along the Thailand coast.

At 1339 local time on the fourth day, Dobie keyed the mike.

"Pan to Hook."

"Hook here."

Dobie sighed with relief. The signal was weak, but it was clear.

"Status," Dobie requested.

"Desperate," came the response.

"How?"

Dobie did not want an extended conversation. He couldn't know who else could be listening on this open frequency. Any ham operator in the world could be listening. Dobie wasn't worried about them, though. It was the local intelligence agency monitoring the frequency that worried him.

"General has abandoned," came Marcel's crisp reply. "Need food and medicine. People dying from beriberi."

"Pan copies. Call in time over seven plus two."

"Hook copies."

Dobie put down the microphone. Marcel had understood they would talk tomorrow, two hours later. He looked across the hotel room desk at Charles.

"We need to get them out," Dobie stated.

"I'll call Mr. Peabody," Charles acknowledged. "Any ideas how?"

Dobie shrugged. Who could he call? And where was Marcel's group of desperate Hmong? Why didn't they walk to Thailand? Dobie knew the answer, though. Both the Pathet Lao and the Royal Lao army would attack a group of desperate Hmong.

"You work on financing and assets. I'll work on operations. I need to find Jeff Nickerson for a start."

Charles looked at Dobie.

"Assets?"

"We'll need an airplane or a large helicopter to get Marcel and his extended family out."

"We also need a list of the Lima Sites to select a pickup location," Charles responded.

"And if they are usable," Dobie countered. "Let's both get a list and compare notes."

"I'll call Mr. Peabody to see what contacts he may have to help. He'll finance it if he gets a story."

"We'll have a story for him."

Charles left.

Two avenues of thought occurred to Dobie. He had two names, who had left the Green Berets and gone to work with the CIA in Southeast Asia. Jeff Nickerson should also have a list of contacts. He wouldn't be a good intelligence officer if he didn't. Dobie would try his names first. But he had to find out if they were still here. That could prove to be a challenge.

Jimbo Atkins knew the same two. He did not know where Jimbo had gone after their Laos mission. Dobie knew Jimbo's two favorite hotels in Bangkok. He didn't know if Jimbo was there. The hotel wouldn't tell him if he called to ask. The best way to find out was to call and ask to be connected. He called one and asked to be connected to his room.

"I'm sorry, we do not have a Mr. Atkins staying with us," came the reply.

The second hotel gave the same answer. The delay in the response, though, triggered an idea.

"If Mr. Atkins should arrive, I'd like to leave a message."

The desk clerk agreed to take a message. Dobie dictated the message.

"Marcel needs his services." Dobie left his hotel number and room number.

Next, Dobie called Jeff Nickerson in Saigon. Jeff wasn't available. He left a message with his name and hotel telephone number. Maybe he would have to go to Saigon to talk in person. But were commercial flights still operating? A military hop would probably require him to go to U-Tapao.

The next day, he tuned the radio to call Marcel.

"Exploring options," he radioed Marcel. "Any usable Lima Site airfields accessible to you?"

"Two six," Marcel replied.

"Usable?" Dobie queried.

"Unknown."

"Confirm it."

"Will do."

"Let's talk in one."

"Hook copies."

Their conversation ended.

Dobie had a week before they would talk again. He hoped he would have a solution for Marcel by then.

For two days, Dobie stayed close to his hotel in case Jimbo or Jeff returned his call. Neither called. Charles reported that Mr. Peabody would finance the rescue of Marcel's family. He was looking for any available aircraft to charter for their mission. Mr. Peabody thought finding pilots would be the bigger challenge. He wasn't sure anyone would fly the plane at a price that would turn a profit from the story in his magazine.

That gave Dobie an idea. Maybe he could find a South Vietnamese pilot who would fly the mission if it meant his family could escape South Vietnam. That would require Dobie to go to Saigon.

The next day, Dobie caught a C-130 to U-Tapao. Another day lapsed before he caught a flight to Saigon. Charles stayed in Bangkok. Mr. Peabody was tracking down contacts who might know people in Thailand. Dobie camped at the Defense Attaché Office to talk with Jeff Nickerson.

"What the devil are you still doing in Saigon?" Jeff asked when he walked into his office.

"I have another project."

Dobie explained the situation.

"Are there any helicopters or transports in Thailand I can charter?" he finished.

"None offhand. But wait a week, and you might have half of those sitting out there on the ramp."

"Can a large helicopter get to Thailand from here?" Dobie inquired.

"You'd have to ask a pilot."

"Is your pilot friend Rick around?"

"He took his family and left. His wife and son survived the C-5 crash."

"That must have been rough. You must know another pilot, though."

"Clicker, Rick's partner, is still here. He's looking for a way out for a Vietnamese pilot and his family."

Jeff told Dobie where to find Clicker and Tinh. A Vietnamese looking to escape made the ideal pilot to help Dobie.

Dobie arrived at Tinh's office to find it empty. No one was around to ask.

Jeff had given him Clicker's hotel. Since he needed a room for the night, Clicker headed there. Spotting the American pilot in the bar or cafe shouldn't be hard, Dobie figured. Hopefully, he wouldn't have to waste over two days to catch him or Colonel Tinh. The Hmong had little time left.

———•———

THE SERGEANT'S IDEA

———•———

Clicker had been trying for a week to find a way for the Ngos to leave Vietnam. Several evacuation flights were leaving daily for the Philippines. Air Force C-130s crammed twice their normal passenger load on each flight, using a "combat evacuation" configuration. They carried no seats, only a floor of empty cargo pallets and tie-down straps for crude seatbelts. It was the same configuration used in the main cargo compartment of that disastrous C-5 flight. Flights by the larger jet transports declined and then stopped.

The big catch remained exit visas. Government red tape trapped the Ngo's applications. A bribe would shake their visas loose. But Lieutenant Colonel Ngo Tinh's modest salary could not afford the bribe. The price for an exit visa continued to climb.

Late on Wednesday, Clicker stopped to buy piastres. The rate was 2,900 to a US dollar, tripling in a week. It was near, if not at, a panic rate. He ran to the Defense Attaché to find Jeff Nickerson. Clicker knew Jeff held the answer to the Ngo's plight. It was his second trip of the day. He had missed the Army intelligence officer in the morning.

Clicker found Jeff in a conversation as usual. Lieutenant Colonel Nickerson seemed to be the Officer-in-Charge of troubleshooting. Clicker could feel the tension in the room. Everyone had the look of "sweating bullets." Not wanting to wear out his welcome, Clicker waited for Jeff to finish his conversation. When his companions scurried away, Clicker walked over to him. Jeff acknowledged Clicker.

"I need a few minutes to check on something," he requested. "But stick around. Don't leave."

Jeff ran out of the office.

Not that I have any place to go, Clicker thought.

The last two comments carried the gravity of orders. Jeff had never been abrupt with Clicker. He had always been friendly and genuine in his desire to help. Clicker attributed that to their mutual friend, Rick Guerri. The Army intel officer and the former Air Force fighter pilot had a bond that Clicker recognized. They had been in battle together. Clicker did not know the where or the what, but the connection was clear to any combat veteran. So, Clicker waited.

Something's afoot, Clicker recognized.

Minutes went by. Clicker found a chair near a corner, sat down, and waited. Thirty minutes dragged on. Finally, Jeff returned. Relief was evident on his face. He scanned the room and spotted Clicker. Clicker rose to meet him, but Jeff led him back to the corner.

"What's up?" Clicker prompted.

"We just put a group from our office on a Herk," he stated. "Ones with no exit visas."

Clicker could not help his eyebrows from rising.

"How?"

"We snuck them by the gate guards and the immigration desk."

Clicker bit his tongue, wanting to ask the "how" of that. He realized that the information was classified as "top secret" with a "need to know." For this office, he fit neither requirement.

"We'll be trying to replicate the process, but we'll have to space the execution out to avoid undue attention."

Clicker fought his desire to ask about the Ngos. He wanted to let Jeff pace the conversation.

"Keep your people close by," Jeff advised.

Clicker had a question he had to ask.

"Is the Embassy on board?"

Jeff carefully formed his answer.

"On the local level, yes. Not necessarily above it."

What the hell does that mean? Clicker wondered.

Then he remembered. An Embassy officer was working at the DAO, one who was "reasonable." The implication was that his superiors were not. Or did the Ambassador want "plausible deniability?" He could state publicly, "No evacuation is ongoing." He could plead ignorance of a subordinate running an evacuation away from the Embassy.

Clicker's hopes for the Ngos soared.

Jeff seemed to read Clicker's thoughts.

"You understand the sensitivity of what I've said?"

"Absolutely!" Clicker responded. "They are staying close to the base. I'll tell them to stand by."

Jeff nodded.

"We have created pickup points for our people. I'll let you know when and where your people need to be."

Jeff walked over to a desk.

"When a window opens, I'll leave a message at your hotel. I'll also put a note in this drawer for you."

He opened the second drawer on the right side of his desk.

"I understand," Clicker replied.

"One more thing," Jeff continued. "A former compatriot of mine was here earlier. I sent him your way. He's looking for a pilot and information for a Hmong rescue mission in Laos."

Clicker raised his eyebrows.

"Hmong? We don't have enough people here to rescue? Who is this guy?"

"A retired Green Beret I served with. Rick and I met with him right after Rick arrived. The guy was running down a class ring from a pilot on the MIA list. A North Vietnamese deserter was looking to sell the ring. Rick knew the missing pilot."

"So what's this guy's name if I run into him?"

"Dobie Starbuckle. I gave him your hotel name. Hope that was okay. I'm guessing he'll find you there."

"I'll be on the lookout for him."

Clicker rushed to Tinh's office. The colonel and Sergeant Khắc were conversing. Tinh motioned Clicker over.

"The sergeant has an idea. Tell Clicker," Tinh prompted the sergeant.

"With Saigon being the last place to fall, the need for transport has disappeared. I've hidden my plane among the wrecks in the boneyard across the runway.

All I need is a pilot to fly it out."

Clicker looked to Tinh.

"Do you know how to fly the plane?"

"I flew C-47s for a short time. I can figure it out."

"How many can you carry?" Clicker asked Khắc.

"Normal passenger configuration is about sixty. But with no seats, double that."

"But your passengers would still need to get past the guards and get on base," Clicker noted.

"Yes," the colonel conceded. "But once the base becomes vulnerable, the guards will desert. At the last minute, his plane makes an excellent option."

"Could it make it to the Philippines?" Clicker queried.

Tinh shook his head.

"Too far. The only option is Thailand."

"You'd want to avoid overflying Cambodia," Clicker noted. "You've read what is happening there?"

"Yes. All the more reason to get out of Saigon."

Tinh turned to Khắc.

"You will want to keep your airplane secure. Someone will grab any flyable airplane."

"My brother and sons are guarding it."

"Good."

"I need to find some fuel and sneak a truck over to the plane," Sergeant Khắc stated. He nodded to Tinh and Clicker and left.

"I've just come from the DAO," Clicker began. "They snuck some of their people without visas onto a plane."

"I was guessing they would find a way."

"Colonel Nickerson said to keep your family ready. If an opportunity opens, he will let me know. We'll have to get to a pickup point outside the gate."

"I'm thinking of getting them to Khắc's plane," Tinh stated.

Clicker shook his head.

"An American plane would be better. With the American President authorizing the evacuation, you'll get to America much quicker. Staying in a Thai refugee camp could mean more than a year of waiting."

Clicker headed back to his hotel, feeling guardedly optimistic. He had promised Colonel Tinh that he would help his family escape. Yet, he had accomplished absolutely nothing. Maybe he had been kidding himself. Still, two alternatives now existed for the Ngos. Using Khắc's plane to fly to Thailand was a backup. But, and it was a big one, passengers without exit visas still had to sneak past the gate guards.

As Clicker walked past the hotel desk, the clerk waved to him.

"You have a message, Mr. Clicker."

The note was brief.

"JN said to talk to you. DS, room 211."

Clicker picked up the single house phone in the lobby and asked for room 211.

"Starbuckle," a firm voice answered.

"Clicker Cruthers. I got your message. Can we meet in the bar in ten minutes?"

"Affirmative. I'll be sitting in a corner."

The guy's brusque manner intrigued Clicker.

All business, he thought.

Ten minutes later, Clicker had no trouble identifying Dobie. Only three other patrons were at the bar. A lone figure sat at a table in the back corner. Dobie rose as Clicker approached.

"Dobie Starbuckle," he introduced himself.

Clicker sat down.

"I understand you are looking to rescue some Hmong," Clicker stated.

Dobie nodded.

"What's their situation?" Clicker pressed.

The bartender arrived to take their orders. Clicker ordered a bourbon. Dobie asked for a Scotch.

Dobie briefly described why Marcel and his extended family were important to Dobie.

"The family saved our asses," he concluded. "Without them, I wouldn't still be here. I want to return the favor."

Clicker nodded in understanding, dropping his initially negative reaction to helping.

"Jeff said you needed a pilot's view."

"I need some mission-essential background information, then some specific intel," Dobie replied.

"Shoot."

"Can a light cargo plane or large helicopter fly a round trip between U-Tapao and south central Laos?"

"How far north of Vientiane?" Clicker pressed.

"A hundred and ten klicks."

As the bartender arrived with the drinks, Clicker did some mental math. He converted the kilometers into nautical miles. Clicker remembered his calculations in his futile efforts to get an engine to Pleiku. He shook his head.

"Too far. You'd have to stage out of Nakhon Phanom or Udorn."

"Great to know. Now, about assets. Any info on available aircraft?"

"Several currently sit right here." Clicker pointed to the table.

Clicker thought of Sergeant Khắc's idea. If he told Dobie about it, would the Special Forces veteran try to hijack the plane for himself? He couldn't risk it. Instead, he decided to be vague.

"The Vietnamese Air Force has several C-47s and C-123s at Tan Son Nhut. You can bet that any flyable plane will head for U-Tapao before Saigon falls."

"How do I get one to Thailand sooner?"

Clicker shrugged.

"Wait a few days; any flyable transport will head there. The helicopters, I'm afraid, will head out to find the US Navy."

"Why is that?"

"For a helicopter, Thailand has to be a direct flight for the large ones. The small ones don't have the range. The big ones would have to overfly the North Vietnamese west of Saigon and Cambodia. They likely wouldn't survive."

Dobie sat silently for a minute, figuring that this information doomed his mission. Clicker sensed his predicament.

"What happens to the planes when they land in Thailand?" Dobie asked.

"Assuming all Tan Son Nhut planes head to U-Tapao, the US Air Force will probably seize them."

Dobie thought again.

"But in the fog of war, an enterprising operation might appropriate one," he mused.

Clicker began to like Dobie.

"A possibility. The big unknown is the timing."

Both sipped their drinks.

"The NVA controls what happens in Laos," Dobie finally stated. "Which means they'll finish the job here first. Laos will quickly follow."

"Then the window to get from U-Tapao to Udorn to Laos and back would be very narrow."

Dobie nodded.

"Why don't your Hmong just hike out?" Clicker asked after a minute of silence.

"Very risky. With the rainy season approaching, the Mekong River becomes very dangerous. Besides the Pathet Lao, the Royal Laotians would threaten any Hmong on the move. Ethnic Laotians persecute them."

"Like the Montagnards in Vietnam," Clicker concluded.

"Walking out is Plan B," Dobie commented.

He downed his drink.

"Seems the best air option is to wait at U-Tapao," Clicker suggested.

"I wish I had a better idea," Dobie admitted.

———•———

A BADLY KEPT SECRET

———·———

Two days of fruitless trips to Tan Son Nhut ensued. Clicker became discouraged again. The emotional rollercoaster wore on the ex-Marine. If he hadn't sent most of his money out of the country, it might have covered the needed bribe. But his US bank had closed its Saigon branch the day he had wired the money home. Only one US bank remained open. It would close any day. He didn't want to drive around with all his money around his waist. Desperate, armed South Vietnamese troops with little prospect of escaping roamed the streets. South Vietnamese Army guards eyed any American approaching Tan Son Nhut jealously. An ARVN corporal would see a wealthy American with a wad of dollars as his escape ticket.

Clicker remembered Da Nang. An hour after their two F-5s had returned, the airliner had limped into Tan Son Nhut. The airline owner had organized the flight to rescue women and children. The crew reported a harrowing tale. People in the wheel wells had jammed the landing gear in the down position. More people had jammed the rear stair door open, so the plane could not pressurize. Armed ARVN troops had ripped women and children off the stairways to the plane and trampled them to get on board.

Little wonder, then, that the American Embassy steadfastly maintained no evacuation was happening. But the clandestine one was a badly kept secret. Vietnamese with exit visas were streaming through Tan Son Nhut's main gate.

Another fruitless day passed for Clicker. But he noticed one important change at the base. He heard several C-130s land. They seemed to land more often than the jet transports had. If they had joined the evacuation in force, the opportunities for the Ngos would increase. Clicker checked with the reception desk of his hotel repeatedly. Whenever a clerk did anything for him, Clicker tipped him in dollars. Their value had now increased to 3,300 piastres.

That night, the Herks kept coming. Twice he counted two landing within an hour of each other.

During his Sunday morning breakfast, he heard two more planes land. As Clicker sipped his third cup of coffee, a reception clerk arrived with a note. Clicker tipped him a couple of dollars. He tore open the envelope. It simply listed an address, a time, and a curt instruction: "Go inside." The note bore the scrawled initials JN at the bottom. It was a pickup place and time from Jeff Nickerson! It looked hand-delivered. Someone must have knocked on his room door after he left for breakfast, then left the note at the reception desk.

The meeting time was at five o'clock that afternoon. Clicker left money for his breakfast and went to the reception desk. He brought his hotel bill up to date, a process he had thought to do every morning. Hopefully, the clerk had not opened the note and then resealed it. If the clerk had opened it, more people would likely be at the rendezvous.

Clicker grabbed his "go bag" and headed to the Ngo's temporary housing. He walked into the shop. An elderly gentleman greeted him.

"I'm looking for Colonel Tinh," Clicker stated slowly.

The gentleman bowed and went through the beaded doorway. A minute later, the gentleman emerged. The prettiest Vietnamese woman Clicker had ever seen followed him. She bowed slightly. Clicker returned the courtesy.

"I am Ngo Anh, Colonel Tinh's wife. You must be Clicker."

Her English was excellent with a French accent. Her beauty stunned Clicker.

Tinh, you devil, no wonder you've never introduced me, was Clicker's first thought. While she wore a loose-fitting top and slacks, he could imagine her in a traditional, form-fitting Ao Dai dress.

He detected a whiff of Chanel No. 19. Clicker recognized it because he had bought a bottle for Huyền at the Tan Son Nhut Base Exchange. He wondered if buying his wife a bottle had strained Tinh's budget.

"I have important information for him … for you," Clicker uttered.

"I don't know when he will return."

"Is he at his office or his planes?" Clicker quickly asked.

"No." Clicker noticed Anh offered no elaboration.

"Can I write a note for him?"

Anh turned and addressed the older gentleman. He retrieved a quill pen and paper. Clicker copied Jeff's instructions exactly, then signed the note. He handed it to Anh. She read it.

"Do you understand its importance?" Clicker asked.

"Yes," she replied. "We cannot thank you enough for your help."

"Do you know where that is?" he inquired, pointing to the address.

She spoke with the gentleman.

"It is very close to here," she stated.

"I'll meet you at the address. It will be important not to be late. And bring any identification you have."

"I understand. We all have passports."

"I'll try to find out more details," Clicker promised.

He bowed slightly and left. He raced to the Defense Office. While the implications of the note seemed obvious, Clicker wanted more details.

Jeff was not in his office. Clicker wandered around the building, hoping to spot him. Exiting the building, he looked toward the flight line. He walked to the military passenger terminal. Jeff was in a conversation with two Vietnamese army officers. He moved so Jeff would notice him, but Clicker did not want to intrude on the conversation.

The army officers left, and Jeff walked over.

"Did you get my message?"

"Yes, the Ngos will be there."

"Do you know how many?"

Clicker had not asked.

"No," he answered.

"Well, no matter. We'll deal with the number we get."

"How will this pickup work?"

"We've been running regular shuttle buses for our employees to come to work. The guards have become accustomed to our bus coming and going. On the trips to the base, we've loaded the children and older passengers in the rear, with employees in front. Around dusk, the back of the bus is in the shadows. In the last two days, the guards haven't gotten on the bus to check IDs. They've just waved the bus through."

"I'll ride in with them and leave with them," Clicker informed Jeff. "So I should sit up front, then?"

"Right. We've moved our processing center to the gym. The theater wasn't big enough. When you get there, the confusion you see will be intentional. We have to get the passengers through our line to get them on a passenger manifest. But of course, we don't want them in the line to have their exit visas checked. So, we create some commotion around that line to slip them by it."

Clicker headed back to the Defense Attaché complex. He wanted to grab some lunch at the snack bar. The idea of calling Rick in the Philippines also occurred to him. As far as he knew, the Guerris still fought for passports for Lei and Thi.

He headed for Jeff's office. Clicker had become a familiar face, so he doubted anyone would question him if he used the phone. No one glanced at him as Clicker picked up the phone and dialed. He heard the clicks as the lines made connections to the hotel outside Clark Air Base.

"Hello," Sue's voice answered.

"Hi, Sue, it's Clicker. Is Rick there?"

"No." The line carried static. "Where are you?"

"Still in Saigon."

"Why are you still there?"

Clicker did not want to talk much on an open line. His answer was circumspect.

"Just working on a small project. Can you give Rick a message?"

"Sure."

"It's a short one."

"Go ahead," Sue replied.

"I may arrive at your station in the next day with the packages."

"That's it?"

"Yes. How are the passports coming along?"

Clicker heard a sigh.

"The bureaucrats remain in charge. They claim they are waiting for verification of the adoption documents from the Saigon Embassy."

"Jerks!" Clicker responded. "Do they think Saigon has the time on their hands for that?"

"Who knows?"

"Has Rick talked with Jeff about getting help?"

"Every time he calls, Jeff isn't in. He concludes Jeff is overwhelmed, so he doesn't leave a message."

"I see Jeff nearly every day. I'll talk to him."

"Great. Thank you, Clicker. I am so frustrated, I could scream."

"I'd better get off the line. Tell Rick I'll call with any update on my trip."

"Bye, Clicker. Stay safe."

When he hung up, Clicker checked his watch. He thought about calling his company's office in Los Angeles. But it would be close to midnight, so only a duty officer would answer. He would call from the Philippines. With nearly four hours until the pickup, he had time on his hands. A big lunch sounded like a good idea. He would miss dinner.

At four o'clock, Clicker headed to the pickup address. Rather than drive his car, though, he left it at the DAO. Someone there might use it. He put the key in the drawer Jeff had told him to check for messages. He'd tell someone about the car when he got in line for an airplane ride out.

Clicker told the taxi to drop him around the corner from the address. He found the building, noting a faded number beside the door. He was thirty minutes early. As his eyes adjusted, Clicker saw it was a clothing shop. Two mechanical sewing machines were in the back. Bolts of cloth lined some shelves. But Clicker noticed a lot of open space on the shelves. The business looked like it had fallen on hard times.

On one side, Clicker saw a dozen people huddled, squatting against the wall. A few children sat quietly among them. A woman came from the back.

"May I help you?"

Clicker was at a loss on how to answer. Was there a code word he should use? His message had not contained one.

"I'm here to meet a bus," he ventured.

The woman glanced at the group along the wall as if asking Clicker if they were his group.

"No, others."

"Others should arrive shortly."

"I'll wait," Clicker responded.

The woman bowed slightly.

Ten minutes later, the front door opened. Anh walked in, followed by the elderly gentleman Clicker had seen at the store. An elderly woman and a couple followed her in. Anh walked over to Clicker.

"Tinh is coming shortly with our daughters and four others."

That made them a group of eleven, excluding the colonel. *A very manageable group*, Clicker thought. He wondered about the fourteen-year-old son. That would make them a dozen, assuming the son was already on the base. Clicker also realized he did not know the ages of the daughters.

The woman from the back approached Clicker.

"Are these your people?"

"Not all of them."

She nodded.

"There is some time before the bus. We have others to come, too."

Yet another group? Clicker wondered. *How many were Jeff and his colleagues going to smuggle onto the base?*

A group walked through the front door, followed by Tinh. Clicker studied the two teenage girls. The older girl stood next to a young man in uniform. Tinh wore his flight suit. The others included a couple about the colonel's age and two young adult women.

Tinh took the elbow of the younger of the two teenage girls.

"Clicker, meet my youngest daughter, Thuan."

"Happy to meet you, Thuan," Clicker replied.

Even in the low light of the shop, Clicker could see the girl blush as she bowed.

"My oldest daughter, Kim," he continued as he ushered the older teenager forward. "And her fiancé, Truc."

"I am pleased to know you, Kim," Clicker replied. Clicker said the names to himself, working hard to remember them.

Truc extended his hand, which Clicker shook.

"Truc isn't leaving, though," Tinh explained. "He remains stationed at the base."

Tinh joined his wife. With the Ngos gathered together, Tinh looked at Clicker.

"Do you know how this will be done?"

Clicker repeated Jeff's explanation. He checked his watch.

"Since Jeff said they plan on doing it around dusk, we have nearly an hour before the bus arrives. The lady here indicated one more group has to arrive." He quickly counted the escapees in the other group along the wall. "Could be a full bus."

"Waiting for dusk is cutting it close to curfew," Tinh noted.

Thirty minutes later, the last group of a dozen refugees arrived. They ranged in age from six to sixty. Clicker surmised they comprised two sets of parents, a couple, and their children. A boy appeared close to fourteen. He hoped his age wouldn't create problems.

Twenty minutes before six o'clock, the waiting groups heard a bus. A figure in US Army fatigues walked in. Clicker noted his name tag identified him as Sergeant Davis. He gathered everyone together and issued instructions in Vietnamese. As far as Clicker could understand, they had not changed. The tech sergeant then motioned Tinh, Truc, Clicker, and two Vietnamese men forward.

"You all sit up front. If the gate guard steps onto the bus, sit up straight, but try to act bored."

He looked at Clicker.

"You have a Department of Defense ID?"

"Yes."

"I want you right behind the driver. If the guard steps onto the bus, be obvious about digging it out of your pocket." He looked at the two Vietnamese men. "Dig out your IDs, too."

Clicker presumed that the two Vietnamese were Attaché employees "sponsoring" all the family members.

"Place anyone younger than sixteen in the back rows. Then, the oldest people. Working-aged people toward the front. Any questions?"

No one had any questions.

"Okay, let's load up."

In ten minutes, the bus was on the move. When the bus drove past the street to the base, Clicker wondered why. Tech Sergeant Davis, who sat across the row from Clicker, picked up a walkie-talkie. While he spoke low into the mouthpiece, Clicker could hear.

"Bravo Two departing Charlie," he called.

Initially, static responded. Then a voice answered.

"Bravo Two, we have an extra stop for you. Drop by Delta to pick up a package."

"Bravo Two copies. A package at Delta. Over." The sergeant released the transmit switch. "Shit. Did you hear that, Bill?" he addressed the driver.

"Roger," the driver responded.

The bus headed away from the base. Clicker looked from the driver to the tech sergeant. Tinh also noticed they were heading away from the base.

"What gives?" Clicker asked.

"Something's up at the gate," Sergeant Davis replied. "We go to a holding point for five minutes." He checked his watch.

The bus pulled to a stop. Clicker wasn't sure exactly where they were, but he figured they were within five minutes of the base. Five minutes passed. The sergeant keyed his transmit button again.

"Bravo Two is at Delta, but there is no package."

"Roger, Bravo Two. Wait for the package."

"Damn." The tech sergeant turned to Clicker and those in the front rows. "We have to abort. Something is happening at the gate, which makes it too risky."

The bus pulled away from the side of the street. Ten minutes later, they were back at the clothing shop.

"Everyone off," the sergeant ordered.

"My son is waiting at the DAO," Tinh said. "Is the bus going back to the compound?"

"Yes," the sergeant replied.

"Can I ride with you?"

"Sure. But you'll be stuck on base because of curfew."

"That's okay," Tinh answered.

"I'll ride, too," Clicker said.

The South Vietnamese Army stop was unusually long. Guards checked everyone's ID closely. The US Marines at the entrance to the DAO checked IDs again.

Jeff met them when the bus pulled into the compound.

"It's off for tonight," he reported. "An extra MP detail is on duty at the gate. South Vietnamese military police captured a People's Army artillery spotter in an ARVN uniform with false papers late this afternoon. As a result, the ARVN has doubled security at the gates. No one without papers gets on base."

"That's not good!" Clicker exclaimed.

Tinh eyed him and nodded.

"The noose is tightening," Jeff continued. "The Communist army is on the outskirts of Bien Hoa. Since they have neutralized the base, they could just bypass it and head to Saigon."

Shit, Clicker thought.

"The good news, though," Jeff resumed, "is that the C-130s are now operating around the clock. A squadron from the States is flying to Clark to assist. It should arrive tomorrow."

Tinh stayed in his temporary office on base with his son. Clicker curled up on the floor in a vacant room. He wondered if the hotel had rented his room.

The next morning, Clicker caught a taxi back to his hotel. He stopped by his newsstand outside the hotel to check on the exchange rate. Clicker found the newsstand boarded up and abandoned.

That, Clicker knew, spelled panic.

———•———

A LAWYER'S IDEA

Rick and Sue had waited two weeks to hear from the Manila Embassy. Mr. Goodwall had not answered the messages that Rick had left. Finally, the phone in their suite rang. The Embassy had new passports for Sue and David. They could pick them up at any time. When Rick asked about passports for Lei and Thi, the caller had no information.

"Could we meet with Mr. Goodwall this afternoon or tomorrow morning?"

The caller did not know. That was another section. Mr. Guerri would have to call that office himself. As soon as he hung up, Rick dialed the embassy officer's number. No, the secretary assured him, Mr. Goodwall had no time for appointments today or tomorrow. But a junior embassy officer was available. Rick made the appointment for the next morning.

That afternoon, the Guerris rode the Clark bus to the Manila Hilton. As soon as the Embassy opened the next morning, they picked up the two passports. Then they waited an hour for their appointment with the junior foreign service officer.

No update was available on the passports for the Vietnamese children. The Saigon Embassy remained busy.

"We will call you when we receive any word," the officer assured Rick and Sue. He had no idea when that might be.

They caught the afternoon bus back to Clark Air Base. In their suite, Rick called the Legal Affairs office on the base. Captain Mills agreed to investigate viable ideas. He would get back to Rick as soon as he had any information. He promised to call a lawyer friend in the States, which might take a few days.

Rick next needed to call his company. Dragon Air was still his employer, although his specific job no longer existed. His contract stated that the company had thirty days to find a new position for Rick. Any job had to fit some narrow restrictions. Rick would not have to sweep floors or clean restrooms in Saudi Arabia. If nothing became available within the thirty days, Rick would receive the rest of his salary for the contractual term. The company would release him from any further service. He was halfway through that thirty-day window.

At ten o'clock that night, Rick placed the collect call to the Dragon Air Los Angeles office. His boss picked up the line. The company had one opportunity for Rick. It was a technical representative for the F-5 in Southeast Asia, based in Singapore. Several countries in the region operated the airplane. The company gave Rick two weeks to consider the offer. His Vietnamese children needed passports before going to Singapore. That made the offer unfeasible.

Since Sue went to bed before the telephone call, he would have to wait until the next morning to talk with her. She slept more than before. Most mornings, he was awake with the children before Sue woke up. She went to bed almost as soon as the children were asleep. The one-bedroom suite was feeling small. He could read only by the small desk light in the main room without disturbing Sue. The other alternative was the bar off the hotel lobby.

On Friday after the Embassy visit, Captain Mills called Rick. He had spoken to his friend. Captain Mills could meet Rick on Monday morning.

As he waited for his Monday meeting, Rick read the *Stars and Stripes*. The People's Army was closing in on Bien Hoa. With no updates from Clicker since Sue's conversation, he wondered what was going on. In the hotel bar, Rick had heard that refugees were arriving daily at Clark. But why weren't Clicker and the Ngos in the Philippines?

A captain emerged through the door next to a sergeant's desk.

"Mr. Guerri?" Rick looked up.

"Captain Rob Mills," the captain said. "Come on back."

In his office, Captain Mills gestured to the chair beside his desk. He sat behind the desk.

"I spoke with my law school friend in Denver. I think he has the solution to your problem."

"Great," Rick responded.

"His advice is to get to the States as soon as possible. If you can get on a C-141, fly as far as Hickam in Honolulu. Get off the plane and go through customs and immigration. The Attorney General has granted an immigration parole admitting

Vietnamese into the US without visas. The President has also authorized the evacuation of at-risk Vietnamese. You should have no trouble clearing immigration in Honolulu. If you also mention your wife and children survived the C-5 crash, I'm guessing you'll sail through."

"I think we can get space-available seats with our DoD ID cards," Rick stated. "Then what?"

"Once in Honolulu, you are in the States. You can work on the adoption process more easily."

"Does your friend know any lawyers who work with the adoption of Vietnamese orphans?"

"He knows two in Denver. A temporary orphanage is operating in the city to unite adoptive parents with their children. They work with the Hoa Sen Orphanage."

Captain Mills handed a slip of paper across the desk.

"Here are my friend's name and office number in Denver. He said to call when you get to Hawaii."

"Thank you," Rick replied. "Why didn't the Manila Embassy provide me with this information?"

Captain Mills shrugged. "Who knows?"

On his way back to the hotel, Rick stopped by the passenger terminal. He learned that a C-141 was departing the next morning. However, no seats were available. It was a flight full of refugees. On Wednesday morning, though, the schedule showed a flight to California. The flight made stops in Guam and Honolulu. It would carry a load of refugees, but space-available seats were open.

Rick rushed back to the hotel to tell Sue the news. Sue smiled for the first time since leaving Saigon.

"If we don't make Wednesday's flight, there will be more," Rick assured her. "Refugees are flowing into the Philippines. The Philippine President wants them removed from his country. Nothing will stand in our way of getting Lei and Thi to the States."

THE HERK

Clicker had flown 280 combat missions over Vietnam and Laos. He prided himself on being the tough, unflappable Marine. Now, he was on the verge of panic. The Ngos looked at him pleadingly every time that he checked in with them. Colonel Tinh, Clicker could tell, was on the verge of panic, too. Clicker sympathized. The family had placed too much faith in him. He had failed.

Back at his hotel in the middle of the afternoon, Clicker sat in the bar. He was on his second bourbon. Thankfully, the bar still had cheap bourbon and Scotch. Clicker perched at the short end of the bar with a view of the door. As he downed the last sip, Sergeant Davis stepped in and spotted Clicker.

"An urgent note from Colonel Nickerson."

He handed Clicker an envelope and immediately left.

Clicker tore open the envelope. The note was brief.

"1700 315 Nyen Tuyn. JN"

It was a different address. Clicker checked his watch. It said three-thirty. Squinting to read the date in its tiny window, he barely made out "28". He had lost track of the dates. He had an hour and a half before the pickup. With his car on base, he would have to depend on taxis.

Clicker made another decision. If this escape failed, he would stay at the DAO. On his way to his room, he stopped by the hotel desk.

"I'll be checking out early in the morning," he informed the clerk. Clicker paid his bill and ambled to the creaking elevator.

Grabbing his knapsack, Clicker walked down the stairs. The stairs exited into the lobby away from the front desk.

On reaching the bottom step, an explosion sounded toward the base. He dashed out the side exit to the street. Another explosion rang out. Reflected sunlight flashed in the sky over the base. He spotted an A-37, the light attack airplane flown by the South Vietnamese. It climbed, then banked back to the base. Clicker saw a pair of bombs fall from it. The plane was bombing Tan Son Nhut! As it pulled up, another A-37 swooped toward the base.

Seconds later, two explosions ripped the air in quick succession. They didn't sound large.

Two hundred fifty-pound bombs, Clicker guessed. But big enough to do damage if dropped accurately.

But why would South Vietnamese planes bomb their base? Only two possible answers existed. An irate South Vietnamese pilot who felt he and his family were being abandoned, or captured planes flown by North Vietnamese pilots. In that case, the battle for Saigon had started. Was it too late to escape?

Over the whine of the A-37s, a C-130 rumbled. Clicker saw it climb. The Herk turned southeast, toward the ocean several miles down the Saigon River. It flew nearly over the top of Clicker. An A-37 turned behind it. Fortunately, the Herk flew at a similar speed as the A-37. If the transport pilot was at full throttle, he might stay ahead of the attacking plane. To the east, Clicker spotted a building thunderstorm.

"Head for the thunderstorm!" Clicker yelled.

The transport plane turned toward the building storm.

What about the pickup? Clicker wondered. He had to assume it was still on. This was the last chance for the Ngos.

Clicker ran into the street to stop a blue taxi. He offered the driver dollars, which were quickly accepted. The taxi sped to the Ngos temporary house, dodging around stopped traffic. A pedicab driver nearly lost the battle to occupy the same space as Clicker's taxi. The cab screeched to a halt in front of the shop. Clicker had forgotten to give the driver an address down the street.

He stuffed the greenbacks in the driver's hand, adding a few extra singles. Their value would have just soared if any black market exchanges lingered in the doomed city.

As Clicker raced into the shop, he found he was breathing rapidly.

Slow down, he urged himself. Hyperventilating before the Ngos would not encourage calmness on their part.

As soon as Clicker walked in the door, Tinh came through the beads.

"We're on again," Clicker blurted. He continued to gasp.

"When?"

Clicker struggled to slow his breathing.

Am I more worried about my ass? he asked himself.

Clicker checked his wristwatch. It was more of a stalling tactic to control himself than an exercise in accuracy.

"About an hour."

Clicker pulled the note from his pocket.

"Here is the address."

Tinh took it.

"I'll ask Anh's father if he knows where it is."

Tinh disappeared through the beads.

Hardly two minutes passed before Tinh reappeared.

"It's an easy walk if we leave in ten minutes," he reported.

"Did you hear the attack on Tan Son Nhut?" Clicker inquired. Tinh's calm demeanor seemed at odds with the current circumstances to Clicker.

"Was that what it was?"

Clicker realized this house was farther from the base than his hotel.

"I saw A-37s dive-bombing the base!"

Tinh nodded.

"I guessed as much."

He seemed to smile.

"Unless the pilots had the benefit of the training you and Rick provided to my pilots, I'm guessing they did minor damage."

Tinh's calmness had slowed Clicker's breathing.

"I saw an A-37 chase a Herk," Clicker reported.

"Lucky it wasn't an F-5," Tinh remarked.

"The Herk headed for a thunderstorm."

"Smart pilot."

Anh came through the beads. She held a brief conversation with Tinh. She disappeared through the beads.

"Anh's mother also knows the way to the address. I suggest we go in two groups. Will you accompany me in the second group to ensure no one lags?"

Truc appeared through the beads, wearing his army fatigues. Tinh was in his flight suit. The man's family was prepared to flee, yet this warrior looked dressed for battle. Clicker, however, wore jeans and a faded tropical shirt.

Anh led the first group, with her father beside her. Kim, Truc, and three others followed. Several minutes later, Thuan and Anh's mother led the second group out the door. Clicker and Tinh brought up the rear of this group.

The pickup point was another modest shop. One other small group waited inside when the Ngos arrived. Clicker glanced around. Everyone appeared eerily calm. His stomach was churning. He felt flushed.

Come on, he admonished himself. *You're a Marine!*

Before he could check his watch, a bus pulled up. Sergeant Davis walked into the shop. He spotted Clicker and Tinh.

"Are your people here?"

"Yes," Tinh responded.

The sergeant walked to the other group. A few seconds later, he turned to the assembly.

"Let's go!"

As the group boarded the bus, Clicker gazed toward Tan Son Nhut. The normal Saigon evening smog filled the air. No unusual smoke drifted up.

Maybe those A-37 pilots weren't so good.

Clicker sat behind the driver again. The tech sergeant with the walkie-talkie sat across. Tinh sat behind Clicker. Clicker couldn't understand the crisp exchanges between the sergeant and his office. In minutes, the bus slowed to a crawl, then it stopped. The ARVN checkpoint was ahead. Clicker saw the Vietnamese soldiers scrutinize a car and a truck in front. They took their time examining vehicles and passengers.

As the bus pulled beside the soldiers, Clicker pulled out his wallet with his contractor ID card. He regretted wearing a tropical shirt. Tinh pulled his military ID from a pocket. The bus door opened, and a Vietnamese soldier climbed onto the first step. He eyed the driver and the sergeant. His gaze shifted to Clicker as his demeanor seemed to stiffen. Clicker held his ID card steady. Then the soldier spotted Tinh. He recognized his rank and snapped a smart salute. Tinh returned the salute. The soldier stepped back and waved them on.

Confusion reigned at the gym. A line extended out of the main doors. Clicker muttered a quiet, "Holy shit" when he saw it. The driver parked by a side door.

"Wait on the bus, please," the tech sergeant instructed, first in Vietnamese, then in English.

He disappeared through the side door. Minutes later, he returned.

"Follow me in," he instructed, again in Vietnamese and English.

Clicker allowed the family to enter first. He brought up the rear with Tinh. The gym was hot. The air conditioning was struggling. To his surprise, the two lines that snaked to two desks several yards apart did not extend through the front doors. Clicker noticed that the line on the left was longer than the one on the right. The sergeant led the group to the shorter line.

He explained the process to the Ngo family in Vietnamese.

"Have your IDs or passports out. This line will put you on a flight manifest. You will receive a card with a number. That is your flight number. It will also contain your name. Guard it. Don't lose it. It is your only ticket out."

He explained it to Clicker, who had followed much of the initial instruction. His many Vietnamese girlfriends had taught him a basic level of the language.

"When you finish here," he continued, "come to me over there." He gestured toward the wall behind the second line.

He then pulled Colonel Tinh and Truc aside. Clicker followed.

"Sir, it would be better if neither of you were here for now. We'll be going to the handball courts through that door."

"But what about the visa line?"

Clicker could detect the concern.

"There will be a distraction in that line, and I'll slip the family out the door there."

The colonel nodded and ambled toward the door.

An hour passed. Then another hour. Finally, the Ngo family was at the passenger manifest desk. The tech sergeant briefly appeared at the desk before going to stand by the door. The DAO staffer processed the Ngos quickly. Each one walked over to the tech sergeant. When Clicker presented his passport, the clerk asked a question in a low voice.

"Are you the last in that group?"

"Yes."

The clerk handed Clicker his boarding card, a paper with his flight number, his name, and passport number.

The clerk coughed, then took two drinks from a canteen on his desk. He coughed again.

"Next," he announced.

Clicker headed to join the group, interested in what the distraction would be. It wasn't anything loud. Clicker only noticed that the Vietnamese at the visa desk seemed to become focused on one individual in the line. The passenger waved his arms. His voice rose.

Tech Sergeant Davis quickly opened the door behind him, which the snaking line to the visa desk shielded. In seconds, the Ngos were through the door with Clicker quietly closing it behind him.

"Everyone here?" the sergeant asked.

Anh looked around, took attendance, and responded.

"Yes."

Her calmness awed Clicker.

A turn through a hallway led them to a group of handball courts. Colonel Tinh waited nearby. The sergeant spoke with someone on the other end of his walkie-talkie. Then he addressed the group.

"Please check your boarding card," he began in Vietnamese. "Make sure it has your name and flight 429."

Colonel Tinh ensured everyone checked their cards.

"Your plane is due to land," he checked his watch, "in about two hours. It will offload some cargo across the runways. Then it will taxi near the passenger terminal. A bus will take you there once we hear it is on its way. You can rest in this court here."

Clicker checked his watch. It read 11:32 p.m.

Across the runways? Clicker thought. *That is the ordnance storage area. What are they bringing in? It seems a little late to bring in bullets and bombs.*

Clicker also did some math. Assuming their flight was a C-130, its estimated time of arrival meant it was already on its way.

"That's good," he said out loud.

"What's good?" Colonel Tinh asked.

"The plane should be on its way here." Clicker looked at the Ngos. "Where is Truc?"

"He had to join his company defending the base," Tinh replied.

Sergeant Davis continued.

"When it is time to board the bus to go to your plane, I'll be back to lead you to it. Anyone missing the bus will miss the flight."

Unable to sit still, Clicker paced the hall. Colonel Tinh left his seat next to Anh in the handball court and intercepted him.

"Does something concern you?"

"You should get on the plane with your family. I can get you a boarding card."

Tinh looked at his wife.

"I wish I could. But Sergeant Khắc is counting on me to pilot his plane with his family to Thailand. And I need to fly one more mission against the Commies."

"Will one mission make a difference?"

Tinh shrugged.

"And if you get shot down?"

"I'll come in low and fast and be gone before they know I'm there."

"And you'll probably miss your target."

Tinh acknowledged Clicker's points.

"I've thought of all those points."

"No wonder you and Rick got along so well. You both won't quit; you both take unneeded risks."

"Rick Guerri inspired my pilots," Tinh commented.

"And almost got himself shot down in a place he wasn't supposed to be. His wife would have collected no life insurance money because of that."

Clicker looked toward Anh and the Ngo family.

"You won't get on the plane with them," Clicker concluded.

"Well, maybe a last mission is a hopeless stunt," the colonel conceded. "But I can't let Sergeant Khắc and his family down."

"Maybe I'll stay here to help you fly that C-123."

"I'd consider it a personal favor if you would leave with them. There will be difficulties you will best be able to help them with."

"Rick and I have discussed sponsoring your entry into the US. It will shorten your stay in any refugee camp."

"Thank you. What does that require?"

"That we will see to your financial needs and help you resettle."

"We can never repay you enough for your help."

"When you get to Thailand, get word to Jeff or Rick. Jeff will probably end up in either Subic Bay or Clark Air Base in the Philippines. Rick is currently at the Angeles Hotel outside Clark. We will try to track you down as well."

"Where do you think you will be with my family?"

"The Philippines initially. But I've read that the Philippine president wants all the refugees out of his country. So we will probably go to Guam pretty quickly."

"I need to talk to my wife and explain this to her."

Clicker sat down on the floor. He tried to catch a catnap. It was going to be a long night.

A crackling bullhorn announcement jarred Clicker awake.

"Passengers on flight 429, your airplane has landed. It will arrive near the terminal shortly."

Sergeant Davis lowered the bullhorn. Clicker noticed the other handball courts had filled with people while he napped.

Clicker joined the Ngo family. Tinh hugged everyone. He then engaged in a quiet discussion with his son. Sergeant Davis walked to an exit with a clipboard. As passengers passed by, he checked off names. A long line formed. Clicker tried to count, but he lost track at seventy-five. He estimated more than twice that number snaked in the line at the exit.

He checked his watch. It said 2:15 a.m. If the plane had just landed, it would take time before it unloaded its cargo and taxied to the terminal. But the Air Force would rather the passengers waited for the plane. With the People's Army of Vietnam surrounding the city, minimizing ground time was imperative.

Buses waited outside the exit. The Ngos and others filled the first bus. It worked its way from the gym toward the flight line. Clicker spotted the passenger terminal. The buses stopped on the flight line side of it. Across the runways, Clicker noted vehicle lights. There wasn't any air traffic, so Clicker concluded their plane was across the runways. He could not see the extent of the damage caused by the A-37 attack. Had that already been nearly twelve hours ago?

Clicker noticed lights moving across the runways to the left of the bus. He spotted a red flashing light among them.

It must be the Herk, he thought.

Clicker then heard another C-130 overhead. A second plane was circling to land. The lights approaching the runway stopped. The second C-130 landed. As soon as it passed the waiting aircraft, the first Herk crossed the runways. Clicker relaxed a little. Their ride out of here was close.

The plane's taxi lights turned toward them on the taxiway parallel to the runways.

WHOOSH! BAM! An explosion erupted behind the bus! Then more whooshing sounds and more explosions.

Clicker recognized the sound of rockets. He looked behind to see explosions impact the DAO compound. The rockets dashed Clicker's hopes in a second. The attack on Tan Son Nhut had resumed. He found himself trapped in the open on a bus full of civilians. Clicker's eyes met those of Sergeant Davis.

Above the din of the explosions, Clicker yelled, "We have to get to some shelter!"

Sergeant Davis tapped the driver's arm and pointed back toward the DAO. As the bus moved, Clicker heard the muffled crump of mortar rounds. The first ones impacted behind the DAO. But the explosions quickly walked toward that taxiing C-130. The booms were now loud. A round exploded in front of the C-130. Seconds later, another round exploded behind it.

"There's an artillery spotter very close!" Clicker yelled to Davis. "They are bracketing the plane!" Clicker looked back at the airplane as a flash lit up its right wing. "They've hit the Herk!"

By now, the bus raced toward the DAO, the site of the rocket impacts. There was no good place to hide.

"We have trenches around the compound!" Davis yelled to Clicker. He stood and raced to the back of the bus. The bus stopped before it reached the buildings. The driver opened the doors and stood.

"Help point the passengers to follow me!" he yelled over the continuing explosions.

The driver ran toward the nearest building, stopping before it. Clicker yelled at Anh to follow the driver. She shoved her daughters forward before jumping down the stairs to the ground. Clicker waved people forward and out the door, pointing to the waving driver. People disappeared behind him as he ushered them into the trench. People ran from the rear of the bus to the driver. Quickly, Sergeant Davis was behind Clicker.

"Everyone is out. Let's go!"

As his feet hit the pavement, a loud explosion knocked Clicker to the ground. Behind the passenger terminal, an orange fireball lit up the terminal.

"The Herk's fuel tanks have exploded!" Davis yelled.

Clicker picked himself up and ran to the trench. Between explosions, Clicker heard a C-130 overfly them. Was a third plane circling to land? Or had the second one taken off under fire? He wondered about the crew of the burning airplane. Did they have time to egress before it exploded?

The explosions from rockets and mortar rounds continued. Clicker heard the mortar rounds start near them, then walk away in a systematic pattern. The spotters were effectively cratering the runways, Clicker knew. Any aircraft evacuation had ended.

The smell of burning rubber and cordite filled the air. Clicker's hearing was gone, but each explosion shook the ground.

It was time for Option Four, the helicopters. But would the Communists allow that?

OPTION FOUR

———•———

The refugees huddled in the shallow trench for nearly two hours. The light of the burning C-130 reflected off the white buildings behind the trenches. Flashes from explosions strobed off the buildings. The artillery concussions moved away. Clicker knew they were hitting parked airplanes and helicopters. The parking spots contained revetments and covered shelters. Hopefully, a few aircraft would survive. Clicker had noticed several unprotected airplanes dispersed around the airfield. At least someone had learned a lesson or two from the other debacles the Army of the Republic had suffered.

As the gray dawn arrived, the shelling stopped. Clicker looked in both directions in the trench. He saw only bodies curled into fetal positions. It was impossible to determine the extent of any injuries. When no explosions occurred for several minutes, he peeked over the ledge. He climbed out warily and inched forward.

Fires sputtered among the remaining hulk of twisted metal and ash that once had been a C-130. Only the charred tail was recognizable. The passenger terminal looked intact with only shattered windows. Wafting smoke obscured further visibility in all directions. Burned gunpowder, metal, and rubber released an overpowering, pungent smell. Clicker's eyes stung.

Sergeant Davis joined Clicker. The curled bodies moved and peered over the edge of the trenches.

"We need to check for wounded," Clicker suggested.

The bus driver dashed to the bus which had miraculously survived the shelling. He ran back with a first-aid kit. Only one bus had sustained minor shrapnel damage. Other bus drivers retrieved kits from the other buses. They walked the trenches, checking for injuries. They stopped a few times to bandage wounds. The walkie-talkie cackled.

"Have everyone remain in the trenches," Sergeant Davis ordered. "Any serious wounds?" he asked the bus drivers.

"Just minor cuts and bruises," each reported.

He chatted into the walkie-talkie.

"I've asked for water to be brought out," he reported. "We're ordered to sit tight. Nobody knows what to expect next."

"Helicopters?" Clicker prompted.

Davis shrugged.

"We can only hope for a quick decision."

The sun rose high and started bearing down on the evacuees.

"If we keep everyone out here in the tropical sun, we'll have heatstroke to contend with," Clicker noted.

A water truck arrived and moved along the length of the trenches. The drivers restricted the thirsty crowd to two drinks each.

After an hour, the walkie-talkie crackled.

"Our backup generators have kicked in," Davis reported to the crew of drivers. "We're ordered to bus people back inside the buildings. Damage to the handball courts prevents us from using them. Let's move them to the Service Club. It's near the tennis courts, where the fences are being removed to make a helipad. The helicopters will land there."

"Are any inbound?" Clicker inquired.

"Negative," Davis responded.

"Why not?"

The sergeant shrugged.

"I'll go see what the plan is."

The buses drove the crowd to the Service Club. Across the swimming pool, Clicker saw the courts were free of any restriction to helicopters. Yet, the morning passed with no helicopters arriving. Colonel Tinh found his family's group. When he arrived, Clicker noticed an intensity he had never seen. Tinh checked all his family members. Only minor scratches and bruises comprised their injuries.

He joined Clicker in the shade by the door facing the courts and pool.

"What now?"

"I guess we are waiting on a decision on a helicopter evacuation," Clicker answered.

An hour later, Sergeant Davis returned.

"The Ambassador wants to come check out the runways himself."

Clicker was incredulous.

"Just how does he expect to get out here? The streets will be mobbed."

"And the ARVN has sealed up the airport tightly. Nobody can leave or enter. Two C-130s are in holding patterns off the coast. If the runways were usable, they will be our ride out."

"Only two planes?" Clicker clarified. He looked around. "Two Herks don't seem like enough. How many people are still inside?"

The sergeant shrugged. "Hundreds. The Embassy must have a thousand around it. We'll rescue more people with multiple helicopter flights. Hopefully, the Ambassador will make the obvious decision once he sees the damage to the runways."

Sergeant Davis left and wandered among the other groups. Past noon, Sergeant Davis hustled back to Clicker and Tinh.

"Choppers are inbound," he announced. "They are bringing in a company of fleet Marines to help us secure the perimeter. We have wounded to evacuate first."

"How serious?"

"We have two Marine KIAs. Civilian casualties also occurred in the handball courts. A rocket slammed into them."

Colonel Tinh swore in Vietnamese.

"We have to move our passengers near the tennis courts," Sergeant Davis explained.

Clicker helped guide the refugees to the buses. Damage to the gym was evident as the buses pulled near the tennis courts.

Twenty minutes later, a large helicopter landed on the tennis courts. Forty armed Marines in combat gear streamed off its rear ramp. Stretcher-bearers brought wounded victims out a door and rushed them up the ramp. Several had IV bags strung above them. The helicopter was on the ground for less than ten minutes. Its rotors bashed the tropical air, and the machine lifted off. Within minutes, another helicopter landed, and the entire process repeated. The passengers were a mix of stretchers and patients walking on their own.

Sergeant Davis's radio squawked. After a brief exchange, he walked over to Clicker and Tinh.

"We've broken your flight into three groups. Your family will board the third helicopter. Choppers are inbound now."

He headed to talk to another group.

Ten minutes later, another helicopter lumbered over the gym and landed on the tennis courts. It disgorged its complement of Marines. Army personnel ushered the first group to the helicopter's rear ramp. In less than ten minutes, it was gone. Fifteen minutes later, another helicopter touched down. Sergeant Davis led the second refugee group to it.

It was now the Ngo's turn. Yet, fifteen minutes elapsed. Clicker waited anxiously. No helicopter arrived. Clicker kept his ears cocked for the telltale whine of incoming artillery rounds. He didn't believe the North Vietnamese bombardment of Tan Son Nhut was over.

An hour passed. Clicker wondered if the helicopters required refueling after each trip. Maybe that was the delay. Alternatively, they could be picking up people at the Embassy. He could see that the wait worried the Ngos. Anh kept looking at the sky. The tropical sun beat mercilessly on the waiting refugees. The sun moved across the sky, so a sliver of shade helped.

Finally, the *whop-whop* of a helicopter reached the anxious group. Sergeant Davis waved the Ngos forward past the swimming pool. Clicker led the way. The helicopter lumbered over the damaged gym and landed on the tennis courts. The rotor wash beat on them, churning the heavy, smokey air. A crew member met them at the bottom of the ramp and pointed forward. Another of the crew led them to the very front. No seats were available, only the bare floor. The crewman motioned for them to sit down. Yelling over the noise of the engines and rotor wash was impossible. In minutes, the helicopter filled with passengers. Clicker felt it lift off. He had moved next to a small window. Nearby buildings gave way to a wider view. Throngs of people lined the base perimeter. He spotted ARVN troops holding them back. Saigon, it appeared, was in a full panic to flee.

The helicopter turned to follow the Saigon River to the coast. The embattled city disappeared, and Clicker saw the swamps south of the city that had hidden bandits over the centuries. After twenty minutes, the helicopter banked. Clicker saw only the ocean. In naval aviation terms, they had gone "feet wet."

Ahead in the South China Sea, the US fleet waited. In the dim light, Clicker looked at Anh and her family. All sat still on the hard floor. They appeared lost. Yet, a burden was lifted off Clicker's shoulders. He had successfully led them through the first step to their new lives. The Ngos had escaped the clutches of the Communists. But how many more steps lay ahead? And would the colonel escape?

—————•—————

PLANES ARE COMING

Dobie had returned to Bangkok almost a week ago. Jimbo had resurfaced to join Dobie and Charles. They met at breakfast every morning to discuss tasks for the day. The trio of retired Special Forces warriors had combed their contacts for anyone in Thailand. Jimbo had found one. Conveniently, he lived near a small civilian airport in northern Thailand. Jimbo could not determine how the veteran supported himself. He proved eager to help them. An airplane of questionable origin would have no trouble buying fuel, he assured Jimbo. Paying a premium price for gas would guarantee it.

Dobie and Charles sat at breakfast wondering why Jimbo hadn't arrived. Dobie shoved the last of his scrambled eggs into his mouth when Jimbo hustled into the hotel restaurant. He yanked out a chair and plopped down.

"Been listening to the news?" he asked.

"Not yet," Charles replied.

"Bad news from Tan Son Nhut. Yesterday afternoon, South Vietnamese airplanes bombed it."

Dobie's coffee cup stopped midway to his mouth.

"Turncoats?"

"Unclear, but that's not the worst. Early this morning, the Commies started shelling the airport in earnest. They nailed a Herk on the ground. The extent of the damage to the runway is still undetermined."

"Shit. We gotta get to U-Tapao ASAP, then," Dobie announced. "Those planes are coming."

He glanced at his watch.

"We leave in thirty minutes. I'll pack up the radio. We'll have to hire a driver to rush there."

"I'll be ready," Jimbo volunteered.

"Good."

"I'll find a driver while you pack up," Charles told Dobie.

Dobie stood, then hesitated. He looked at his comrades.

"What if we bought a car? We'll need transport when we get there."

"Mr. Peabody won't mind us using funds to expedite," Charles commented. "Good."

Dobie looked at Jimbo.

"You speak the best Thai. See what you can do."

Jimbo gave a casual salute.

"But finish your breakfast first. Let's reconvene in the lobby in an hour."

Two hours later, the trio piled their luggage into a battered Chevy. Jimbo had negotiated with a local mechanic. Dobie nodded in satisfaction.

"You drive," he instructed Jimbo. "I hate driving on the wrong side of the road, especially with the steering wheel on the left."

Three hours later, they pulled up to the main gate of U-Tapao Royal Thai Air Base. They showed their retired IDs to the Thai guard. Jimbo steered toward the flight line. Dobie wanted to scout the likely location where the Thais might park airplanes. It wasn't hard to locate.

"Looks like some airplanes beat us here, boss," Jimbo observed. Several South Vietnamese Air Force cargo planes stood on the grass at the south end of the flight line. Beside them, several tents stood. Crews worked assembling additional tents. Portable restrooms lined one boundary of the tent city.

"We have to get over there to look for our guy," Dobie stated.

Down a block, a street ran to the flight line. Jimbo drove to the gate. A Thai guard and an Air Force Security Policeman stopped them.

"IDs, please," the Thai guard demanded.

The trio pulled out their IDs. The guard studied them. He passed them to the Air Force guard.

"I'm sorry, the flight line is restricted to authorized personnel," the American informed them.

"Our friends from Tan Son Nhut have arrived here, Sergeant," Dobie lied. "We are their sponsors for the States. We need to find them."

"I'm sorry, but you'll have to inquire at the refugee administration desk."

"Where is that?"

"It is in the base operations building, four blocks down. It's the building with the flagpoles in front."

Recognizing that they would not talk their way past this guard post, Dobie smiled.

"Thank you, Sergeant."

The guard passed the IDs to Jimbo.

They found the refugee desk. The Thai official at the desk was not helpful. Jimbo spoke to him in a mixture of Thai and English.

"He says so many refugees have overwhelmed the processing system. We need to give them a few days to catch up."

They walked back to the car.

"It will only get worse in a few days," Dobie concluded. "Marcel doesn't have a few days."

"Let's try the Air America hangar," Jimbo suggested. "They might be more helpful. I remember where it is."

The hangar was a tattered building with a single door facing the street. The ten-foot chain-link fence along it had two strands of barbed wire at the top. Dobie tried the door. It didn't budge. Dobie pounded on it. A minute passed before Dobie noticed the eyehole darkened.

"Lieutenant Colonel Starbuckle is here to meet Cowboy," Dobie announced.

A latch rattled, and the door opened.

"Cowboy isn't here," an unshaven face reported through the small crack that had opened. Anticipating a question, Dobie flashed his retiree ID card. "Can we come in to talk?"

"State your business," the face demanded.

"Cowboy said to come here. We're here to help a couple of key refugees," Dobie pronounced.

The face hesitated a second, then swung the door open and stepped back. It opened into a small office with a single desk and two chairs.

"Cowboy won't be back for a few days."

"Perhaps you can help us," Dobie stated. "We are here to meet a specific plane from Tan Son Nhut, a C-123."

"I don't know anything about any C-123s," the face brusquely declared.

Dobie shrugged, trying to act calm when he wanted to punch the guy. But Jimbo's preferred approach would not help them. Dobie cast a glance at Jimbo. He didn't want Jimbo to lose patience. Jimbo gave a subtle nod.

Dobie didn't want to give any more information. The Hmong general was a key CIA asset in Laos. Dobie knew anyone here with Air America was likely involved with any rescue of the general. He didn't want their airplane or pilot commandeered by the spooks. He quickly concluded that stopping here had been a mistake.

"Okay. If you see Cowboy, tell him Dobie came by. I'm in town."

Dobie turned and led his group back to the car.

"The guy seemed a little jumpy to me," Jimbo observed. "Something must be up."

"I should have known better," Dobie admitted. "Let's find a lone Thai guard who may be more accommodating."

In ten minutes, Jimbo pulled the car to the edge of the tents. A Thai guard proved willing to assist, aided by the twenty dollars Jimbo slipped to him. While Charles stayed with their car, Dobie and Jimbo scurried among the tents. They searched for anyone who knew anything about the pilot who flew them. Late in the afternoon, they met Charles at the car.

"Let's go find a hotel and chow," Dobie ordered. "We'll have to try again tomorrow."

———•———

THE COUSIN

———✦———

Lieutenant Colonel Ngo Tinh knew he was in trouble. Had this idea been a rash act of vengeance? The crumbled handball courts where his family had waited and their destroyed airplane ignited a fuse of revenge. Twice, in a matter of minutes, the Communists had targeted his family. As soon as his family's helicopter disappeared, he ran to an F-5. He berated the crew chief to fuel it and ordered two pylons of cluster bombs. Even with the light bomb load and minimum fuel, he had nearly crashed on takeoff from the taxiway. Once he completed this desperate mission, he could not land on the cratered runways. He planned to eject at a low altitude over them.

Tinh descended low over the battlefield. To get a good look, he had slowed the sleek jet almost to landing pattern speed. He had one pylon of three cluster bombs remaining on his right outboard station. He needed a direct hit with it. The South Vietnamese troops below had stayed to fight to defend Tan Son Nhut. He had to help them. Without a direct hit on their foe, the enemy would overrun the ARVN troops. Truc, his future son-in-law, waited at the base for any Communist troops who survived this battle.

To his right, Tinh saw an AC-119 gunship firing at the enemy. They were the only two airplanes supporting the South Vietnamese fighters. One of his other pilots had been ready to join the fight. But they could find no bombs to arm the other F-5.

Ahead, Tinh saw the massed enemy. Two tanks supported the People's Army of Vietnam troops. The arrogance of the North Vietnamese army calling themselves that still irked him after twenty years. One tank had started on a bridge crossing the Dong Nai River. If he could hit that one on the bridge, it would block the bridge and snarl up their advance.

He shoved the throttles forward, lit his afterburners, and raised the nose to climb a little. More altitude would increase his accuracy. He rolled inverted in the climb to keep his target in sight. Pings told him he was taking small arms fire. Another two seconds ...

He pulled the jet back toward the earth and rolled upright, retarding his throttles. He centered the lead tank in his bombsight. More pings! He dropped the bombs.

As he pulled the nose up and rolled left, his peripheral vision caught a streak of smoke off his right wing. The nose sliced above the horizon, and he shoved the throttles into afterburners. He banked steeper and pulled. His slow speed and low altitude made him vulnerable to the Strela missile. The shoulder-fired anti-aircraft missile usually wasn't a threat to high-speed, maneuverable fighters. But he had sacrificed his advantage to ensure accuracy.

The F-5 shuddered as the missile exploded. The right engine fire-warning light flashed. He left the throttles in full burner. He needed all the thrust available to turn toward the friendlies. His left engine fire light illuminated. Colonel Tinh ignored both lights. The caution panel lit up.

He knew he was through flying this jet. He was a passenger now. It needed to carry him away from the enemy before he had to eject. But an explosion shook him. The jet yawed and rolled. Maybe he had flown far enough.

He moved his hands to the ejection seat armrests, pulled them up, and squeezed the triggers. The rocket-powered seat shot him out before the jet rolled on its side. He had a slim chance that his chute would open before he hit the ground. Still, Lieutenant Colonel Ngo Tinh felt a sense of satisfaction. He had done all he could to save his doomed country. If he never returned to his beautiful wife, she would understand. She would fight to save their family wherever they landed. He would miss seeing her beauty in her colorful Ao Dai dresses.

Tinh felt a slight tug as his chute opened. He looked to the ground, which rushed up. Tree branches slapped him as he plummeted into them. One jerk. Then another. He crashed to the ground.

He lay in a heap for several seconds.

Move, a brain wave ordered.

He reached for the quick-release buckles on his shoulders. Popping them open, he pulled down. He felt the tug of the chute release. Rolling over on his hands and knees, Tinh heard and felt the loud thud on the back of his helmet. He scrambled forward. Another blow hit him in the back. Arms pulled on his legs. He sprawled forward, and a mob descended on him. He was not among the friendly troops. These were the comrades of the soldiers he had just bombed.

As he had climbed into his jet for this mission, one random thought had jumped into his brain. If shot down, he would fight to the death. His adversaries, though, did not allow him the opportunity.

They jerked off his helmet, and blows rained on his head. His back was a favorite target as well. Tinh tried to raise his arms to protect his head. He needed to roll away, assess the adversary, and counterattack. But his attackers cinched his arms behind him. Ropes wrapped around his legs. Despair descended on him as he felt himself bound and unable to fight. The blows fell unimpeded.

As he approached the edge of consciousness, a loud voice boomed. He did not understand the words, but the blows ceased. More indistinct orders issued from the source. Hands dragged Tinh across the rough forest floor. Straps pulled across his chest, and he felt the rough bark of a tree against the back of his head. Another rope pressed under his chin and slid to his throat. His head banged against the rough bark again. The rope around his neck pulled tight, but enough slack allowed him to breathe.

Tinh blinked, trying to clear his head. Hands searched the chest pockets of his flight suit. His small wallet came out. It contained his identification card. More orders came from the command voice. Hands ripped his ID tags from his neck.

Seconds passed before more orders. In the shadows of the trees, Tinh saw two faces examining him. The mouth of one face formed a superior sneer. The other wore a perplexed expression. That face was familiar to Tinh. It brought back a forgotten memory from over twenty years earlier.

He had been on a riverbank near his village west of Vinh. He was drinking homemade rice wine with this man. Both had been young. The perplexed face now looking at him was Nguyen Quyên. He was the son of his mother's older brother. Quyên was two years older than Tinh. As boys, they had gone to school and had flirted with local girls together, out of sight of their traditional parents.

Tinh's memory was the last time he had seen this cousin. It had been a parting of ways, figuratively and literally. Tinh's father planned to flee south with his family. His father warned him to tell no one of the decision. Nguyen Quyển's family was staying. His father had been away for a few years, fighting with the Viet Minh against the French colonialists. In a hushed voice, Quyển was telling Tinh of his own decision. Quyển was leaving to join his father.

"We have to defeat the French oppressors," Quyển had argued.

Tinh recognized the Viet Minh party line.

"You know the Viet Minh are only tyrants from our people," Tinh had reacted. "We will trade one dictator for another."

"Maybe, at first. But when the revolution against the French is secure, it will no longer be necessary."

Tinh had scrutinized his older cousin. He couldn't tell if he believed his statement.

"The Minh need fighters who aren't hardcore Communists to ensure the tyrants are replaced. That can only come from within. Otherwise, we will continue to fight a civil war. Both sides will become hardened in their positions. Neither will compromise then."

"Do you believe the Communists will tolerate reformers?" Tinh had asked incredulously.

"Of course not," Quyển had replied. "That is why the reformers will have to pretend to be the most hardened Marxists."

Tinh had not thought of this conversation in over ten years. Then, another cousin had fled North Vietnam with his family for Saigon. Tinh had welcomed them into his home. Tinh had asked about Quyển.

"He is advancing rapidly," was the response. "Quyển has an excellent tactician's mind, like his father. He has led his soldiers to many victories. I think he will go far."

Tinh had thought that Quyển must be pretending very well. Or maybe he had stopped pretending.

Now, as Quyển and his comrade studied him in the jungle, Tinh realized he was about to learn which was true.

"We do not have time for prisoners," the comrade sneered. "Let's let our comrades finish him."

The comrade struck Tinh across the face with a rattan switch he carried.

The asshole carries the switch like a swagger stick, Tinh thought. He glared back.

"If he would become enlightened," Quyên added, "he will be useful when approaching Tan Son Nhut."

Tinh studied the dark insignia on both soldiers' fatigues. He thought Quyên wore the higher rank.

"He appears defiant already," his cousin observed. "Yet we can try another approach before giving up. I'll see to him when we have driven the reactionaries back."

He turned and issued orders to two soldiers. One soldier pulled Tinh's boots off. The soldiers then sat on either side of Tinh, pointing their AK-47s at him. Quyên and his comrade whirled and walked away.

Tinh heard the battle rage for another hour. The light faded before the sounds moved farther away. The explosions became less frequent. Tinh's head ached, and his parched throat burned. He inspected his legs. Blood stained his ripped left flight suit leg. He flexed his leg muscles and shifted. Both legs reacted with no increase in pain.

Good, no broken bones.

Tinh began evaluating his chances of escaping. With darkness falling, the best opportunity would be sooner rather than later. He knew the surrounding area. While trees surrounded him, he knew he must be close to the river east of Saigon. He had not noticed the river before he had to eject. Tan Son Nhut had to be twenty-five kilometers west. He would not have far to go to reach friendly troops.

Another hour passed. The light faded. Tinh knew the time to escape was rapidly closing. His captors would have no qualms about shooting him. Even his Communist cousin could be capable of that.

As he sat against the tree, Tinh watched his guards. Their interest in him had waned as Tinh had stayed still. He wiggled his bound wrists behind him. It felt like they were bound with a rope. That would be easier to tear than leather or web straps. He rubbed the rope against the rough tree bark. If only there was more noise from the battle to hide the sounds he made. He looked straight ahead so he could keep both guards in his peripheral vision. Whenever one looked his way, he stopped moving his hands. He could feel the ropes loosening behind him. The growing dark would help.

A plan formed in his mind. When he got his hands free, he had to untie his legs and get out of the rope holding him against the tree. Then, he would lure one guard over by feigning a convulsion. When the guard leaned close to him, he would grab the man's throat with both hands, squeeze, and twist to break his larynx. He would grab the rifle, point it at the other guard, and signal him to be quiet. *Then what?*

Before Tinh could devise the rest of his plan, another soldier walked toward them. His hopes sank. He could not overpower a third guard. In the dim light of dusk, he saw a shadow approach the guards. The shadow said something, and the guards moved several feet away and separated more. The figure turned and walked to Tinh. With the guards now farther away ... if only he had his hands free.

The figure knelt beside Tinh, but turned slightly, checking on the guards.

"We only have a few minutes before we have to move," Quyển stated.

Tinh remained quiet.

"I'll insist on maintaining control of you," Quyển continued. "You have to act compliant. Give me no reason to increase the guard on you."

The conversation sounded strange to Tinh.

"I'm through with this war," his cousin went on. "It's over anyway. In a matter of days, maybe hours, Saigon will fall."

Quyển looked around, as if he was ensuring no one was close enough to overhear.

"I've lost all my family to this war. My sons first. Then my wife and daughters. They died when our town was bombed. That was the official explanation. But it was a lie. They died when a surface-to-air missile fell back to earth and hit next to them. The missile came from twenty miles away."

Tinh became curious. This conversation was leading somewhere.

Quyển finally turned to face Tinh.

"I have no stomach for what will follow in Saigon."

Quyển must have seen Tinh's wrinkled brow in the dark.

"It will be the same as in every town we have conquered. We will kill the leaders to ensure the ones we install will follow orders."

He stopped to check around them.

"Your appearance has given me an idea of how we both can escape this war. And this lost country."

Tinh tried to study the face of his cousin in the dim light.

"The Americans are no longer flying helicopters into Tan Son Nhut. All the helicopters are now going to the Embassy. By tomorrow morning, we will convince them to abandon that, too. If we find an airplane, I expect you could fly us out."

Tinh hoped Khắc's plane would still be there if he could get to Tan Son Nhut quickly.

Four soldiers suddenly appeared from the trees and approached the guards. They then turned toward Tinh and Quyền. As they approached, Quyền stood and walked toward them. A hushed conversation ensued. The soldiers glanced toward Tinh twice during the exchange. The group approached Tinh.

"You refuse to tell me about the defenses at the air base," Quyền proclaimed, gesturing to Tinh. "But you will."

In the dim light, Tinh noticed Quyền's stoic face show a hint of a smile, which was not visible to the soldiers. Quyền turned to them.

"Keep him guarded well. I am not finished interrogating this prisoner. He will be useful to us. Make sure he doesn't escape."

Quyền turned and walked away, leaving two of the soldiers with Tinh.

As his cousin left, Tinh had to ponder. *Did Quyền want to defect? But how does a commander surrender to a prisoner? And was the smile real or only shadows in the dim light playing tricks?*

———•———

A FAMILIAR CARRIER

———⊢———

C licker lost track of time as the helicopter whirred toward the US fleet in the South China Sea. He checked his watch. The date and time engraved itself into his mind, April 29th, 1700 hours.

Finally, Clicker felt the helicopter slowing. Then his stomach told him they were descending. He looked out the small window. A familiar sight came into view, the flight deck of a US Navy aircraft carrier. The helicopter lurched.

The ramp opened, and sailors stepped in. They rushed people off the helicopter. Their brusque manner angered Clicker.

Come on, guys, he thought. *These people have just escaped death or imprisonment.*

Down the ramp, Marines shoved the crowd to the side of the ship. Clicker looked around. He had been on this aircraft carrier before. Of his two tours in the Vietnam War, one had been on this carrier.

The Marines escorted the refugees to the aircraft elevator. As the elevator started moving, Clicker heard the roar of a helicopter departing. He now understood the rush. More people waited in Saigon for its return.

He kept the Ngos together, ushering them through familiar space. They walked through the hangar deck. Past two watertight hatches, they stopped. Sailors had cleared a work bay for them. The smell of oil and aviation fuel permeated the air.

A heap of blankets stood along one wall. Next to it stood a pile of sailor work uniforms. The ship's crew had stacked the pants and shirts separately. Various rank insignias adorned the sleeves of short-sleeved and long-sleeved shirts. Faded dark blue pants lay beside them. Both pieces carried the look of many trips to the ship's laundry. Sailors had donated their older uniforms. Fortunately, they had thought to string cords through the loops for belts.

Clicker snatched six sets of clothes and six blankets. The clothes would be too large, but a custom fit did not matter. He passed a set to each of the Ngos.

He grabbed a blanket for himself.

"Just hang on to them," he instructed. "This space lacks precise temperature controls."

Clicker selected a space along a wall close to the hatch. He sat down. The Ngos followed his example. They waited for the next leg of their trip.

Throughout the afternoon and into the night, people continued to arrive. The space became crowded. The piles of clothes and blankets quickly disappeared. He had not grabbed clothes for himself; a step he regretted as the mass of bodies warmed the space. Air circulation was nonexistent. The odor of perspiring bodies filled the compartment.

Sleep became impossible during the night. The vast ship rolled gently, and the air quality continued to deteriorate. Seasickness took its toll on the crowded refugees. Clicker understood that US Navy ships did not contain space for thousands of extra inhabitants. The ship's captain was doing his best to accommodate the guests.

He hoped they would eventually head for Subic Bay, the Philippines. As he recalled, the trip took more than a day of sailing. Or would they? Could the US fleet abandon its post off the coast of Vietnam at this crucial time? Not likely, he concluded. So what then? The task force commander would shed the extra passengers as soon as practical. They could only interfere with his mission.

By midnight, the flow of refugees into their space slowed. Everyone struggled to keep a small space on the dirty floor. Anh encouraged her children to lie down and try to rest. She sat against the wall with her children between her and Clicker. Yet, she glanced at him often, questions evident in her face. He had no answers for her.

When the flow of people stopped, Clicker stood. He leaned close to Anh. He still caught a whiff of her perfume.

"I'm going to see if I can find out what's next. I'll be back."

She nodded.

Clicker weaved through the bodies on the floor to the hatch. He stepped into another crowded section of the hangar deck. He worked his way to the elevator to the flight deck. Before he arrived there, he encountered a cord and two US Marines.

"Sorry, sir, but you cannot leave."

"I'm trying to find out what's next, corporal."

The Marine eyed him.

"Refugees are still arriving here and on other ships."

"Will we head for Subic, then?" Clicker asked.

"Sorry, sir, we haven't been told anything."

"The passengers need water," Clicker continued.

The corporal looked past Clicker.

"I'll request some, sir," he answered. The corporal relaxed. "Do you mind my asking how you became a refugee?"

"It's a long story, corporal. But I'm very familiar with the operations on this aircraft carrier. Now, I'm helping a friend by getting his family out of harm's way."

"It's a classic case of SNAFU," the corporal volunteered. "You'd have thought someone would have figured out this could happen and prepared us better."

"The soldier knew someone had blundered," Clicker quoted.

The corporal gave him a quizzical look.

"It's from a poem written over a hundred years ago," Clicker answered.

"I'll ask for the water," the corporal stated. He turned to the private next to him and issued instructions.

"Thank you."

Clicker worked his way back to the Ngos. Anh's head bobbed as she dozed. He resumed his place on the opposite side of the children from her. Her beauty and poise awed him. A realization struck him: both ran deeper than her physical features.

When she had looked at him, even with the questions in her dark eyes, he had seen a fierce determination. His presence would not determine whether her family survived this ordeal. She would see to that. His presence could make it easier. Why had he never met a woman like her? Or had he, and he never noticed? Or had he been looking in the wrong places?

Clicker spent the rest of the night with his thoughts. They jumped randomly to different times in his life. He recalled events that led him to the present. The incident that caused him to leave the Marine Corps popped into his mind. Being a Marine pilot filled his search for adventure. It was his off-duty exploits that had cut his career short. Why had he found that admiral's seventeen-year-old daughter so enticing? The young lady possessed far more experience than the admiral knew.

The Ngos stirred occasionally. A daughter would awaken and stare into space. Then Tinh's son would look around. The boy looked overwhelmed.

As he looked at the Ngo group, Clicker realized that Anh's attention remained focused on her three children and her parents. The group who had arrived with Tinh at the shop must be a sibling and family, Clicker guessed. It was unclear whose sibling. They stayed close together. The other couple clung to each other.

Clicker remembered that Tinh once mentioned an older son. Where was he? His impression was that he had been the oldest child. Clicker replayed the two times the son had arisen in conversations. Tinh had spoken about him in the past tense. Clicker could only conclude that the son had died in the war.

Early in the morning, Clicker sensed a change on the ship. It was subtle. Throughout the night, he had heard planes landing above them. The sound of the catapult rumbled in a pattern. Clicker checked the time.

"0730," he muttered to himself. "April 30th."

He heard the sounds of aircraft recovery operations, but the catapults did not roar. The ship had recovered its air armada, and it had launched no planes.

Evacuation flights must be over, Clicker realized.

The circadian rhythms of the passengers awoke the few who had slept. Marines and sailors appeared through the hatch and cleared a space. Then, large kettles and large coolers arrived. Sailors supervised the distribution of a meager breakfast. Importantly, water was on the menu. The breakfast lacked eating utensils, but forks and spoons were foreign to the Vietnamese. Sailors spooned rice into a variety of bowls and canteen cups for the passengers. Insufficient numbers of them, though, required families to share one. Anh took one for her family. Clicker's canteen cup from his knapsack came in handy. He shared his cup with Bao. While insufficient, the food and water provided some fuel for the journey ahead. Clicker ensured Anh kept her canteen cup. She stuffed it into her small satchel.

Hours passed before movement through the hatch caught Clicker's attention. He noticed people moving. Another phase of the journey began. Another hour passed before two Marines stepped through the hatch. They directed people out.

"Let's go," Clicker motioned to the Ngos. "Take the clothes and blankets."

Through the hangar deck, the sailors and marines escorted them lower in the ship. Clicker knew where they were going. They were leaving the carrier. Several decks down, they stopped. Sailors led groups into landing craft, which they launched off the stern of the ship. Large numbers of people crowded into the flat-bottomed boats. As their boat departed, the ride became rough. The design of the landing craft did not suit the open sea, unlike a large ship's relative stability. Seasickness quickly broke out among the passengers. Clicker could only hope the ride would be short.

It wasn't. The craft bounced and heaved. It crashed through the waves. They were in a hurry. Kim and Thuan began crying from the discomfort. Anh hugged Kim. Thuan leaned against Clicker. He tried to comfort her. Bao sat stoically. Then the ride smoothed out.

"Put on the extra clothes," Clicker ordered. "Tie the blankets over your shoulders. We will have to climb out of the landing craft. You will need your hands free."

When the children hesitated, Anh repeated Clicker's instructions in Vietnamese. Thuan's shirt was covered with vomit. Anh helped her remove it and put on the large sailor shirt. Clicker realized that he had grabbed long-sleeved shirts for them all. He helped Kim and Bao roll up the long sleeves and pant legs.

A shadow fell over the craft. Clicker looked up and saw that the craft had pulled beside a large merchant ship. Rope ladders hung off its side. They would have to climb up to the deck of the ship.

"Take off your sandals," Clicker instructed. "Shove them into your shirts. Your bare feet will grip the rope better."

Anh again repeated his directions in Vietnamese. Others near them heard Clicker's idea and copied it.

The craft bobbed against the merchant ship, banging against it before bouncing away. Clicker worried about the grandparents. Could they make the climb? Would any of the elderly refugees arrive at the top? It looked to be ten to fifteen feet, but the bobbing of the ships caused the rope ladders to swing.

"Help your grandmother," Clicker instructed Bao. "Climb right behind her."

The boy looked unsure. Clicker helped the elderly lady to grab the ladder, then he led Bao to it right behind her. Bao rapidly understood. He climbed with one arm and supported his grandmother with the other. Clicker held his breath.

A shriek pierced the air from the other end of the landing craft. Clicker turned to see another older woman fall from the ladder. She hit the bottom of the craft with a loud thud. Blood pooled next to her head. She remained motionless. Clicker knew he could do nothing. He led Kim to the ladder and helped her start climbing. Bao pushed his grandmother over the edge of the ship. They both disappeared. Finally, the Ngos were up the ladder, and Clicker scampered up.

A platoon of Marines scattered themselves around the deck. They directed the refugees below to an empty hold. Another grimy, hard floor awaited them. Clicker remembered his carriers had taken thirty-five hours to reach Subic Bay. Was the merchant ship faster or slower?

Clicker feared that a hard trip awaited them. He felt himself growing close to the Ngos.

ESCAPE

—•—

Tinh watched Quyển walk away, trying to imagine what the suppressed smile meant. One soldier walked to Tinh and untied the straps securing him to the tree. The soldier loosened the ropes around his legs so he could walk.

"Stand," he commanded.

Tinh had trouble getting his feet under him. His body ached. Back spasms made walking painful. His shoulders throbbed. He worried about the ropes holding his wrists behind his back. Would the soldiers notice how loose they were? As if reading his mind, the soldier stepped behind and untied the ropes. He gave no sign he noticed they were loose. The soldier tied Tinh's hands in front, but also looped a rope around his arms above his elbows and behind his back. It gave Tinh slight movement of his arms. Tinh guessed they would be walking. The guard shoved Tinh forward.

"Walk."

As Tinh had suspected, they were in a forested park surrounded by a city neighborhood. When they reached a street, the soldier prodded Tinh to walk down the middle. Military vehicles clogged the road. Ahead, Tinh could make out an outline of a tank. He calculated they were moving toward Saigon, close to the river east of the city.

Crossing a bridge, he saw the little light reflect off a narrow stream. Tinh was grateful his captors had not blindfolded him. This was a narrow channel. He had landed on an island with this channel on the west. The major river curved from the north to the east of the island. He knew all the bridges leading to Saigon. The tank he had bombed was right behind them. No wonder Quyển's comrade had suggested they kill him.

While Tinh could walk clumsily, he could not run. He needed to loosen the bindings on his legs and hands. The ropes were well-positioned to restrict his movement. He had to be content with rubbing the bindings on his wrists together to loosen them. Tinh tried to keep track of who and what was behind him to know if slipping away in the dark held any promise. The best way to do that, he calculated, was to trip and fall to look behind.

The first time he fell, the reaction was swift. Rough arms jerked him back to his feet. Soldiers surrounded him. He had to bide his time. When they met some resistance, they would shift their attention from their prisoner.

Tinh plotted the timing. The column was moving at a quick walk but halted frequently. At a brisk pace, Tan Son Nhut was a four- to five-hour walk. A slow walk might take six to eight hours. He would need a bike or scooter to stay ahead of the invasion force after his escape.

Tinh's eyes roved from one side of the street to the other. The population had fled this highway, leaving it to the invading army. As the evening wore on, the curfew further emptied the streets. An abandoned bike or scooter was unlikely. Refugees would have used all available to flee. So he had to get off this route when he escaped. Tinh knew this major highway went straight for another ten kilometers. Then a couple of sharp turns would lead them to the last major bridge across the Song Sai Gon, the Saigon River. His escape had to happen within this ten-kilometer stretch.

The challenge, Tinh knew, was that this highway was one of only two roads that ran for any distance. The only other road going west for any distance was south of them. All other streets were local ones that came to dead ends near parks or streams. So, his escape would have to be to the south. He also remembered that two or three other roads crossed this highway that led to the other western route. His escape would have to be at the first one. He had to recognize it when they crossed it. But would he?

The convoy walked for about two hours before gunfire in front caused it to halt. The invaders had encountered a pocket of resistance. Soldiers behind Tinh moved ahead. After several exchanges of gunfire, Quyền and the other senior officer appeared out of the dark.

"It is time to find out what the prisoner will tell us," Quyền told his comrade.

"I will help," the companion replied with a smirk.

From this soldier's attitude, Tinh surmised he was the unit's political officer.

That role advanced party dogma and ensured compliance. It reported up a separate chain of command.

Quyển grabbed Tinh's left arm and led him to a building on the left side of the street. He broke down a door and threw Tinh to the floor. Quyển drew his pistol, knelt next to Tinh, and placed a map on the floor. He lit a lantern from a nearby table. He pointed the pistol at Tinh's head.

"What is another route to Tan Son Nhut?" he demanded. The companion crouched close.

Without warning, Quyển shifted his pistol and shot the companion in the head.

"I've been waiting a long time to do that," he remarked, turning back to Tinh. "This commissar has punished my soldiers repeatedly for not reciting his lies with enough enthusiasm."

He holstered his pistol. Quyển gestured to the still body with the pool of blood next to the head.

"He would have enjoyed the killings that will follow the Communist victory."

Pulling a knife from a pocket, he cut Tinh's bindings.

"Is your family safe?" he asked.

"They should be on an American ship by now."

"Good." Quyển picked up the map. "How do we get to Tan Son Nhut ahead of this army?"

Tinh recovered from his shock. He pointed at the map.

"This road," he replied, finding the first cross street to the alternative route. "Where are we in relation to it?"

"It's about a hundred meters ahead. There is resistance past it. How do we get there and away from them?" Quyển motioned his head toward the door.

"We have to go south a block or two, then pick our way through the neighborhoods. To get to Tan Son Nhut, we need a scooter or bike."

"Let's get moving," Quyển answered. "Take his sandals and pistol."

Tinh removed the sandals and pistol from the dead political commissar. Quyển went through a second door in the room toward the rear of the building.

"Here is a side door."

Both men exited the building and threaded their way between buildings, away from the marching army.

The pair scooted from one building to another, finding passages between buildings that headed south. Tinh led the way. They traveled for an hour before they came to a wide street crossing their path. Tinh studied it, looking both ways.

"I know this street," he informed Quyển. "If we go to the right, we should find the street that heads west toward the river."

The dark street was deserted. They soon came to the wider street running west. A few lights illuminated the way, but the street appeared deserted. Glimpses of light came from several buildings as they passed.

"We need faster transportation," Tinh noted.

He looked between buildings as they passed each one. After another hour of walking, Tinh stopped.

"Here's what we need."

He walked to an alley and came back with a pedicab. Tinh sat on the bicycle seat, motioning for Quyển to the passenger seat in front. As he pedaled down the street, artillery booms sounded northeast of them.

"They've started shelling the airport," Quyển observed. Seconds after the shelling began, explosions lit up the dark horizon toward Tan Son Nhut.

"I hope some taxiways remain intact," Tinh said.

"They'll focus on the runways initially, then on locations of parked planes, fuel, and ammunition," Quyển noted.

"I'm sure you have artillery spotters inside the air base," Tinh commented.

"They do. They'll be radioing adjustments to the gunners."

"I hope they miss the airplane that I hope is there and the taxiway near it."

"You have an airplane to fly out?"

Tinh told him about the crew chief.

"We have to get there before the shelling damages it."

Tinh suddenly stopped pedaling and braked to a stop. He looked left, then right. He spun into the dark alley to their right.

"What's wrong?" Quyển inquired.

"A military police jeep two blocks ahead."

He got off the bike and peeked around the corner of the building. He turned back to Quyển.

"You need to get out of your uniform."

Quyển unbuttoned his shirt.

"I'll turn it inside out."

"Fortunately, the jeep turned to head away from us. I don't think they saw us."

He continued watching around the building's corner. Quyển knelt and peered down the street, too. Both could see only the silhouette of the vehicle in the darkness. Then they saw it turn in their direction. Tinh looked into the dark alley.

"Let's get deeper into the darkness."

Tinh began pushing the pedicab. Its wheels squeaked. He shoved it into an alcove.

"Better if we leave it here," he advised as he led Quyển down the alley. Another recess in the buildings appeared. Tinh crept into it. Quyển followed him. Tinh dropped to one knee.

"You don't have my ID or dog tags?" he queried Quyển.

"No."

"If they find us, we'll be shot as saboteurs."

Tinh drew his pistol. Quyển drew his sidearm as well. They waited in silence. The military police jeep crept along the street and stopped at the alley's entrance. One soldier stepped out, and a bright flashlight flicked on. Tinh and Quyển ducked back into the recess.

They saw the beam of light flash around the alley, lighting the building across from them. The beam disappeared momentarily. Then it settled on the ground in front of them. Both men flattened themselves against the wall. It lit up the wall next to them. Each held their breath. It disappeared again, and they heard footsteps walking away. A tense minute later, they heard low talking. Gears ground, and the jeep drove away.

Tinh leaned forward to peer around the corner. But Quyển, feeling rather than seeing Tinh move, extended his arm to stop Tinh. They stood in silence for another minute. The flashlight suddenly flicked on and flashed around the alley.

A low voice said, "It's clear."

Footsteps receded, and they heard the jeep drive away. Another minute passed. Quyền leaned forward and looked around the corner.

"They've left."

Both men holstered their weapons.

"Close call," Tinh remarked.

The thump of artillery continued to their east. As Tinh walked the pedicab to the street, flashes lit up the sky to their west.

"They will keep up the barrage for a couple of hours," Quyền commented. "How far do you think we are from the base?"

Tinh shrugged. "Ten kilometers. In another kilometer or two, this road turns north at an angle. It joins the road your army is on near a major intersection. If the South Vietnamese Army is going to fight, they'll have an ambush set there. Our shortest route to the air base is going north at the intersection."

"If they plan to fight, I don't think that a single military police jeep would wander around. They would have patrols checking this area, looking for a flanking force. I'd guess that Jeep is out all alone. Your army has probably fled. That's been the pattern. I expect that the resistance we met when we escaped is the only force stopping the attack on the base."

"Then we had better get moving if we want to beat them there," Tinh remarked.

He climbed onto the pedicab, and Quyền sat in the passenger cab. They reached the turn to the north quickly. Tinh stopped. He listened. The only sounds were the explosions of the artillery. Quyền stepped out and drew his weapon.

"Let's walk slowly," he whispered.

Ahead, they could see the major road in the flashes of the explosions. They reached the road. It seemed quiet.

"Once the force clears out the resistance back there," Quyền said, pointing to their right, "a scouting patrol will check this intersection. We'd better move."

They climbed onto the pedicab, and Tinh pedaled north. Another major intersection appeared. Tinh turned left. The Army of the Republic of Vietnam was nowhere to be seen.

"We'll come to the bridge across the Saigon River," he told Quyền in front of him. "If the army has blown it, the next bridge is a long way south."

They reached the bridge and crossed it. Nothing would impede the invading army when it rolled into Saigon. Thirty minutes past the bridge, Tinh slowed the pedicab to a walk. The explosions lit up the sky.

"Will the artillery avoid hitting the army's road to the base?" he asked Quyên.

"Most likely. They're likely to shell it only if they meet resistance."

"Then we'll creep up as close as we dare. In the shelling's chaos, the guard posts are probably abandoned, if not destroyed."

"Looks like we are a couple of kilometers away," Quyên remarked. "Where on the base is this airplane?"

"If it survives the shelling, it will be in a group of abandoned and destroyed airplanes north of the runway. Our passengers will be hiding among the wrecks."

"Clever place to hide it," Quyên noted. "The artillery spotters are not likely to waste shells on wrecked airplanes."

"How long have you had spotters at the airport?"

"A couple of days."

Tinh turned right, and the explosions were close in front of them.

"The main gate is just ahead," Tinh shouted. It was difficult to hear over the din of the bombardment. "Tell me when you think we are close enough."

The ground now shook beneath them. Flashes of the rounds destroyed their vision. Quyên raised an arm.

"Let's wait behind that wall," he gestured to their right. "This could go on until dawn."

As Tinh sat down with his back to the wall, he realized how tired he was. He had been awake for at least thirty-six hours. He had rested while he waited with his family for their evacuation flight. But he felt too keyed up to get any actual sleep. Dozing on the ground at the airport did not provide rest. Now, napping would be impossible. The loud explosions continued to reverberate and rock the ground. He had nothing with which to plug his ears. Still, he closed his eyes.

Tinh had no sense of how long they sat against the building. Debris fell from the roof and the concrete wall. Suddenly, silence ensued. Tinh and Quyên looked at each other.

"If it doesn't start again in a few minutes, it means they have finished. They will move forward, dragging the guns with them."

They waited several minutes. No shelling started.

"Let's go," Tinh directed.

Standing required great effort. His muscles twitched; his legs cramped. Tinh willed himself to go on. *I can rest after we take off*, he told himself.

"Do you want me to peddle?" Quyên asked. "You can point the way."

"Yes." Tinh sat in the passenger seat, and Quyên straddled the seat.

"Straight up the road," Tinh ordered.

They began to run over clothing on the road. Tinh signaled to stop. He leaned out to pick up a piece. Quyên did likewise. They inspected the clothing. Weapons littered the road as well.

"Army uniforms," Tinh noted. "It means the soldiers have deserted."

He held a shirt up to size it. Quyên grabbed an M-16.

"You better take off your uniform and put this on," he told Quyên, handing the shirt to him. "It would be a shame to get shot by the one soldier who didn't drop his weapon."

Quyên quickly changed shirts. Then he pedaled on. Five minutes later, Tinh held up his hand. Quyên stopped.

"Just ahead is the army checkpoint before the main gate."

He studied it in the dark. He couldn't tell if it was manned. Tinh twisted in his seat. "Let's have our weapons easy to draw if we need them. I'll order anyone there to let us pass. I'll say we are going to get an airplane to support the army. Don't shoot unless I start it. Let's pedal up to it with some urgency."

Quyên nodded. He reached for the M-16, checked the magazine, and chambered a round. He handed it to Tinh. Quyên unsnapped the strap holding his pistol in the holster. The pedicab lurched forward as Quyên pedaled fast.

As they approached the guard station, Tinh could see two soldiers at it. As they pulled up to them, one stepped in front of the pedicab, M-16 at the ready position. Quyên slowed to a stop.

"I'm Lieutenant Colonel Tinh. We need to get to another airplane to support the army. Let us through."

The soldier studied them. He looked at Tinh, then inspected Quyên. Tinh was glad that Quyễn wore the army shirt. Its insignia was that of a corporal.

"The runways are not usable," the guard informed them.

"I'll find a taxiway to take off from. I know my squadron has airplanes ready."

"Where are you coming from?"

"I flew yesterday afternoon. I was shot down. It took me until now to work my way back. This soldier offered me a ride."

The guard thought it over.

Finally, he said, "Go on. I don't think you'll find any airplanes left."

He stepped aside and saluted Tinh. Tinh returned the salute as Quyễn pedaled past. No one guarded the main gate. Tinh motioned straight ahead. He thought of going straight along the taxiways but decided against it.

To keep his energy after his adrenaline stopped surging, he needed some food. He motioned Quyễn to the right toward the Defense Attaché buildings. They had a snack bar. If looters hadn't emptied it already, it would be the only place to find something to eat.

He directed Quyễn to the right. Fires smoldered to their front.

"Either your army shelled it or the Americans blew it when they left," Tinh commented.

"Could be both," Quyễn replied. He stopped the pedicab.

Tinh pointed to the Service Club. He hoped that the shelling might have spared it. And he remembered seeing cases of Army C-rations stacked in the halls.

"We'll make a quick stop for something to eat and drink. Stop here."

He jumped out of the seat and strode to the door, motioning Quyễn to follow. The battery-powered emergency lights were on. It looked intact. The looters hadn't arrived yet.

Inside, Tinh spotted the cases of C-rations. Grabbing the small can opener on top, he rummaged through the top case. He grabbed canned fruit, crackers, and tins of peanut butter. He left the canned Spam and stew. Finally, he grabbed water bottles from a case.

Tinh pried open two cans of fruit, giving one to Quyễn, and then drained two bottles of water. He stuffed cans into his flight suit pockets. In minutes, he was ready to go. The pair raced out the door to the pedicab. He had one other stop to make at a small office he had spotted on his visits. Hopefully, two other items he needed would be there. The C-123 required a headset to talk on the radio. Some kind of navigation chart for Thailand was a necessity, as well. He had carried one with him on his flight, but that one had gone down with his F-5.

"I'll drive again," he said as he straddled the driver's seat. Quyển climbed in, and they headed toward the main buildings. He inched around the debris. He located the remains of the building he wanted. The building was too destroyed for him to enter.

Tinh had to hope that Khắc had a headset. He pointed the pedicab toward the tarmac.

———•———

THE AIRPLANE

―――

Tinh pedaled to the ramp and spotted the glow of embers in the smoldering C-130. He headed straight toward the burned hulk. Other fires burned around the airport, which offered the only flickering light on the dark airfield. Beyond the burned airplane, Tinh noticed a windsock. The wind was light, and he made a mental note of its direction.

Quyển checked his watch against the light of the surrounding fires. They had about an hour before the dark gave way to predawn light. If the airplane and the crew chief were still here, they had to find it quickly. Then they would have enough time to rush everyone on board and leave before sunrise. Quyển had said that shelling would resume at dawn.

Tinh rounded the remains of the burned C-130 and pedaled toward the runway. The air base's graveyard was across the parallel runways and to the left. As the pedicab crossed the runways, Tinh looked left and right. Was there enough space between the holes for a short-field takeoff in the C-123? The fires did not provide enough light to tell.

Across the runways, he turned left onto the parallel taxiway. The graveyard was halfway down the taxiway. His eyes searched in the shadows on his right for the wrecked airplane hulks. In another few hundred feet, he saw them. He angled to the edge and slowed. Could he find the undamaged airplane among them? The crew chief would have taxied the plane here, so it had to be just off the taxiway.

He spotted the silhouette of a C-123 and braked to a stop. It looked deserted. The nose wheel was almost flat. He turned and coasted to it. In the murky light, he saw an open engine panel on the left engine. Was this the right airplane?

"Is that the airplane?" Quyển asked.

"Not sure."

Tinh stopped and approached the plane. As he neared the crew door, a shadow emerged from the dark.

"Get away," it ordered.

Tinh saw an M-16 pointed his way.

"I'm looking for Sergeant Khắc," Tinh responded.

The M-16 barrel lowered slightly.

"Why?"

"I'm to meet him at an airplane," Tinh responded.

"Why?" the shadow demanded.

This game of questions is wasting time, Tinh thought.

"He wanted my help."

"Why?" the shadow demanded again.

"Drop the gun or you are dead," Quyển ordered from the darkness on Tinh's right.

Before the shadow responded, another voice behind him spoke.

"It's okay, Hai."

Sergeant Khắc emerged from the darkness.

"Colonel Tinh is our pilot."

The crew chief walked to Tinh.

"You'll have to forgive Hai," he began. "He has kept the airplane secure. We have had a lot of interest in it."

"Is it flyable?" Tinh asked, pointing to the nose wheel. He glanced at the open engine panel.

"A little camouflage," Khắc responded. "I heard you went down. I thought we were doomed."

"My cousin found me," Tinh replied. He motioned to Quyển in the dark. "He needs to come with us."

"Okay," Khắc replied.

"Can you get the plane ready?"

"I'll pump up the nose wheel and close the panel."

"Fuel?" Tinh quizzed.

"As you ordered, sir."

"The passengers?" Tinh continued.

"All here."

"Did Private Truc get here?" Tinh asked.

"No," Khắc replied.

Tinh's shoulders slumped. Then he motioned Hai and Quyển over.

"Here's my plan," he began. He turned to Quyển. "Are there troops with missiles west and south of us?" he asked his cousin.

"Saigon is surrounded. Only the swamps between the city and the sea do not contain the People's Army."

"How close are they to the American embassy and palace?"

Quyển shrugged. "In the last few hours, you have to assume close."

"Do you have a flare pistol and flares?" he asked Khắc.

"Only two flares and the pistol."

"What about a headset?"

"I have one."

"Quyển," Tinh continued, "I want you lying on the ramp with the flares as we fly out, looking for any missiles coming up. Shoot at them." He turned to Hai and Khắc. "Get one more passenger who can handle a gun."

They looked at each other and nodded. Tinh unbelted his gun holster and handed it to Hai.

"No one else gets close to the plane. Once we start engines, they'll come at us. Position yourselves in the troop doors. Quyển will cover the ramp."

Everyone nodded. Tinh turned to Khắc.

"It will get light soon. As soon as we have enough light, we need to leave. I need to find enough taxiway for takeoff. I want you in the copilot's seat," he finished, gesturing to Khắc.

"Yes, sir," Khắc replied.

"Sergeant Khắc," Tinh stated, "I need your help to fly this airplane. It will not be disrespectful for you to tell me something I need to do. Is that clear?"

"Yes, sir," Khắc repeated.

"Good. Let's get everyone on the airplane," Tinh ordered.

Khắc and Hai turned to the tail of the plane.

A minute later, shadows emerged from the wrecked airplanes and started climbing into the airplane. They used both troop doors and the ramp. They were eerily quiet. Adults lifted children into the troop doors. Several carried a single small bag. Tinh knew the bags would contain their life savings, converted into gold chains or diamonds of dubious quality. He had sent his wife out with their savings in a pouch strapped around her waist.

"Can we make it?" Quyến asked.

"If the gunners have left me enough taxiway," Tinh answered.

"They would have focused on the runway and airplanes."

Several minutes passed. Khắc approached them.

"Everyone is on board."

Tinh looked to the sky, then the ramp.

"I'll check the taxiway."

"I'll come with you," Quyến stated.

They walked to the pedicab. Tinh looked both ways.

"The taxiway was cratered the way we came. I hope it's better in the other direction."

Tinh pedaled down the taxiway, straining to examine it. He weaved in both directions to survey the damage. Along the graveyard, the damage looked limited. A few hundred meters beyond it, craters littered the taxiway. He stopped the bike. He studied the pattern of the holes. Beyond them, the taxiway looked clear in the dim light. Tinh paced off the distance of the craters from the edge of the taxiway. He nodded.

"I think we have room."

He pedaled a little further down the ramp. Tinh stopped and looked at the sky. The blackness was receding. In the distance, an airplane engine started. Then the pulsating *whop* of helicopter blades reached them. Tinh and Quyến exchanged glances.

"As my American friends would say," Tinh started. "It's time to get out of Dodge."

Quyến gave him a puzzled look.

"Time to go," Tinh explained.

He pedaled furiously back to their airplane. The light continued to improve. As soon as he saw the plane, Tinh raised his left arm and made a circular motion with his hand. Seconds later, the rumble of a small engine started. Then, an aircraft engine backfired, and the right propeller of their plane started turning. Seconds later, the left engine coughed and blew black smoke, and its propeller turned. Despite the tension he felt, Tinh smiled. Sergeant Khắc had been watching. The crew chief had heard the helicopters start and knew it was time to go. By the time the pedicab reached the airplane, both engines were idling. Tinh stopped.

"Get to the back. We are leaving," he ordered his cousin.

Quyển grabbed the M-16 off the pedicab seat. Tinh pushed the pedicab past the left propeller as Quyển rounded it and ran to the troop door. Tinh rushed up the steps. As he pulled the door closed and latched it, the whine of the small jet engines reached his ears. This C-123 had small jets mounted outboard of the main engines. The crew chief expected they would need them for takeoff. Tinh bounded up the steps to the cockpit and climbed into the left seat. He scanned the engine instruments as he buckled his seat belt. Unfamiliar with the instruments, he turned to the crew chief in the right seat.

"Everything good?"

"Yes, sir."

Tinh looked down.

"Parking brake?" he asked.

Khắc pointed to the lever. Tinh jiggled it. It moved. He looked at Khắc, who gave him a thumbs-up. Tinh moved the throttles forward, and the plane began rolling. He looked down to his left and grabbed the nose gear steering wheel. With it and the brakes, he pointed the nose of the transport down the taxiway. As he added power, figures rushed from the right out of the hulks of wrecked airplanes. They raced toward them. Above the roar of the engines, Tinh heard the sharp reports of an M-16. The figures hesitated, and then they were past them. Tinh strained to spot the craters in the taxiway in front of them. If he hit one, their escape was doomed.

Tinh shoved the throttles forward. The plane accelerated. He gingerly eased it past a crater in front. As the airplane gained speed, Tinh gently steered around others. He steered the plane to the edge of the taxiway. Releasing the nose steering wheel, Tinh cradled the yoke with his left hand. Now, only gentle turns with the rudder pedals were possible.

"Call takeoff speed," he yelled to the crew chief. He hoped the chief knew the speed.

Seconds later, the chief yelled, "Five knots still!"

A large bump shook the airplane. It swerved left. Tinh immediately eased the yoke back. The rough roll smoothed out. Tinh recognized they had lifted off the taxiway. Below takeoff speed, he was in ground effect. He was riding the cushion of air rushing under the wings, keeping the plane off the ground. Floatplane pilots used ground effect to break free of the tug of the water before the aircraft would fly on its own. The plane wasn't ready to fly yet. A few more seconds ...

"Takeoff speed," Sergeant Khắc yelled.

Tinh eased the yoke back slightly. They were flying now!

"Gear?" Khắc asked.

"Wait," Tinh commanded. Raising the gear would help them accelerate and climb. But that last thump concerned Tinh. He needed to know if it had blown the left tire.

"See if someone can check the left tire," he ordered. Tinh checked their altitude. With the city surrounded, Tinh leveled off five hundred feet above the rooftops. He eased the plane into a gentle left turn toward the middle of the city. It was their only safe route out. Khắc turned and rapidly spoke to someone behind them.

Tinh kept the plane at twenty knots above takeoff speed. He didn't know the limiting speed with the landing gear down, but he didn't want to blow the landing gear doors off the airplane. Damage was likely if they blew off. As the plane turned, he searched the city for the American embassy. Turning to the east, the sky brightened with the approaching dawn. Sweat dripped into Tinh's eyes. His wet palms cradled the yoke.

Don't clench it, he ordered himself.

Tinh spotted the embassy in the dawning light. He planned to fly between it and the Presidential Palace. As the embassy swung to the left side of the windshield, Tinh rolled the wings level. A bright sun exploded over the horizon. He didn't have his sunglasses, so he squinted. The sun was a large yellow chrysanthemum filling the eastern horizon. Tinh's mother had placed bunches of the flowers on their doorstep at Tet. She explained they would bring equilibrium and stability for the new year. He could only hope that they would usher these qualities into the new life he flew to.

As he looked toward the US Embassy, a helicopter lifted off its roof. It turned toward the Presidential Palace.

The pilot knows the way out, he figured. *I'll follow him to the coast.*

As Tinh banked to follow the helicopter, he spotted two smaller helicopters on each side of the large one. Then, a glint high above grabbed his attention. He looked up and spotted two dark spots.

Of course, he thought. *The Americans have air cover. If only we had such assets, maybe I wouldn't be running away now.*

He did not need a US Navy fighter pilot on his tail with a twitchy trigger finger. Tinh aimed for the river which led to the sea, staying to the left of the helicopters. He could fly parallel to them and not look threatening. He turned to the crew chief.

"Let's turn on the radios," he ordered.

The crew chief reached to the center console between them and twisted two knobs. Tinh plugged the headset into his radio/intercom panel and put one headphone over his left ear.

"We need to have the Guard channel on," he explained. He motioned above them. "There are US fighters up there. If they talk to us on the emergency frequency, we want to hear them."

The crew chief craned his neck to look.

"I don't see them," Sergeant Khắc stated.

"They are there. I saw them."

On cue, Tinh heard, "Taco One on Guard. Charlie One Two Three near the Embassy, state your intentions!"

A Navy fighter was calling them.

Tinh keyed the microphone switch on the yoke.

"Charlie One Two Three over the Embassy is a refugee flight. Our destination is U-Tapao."

"Roger," came the reply. "Call if you need assistance."

Tinh felt a glimmer of hope. Now he had air cover, at least for a few minutes.

As the Embassy slid past on his left, Tinh looked down. At five hundred feet above, it gave him a clear view of the chaos surrounding it. Hundreds of people clambered over its walls. Thousands lined the perimeter and the streets. As his aircraft slid by, a group charged through a door on the roof. He spotted heads turning skyward.

Further left between the rooftops, Tinh spotted the bridge to Saigon, which he and Quyển had crossed two hours earlier. North Vietnamese tanks approached it. The other side of the American helicopter seemed like a better idea. He wanted to steer clear of the People's Army of Vietnam. As he banked right to cross behind the helicopter, he hoped the Navy fighters above did not misinterpret his move.

Then he spotted tracer rounds arcing toward the helicopters from the left. They arced below and behind. Tinh eased the nose lower.

Movement behind him caught Tinh's attention.

"I can't see the tire," he heard.

Tinh looked to the crew chief. Time to raise the landing gear. But he had wanted to know the status of the tire first. Tinh feared the swerve on takeoff indicated a blown tire.

Guess I'll have to assume a flat tire.

He reached for the gear lever and raised it. Then he shoved the throttles forward. He stayed low until the swamp and away from any potential missiles that might come their way.

As the wide river slid below the nose, Tinh rolled right to follow it to the sea. He did not see the streak of smoke rise from the city on his left and head his way.

———•———

THE FLIGHT

Quyển lay on the raised ramp of the airplane, peering out the open cargo door. He swept his eyes from left to right, looking for any telltale streak of smoke. Tinh was flying a few hundred feet above the rooftops as the plane rolled out of its turn after takeoff. The airport slid out of view. Quyển looked to his right, where the closest concentration of the People's Army advanced.

A bridge came into view between the buildings. PAVN tanks drove to it. That was where a missile would most likely come from. Yet, Quyển could not ignore other directions. But his scan always returned to the bridge, even when it disappeared between the buildings.

After a few minutes, he felt the plane bank again, this time turning to his left as he faced rearward. Then he heard the M-16 behind him fire a short burst. He turned. The man kneeling in the troop door excitedly pointed out when he saw Quyển look. It was the signal they had arranged if one scanner thought he saw a missile.

Quyển scrambled to the door on his knees, not wanting to stand up and risk falling toward the open door. A single white strap crossed the door, but sizable gaps gave enough room for a man to fall through. By the time he reached the door, the scanner excitedly pointed behind them. The plane had turned far enough that Quyển crawled back to the ramp.

A streak of white smoke had risen above the buildings and was coming straight for them. It was a missile. Quyển pointed the flare pistol at it and fired.

The flare streaked out to the smoke. Quyển snapped the barrel of the flare pistol down and pulled out the spent casing. He grabbed his last flare from his shirt pocket and jammed it into the pistol. The barrel snapped back into place.

Quyển hesitated for a second. He didn't want to shoot his last flare if it wasn't necessary. The plane rolled out of the turn. Quyển could see they were over the river, and they were heading south, following it to the sea. The danger was much less ahead. He studied the path of the smoke. Did it follow his first flare? He could not tell. The last flare streaked away as Quyên pulled the trigger.

Now, he could only hope the missile would track one of the two flares. Otherwise, their flight was going to be brief.

Time slowed as Quyên studied the path of the missile and the diverging tracks of his flares. The missile turned away from the airplane to track a flare.

Quyên spotted a speck in the sky over the area of the missile's source. Then, explosions erupted on the ground. Another speck pulled out of a dive. Seconds later, more explosions.

A hand began slapping Quyên's shoulder. He looked to see a jubilant smile from the scanner holding the M-16.

"Good shooting!" the scanner yelled.

They were safe, as long as no units of the People's Army had penetrated the jungle and swamps below. Quyên felt confident that the path was clear. This would have been the route all those helicopters had taken. It was likely that other US Navy fighters had neutralized any threat along the river to the ocean. Quyên identified a collection of bomb craters along the shore. They looked fresh. For once, Quyên was glad to see American air power at work.

In the cockpit, Tinh had not heard the M-16 above the roar of the engines. The crew chief did not have any headsets for them to communicate with the back of the airplane. Tinh would never know if a missile tracked them from the rear until it exploded.

Still, as he followed the course of the river south, he kept the American helicopters ahead and to his left. He leaned forward to scan above him. He saw no Navy fighters, but he knew they were up there. The two gunship helicopters continued to fly on either side of the large helicopter.

Looking to his left toward the sun, Tinh saw a swarm of bugs around the red-orange ball. But they weren't bugs. They were a swarm of helicopters that had left Tan Son Nhut before them. South Vietnamese pilots were flying every available helicopter, overloaded with people, Tinh knew. Everyone flew east in search of the US Navy fleet. It was their best chance of escape. They hoped to land on any aircraft carrier or a ship with a heliport.

Tinh raised the nose of his plane.

Time to get higher, he decided. The PAVN wasn't in the swamps below, Quyên had assured him. But the swamps had been home to every thief, pirate, and outlaw for Saigon's entire existence. Those people carried weapons. Tinh did not know the best climb speed for this transport, so he would have to guess. But the sooner he could climb above four thousand feet, the better. Until then, any rifle bullet could find them.

So far, the ride had been gentle with few bumps. As the sun rose and heated the terrain below, it would get rougher. Airsick passengers would make the flight an ordeal. Climbing higher would find smoother air. It would be much cooler as well.

In his hurried look at the C-123's flight manual, Tinh had decided that ten thousand feet was a good altitude for the flight. Without a pressurization system, climbing higher would create an oxygen deficiency for everyone. It was as high as he could climb to stretch their fuel.

"Let's close the doors," Tinh told the crew chief.

"I'll have to do it."

"Make sure we have max air circulation."

"Yes, sir," Sergeant Khắc replied. He reached to the overhead panel between them. Then he climbed out of his seat and crawled to the cockpit door.

As the transport climbed, Tinh kept his scan alternating between the outside and his flight instruments. He didn't have that instinctive feel for the airplane like he had for the F-5. The plane bounced continuously, and the noise was deafening.

Suddenly, a Navy A-7 passed on his left, rocking its wings. Tinh spotted a rack of bombs under each wing. Outboard each of those racks, Tinh saw an empty rack. The Navy had dropped bombs somewhere. Tinh banked left, then right, hoping the fighter's wingman behind him would see his friendly wave.

"Charlie one-two-three over the river, Taco One on Guard."

The Navy flight lead was calling him again. Tinh pushed his mike button on the yoke.

"Taco One, Charlie one-two-three, go ahead."

"Tell your tail gunner nice shooting at that Strela. We appreciate it."

"Will do," Tinh replied. *So Quyên has earned his passage by distracting a missile meant for us.*

The second A-7 passed on their right and rocked its wings; then the jets were gone. Several minutes elapsed before Sergeant Khắc climbed back into the right seat.

"We shot down a missile," he bragged.

"So I heard."

The crew chief looked disappointed that Tinh already knew.

"Two Navy fighters came by," Tinh explained. "They told me."

Khắc looked out front, then out the side window.

"I don't see them."

"They are tigers in the jungle. You don't know they are there until they pounce."

Fifteen minutes later, the plane was still climbing. It felt sluggish, so Tinh eased the nose lower. Their climb slowed to a crawl. Tinh worried about how overweight they were. The coast slid below them, and a minute later, Tinh banked right to head south. He looked at the center console for an autopilot. There was nothing that looked like one.

"Do we have an autopilot?" he quizzed Sergeant Khắc.

The crew chief shook his head.

"No."

It's going to be a long flight, Tinh realized. His energy was fading fast. He knew he could not make it to Thailand without a nap. He had lost track of how long he had been awake. The adrenaline that had been fueling his body was gone. He needed rest before he hallucinated.

As the plane settled on the southern heading, Tinh looked at the coastline out the right window. He estimated they were a couple of miles from land. Too close, he knew, until they climbed higher. He had to assume any forces along the coast weren't friendly. South Vietnamese troops were as likely to shoot at them in frustration as the PAVN were. He banked left to increase his distance off the coast. Tinh studied the coastline as far as he could see. It was one hundred miles to the southern tip of Vietnam. At ten thousand feet, Tinh knew it was safe to cut across the southern tip of the country.

When the plane reached ten thousand feet, Tinh leveled off and let the airspeed build to reach cruising speed. He inched the throttles back. It would take trial and error to find the setting for his cruise speed. Tinh fiddled with the trim wheels for the ailerons and elevators. The plane needed to stay on the heading and altitude when he let go of the yoke. Finally, he was satisfied; he tapped Khắc.

"I need to nap, or we'll never make it," he began his explanation. "I've trimmed the airplane, so it should stay on course and altitude."

Tinh stared straight ahead for several minutes. He was forgetting something. But his foggy brain couldn't remember what. He needed rest. His bloodshot eyes went out of focus.

What was it? He knew it was something important. His mind wandered to his wife and family. He had not had the luxury of worrying about them since Clicker rushed them aboard that helicopter. *How long ago was that? Was it a day ago?* He could not figure it out. He hadn't slept since then. His head fell forward. He snapped it up with a start.

Even in his sleep-deprived state, his flying habits suddenly kicked in.

Level off checklist. Set power and fuel. Fuel! That was it! He studied the fuel flow instruments for each engine. They were guzzling precious fuel! If he didn't lean the mixture, they'd be ditching in the sea well before Thailand! And those small jet engines were gas guzzlers, too.

"We need to shut down the jets," he shouted to Khắc.

The sergeant reached up and moved two switches. The airplane didn't slow; it descended slowly. Rather than pull back on the yoke, Tinh inched the throttles ahead to stop the descent and regain the hundred feet of altitude. He readjusted the elevator trim wheel next to his right thigh.

"Do you know how to lean out the fuel mixture?" Tinh asked the crew chief.

"Yes."

Khắc reached for two levers on his side of the power quadrant. He nudged them back, studying the engine instruments.

Tinh's confidence in the crew chief grew. This sergeant knew his airplane. Tinh watched the fuel flow drop. He also watched the cylinder temperature gauges. It had been years since Tinh had leaned a piston engine's fuel consumption.

Khắc said nothing as he made the final adjustments. Finally, he was satisfied. Tinh took a pencil out of his pocket and a scrap of paper. He jotted down two sets of numbers, the fuel flow rates before and after the crew chief adjusted them. Next, he wrote the time on the clock next to the numbers. It didn't matter if the time was correct. The clock only needed to keep time. Tinh jotted down their takeoff time as well. He needed to track their fuel burn along the flight. If they were burning too much fuel, he wanted to know. Not that he could do anything about it.

If they ran low on gas, he had only two bad choices. Ditch in the water, so everyone could drown. Or head to shore and crash land. He had no intention of doing that. Both Vietnam and Cambodia would only offer cruel deaths. He knew what the Vietnamese Communists would do to escaping military men and their families. The Khmer Rouge had conquered Cambodia just two weeks earlier. They were crueler than the Vietnamese Communists.

When the airspeed stabilized, Tinh adjusted the flight controls and trim tabs again. He let go of the yoke. Satisfied, he turned to Khắc.

"I need to sleep. You will need to watch the airplane."

Khắc looked unsure. Tinh pointed to his altimeter and then to the altimeter in front of the crew chief.

"We are at ten thousand feet. See the small pointer under the long one at the zero?"

Khắc looked from Tinh's altimeter to his own.

"Yes, sir," he acknowledged.

"The long pointer needs to stay between the seven and the three." Tinh pointed to the numbers. "If it doesn't, wake me up."

Khắc's eyes widened.

"See, the large pointer is just moving up and down a little, but that is okay."

"Yes, sir," came a hesitant reply.

Tinh gestured to the coast off the right side of the airplane.

"We need to stay about the same distance off the coast. Wake me up if we drift away so you can't see it. If we drift so we are almost over it, wake me up."

Tinh looked east out his side window. Thunderstorms climbed from the ocean to altitudes high above them.

"See those storms to the east?"

"Yes, sir."

"We don't want to be close to them. If they move close to us, wake me up."

Khắc nodded, still looking unsure. He looked at the man kneeling on the floor behind the center console. Tinh turned to him.

"Can you help him?"

"Yes, sir," came the answer.

"Okay," Tinh said to Khắc. "Repeat what I told you."

Khắc hesitated, then repeated the instructions. Tinh helped him when he hesitated once.

"Good," Tinh assured him. He paused and looked at the clock on the instrument panel. "Wake me in forty minutes. We should be near the tip of Vietnam. We need to turn west." Tinh pointed to the right, out the windshield.

Khắc nodded again. Tinh looked at his helper behind them.

"Okay?" he asked.

"Yes, sir."

Tinh nodded and turned to the front. He checked the airplane's altitude and heading to see how it had wandered during his explanation. The altitude was a little lower, and the heading was within two degrees of where it had been. A two-degree difference in heading, Tinh knew, would keep the plane within a couple of miles of his course. Tinh slid his seat back a couple of inches so he wouldn't bump the controls while he napped. He fiddled with the seat to recline it slightly. Tinh tightened his seat belt and locked his shoulder harness. His eyes closed, and he was asleep in a minute.

———◆———

SLEEP

—•—

Tinh awoke with a start.

Now what? he wondered. He was going to chew out whoever had disturbed his sleep.

When his bleary eyes focused, the glare made him squint.

Why is it so bright? And where am I?

He stared straight ahead, trying to make sense of where he was. Then somebody tapped him on his right arm.

"Colonel Tinh," he heard. The smell of old metal and oil brought him to his senses.

Sergeant Khắc was staring at him.

"What is it?"

"The land has just passed our wingtip."

Tinh leaned over to look past Khắc out the window. He could see no land. Tinh grabbed the yoke with his left hand and rolled the plane to the right. He kept looking out the window. In a few seconds, he spotted the southern tip of Vietnam. He checked his heading indicator, then his altitude. The plane was descending. He eased the yoke back as he rolled out on a northwest heading.

When the plane regained altitude and the nose steadied on the heading, Tinh studied the engine instruments. He didn't know what numbers to look for, but several contained green arcs for the normal ranges. He compared the same instrument for both engines. Any difference would be a warning to check closer and ask the crew chief about.

The left engine's oil pressure wobbled below the level shown on the right engine. He pointed to it.

"Has that been happening for a while?"

"For about five minutes," Khắc replied.

"Guess we should watch it."

Tinh checked the clock. He had slept less than he expected. They must have had a tailwind. That meant the wind would now nudge them away from the land. He had calculated that a northwest course fifty miles off the coast of Cambodia would be direct to U-Tapao. He studied the coastline, trying to guess its distance. His experience told him that at this altitude, the horizon would be one hundred nautical miles away. So he needed to see the land easily.

Tinh next looked at the overhead panel to check the fuel. On his piece of paper, he jotted down the time and the total. Next to it, he wrote "southern tip." Then he calculated how much fuel they were burning. Khắc watched him with interest.

"Our fuel burn looks right on schedule," he informed the crew chief. "Maybe you should scan the engines," Tinh suggested. "And check if my cousin is awake."

Khắc unbuckled and headed to the cargo compartment. Tinh knew they had very few options if anything was wrong with the airplane. But more time to think through a problem always meant a better decision.

Several minutes elapsed before Khắc returned.

"Everything looks good?"

"Yes, sir."

"Nothing suspicious about the left engine?"

"No, sir."

"Was my cousin awake?"

"He is sleeping on the ramp."

Tinh nodded. His eyes burned from fatigue. His arms felt heavy. While his mind tried to think through what he needed to do to get this plane to Thailand, focusing was difficult. His thoughts kept jumping from one item to something completely different. His catnap had had little effect on his exhausted body. He needed more sleep. And some tea or coffee.

"How are you doing?" he asked the sergeant.

"Very tired."

Tinh could guess that the crew chief had not slept the night before. Guarding his airplane would have been his highest priority.

"Why don't you lean back and rest," Tinh suggested. "I'll monitor the airplane."

Khắc nodded and reclined his seat.

"I'll be fine with an hour's nap."

Tinh gave him a thumbs-up.

To keep his mind awake, Tinh started thinking through scenarios for trouble. It was a pilot's trick to stay alert.

If a serious problem developed with the aircraft, no good options existed. He had not asked whether the plane carried any life rafts. Even if it had one or two, the number of passengers far exceeded any capacity for them. Turning to the coast was as bad an option as ditching in the ocean. No one knew what the Khmer Rouge in Cambodia was up to since their victory a few weeks earlier. But Tinh had heard that refugees crossing the border into Vietnam told horror stories. Executions and starvation were running rampant in Cambodia.

Tinh experienced a sense of déjà vu. Hadn't he already thought of that problem? It didn't matter. Staying awake mattered.

The conclusion was obvious: any problem that forced the plane down meant certain death for all. Tinh looked across at the snoozing crew chief. Sergeant Khắc had shown shrewd judgment in getting his airplane ready for an escape. He had sought Tinh to fly it. Tinh could only hope that the plane would stay in the air.

He tried to figure out an ETA to U-Tapao. Tinh had spent fifteen minutes one day figuring out his route and required fuel. He looked at his notes, then at the clock low on the instrument panel. They had been airborne for an hour and forty minutes. That left … Tinh thought. What had he figured their total flight time should be? His flight planning notes were in his F-5 crash.

He could not remember. Tinh looked out the right window. How far was he really from the coast? Had it moved farther away while his thoughts had meandered? He checked his heading. He had turned to the heading he remembered from his planning. But he had planned to cut across the tip of the country. They were south of where he wanted to be. And he judged they had a crosswind blowing them farther south. He rolled the plane into a shallow right turn.

He studied the coastline again. Once he was comfortable with its distance, he should draw a line where it was. Tinh looked around the cockpit. Was there anything he could make a mark with? Nothing was evident. He held up his index finger with the tip touching the coast. He looked to see where the bottom of the window was on his finger.

Halfway to U-Tapao, he remembered he had to turn slightly right. It was by a large bay on the coast. He had to see the bay clearly, so he rolled several degrees right again. When he could easily see the features of the land, it would be time to fly parallel to the coast.

His biggest challenge: getting more rest. But he had to stay awake to navigate and fly the airplane. How much could he count on Khắc to monitor the airplane? If he let him sleep along with Quyển, then they could stay awake and work together while Tinh slept more. But who could keep him awake now? He looked around the flight deck. One person had curled up on the only floor space.

Tinh turned to look out the windshield. His eyes went out of focus. They closed. Suddenly, he jerked his head up! He had fallen asleep. How long? He checked the clock. Then he compared it to the time he had written in his notes. It was ten minutes later. But he didn't know how long his thoughts had wandered. Tinh did an instrument scan. The plane was four hundred feet high. Not a problem. His heading was off by ten degrees. He looked right to check the coastline. Its features were clear. He rolled back to parallel the coast.

His eyes felt so heavy. He needed sleep, blissful sleep. Tinh slapped himself on his right cheek. If only he had some water to splash on his face. His passengers needed any water on board, though. They were all dehydrated. He slapped his left cheek harder. Then he felt the large lump in his flight suit's leg pocket. The can of fruit. He had forgotten about the C-rations. He pulled it from the pocket. Opening it with the small can opener was difficult. But the can held some liquid and some calories. Both items his fatigued, aching body craved.

What else could he do to keep busy, to keep his mind working? He looked at the radio panel. If he dialed in the navigation station at U-Tapao, the plane could go straight there when they got into range. He stared at the frequency dial. What was the frequency? He couldn't remember it. He stared, thinking the numbers on the dial would jog some memory. They didn't. The frequency would differ from all the other ones he knew. Maybe going through those would trigger his memory. He started with Bien Hoa. Then he thought of Tan Son Nhut. Then

Da Nang. What had Da Nang's channel been? He couldn't remember it. He continued staring at the frequency knob. No numbers came to mind.

He removed his left hand from the yoke. The plane tilted to the left. He fiddled with the trim wheel so it leveled out.

If I could find a Bangkok radio station, I can home in on it.

A U-Tapao station would be better, but Bangkok stations had stronger signals. Bangkok was straight past U-Tapao from this direction, so homing on Bangkok would take them to U-Tapao. The coast of Thailand turned north at U-Tapao. From ten thousand feet, he couldn't miss it.

He looked down at the radio panel to find the correct one. This plane had two of the radios. He turned on one and dialed in Saigon's radio station. He remembered its frequency. A propaganda broadcast came through his earphones.

The Communists have captured the radio station, he knew. An announcer reported that "the glorious comrades of the People's Army of Vietnam" had captured the Presidential Palace. The former president of the Republic of Vietnam, his president, ordered the Army to surrender.

Tinh's heart sank. He had known it was inevitable, but hearing his president order the surrender broke him. He began sobbing. Through his sobs, he heard the announcer repeat the order to surrender.

"Our comrades in the People's Army will welcome you. You will receive humane and lenient treatment," it promised.

As he absorbed the surrender, his mind jumped to his wife and family. He had no news about them. How long had it been since he had hugged his wife and children and sent them to that thundering helicopter? He did not know. They must be on a US Navy ship now, sailing to … where? Where would the ship take them? How would he ever find them?

He had waited too long to get them out. Some illogical sense of duty had prevented him from admitting defeat and sending his family to safety earlier. But to safety where? America? Would America take them? The American Ambassador had delayed deciding on an evacuation. What had he been thinking? Would any country welcome refugees with little money and few skills? All he knew how to do was pilot airplanes. His job in his young days had taught him to cut trees.

His mind jumped to Clicker and Rick. He could only hope his American friends would help him and his family. Both had tried to convince him to send his family out sooner. They had run high risks for his lost country. Both had flown hundreds of combat missions for a lost cause. Rick had almost lost his entire family. At least Rick had finally put his family ahead of the lost cause and had flown out with them. Yet, Clicker had stayed. And he had agreed to go with Tinh's family and look out for them. What had Tinh ever done for them? How would he ever repay them?

Tinh's body slumped in his seat. He felt defeated, even in his successful escape from his lost country. His mind and his body were exhausted. He had not one ounce of strength left with which to fight. He was on a hopeless flight from evil, and he was the only one on the airplane with the skill and knowledge to pull it off. But he had been awake for over forty-eight hours in a stress-filled scramble. His family had escaped. That was enough. He had no strength to continue. As he cried, his head slumped forward and his eyes closed. Sleep overcame him, and Tinh felt strangely at peace.

He did not notice that as his left hand fell from the control yoke, it nudged it forward. The plane began a slow descent toward the ocean ten thousand feet below.

———•———

THUNDERSTORM

——◦——

Tinh woke up suddenly. Something pierced his lap and his shoulders. As he opened his eyes, a bright flash blinded him as an explosion deafened him. A second later, a force slammed him into his seat. Then he was floating, with a slicing pain across his hip bone.

Where was he?

Despite the roar of the engines, Tinh heard screams behind him.

He slammed back into his seat.

Tinh looked to his left. Nothing but gray. He looked to his right. Sergeant Khắc stared at him, eyes wide and mouth open. A look of terror. The face startled Tinh to his senses. Lightning flashed in the window past Khắc. Tinh remembered where he was.

He grabbed the control yoke with both hands. His eyes studied the flight instruments in front of him. They were in dark shadows, making them impossible to read.

"Instrument lights!" he shouted.

Khắc didn't hear him above the wind and loud thumps all around. Hail pummeled the plane. Tinh leaned forward. His head banged against the top panel.

Looking closer, he saw the plane was rolling. Tinh moved the yoke to level the wings. He studied the altimeter: five thousand feet and increasing rapidly.

Tinh came as close to panic as he ever had in an airplane. He had fallen asleep at the controls, and the plane had descended from ten thousand feet. But that was the good news. He had plenty of air between him and the ocean. The danger came from the thunderstorm. While he had flown close to storms, he had never entered one. Pilots avoided this force of nature. Until aviators had learned to respect these monsters, thousands of skilled pilots had died in them.

Tinh needed radar to tell him which way to turn to escape. But the C-123 did not have radar. He was flying blind.

Lightning flashed in front, immediately followed by the crash of thunder. A bolt of lightning pierced through the dark clouds to his right. He had to decide. Two of these flashes had been on his right. Tinh rolled the plane left. He lost the battle to keep the airplane level. It still climbed. He added power. Suddenly, the plane stopped climbing. Tinh floated in his seat at the sudden change.

He checked his compass heading. They had been flying northwest. Turning to the southwest seemed like the best direction. He did not want to turn further south and reverse course. They did not carry enough fuel to fly directly away from their destination. He had to hope that turning ninety degrees would carry them out of the storm.

He saw no lightning in front now, but the plane bounced around, nearly out of control. Tinh kept his eyes on the attitude indicator, fighting to keep the wings level and the nose on the artificial horizon. He checked the altimeter. The plane had descended back to five thousand feet. Tinh advanced the throttles farther. If they climbed, they might break out of the cloud. Then he could see where the towering thunderheads were. While his F-5 might have been able to climb above small thunderstorms, this airplane couldn't. His best hope was getting above the lower clouds around the storm.

Two more minutes of flying convinced Tinh that he had guessed correctly. The bouncing continued to ease. He still fought the turbulence, though, to keep the wings level. The dark clouds became lighter. Another minute passed, and only white cotton balls surrounded them. They must be climbing closer to the tops. Then the clouds thinned, and Tinh saw wisps of clouds. Abruptly, they were out of the cloud, although the plane remained surrounded by large cotton puffs.

A plume appeared in front, and they punched into its top. The updraft drove Tinh into his seat, and his hands slipped off the yoke. Then they were in the clear, and Tinh floated above his seat for a second. He looked around the windscreen. Tops of puffy white clouds surrounded them. Tinh leaned forward and looked up to find the blue sky. The fear that had gripped him receded. They were close to popping out on top of the clouds.

As the plane climbed through eight thousand feet, they popped out. Tinh studied the cloud tops around them. The darkest ones were to their right, and those climbed higher into the sky. He saw them brighten as lightning flashed inside the gray and black towers. It was too soon to turn back to the right.

Tinh saw that the fear had left Khắc's face. A figure inched beside him to look out the window. The face was bloody from a nasty cut on the forehead.

"Do you have a doctor or nurse among the passengers?" Tinh inquired.

"I have an aunt who is a nurse and a cousin who is a medic."

"If you have a first aid kit," Tinh instructed, "make sure they get it. We have injuries among the passengers." He nodded to the figure next to Khắc. "Also, please check on the condition of the airplane."

"Yes, sir." Khắc unbuckled and headed back.

Tinh looked at the clock. He jotted the time on his makeshift flight log. They had been flying for more than one hour and thirty minutes since they passed the tip of Vietnam. He racked his brain for the courses and times he had calculated for this flight. They had flown farther south than he had intended. He had tried to compensate for that. Now they were going farther west than he had planned.

What does that do to our fuel situation? Uncertainty about their exact position led to one conclusion. They would be dangerously low on fuel by the time they reached U-Tapao. He hoped they had enough to even get there.

Tinh tried to picture the route he had sketched on his aeronautical chart. The thunderstorm must have been off the coast by the big bay he had hoped to see. Soon, the direct course to U-Tapao would be north-northwest. He looked out the right window to study the clouds. The towering columns were off the wing. The tops of the clouds drifted lower as they went north.

Tinh rolled the plane to turn due west. He studied the clouds again and turned another twenty degrees north. He looked for the coastline. It was not visible. The clouds below obscured it. He had no idea how far away it was. He turned to a northwest heading again, putting the high clouds of the thunderstorm off his wing. As soon as the thunderstorm disappeared, he would turn north-northwest. A few minutes later, Tinh rolled the plane north as he approached ten thousand feet. He reset the throttles. Then he nudged the trim wheels for the ailerons and the elevators until he was satisfied. When he took his hand off the yoke, the plane did not roll or change altitude.

A hand tapped his right shoulder. He turned to find Quyền crouching behind the console.

"What happened? That was a rough ride for a bit."

"I fell asleep, and we wandered into a thunderstorm," Tinh admitted.

Quyền nodded.

"I woke up a foot off the ramp where I was sleeping. I'm surprised hitting the floor didn't knock me out."

"How bad are the injuries back there?"

"Pretty bad. I don't think one older man will make it. A woman who is a nurse says he has a severe concussion."

Tinh's head slumped as he listened.

"Don't blame yourself," Quyền assured him. "You flew us out of that storm. Get half of these people to Thailand, and you'll be a hero."

Tinh still shook his head.

"Any idea of how long until Thailand?" Quyền inquired.

Tinh shrugged his shoulders.

"Perhaps one hour and twenty minutes. We have to be less than 200 nautical miles." He did a quick calculation. "About 360 kilometers."

Tinh paused. "If I remembered the navigation station frequency, I would be more precise." Tinh looked at the navigation radio and fingered the channel dial. *What was that channel number?*

"Don't try too hard to remember it," Quyền suggested. "It'll come to you if you don't think too hard."

"I hope you are right."

Tinh reached for another radio dial.

"A powerful radio station from Bangkok or U-Tapao would give us the correct course."

"Let me try," Quyền offered. "I've learned to speak passable Thai."

Tinh pointed to the radio.

"A radio station should be in the frequency range of 500 to 1400."

Quyền smiled.

"We listened to stations on the road south. I'll try those."

Tinh took off his headset and handed it to Quyên.

"You'll need this."

Quyên donned the headset and started tuning the radio. In a few minutes, he tapped Tinh.

"I found a Bangkok station. It's weak, but the signal sounds steady."

Tinh looked at the instrument panel for the compass indicator. A thin pointer on the right indicator pointed straight ahead, between the numbers 33 and 0 on the compass. Tinh brought the picture of the navigation chart into his brain. They would pass over U-Tapao if they followed that needle to Bangkok.

Tinh's spirits soared. *We might make it!*

He turned to Quyên and pointed at the needle.

"It points to the radio station," he shouted. "U-Tapao is right along the way!"

Quyên smiled. He patted Tinh on the shoulder.

"I knew you'd find the way to U-Tapao!" he exclaimed.

Three numbers jumped into Tinh's mind: one zero five. He quickly reached down to the navigation radio dial and put them in. He looked at the compass needle that would point to the station. It wobbled near the top, but it didn't lock onto any heading.

Too far out, Tinh concluded. He checked the clock and did a quick calculation. He jotted down the time that Quyên had found the radio station. Next to it, he wrote, "180 nm?" He reached for another instrument in the center of the panel in front of him. In it, he dialed the number "345" which he estimated should be the course to the navigation station at U-Tapao. The bar that showed the course line wavered, but like the compass needle, it did not lock on.

Tinh rechecked the clock. *Another twenty minutes,* he guessed. *Then it should lock on.*

Quyên handed the headset back to Tinh as Sergeant Khắc climbed into his seat.

"How are the passengers?" Tinh inquired.

"One old gentleman has died," Khắc reported. "We have a couple of broken arms so far. My aunt and cousin are working their way through the injured."

"Do you have a flight manual for the airplane?" Tinh asked Khắc.

"Yes."

"Please hand it to me. I need to look at it. What about tie-down straps in the back?"

"A few."

"Have them stretched across the floor near the back. Have the injured slide under them for seat belts. If we have a flat tire, the landing might be rough."

With a possible flat tire, Tinh wanted to be sure of his landing speed. The procedure for landing an airplane with a flat tire was generic across aircraft: keep the flat tire off the runway as long as possible. But speed control was crucial to minimizing damage and injuries. Tinh recognized he had graduated from fighter pilot to test pilot.

Thumbing through the flight manual, Tinh found what he wanted.

Quyển tapped him and pointed to the course indicator. It had steadied slightly off-center. Tinh adjusted the course knob, and the needle steadied in the center of the display. He compared the course to the radio beacon compass pointer. They read within a few degrees of each other. Tinh searched the instrument panel. There had to be a distance meter telling him how far he was from the navigation station. He found it. It read 105!

He quickly noted the time, then jotted the time and distance on his notepaper. Then he looked up at the fuel panel to determine his fuel status. Scribbling the numbers down and doing a quick calculation, Tinh was certain where he was from U-Tapao. He had navigated flawlessly. Only one question remained: Did he have enough fuel? If the fuel gauges were accurate, they would just make it. If not, he guessed there was a fifty percent chance they had slightly more fuel than they needed. It was the other "flip of a coin" chance, though, that worried him.

If the navigation station was in range, the air controllers might be in range, too. Tinh checked the frequency selector. Then he clicked the microphone button on the yoke.

"U-Tapao Approach, this is Charlie one-two-three tail number two five seven five on guard, do you read?" Tinh transmitted. He waited. When no one answered, he keyed the mike again and repeated the call.

"Aircraft calling U-Tapao Approach on Guard, say again."

An American voice answered him!

Tinh's spirits soared. He repeated his information.

"We are inbound to your station from Saigon," Tinh finished.

"Provider Two Five Seven Five, U-Tapao Approach copies. Please contact us on two-seven-three-point-three." Tinh noted the controller used the name for the C-123 in his call.

Tinh repeated the frequency, then wrote it on his paper. He dialed the frequency into his radio. He keyed his mike.

"U-Tapao Approach, Provider Two Five Seven Five. How do you read?"

"Loud and clear," the controller answered. "State your position."

Tinh read his distance and direction from the airport.

"Provider Seven Five, are you able to squawk three one two three?"

Tinh looked at the center panel for the radar transponder. He dialed the code into the radio. Sergeant Khắc watched him. Tinh smiled and gave him a thumbs-up.

"Provider Two Five Seven Five, U-Tapao Approach, radar contact eighty-nine miles south of U-Tapao."

Tinh's eyes nearly teared up as he heard the controller confirm he saw the airplane's radar return. He was a child again, taking his mother's reassuring hand.

Tinh acknowledged the controller's call.

"Provider Seven Five, expect a straight-in visual approach to runway three six," the controller continued.

Tinh had to tell the controller about their situation. He had injured passengers who needed medical attention, and he had a possible flat tire. A flat tire would strand the airplane on the base's only runway and close the airport to other airplanes.

Tinh keyed his mike and gave the controller the information.

"Stand by," was the response.

Were they now going to deny him permission to land? Tinh quickly decided. Permission or not, he was going to land. He would look for a taxiway to put the plane down on to spare the runway. He had neither the fuel nor the intention to fly anywhere else.

It seemed like an eternity before the controller called again.

"Provider Seven Five, you can land on the parallel taxiway west of the runway. Land on the near end of it. Medical help will meet your aircraft."

A sense of relief enveloped Tinh. He turned to his cousin, who knelt behind him.

"Would you go back and tell everyone we will land at U-Tapao in about thirty minutes? I am talking to the airport. Check that the injured are under straps near the ramp. We will have them off the airplane first."

Quyển nodded.

"I'll stay back to help."

The next twenty minutes elapsed quickly. The coast of Thailand came into view. Tinh picked out where the air base would be, just east of the point where the coast turned north. His next decision was when to descend. He did a couple of quick calculations. A normal glide path would put him at three thousand feet at ten miles from the airport. But Tinh wanted to stay well above that to increase his gliding range. The uncertain fuel amount worried him. He decided on his descent rate and the point to begin.

"Remember, Sergeant," Tinh advised the crew chief. "I need your help."

He wanted help in lowering the landing gear and flaps. Importantly, he wanted the crew chief to call the airspeed frequently. Tinh needed to focus on the stick and rudder skills to make a smooth approach.

"You have a speed control indicator," the crew chief informed him. He pointed toward the panel in front of Tinh. Tinh found it next to the airspeed indicator.

When the distance showed ten miles, Tinh started his descent. The controller gave Tinh a new frequency to contact the control tower. The plane descended rapidly as Tinh worked hard to keep the plane on speed and on the descent rate he wanted. At three thousand feet, the left engine coughed. The plane yawed to the left. Tinh fought to keep the wings level and tapped his right rudder to straighten the nose.

Tinh recognized the problem immediately. He had not put the fuel selector on cross-feed to ensure that both engines burned the remaining fuel. The left fuel tank must be empty. The engine coughed again.

"Left engine flame out!" Khắc shouted.

"Shut it down!"

Tinh glanced as the crew chief reached for the emergency shutdown handle, ensuring Khắc grabbed the correct one.

With the engine shut down on the same side as a possible flat tire, Tinh knew keeping the airplane on the taxiway would be a major challenge.

"Flaps and gear!" Tinh ordered.

The flaps rolled down, slowing the plane's descent. The rumbling of the gear into the wind assured him it was extending. Khắc called out the airspeed. They were still fast, but Tinh didn't mind. He could slow down by leveling off over the taxiway. He kept his aim for the start of the taxiway as the plane raced to it.

Tinh eased back on the yoke, and the plane slowed. He tried in vain to keep the nose pointed straight down the taxiway.

Hold it off! he thought as the taxiway rushed up. He banked slightly to the right, trying to hold the possible flat tire off longer. His right wheel touched. The plane lurched. Then his left wheel touched the concrete. The plane did not swerve. The tire was okay!

Tinh let the nosewheel lower to the taxiway, and he tapped the brakes.

"Reverse," the crew chief advised.

Unsure of how to do that, Tinh simply shouted, "Go ahead!"

The crew chief eased the throttles back, and Tinh felt the airplane slow rapidly. His feet alternated on the rudder pedals to keep the plane on the narrow taxiway. The plane stopped, and Tinh slumped in his seat. A US Air Force ambulance pulled onto the taxiway and raced behind the airplane.

Sergeant Khắc pulled the right engine's emergency handle, and the engine stopped turning.

"Parking brake, sir," he advised Tinh. When Tinh looked for it, he felt the brake pedals move down. Sergeant Khắc reached over and pulled the parking brake handle.

"Nice landing, sir."

Tinh smiled meekly.

"Thank you for your help."

Tinh unbuckled and struggled out of his seat. His knees wobbled as his fatigue overpowered him. He stood at the rear of the flight deck. People streamed through the crew door. On the ramp in the rear, Tinh saw medics loading people onto stretchers. Passengers helped the injured down the ramp.

Tinh nodded as stoic passengers filed past him. One elderly lady paused and bowed to Tinh. He waited until the airplane appeared empty. Then he stumbled through the compartment to ensure that everyone was off. It was then that the smell hit him. The pungent odor churned his stomach as he saw vomit everywhere on the floor. His sandals slid as he could not avoid stepping in it. He could also see bloodstains. His passengers had survived a harrowing ride to freedom. As Tinh stepped off the ramp, his legs buckled. He went to his knees on the hot tarmac. Unable to move, he sat there and sobbed.

———•———

THE SOLDIER KNEW

—◦—

Dobie, Charles, and Jimbo waited anxiously at U-Tapao. For two days, they raced among the cargo airplanes arriving from Tan Son Nhut. All were battered planes, needing major repairs. They paid special attention to the few C-123s, which were newer than the C-47s. Spotting the pilots was difficult. Only a few wore flight suits. No one wanted to talk to an ex-American soldier. Most pretended not to understand the Vietnamese that Dobie and Jimbo spoke.

Today seemed like the day. Tan Son Nhut had experienced its first attack two days earlier, and the Americans launched their helicopter evacuation the previous day. Today had to be Saigon's last gasp.

Over the prior days, Dobie had spoken with Marcel. His extended Hmong family was at Lima Site 26. Only two thousand feet of its landing strip was intact. Dobie hoped it would be enough for a C-47 or C-123. The site held a few groups of Hmong. Their rumor mill buzzed, expecting the Hmong general was ready to flee from a different location. Most Hmong were going there, hoping the general would take them.

With Saigon defeated, the Pathet Lao and their Vietnamese allies would certainly finish the war in Laos. If the Americans had not saved Vietnam, the Hmong knew to expect no aid. Yet, the Hmong long ago concluded that there would be little outside help. Several groups were trekking south toward the Mekong River. Laotian troops ceaselessly harassed those groups. The Royal troops viewed the Hmong as competitors for any refugee aid. The Pathet Lao routinely murdered the Hmong.

Dobie awoke early. He felt antsy, like before a big mission. He had not even felt this agitated before the hike for the ring. Maybe it was his concern for Marcel, over which he had only a marginal impact. He had to depend on others to get him out. Maybe it was because today his war was ending in defeat.

Jimbo beat him to breakfast, though.

"Woke up early, Sergeant?"

"Yes, sir. Couldn't sleep."

"I had trouble, too."

"Fucking Commies," the retired Special Forces sergeant responded. "How the fuck did we let them win!"

"The soldier knew someone had blundered," Dobie quoted.

Jimbo's head drooped.

"We sensed this was coming way back then," he admitted. "So many asinine decisions."

Charles joined them. Dobie looked at him.

"Charles," he started, "we have a critical mission today."

"I'm all ears," Charles replied.

"The last of the Saigon airplanes has to arrive today. We have to find the plane and the pilot to help us."

"They might not arrive here together," Charles added.

"I hope we can talk our way onto the flight line again," Dobie added. "If the plane and pilot don't arrive, we'll have to look through the refugee camp."

"That will require finding a needle in the haystack," Jimbo grumbled.

"Does anybody have a better idea?" Dobie demanded.

No one did.

The trio finished breakfast. As they had done since arriving, one always stayed in Dobie's room with the radio. It was too essential to allow anyone to steal it. Dobie and Jimbo headed to the Chevy. The challenge lay ahead, getting past the flight line security.

Dobie spotted the gate guarded by the lone Thai security guard they had bribed yesterday.

The guard examined the Americans suspiciously again.

"We are expecting former comrades to arrive from Saigon today," Jimbo explained again.

The guard looked expectantly at Jimbo. Jimbo slipped him two twenties. The guard stepped aside.

"Last time," the guard muttered in Thai.

Jimbo nodded and smiled at him.

"No shit," he muttered to Dobie.

First, the duo studied the planes parked along the taxiway in the grass. Maybe it was lucky their plane hadn't arrived yet. It would be trapped behind all the later arrivals. Only a couple looked new from yesterday afternoon.

Desperate bastards risked a night takeoff and flight, Dobie concluded.

A group of refugees struggled to raise additional tents. The odor from the portable restrooms drifted over the camp.

No one thought to put those downwind of the tents, Dobie realized.

Dobie and Jimbo wandered among the refugees, asking about the pilot who had flown them here. Again, no one would help.

As they met at the car, Jimbo looked south over the sea. He shielded his eyes from the noonday glare.

Dobie tapped him.

"An airplane must be coming in," he declared. "A fire truck and ambulance have pulled onto a taxiway."

He pointed for Jimbo. Both men then looked south. Several minutes passed.

"I see a plane," Jimbo reported.

Dobie spotted it. As it grew closer, Dobie tapped Jimbo's shoulder.

"Looks like a one twenty-three."

He looked back at the taxiway.

"A second ambulance is here. They must have several injured passengers. Let's go meet it."

As Jimbo rounded the tents, he stopped.

"The ambulances and fire truck aren't pointed to the runway," he observed.

Dobie looked at them. Then he looked back at the approaching airplane.

"He's lined up on the taxiway."

They watched as the C-123 floated past them and landed on the taxiway.

"Damn," Dobie stated. "He shut down his left engine. The pilot didn't want to crash on the main runway."

Jimbo turned the car onto the taxiway and followed the airplane. As the plane passed the emergency vehicles, they pulled out to chase it. The plane stopped quickly, and the rear door and ramp opened. Firemen rushed toward it, dragging hoses. Medics dragged litters out of their ambulances. Jimbo stopped the car.

"Let's let them finish," he stated.

One passenger spoke with the firemen. It was a brief conversation, and the firemen started reeling up the hoses and walked back to the crash truck. Medics rushed into the airplane. Soon, they reappeared, carrying passengers on the stretchers. Spotting the car, one medic ran over to Dobie and Jimbo.

"Can you drive a couple of walking wounded to the hospital? We have a full load of stretchers."

"Sure can," Jimbo responded. He eased the car forward beside an ambulance.

"I'll stay here," Dobie stated as he opened his car door. "I'll find the pilot."

Medics walked three passengers to the car. All wore bandages on their arms, legs, or heads. As Dobie helped a frail woman into the backseat, he smelled vomit and spotted it on her clothes. He looked at the medic.

"Must have been a rough flight."

The medic nodded.

"The floor is covered with vomit and blood," he commented. "They fell asleep in the cockpit and wandered into a thunderstorm."

Dobie studied people still wandering out of the airplane. Someone in uniform walked under the wing. He appeared to inspect the airplane. That was different. On the airplanes over the last two days, a crew chief never checked the plane. Dobie's hopes about this airplane improved.

By the time Dobie reached him, Khắc was checking the landing gear.

"Is this your airplane?" Dobie began.

Khắc looked up.

"Yes."

"Is it in good shape?"

"So far, everything looks good."

"What about the left engine?"

"The left engine ran out of fuel."

"Where is the pilot?"

"I think he is still inside."

Dobie studied the crew chief. He saw bloodshot eyes. His speech sounded slurred.

A jeep parked at the nose of the airplane. Thai security police began directing the passengers toward the tent city.

"I'd like to speak with the pilot," Dobie stated. "Can you take me to him?"

Khắc led Dobie to the ramp as a figure in a flight suit stumbled down it. The sergeant stopped.

"He's our pilot."

Dobie stepped forward as Tinh stumbled and fell to his knees. The crew chief started forward; then he stopped. Dobie recognized the utter exhaustion in the pilot. He waited as Tinh's shoulders heaved. The Green Beret had seen this before. It was battle fatigue in a commander who had fought longer and harder than he ever imagined possible; when he had survived against all odds and some of his men had not; and when your mind and body tried to understand.

Dobie knew this was the man he was searching for. Here was the pilot who would pluck Marcel and his family from the jaws of death.

Dobie allowed Tinh his moment. Khắc stood, unsure of what to do. He had never seen a superior officer collapse.

"Tell me about your flight," Dobie prompted him.

"I didn't think the Colonel would return from his last mission. We heard the enemy had shot him down."

"A last mission?"

"After the Americans started flying the helicopters, Colonel Tinh flew an F-5 against the People's Army attacking Saigon. He had promised to fly my airplane here right after he finished. But he did not come back."

"So he went down? Where?"

The crew chief shrugged.

"It had to be just east of Saigon, where the invading force was."

"But then he showed up?"

"Yes, before dawn this morning. He and another showed up at our plane. We had given up hope of escaping. But he came. I think he spent the entire night getting back to us. We can never thank him."

"Then, he hasn't slept for …" Dobie did some quick math, " … forty or more hours?"

"None of us slept last night. We had to keep others from taking our plane."

A Thai security guard approached the group. He pointed to the tents and nudged Colonel Tinh. Dobie stepped over to the guard.

"We will take him over," he told the guard in broken Thai.

"Must go. Now," the guard replied.

"What will you do with the airplane?" Dobie asked.

"A truck will come to pull it over to the others."

Dobie stepped over to Colonel Tinh and squatted.

"Colonel Tinh, my name is Lieutenant Colonel Starbuckle."

Colonel Tinh looked up. Playing a hunch, Dobie continued. "Clicker asked me to watch for you. To help you get to America."

"You've spoken with Clicker? My family is okay? Did they get to the Philippines?"

The colonel was unknowingly calling Dobie's bluff.

"No, I'm sorry, I haven't heard. I only spoke with him before."

Tinh's shoulders slumped. The Thai guard reached out again, but Dobie held up his hand to the guard.

"We need to go over to the tents," he explained to Tinh. "We can talk there."

They stood. Khắc stepped closer. They began walking to the tents.

"Can you watch your airplane?"

The sergeant nodded.

"I want to make sure it stays safe."

A dedicated crew chief, Dobie noticed. Good.

A plan outline emerged in Dobie's mind. The devil, he understood, was in the details.

"Let's follow whatever orders they give us here," he said, gesturing toward the tents. "Then we secure your airplane."

The crew chief nodded.

"After a rest," Dobie continued, "I have a proposal for both of you. One that will hasten getting you and your families to America."

Tinh's bleary eyes appeared interested.

From the little that Khắc had said, Dobie recognized he had another story for Ashley Peabody. With the story of the Hmong rescue, Peabody would do anything for these men and their families. His magazine would include stories possessed by none other. He would sell millions of magazines.

Dobie stayed with Colonel Tinh and Sergeant Khắc for an hour. The refugee camp experience was novel to Dobie. He had seen them before, but always from a distance. The chance to escape and bypass this experience would become an important incentive to Tinh and Khắc. But would it be enough of a motivator for the danger it would involve?

After Tinh and Khắc settled into their tent, Dobie felt he could leave. He pulled Khắc to the side.

"I'll find out where they park your airplane. I want it in a place we can access and move it."

The crew chief gave him a questioning look.

"I'll be back tomorrow," he assured the sergeant.

Dobie walked to the taxiway. A tow tractor was hooking up the airplane. Dobie headed toward it. Out of the corner of his eye, he spotted their Chevy. Jimbo stood next to it. He waved to him to follow him. Jimbo trotted to catch up.

"What's up?"

"I've learned Colonel Tinh and Sergeant Khắc's tent assignments. We have to maintain control of their airplane."

Jimbo's better mastery of the Thai language would be crucial now.

"Get some bills available," Dobie stated.

They reached the tractor before it moved.

"Where are you moving it?" Jimbo queried the driver in Thai.

The driver pointed to the mass of the other airplanes.

"We would appreciate it if we could help," Jimbo continued, clearly reaching into his pocket.

The driver eyed him suspiciously. Jimbo pulled two bills out, allowing the driver to notice.

"How?" was the driver's simple question.

"So it will not get blocked," Dobie said quietly to Jimbo.

"Where will you park other airplanes?" Jimbo inquired of the driver.

He gestured to one end of the line of airplanes.

Dobie eyed the arrangement. He conferred quietly with Jimbo.

"How about in the middle, in front of those already there?"

Jimbo nodded. He then directed the tow truck driver to the spot, adding another bill. The driver, though, didn't move. Jimbo slipped him the first two bills. The driver nodded.

As the driver unhooked the plane after moving it, Jimbo walked over. He added another bill. The driver smiled.

"No more planes around it, please," Jimbo added. He received a nod in response.

As soon as Dobie returned to the hotel, Charles phoned Ashley Peabody. Charles explained Dobie's ideas for the story possibilities. Peabody became enthusiastic about the prospects. Importantly, he would make the calls to bring these families to America to limit their time in the refugee camps. His Rolodex contained a few names to call.

BACK TO THE US

Wednesday morning, the Guerris arrived at the Clark Passenger Terminal early. Rick wanted to be first in line for the few space-available seats. They were successful.

Rick and Sue had listened to the updates from Saigon the day before on the Armed Forces radio station. They clung to the updates on the helicopter airlift, yet it could not provide much detail. *Stars and Stripes* carried the story as well. They were relieved to read that the C-130 crew had escaped after being hit by artillery fire. But as of the morning report, the final status of the evacuation was still unclear.

Rick and Sue heard no word from Clicker. They would have heard from him if he had made it out on one of the last C-130s. The news of the bombing and shelling of Tan Son Nhut alarmed them. Now they could only hope that he and the Ngos had been on one of those helicopters. That would put them on a Navy ship. Presumably, those ships would sail to the Navy's large base at Subic Bay, just across a mountain range from Clark. The Guerris, though, would be on a C-141 flying to Hawaii.

Rick had left a note for him at their hotel lobby. He could only assume Clicker would call the hotel if he arrived in the Philippines. They also worried about Jeff Nickerson. Rick knew Jeff would be one of the last to leave. He prayed he would not have another friend captured by the Communists.

At a quarter to ten, passenger service announced a delay for their flight. The aircraft had a mechanical problem. Rick asked about an estimate of the length of the delay. No information was available.

Rick noticed no other passengers in the terminal. They were the only space-available passengers. Two hours later, the PA announced their flight number. Several other buses pulled behind their bus. As they walked to the airplane, Rick and Sue saw the anxious faces of Vietnamese men, women, and children staring at the large jet transport. It looked to be a crowded flight.

Rick gestured to Sue and the boys. "Let's get on board. We'll want to be at the front."

As the passenger service airman led them to the ramp, Rick was disappointed to see troop seats again.

The facilities lacked a loaded pallet of restrooms. Still, the C-141 had facilities superior to the "honey" bucket and urinal of a C-130. As the family settled into seats at the front, a familiar figure came down the cockpit stairs.

"Ann?" Sue asked.

Lieutenant Ann Jagger rushed over.

"We meet again!" Ann exclaimed.

Sue gave her a big hug.

"How's the foot?" Sue asked, checking where her cast had been.

"Just a light walking cast," Ann replied.

"And you're still flying," Rick observed. "Don't you believe in DNIF status?"

"Duty Not Involving Flying doesn't suit me," Ann laughed. "Guess who our aircraft commander is?"

"Not Gear Check," Rick replied. To Ann's puzzled look, he added, "Dan Price?"

"Poke your head into the cockpit. I'm sure he won't throw you out."

Rick climbed the stairs to the cockpit. As he scanned the two seats, he noticed the copilot had one headphone off.

"Copilot, be sure the pilot lowers his gear before landing."

A surprised lieutenant looked at this civilian in the cockpit. Before he could respond, though, a voice from the left seat spoke up.

"Tell that fighter jock to sit down, shut up, and keep his feet off the seats!"

Dan Price twisted out of his seat and extended his hand.

"Welcome aboard again. I thought you'd be back in College Station by now."

"It's a long story. The Manila embassy had no clue what to do for two adopted Vietnamese children. So we are going to smuggle them into the country."

"I don't think you'll have any trouble," Dan assured him. "Are Sue and the kids on board, too?"

"Up front in economy class."

"Did you see Ann?"

"She told me you were in charge of this gaggle."

"Bring Sue and the baby up here. We have a spot on the bunk." He motioned to the seat at the rear of the cockpit.

"She'll appreciate that."

"Are you going all the way to Travis?"

"We're stopping in Honolulu for a vacation. I have the name of a lawyer I can call to make sure our adoption is all in order."

"Good luck. If you'll excuse me now, I must get this flight out of here. Send Sue up."

Rick nodded and returned to Sue and their children.

"Dan Price says he has a seat up there for you and Thi," he informed Sue.

"It's okay?" she asked.

"He's the boss," Rick assured her.

Sue gathered the small bag for Thi and stood. Rick took the bag.

"I'll bring this up."

A refueling stop in Guam interrupted the flight to Honolulu. The passengers had a one-and-a-half-hour break to stretch their legs. Then they climbed aboard for an eight-hour flight to Hickam Air Force Base in Honolulu. The Guerri family dragged themselves off the airplane in the dark the following morning in Hawaii. The airport bustled with activity, though.

At the Customs and Immigration Desk, Rick handed their three passports to the official. He studied them and stamped them.

"Passports for the other children?" he asked, looking from Rick to Lei and Thi.

Rick handed the adoption papers to the official.

"We did not have time to get passports processed for our adopted Vietnamese children," he explained. "We were lucky to get new passports for my wife and son after they lost theirs in the C-5 crash."

The official raised his eyebrows. He looked at Sue and the children.

"Did they all survive the crash?"

"Yes, we did," Sue responded.

He handed the passports and adoption papers back.

"Be sure to get passports issued for the Vietnamese children if you plan to travel out of the country again."

"That is our priority," Rick answered.

"Good luck to you," the official responded, motioning them to walk through the turnstile.

On their way to the taxi stand, Rick spotted a newspaper rack.

"Saigon Falls to the Communists!" blared the headline.

Rick grabbed a paper. He directed the taxi to the military hotel on Waikiki Beach. On the way, he skimmed the lead story.

"Well, I guess the Vietnam War is finally over," he commented.

"I worry about Jeff and Clicker," Sue replied. "Does it say anything about people being left?"

"It has pictures of the Embassy overrun by a mob," Rick reported. "It says the last Marines left at dawn yesterday. By noon, the South Vietnamese Army had surrendered."

The hotel appeared quiet as the taxi and the dawn arrived at the hotel simultaneously.

"All our standard rooms are booked," the clerk informed them. "I have a Deluxe Ocean Front with a balcony available."

"That's perfect," Rick stated.

Sue immediately took a shower. Then she bathed the children. By the time Rick finished washing the grime from Air Force travel off his body, his family was asleep. He finished reading the stories about Saigon in the paper. Soon, he was asleep next to Sue.

Mid-afternoon arrived before Rick stirred. Everyone quickly woke up, groggy from jet lag, and hungry.

A hotel café was open, so they ate a meal. Sue wasn't sure whether to order breakfast or lunch for the boys. Lei wanted a hamburger. On the way back to the room, she stopped in the hotel shop. She bought a new one-piece swimsuit. She resolved to relax while Rick dealt with the lawyer. They planned to spend a week recovering from their ordeal.

Yet, Sue and Rick knew their trip was an easy one. Hundreds of Vietnamese refugees were on their way to resettlement camps in the United States. The refugees would be in the United States, but every family faced an uncertain period of adjustment.

They heard no news of their friends' escapes from Saigon. Clicker, Jeff, and the Ngos remained on Sue and Rick's minds.

The first morning after breakfast, Rick pulled out the lawyer's name. He dialed from the hotel suite. He left a message since the lawyer wasn't available. At seven the following morning, the phone rang in their suite while Rick was convincing David to get dressed. Sue woke and answered the phone.

"Rick," she called from the main room, "it's that lawyer."

Rick rushed to the phone. He jotted some notes on the desktop pad and hung up.

Sue watched expectedly.

"What did he say?" she asked as Rick replaced the phone in its cradle.

"A lawyer from Denver will call us. He is handling adoptions for Hoa Sen's children in Denver. He will make sure we follow the proper steps."

Rick saw the relief on Sue's face.

"It won't be immediate, though. We need to get another notarized copy of the adoption documents. The Denver lawyer will want them."

He picked up the phone to dial the front desk.

"Is there a notary public in the hotel?" he asked.

He nodded, said thank you, and hung up.

"There is one at a bank down the street. Can you watch the children after breakfast so I can go there?"

"I'll take them to the beach."

Two hours later, Rick walked to his family on Waikiki Beach.

"Did you get copies made?"

Rick held up a large envelope.

"Right here. I'll mail a set to the lawyer and take our copy to the room. Then I'll join you here. I could use a week on Waikiki."

After two days on the beach, Rick thought Sue was recovering from the effects of the crash. But he awoke in the middle of the night to find her crying on her pillow. Her back was to him, but her shoulders shuddered, and he heard her sobs. He placed an arm around her.

She rolled over, and he felt the tears on her cheek. He tried to comfort her and gave her tissues.

"Oh, Rick," she sobbed. "I keep asking myself: Why did Mai have to die in the crash? She was getting a child back into his seatbelt when we hit. How do I ever tell Lei I killed his mother? Why did I survive?"

"You can't blame yourself. It's not our fault that the Air Force sent a flawed airplane."

"Have you seen how lost Lei is? Today, he was just sitting on the beach staring at the ocean. How can we ever love him enough to make it up to him?"

———•———

MR. EUGENE

The trip on the merchant ship became an ordeal for Clicker and the Ngos. The thin blankets made poor mattresses on the grimy deck. Crowded conditions made the air stagnate in the hold. The ship rolled and bounced. Throughout a miserable night, an epidemic of seasickness erupted. The scarcity of food did little to relieve the nausea. Water remained in short supply.

A windy morning greeted everyone early on the heaving merchant ship. The refugees appeared to get their sea legs as cases of seasickness diminished. Clicker noticed Bao's face contained a lost look. He fidgeted with a knife he took from his pocket. He unfolded and folded its two blades, a two-inch one and a smaller one. Clicker recognized it as a red Swiss Army knife. Bao unfolded the other two components and studied them. Clicker figured Tinh had bought it in the BX.

"Do you know what those two small parts do?" Clicker asked. He pointed at them.

Boa shook his head. Clicker opened one of them.

"This is a can opener," he told him.

Boa didn't understand. Clicker pantomimed holding a can and opening it. Boa nodded. Clicker closed it and opened the other part.

"This is a bottle opener," he said. Again, he pantomimed the act of opening a bottle.

Clicker pointed to the point. "And this is a screwdriver," he noted. Bao didn't understand. Clicker pantomimed tightening a screw. The boy still didn't understand. Anh translated Clicker's explanation. Bao gave a hint of a smile.

"You'll want to tie the knife to a belt loop so you won't lose it," Clicker noted.

Clicker held a long end of the cord from the boy's waist. He made a cutting motion with a finger. Bao understood and cut the cord. Clicker unwound strands to braid a thinner cord. Then he tied one end to a belt loop and the other to the ring on the knife.

"Thank you," Anh told Clicker. She looked at her son. "Bao doesn't understand why his father is not with us."

After a pause, she added, "He misses his big brother, too."

Clicker wanted to ask, but he felt it would be prying. Anh went on.

"Tan died in the war two years ago," she explained. "With Tinh flying a lot and gone often, Tan taught Bao many things a father usually teaches a son. They were very close. Now he is afraid his father will die, too."

Clicker said nothing.

"I haven't been able to explain to Bao why Tinh did not come," Anh continued. "I'm not sure I understand."

Clicker looked from Anh to Bao.

"At first I wasn't sure either. But I have had time to think lately."

Clicker looked at Bao.

"I've known your father for less than a year. But he has taught me things. One characteristic I have seen Tinh show his men is duty … and honor." He stopped. "That's two, I know, but they are very much alike."

He stopped as Anh translated it for Bao.

"I encouraged Tinh to leave with us," he told Anh and Bao. "But he said he still had a duty to perform. Bao, your father is a soldier. He saw other soldiers continue to fight for your country. His obligation compelled him to stay. When other soldiers need his help, your father can give but one reply. He would lose his honor if he left."

Tears formed in Anh's eyes as she translated for Bao. When she had finished, she reached out and hugged her son closely.

"Thank you, Mr. Clicker," she finally said. It was the first time she had addressed him directly. She hesitated. He could tell she wanted to ask him a question.

"You're welcome, Anh," he replied, hoping it would encourage her.

"Clicker, what does the name mean?"

Clicker smiled.

"It's a nickname my friends gave me years ago."

Her face showed he needed to explain. He clicked his tongue.

"I do that a lot," he explained, clicking it again.

The hint of a smile formed on Anh's face. "What is your given name?"

"Eugene," Clicker explained.

"What does that name mean?"

Clicker smiled. "It means good or well-born. I'm not sure I've lived up to the name."

"It is a much better name," Anh stated. "May I call you Mr. Eugene?"

"Eugene would be fine."

Anh looked at her daughters. Kim sat with her head down, her chin resting on her knee. She looked to be on the verge of tears.

"Kim worries about Truc," Anh stated. "While Tinh arranged for Kim to meet him, she learned to love Truc in a short time." She paused. "Kim sees a lot of her father in Truc. He has a sense of honor as well."

When they climbed out of the hold for their first meal, Anh hung on to his offered arm. He steadied Kim and Thuan as well. Bao helped his grandparents.

Clicker ushered the Ngos up with the first group. Marines prepared the food in large metal cans, which stood over large burners. They dumped bags of rice into the cans and added water. The Marines grabbed large cans and dumped them into the rice. Clicker led Bao over.

"Get your knife; we can help."

Bao understood. He pulled his knife from a pocket and unfolded the can opener.

"We would like to help," Clicker told a Marine.

The Marine handed Bao a large can of Spam. Bao initially struggled with the knife and can, but he quickly figured out how to use the can opener. Bao handed the can to the Marine. Clicker grabbed the empty cans. They had a practical use because he saw no bowls.

Clicker would never again look at rice in the same way. Tossing in Spam added some taste and protein. Like the rice and sardines in Clicker's survival school, rice with Spam was a survival ration.

———•———

TINH'S DECISION

----·|----

Dobie checked in with Tinh and Khắc for two mornings. The colonel recovered from his ordeal. On Saturday, Dobie explained to Tinh the need for the airplane and the pilot.

"Sergeant Khắc has to come, too," the colonel explained. "I do not know this airplane well enough. I can fly it, but Sergeant Khắc knows everything else."

The response encouraged Dobie. It showed that the colonel considered a risky mission worthwhile if it meant another family made it to America. Dobie worried about the Sergeant. *Did he have the same warrior spirit?*

With Marcel's family in constant danger, time was crucial. Yet, pushing the colonel and the sergeant could only result in a "no" answer.

"Please think about it," he implored in a conversation with the colonel and the sergeant.

When Dobie returned to the hotel, Charles had troubling news.

"We are operating the radios past their range," Charles reported. "It was hard to hear all that Marcel said. But it sounds like forces are putting pressure on the Hmong everywhere. He's afraid they are being pushed into confined areas for a last battle. The rumors are widespread that the Hmong general is more interested in his escape than fighting."

"How's Lima Site 26?"

"So far, the pressure is farther east where the general is."

"You gotta push for a decision, boss," Jimbo interjected. "The vise will close on Marcel quickly."

"We need to find another pilot ASAP," Charles suggested.

"But where?" Dobie countered.

Charles shrugged.

"By the way, you got a call this afternoon. Some guy named Clicker."

"Clicker?" Dobie asked.

"That's what he said."

"What did he say?"

"Just left a number."

"Where?"

"Olongapo, the Philippines."

Dobie grabbed the message and dialed the front desk.

"I need to place a call to the Philippines," he told the operator.

He listened.

"Yes, thank you. I'll be here waiting."

Ten minutes later, the phone rang.

Dobie grabbed it. Clicks sounded from the international phone circuits. Finally, a hotel operator in the Philippines answered. Dobie looked at the message.

"Please connect me with Mr. Cruthers," he requested. More clicks ensued.

"Cruthers," a voice answered.

"Clicker, this is Dobie Starbuckle. I got your message."

"Based on our conversation, I guessed you would be in a hotel outside the base. I'd appreciate it if you'd look for a Vietnamese pilot there for me. He's expected to fly a C-123 to U-Tapao."

"Colonel Tinh?" Clicker asked.

"Yes!"

"I've been checking on airplanes landing here. He arrived on Wednesday afternoon. He said you had left with his family."

"Yes, they are at a camp here at Subic Bay," Clicker replied. "The grapevine reports our group leaves for Guam soon. His wife has begged me to find him."

"The Commies shot down the colonel," Dobie reported. "But he escaped to Tan Son Nhut and flew the airplane and passengers out. It was a rough flight. Do you plan to go with his family to Guam?"

"If I don't stay with them, the thousands of refugees will swallow them. I plan to sponsor them to spring them from the refugee camps ASAP."

There goes my big inducement to the colonel, Dobie reflected.

"I'll tell the colonel his family is safe. Will you be in a hotel on Guam?"

"Yes. Assuming we go to the Navy Air Base there, I will be near it. The gossip says a refugee camp is under construction nearby."

"To get my group out, I need the colonel to pilot the plane. I don't have time to find another pilot. We will need to base out of an airport closer to the border, though. Comms are too difficult this far away."

"Where can I reach you next?"

"Not sure. I'll leave a message for you at the front desk here when we leave."

Dobie hung up.

"We need Colonel Tinh to decide," he stated. "Jimbo, come along. I'll talk to the colonel alone, though. We don't want him to feel like a gang is pressuring him. We need to find a fuel truck to gas up the plane. You work on that."

He looked at Charles.

"Do you think Peabody has any contacts acquainted with a pilot? He has to get here quickly."

"I can ask."

"Okay. Work on that while we go to the base. We need a backup plan if Tinh won't go."

Dobie and Jimbo rushed to the base. Access to the refugee camp was easier than they expected. Trucks were driving back and forth carrying supplies.

Looks like they are planning on it being here a while, Dobie concluded.

Jimbo dropped Dobie near Tinh's tent. Then he went looking for a fuel truck with a driver to bribe. Dobie found Tinh sitting on a cot.

"Can we talk outside?" he asked.

Once outside, Dobie ignored the Vietnamese preference for small talk before dealing with business.

"I spoke with Clicker. Your family is in the Philippines. Soon they will go to Guam."

Tinh's eyes brightened.

"Everyone is okay?"

"It appears so. Clicker will fly to Guam with them. He hopes to get them out of the refugee camp on a plane to the States."

Dobie paused so Tinh could absorb the news. Then he continued.

"I have spoken with Mr. Peabody, who is financing my operation. He will pay for the story of your family's escape and your escape from Saigon with Sergeant Khắc. Mr. Peabody will also work to get you to America. Have you considered our request to help us rescue our friends in Laos? They saved the lives of my team a couple of months back. Now they need our help."

Dobie hoped that his directness had not made Tinh inclined to say no. He allowed the silence that followed to linger.

"Give me the details of what this flight would involve," Tinh finally requested.

No definitive answer, Dobie realized. *But not a "no."*

Dobie explained where Marcel was in Laos and where refueling would occur in northern Thailand.

"Are maps or charts of Thailand and Laos available?" Tinh asked.

"Topographical maps of the site," Dobie answered. "We found old aeronautical charts of Thailand and Laos."

"How old?"

"Less than a year."

Tinh nodded.

"And I need the aircraft manual from the airplane."

"Will Sergeant Khắc come?" Dobie was compelled to ask.

"If I agree." Tinh looked Dobie in the eye. Dobie recognized the importance of this for a Vietnamese. "But I need to be sure this is a viable mission."

The response encouraged Dobie.

"Whatever you need," Dobie replied.

"I need paper and a pencil," Tinh requested. Dobie pulled a pen and a small notebook out of a pocket.

Tinh jotted a couple of notes. "The first trick is stealing the airplane."

Dobie nodded.

"Just before dawn would be easiest. I'll need enough light to see the taxiway to take off. Hopefully, we can be gone before base security realizes what is happening."

"I've concluded the same," Dobie acknowledged. "Can you come to the plane with me now to get what you need?"

"Let's go," Tinh replied.

The pair arrived at the airplane to find Jimbo sitting against a landing gear. He stood when Tinh and Dobie arrived.

"What's up?"

"We need the flight manual," Dobie explained.

"One more thing, boss," Jimbo said. "The cargo compartment needs a serious cleaning. I've asked around. A fleet service team will sneak over after dark. I requested a fuel truck, too. We'll see if they show. But we need the crew chief."

"I'll inform Sergeant Khắc," Tinh noted. "He knows how much fuel to pump."

"The charts are in the car," Dobie reported.

"If it's a feasible mission, we can leave early in the morning," Tinh stated. "I'll get the flight manual, then look at those charts."

Tinh climbed the crew steps and returned in seconds. They walked to the car on the edge of the grass. Dobie pulled maps and charts from a tattered knapsack.

"Do you have a compass?" Tinh asked. Dobie pulled a compass out of the pack.

Tinh sat in the back seat and unfolded the maps. He noticed circles drawn around two airfields on the Tactical Pilot Chart.

"What are these?"

Dobie pointed to the northern airfield.

"That's Lima 26, where our passengers are. The one to the southeast is where the Hmong general has his headquarters. Pathet Lao and PAVN forces are moving toward it."

"From which direction?"

"Our intel indicates from the north and east."

"South of Lima 26 is clear of hostiles?"

"Based on our information."

"Are you familiar with Lima 26?"

"I operated from there years ago."

Tinh studied the aeronautical chart.

"What's the surrounding terrain?" he asked.

"Lima 26 sits in a valley, with higher mountains to its west."

"Let me see the grid map."

Dobie pulled his map from the pack. Tinh studied it.

"What about the runway's condition?" Tinh finally asked.

"A report says two thousand feet are usable."

Tinh measured, drew lines on the chart, and jotted numbers next to them.

"We will need to refuel before we get there. It can't be a military base."

Dobie pointed to an airport symbol in northern Thailand.

"We know a contact here."

Tinh drew a line from it to a circle south of the Lima Site. He measured and jotted.

"Flying from Lima 26 to here will be too far," Tinh stated. "Where do you propose we take the passengers?"

"The Thais are very hostile toward refugees," Dobie replied.

"I've noticed."

"It will be best to land at a base with US forces and surrender to them. Udorn is the closest Thai base."

Dobie pointed to the air base in northern Thailand on the chart.

Tinh stayed quiet for a minute.

"Not getting back here might be an issue for Sergeant Khắc," he finally stated. "He'll be separated from his family."

"Does he have a complete list of them?"

"I doubt it."

"He needs to write one down. We'll need it to free them from the camp. We might also convince the US commander to move us back here after we surrender."

Tinh opened the aircraft flight manual. He studied several pages, traced on graphs, and jotted notes on the pilot chart.

"We had a flare pistol on the plane," Tinh stated. "We need to see if it is still there. If so, we need flares for it. Otherwise, getting another one is helpful. Using it will help avoid getting shot down by a missile."

"We can check on other planes here."

"How many on your team are coming with us?" Tinh asked.

"Aside from Jimbo and me, there's Charles. But he will stay where we refuel. He's our 'get out of jail' card. He works for our sponsor."

"Besides Sergeant Khắc, I have one more. He will be our tail gunner. He saved us from a missile flying out of Saigon."

Dobie nodded. He liked the way this fighter pilot operated. Tinh drew up a plan, considering contingencies. He understood one crucial tenet of war: no battle plan survives contact with the enemy.

Tinh folded up his chart.

"I suggest your third team member gets here tonight. We need to be ready to leave before dawn. We all need to spend the night on the airplane. I'll get Sergeant Khắc and Quyền, my third member."

"I'll tell Jimbo, then go pick up Charles," Dobie stated.

Tinh handed the airplane flight manual to Dobie.

"Put this on the small table in the cockpit." He pondered for a moment. "Do you possess weapons? The Thais confiscated the ones we had. We may need to defend the plane while on the ground."

"We carry handguns, but we need more ammo. Our passengers should be able to defend the plane."

Tinh gave Dobie a salute.

"I'll meet you at the plane around dusk."

With that, Tinh walked toward the refugee camp while Dobie headed for the airplane.

As Tinh approached the tent area, he saw worrying activity. Thai workers were busy building a fence around the refugee tents. Their refugee camp was about to become a prison. The smell of poor sanitation also grew. Tinh saw no construction of additional toilet or shower facilities. The Thais clearly considered a fence more important.

———◆———

ON TO GUAM

A fter thirty-eight harrowing hours, the merchant ship slowed. Clicker climbed the stairs out of the cargo hold to see where they were. As he reached the top and looked around, a hazy sun rose above the horizon. By his estimation, they should be in Subic Bay. The ship stopped, and Clicker heard the rattling chains of the ship dropping its anchor. They weren't in a bay. He saw an opening to a bay and a tropical forest lining the shore. It had been nearly five years since his last visit to Subic Bay, so he could not be sure this was it.

Clicker looked at his watch. It read 0600. He squinted at the small date window. The day was May 3rd. They had been traveling for four days. No news of Saigon had reached them. But the city and the country must have fallen to the Communists by now.

The ship remained stationary for no apparent reason. Marines on deck prepared and served another subsistence meal. Spam had given way to canned sardines and tuna in the rice. Water remained rationed.

Clicker approached one of the Marines.

"What is the news from Saigon?" he asked.

"Sir?" came the reply.

"Has the city fallen?"

"Yes, sir. It fell three days ago."

"Where are we?"

The Marine pointed to the opening of the bay.

"Subic Bay is there."

The delay gave Clicker time to plan his steps once the refugees reached shore. He expected restrictions on movement for the refugees. His official US passport and Department of Defense ID should allow him freedom of movement. A run to the Navy Base Exchange was first on his to-do list.

Hours passed.

What is the damn delay? Clicker fumed.

The Marines had no answers. They were in the dark, too. The refugees spent another morning on the ship. Sanitary conditions deteriorated further. The makeshift latrines overflowed. Clicker and a Vietnamese man organized the dumping of the contents overboard. Clicker guessed the man was a former military leader. Anh's father insisted on being part of the chain that passed the buckets up. He ordered Bao to participate.

Shortly after noon, movement on deck told Clicker their sea ordeal would be ending. Slowly, the Marines moved groups out of the cargo hold. The spirits of the passengers improved as the hold emptied of people.

Finally, a Marine corporal waved to the group that included the Ngos. On deck, Clicker guessed the reason for the slow progress. The US Navy had only two boats to transport the refugees to shore. Anchored outside Subic Bay, the ride to the shore took nearly an hour.

On the dock, a contingent of Marines herded the refugees to buses. They arrived at athletic fields where a tent city stood. Barricades surrounded the encampment. Was their purpose to keep the curious out or the population in? Clicker could not help feeling that the place felt more like a prison than a temporary shelter.

At a processing table, clerks recorded the names of every refugee. Two Navy corpsmen sat at another table. By the time Clicker stood at the front of the line, he had not arrived at a decision. He wanted desperately to go to a clean hotel with a full bath and clean sheets. But he was afraid of being separated from the Ngos. He feared he would never find them again in the throng of refugees.

As the clerk studied his passport and ID, Clicker reached a decision.

"Mr. Cruthers, if you will step over to see Mr. Jones," the clerk stated, pointing to another table. "Transportation to the base hotel or gate will arrive shortly."

"Thank you, but I need some information," he replied. "I am sponsoring the Ngo family to immigrate to the States." He gestured to Anh and the family behind him. "I don't want to become separated from them. Can they accompany me to a hotel off base?"

The clerk did not hesitate before answering.

"That won't be possible," he stated curtly.

"Is someone here with authority whom I can speak with?"

"Not at the moment."

Bullshit, Clicker thought. *Stay calm,* he encouraged himself. *Now what?*

Besides a BX run, Clicker had other items to accomplish.

"May I visit them later today?"

"If you speak with Mr. Jones, he can assist you."

"I'll wait until you register the Ngos," Clicker stated. "I need to know their assigned tent."

Clicker stepped aside. Walking with them to their tent felt necessary. He did not want to cause a delay. Anxious people and others still on that stinking boat waited behind him.

Anh stepped to the table.

"Do you need an interpreter, ma'am?" the clerk immediately inquired.

"No, I do not," she stated clearly with her French accent.

She retrieved passports and other documents from her satchel. The clerk inspected them and recorded all their names. Then, he handed her a pile of forms.

"These are applications to immigrate to the United States. Prepare them at your first opportunity. We have volunteers to assist if needed. Keep them with you until you have completed them. You will have an opportunity later to submit them."

He shuffled more papers, recording other information as he did. Finally, he finished. He handed additional forms to Anh.

"Your assigned tent is here," he instructed, pointing to the top form. Pulling another form from the pile, he concluded. "Camp regulations are here, in English and Vietnamese."

He gave her a few seconds to absorb the information. Then he pointed to a gate to the side.

"Directions to your tent are available past the gate." He pointed with his index finger.

Ignorant bureaucrat, Clicker steamed. *He has no clue that pointing with your finger is a rude gesture to the Vietnamese.*

Clicker followed the Ngos through the gate. Two women, an American and a Vietnamese, met them. Clicker assumed the American was a Navy wife, and the Vietnamese was an interpreter.

"We can show you to your tent," the Vietnamese lady said in Vietnamese. "We will also show you the closest facilities. Please ask questions you may have."

As they walked, Anh started asking questions. She started with the American woman.

"I speak English, and my children speak a little. My parents do not speak any." She looked at the Vietnamese woman. "So, thank you for helping us."

The American kept glancing at Clicker. Anh continued.

"Our good friend, Mr. Eugene, has been such a help to us during this trip. He has been so kind to sponsor our immigration to America. Will he be able to visit us regularly?"

"I'm Cheryl Robson," she introduced herself. "I think Eugene will talk his way in to visit you."

"Mr. Eugene flew with my husband near Saigon," Anh continued. "We owe him so much."

"Your husband's a pilot?" Cheryl inquired. "And you, too?" she added, looking at Clicker.

"Colonel Tinh could not leave with his family," Clicker stated. "I was glad to accompany them. And yes, I instructed some of Colonel Tinh's pilots."

"My husband is a Navy pilot," Cheryl volunteered.

They arrived at the tent. Clicker noted its number. Cheryl explained the location of the nearest latrines and other limited facilities. Clicker wondered how long the Navy expected the Vietnamese to be here. He guessed it wouldn't be long. He expected the Ngos would stay in more camps before they settled in the States.

After Cheryl Robson and her companion left, he gave Anh an outline of his plans.

"I'll make a run to the BX to buy a basic change of clothes. I can only guess at sizes. Do you prefer sandals or American-style tennis shoes?"

Anh interpreted and told Clicker their preferences. The children wanted tennis shoes. Anh opted for them as well. Her parents preferred sandals. His challenge was to guess the sizes. The smallest adult sizes of clothes would probably fit them. He placed his foot next to each of theirs to get an idea for shoes. He decided that too big was better than too small.

"I also want to make some calls to locate Tinh," he stated. "It will be hard, though, since everyone we know is on the move. But I promise to try."

"Thank you, Mr. Eugene," Anh whispered.

Clicker rushed to the gate of the tent city. He saw no point in asking about access. He would just walk in and dare someone to stop him. The most critical information he needed to know was how long the Ngos would be there.

He raced to the Base Exchange to buy a change of clothes: pants, shirts, jackets, and shoes. He bought new clothes for himself, as well as a razor and shaving cream. Water bottles also seemed to be a good idea. He found two one-liter bottles, as well as iodine tablets. He was the last customer at the BX. The manager had to unlock the doors to escort him out.

Next, he found a hotel close to the gate to the base. Before doing anything, he showered and shaved. His body odor annoyed him.

Early the next morning, the hotel manager helped him compile a list of hotels near the U-Tapao Air Base. The hotel earned a healthy profit from phone calls, especially international ones. Dobie's report that Tinh was in Thailand elated Clicker. Tinh would be there for some time. Clicker guessed the Thais would take weeks to figure out how to address their refugee problem.

Anh cried when Clicker told her that Tinh was safe in Thailand. Bao hugged his mother and cried with her. Clicker did not mention the possible Hmong trip. Kim remained subdued. No news was available about Truc, her fiancé. She only knew his unit formed the last barrier to the Communist forces attacking Saigon. Anh shared her worry.

With the first two items accomplished, Clicker headed to the Officer's Club bar. It seemed to be the best place to hear rumors about the refugee camp. He did not have contacts to collect any official information. Jeff Nickerson would be a useful source, if he knew where Jeff was. But the dash from Saigon had swallowed Jeff up.

The bar, Clicker reasoned, would be where personnel on temporary duty would gather. He was interested in any cargo plane aircrews or crews from any ship with space for passengers. On the way, Clicker asked his taxi to swing by the flight line. He searched for Air Force cargo planes. No planes were on the ramp. The problem, Clicker recognized, was the proximity of Clark Air Base across a mountain range. The Air Force would keep its airplanes there. It was a quick hop over the mountains to the Cubi Point Naval Air Station, the airstrip for Subic Bay Naval Base.

Clicker paid the taxi to wait while he dashed into the airfield's passenger terminal. He wondered about the likely destinations for any refugees, asking about flights to Guam or Hawaii. Signing up for any space-available seat, he left his hotel number. He could only hope he would hear about any refugee flights. He wrote down the telephone number of the passenger terminal desk.

Personnel on temporary duty filled the club bar. Clicker wandered among several groups, striking up conversations about their reason for being there. He bought rounds of drinks, even as his available funds dwindled. Clicker's story of the dash from Saigon interested all listeners.

He heard two pieces of useful information. The President of the Philippines was unhappy that the Americans brought Vietnamese into his country. He demanded their immediate departure. An Air Force captain provided the second useful tidbit. He commanded an aerial port detachment at Cubi Point on temporary duty. He reported that flights to Guam would begin immediately. Clark Air Base also prepared to evacuate the refugees from a tent city on the base.

After a quick hamburger at the bar, Clicker rushed to retrieve his knapsack from the hotel. He decided to spend the night at the camp. It was the only way to guarantee that the Ngos would not disappear.

As he reached their tent, the arrival of camp officials validated Clicker's decision. They were to leave at 0800 hours the following morning to board a C-130 for Guam. Clicker's presence confused the official. He was not on his list.

"Well, I wouldn't worry too much," the official finally admitted. "The flight has no assigned seats."

The next morning at 0730, Vietnamese and one American lined up to board the bus to the flight line. A passenger service representative checked names.

Clicker remained missing from the list.

"Mr. Eugene has traveled with us since we left Saigon," Anh assured the airman.

Then Clicker spotted the Air Force captain from the bar. He waved him over. The airman explained that Mr. Cruthers was not on the passenger manifest.

"You want to travel with the Ngos to Guam?" the captain asked Clicker.

"Yes, sir, I do."

The captain turned to the airman.

"Add him to the manifest."

When Clicker followed Anh off the bus to the C-130, he understood the statement about seat assignments. The Herk had no seats, only a bare metal floor. White tie-down straps spanned the width of the floor at regular intervals. This was a no-frills flight configured for maximum passenger capacity. Yet, it was a vast improvement over the cargo hold of the merchant ship. The Air Force, at least, took pride in the cleanliness of its airplanes.

Spotting the honey bucket as he entered the airplane, Clicker was glad he had suggested everyone use the latrine before boarding the bus. Clicker touched Anh's elbow to lead her and the family as far forward as possible. The thinness of her elbow surprised him.

He also saw blankets spread around the floor. Clicker grabbed four as they worked their way forward.

The flight crew wasted no time. The loadmaster raised the ramp, and he advised everyone to sit and slide under a strap. He also passed out a package of earplugs and showed their use. Consequently, no one mistook them for chewing gum. Anh made certain her parents understood.

Clicker also spotted airsickness bags scattered around the airplane. The Air Force preferred to keep its airplanes clean. To avoid the power of suggestion, the loadmaster skipped a demonstration.

After the pilot started the engines, another loadmaster climbed up the steps of the crew door. As he worked his way past, Clicker tapped him on the shoulder.

"How long to Guam?"

"Five hours and fifty minutes."

In contrast to the prison-guard demeanor of the Marines on the ships, the Air

Force crew worked to provide some comfort during the flight. They didn't offer an in-flight meal, but they had strapped five-gallon water coolers to stanchions in the cargo compartment. Importantly, paper cups made drinking easy. When the loadmaster noticed passengers shivering, he spoke into his headset. Shortly, the temperature rose to a comfortable level.

Kim, Thuan, and Bao curled up with blankets to sleep for much of the flight. Anh's parents chatted with each other. Clicker caught Anh's glance once. She smiled at him. He liked her calling him Mr. Eugene.

Alone again with his thoughts, a quote jumped into Clicker's mind. He suspected it came from a piece of literature his education had forced upon him. It was about some people achieving greatness, while others having greatness thrust upon them. Here was a humble Vietnamese wife leading her family to safety amidst the chaos of war. Her poise in the battle inspired him to help her in every way.

Just my luck, he mused. *I'm falling in love with another man's wife, a man I respect.*

———•———

LIMA SITE 26

Tinh decided to take off earlier than dawn. Actions by the Thai authorities over the past twelve hours prompted his decision. Besides the new fence, Thai officials posted regulations around the refugee camp. The directives required written authorization for camp residents to depart the area. Armed guards roamed the perimeter near the unfinished portions of the fence. Tinh, Khắc, and Quyển had to sneak past the sentries in the dark to get to the airplane. Likewise, Dobie, Jimbo, and Charles drove past a security gate with the car's lights off. Sneaking onto a Royal Thai Air Base flight line with loaded weapons and a high-quality radio could land them in a Thai jail.

When the cleaning team saw the mess on the cargo compartment floor, their price doubled. They demanded half before beginning. Fortunately, the team brought a portable light. Dobie wished he had parked the plane farther from the refugee camp.

Jimbo's fuel truck did not arrive until 3:00 a.m. The cleaning team had just finished. The driver extracted a bonus before he allowed the fuel to flow. Dobie surrendered a small gold baht chain to satisfy him. Khắc accomplished refueling using only a small flashlight. Jimbo took great care to ensure no beam flashed toward the camp.

Dobie drove the Chevy along the taxiway with its lights off, stopping whenever directed by Tinh. The pilot wanted to ensure that it was clear for takeoff. Tinh looked for small obstacles that would not be visible in the predawn light. With Tinh satisfied, Dobie parked the car out of sight between two airplanes next to their C-123.

The cleaning team could not remove all the odor from the plane. Dobie hoped the smell would dissipate once they were in the air. Khắc left the upper rear cargo door open. Once they started the engines, he planned to crank the airflow to the maximum.

At fifty minutes before dawn, Tinh looked across at Khắc.

"Let's start engines."

Khắc turned on the battery and flicked the switches to start the engines. Tinh turned on the radio. If the tower called, he had no intention of answering. But he wanted to hear what they might say. With the lights off, Tinh hoped they wouldn't even notice them.

Khắc started the piston engines in quick sequence. As Tinh rolled out of the parking space, Khắc started the small jet engines. Tinh straightened out the nose.

"Everything good?" he quizzed the sergeant.

"Good."

"We're rolling."

Tinh advanced the throttles, and the plane accelerated. The takeoff went smoothly, and the radio stayed silent. Tinh climbed high enough to clear any building or tower ahead. However, he wanted to stay low to minimize any radar spotting him. He did not know if the Thai Air Force had F-5s on alert, and he preferred not to find out.

"Let's shut down the jets," Tinh instructed.

After twenty minutes with no calls on the emergency frequency, Tinh eased the plane into a climb for the rest of the flight to their refueling airport. The airport had a radio beacon station, so Tinh dialed the frequency into the navigation radio. Khắc adjusted the engine controls to reduce the fuel burn.

An hour later, the navigation needle pointed straight ahead as the radio locked on a strong signal. Tinh deviated from his direct course to it, though, to avoid following a section of a highway. He preferred to remain out of sight of any highway traffic. Ten miles away, he called the airport tower; the tower cleared him to land with no questions. Tinh wished they had found paint to cover the Vietnamese Air Force insignia on the airplane.

Jimbo directed Tinh to the location on the airport that his contact had given him. Unable to contact the friend, Jimbo hoped that the vague timing he had provided would not be a problem.

"When you see a C-123 arriving from the south, it will be us," he had communicated.

Ten minutes after they parked, a bicycle pedaled to the airplane. Jimbo shook hands with the American and exchanged a few words. The bicycle pedaled away, but it returned in five minutes, leading a fuel truck.

Dobie, Jimbo, and Charles chatted in the cargo compartment. Charles picked up two packs, one holding the radio. He departed the airplane. Charles planned to hail a taxi and check into a nearby hotel. He would be the rescue group's link to Mr. Peabody if further help became required. He would also report the mission results to Mr. Peabody, who waited in Manila.

While Sergeant Khắc supervised the fueling, Dobie asked Tinh to turn on the plane's high-frequency radio. He needed to contact Marcel to give them an estimated time of arrival. Tinh estimated how long the refueling would take to calculate the time Marcel should expect them. Tinh wanted the passengers at the south end of the usable runway. He planned to land to the south, turn around, load the passengers with the engines running, and take off to the north. The terrain climbed more gently to the north out of the valley. Minimum ground time was essential. He also asked that Marcel mark the usable section of the runway with cloth panels or poles. Remembering the chaos at Da Nang, Tinh warned Marcel to be ready to defend the airplane against a mob.

When they finished the radio call, Khắc climbed into the cockpit.

"We have the fuel," he reported. "I also added oil to both engines."

"Let's wait five minutes," Tinh ordered. "Then check for any water in the tanks. Better to learn that now than after we take off."

Khắc nodded. He understood. The preflight of every airplane required a check for water at the bottom of a fuel tank. All airplanes contained small valves to drain a fuel sample. In locations where the fuel quality was a question, the step became critical.

While they waited, Tinh issued instructions for their landing, loading, and takeoff at Lima 26.

"Did you find any flares?" he questioned Dobie.

"No."

"We'll just have to hope we don't have any missiles coming after us."

He gathered his thoughts.

"After we land, I want Khắc to open the cargo door. As soon as we turn around, lower the ramp. Get the passengers on board ASAP. When we are full, we go. Raise the ramp." He pointed to Quyên. "I want you back there. Jimbo, too. Dobie, you watch from the top of the stairs to the cockpit. When Khắc raises the ramp, Quyên, wave both your hands over your head to tell Dobie. Hang on in the back. We'll be going."

Tinh looked at each of them. They understood.

"We must keep people from climbing into the landing gear. Figure out how to do that best. Shoot anyone who tries. They will die anyway, and they will kill us all if they get tangled in the landing gear."

Five minutes later, Khắc and Tinh left the cockpit. They found small amounts of water in the fuel tanks. Khắc drained samples until the water was gone. He looked at Tinh.

"Another five minutes," Tinh instructed. "We have to be sure."

Five minutes later, Khắc and Tinh checked the fuel again. They scrutinized each sample. Tinh nodded.

"Let's go."

The takeoff was quick. He turned northwest toward the Mekong River and Laos. Tinh selected an altitude above any danger from rifle fire, but low enough that radars would not spot them. His route avoided larger settlements and any significant roads. The last forty miles would be the tense period. The Hmong general holed up fifteen miles east of the route he planned. He hoped Marcel had not missed intelligence on hostile forces near him.

Twenty minutes after takeoff, the mighty Mekong River slipped below them. They had entered Laos. Ten minutes later, Tinh spotted a long lake. He handed his headset to Dobie, who crouched in the small space behind the center console. At the lake's northern tip, Tinh banked right to head to the landing site. Dobie called Marcel to tell him to get ready. They were less than twenty minutes away. Halfway to the site, Dobie pointed out the right cockpit windows. A smoky haze covered the hills and jungle. Two plumes of smoke rose from the jungle and the mountains on the horizon.

"Looks like the general is under attack," Dobie reported to Marcel.

Above the din of the engines, Dobie shouted, "Marcel says it's all calm around them. They have several extra people to come with us. He doesn't expect any trouble on the ground."

Tinh hoped Marcel was correct. He searched ahead, not knowing just what to look for to find the airfield. All he knew was that the field was in a valley. He planned to overfly it to give them the best chance to spot it. Then he would bank into a tight spiral down.

His lack of experience with the airplane made him nervous. He had studied the final approach airspeed. But he didn't know how well the plane slowed in a tight spiral to the runway. He did not have the mental picture to roll out on the final approach.

Suddenly, Dobie shouted.

"There it is! Off the nose to the right!"

Tinh rolled several degrees right, searching over the glare shield. He wanted it on his left side. As he rolled the wings level, he saw it. He pulled the throttles back to slow the airplane.

Used to piloting a fast jet into airports with long runways, his first thought was, *That is a short runway! What have I gotten myself into?*

The dirt runway disappeared below the left section of the windscreen; then it slid through the small windows near his left leg. A few seconds later, Tinh rolled into a steep left bank. With four thousand feet to lose, he was unsure how many turns that would take.

The airplane spiraled down. Tinh wanted to stay over the northern edge of the runway. He checked his altitude, his airspeed, and the runway. The plane didn't slow. He was descending too fast. Slowing his descent rate, he checked the airspeed. It dropped.

"Flaps!" he shouted to Khắc.

The wing flaps would create drag to slow the plane and allow him to slow safely. The plane shuddered as the flaps rolled out. Air pockets over the hills and changing terrain jostled them.

"Airspeed!" Khắc shouted.

His airspeed was too slow. He increased the descent rate while nudging the throttles forward. The runway disappeared as a ridgeline came into view. That was west of the runway. He circled over the ridge and let the airplane swing to the east. His altitude showed another thousand feet to lose.

He shoved the throttles forward, unsure how much was enough. The plane leveled off and climbed. Too much. He pulled them back an inch. The runway was not visible.

"Runway?" he shouted to Khắc.

Dobie, still staring out the right window, pointed down. Tinh waited a few seconds before banking left. He would fly parallel to the runway. The plane approached his altitude.

Check airspeed! his experience shouted. *Too fast, now.*

Tinh rolled out and looked off his left shoulder. He should see the runway. Nothing. He only noticed the valley floor and the ground climbing west of the runway. That meant it was right behind them. Tinh made a tight left turn.

Airspeed! Altitude! Tinh checked them in quick succession. He had climbed in the turn. He was thrashing around in the sky. The plane swung around, and Tinh spotted the runway. He aimed for it.

"We'll fly over the runway to spot the good part," he shouted to his crew. "Help me find the markers."

He lined up to the right, so he would have the best view. Halfway down the runway, he spotted two brightly covered panels on the edge.

Is that the beginning or end of the usable runway? Tinh wondered.

As the end of the runway slid by, two more colored panels appeared. The last half of the runway was the usable portion. Tinh turned left in a slow, wide turn, keeping the end of the runway in sight.

Airspeed! Altitude! He reminded himself. *A little fast. Too low!*

Tinh gently corrected as he rolled out of the turn.

As the approach panels slid by his left, Tinh reached for the landing gear lever and lowered it. He nudged the throttles up. The gear rumbled into the slipstream.

Now, basic stick and rudder skills, he told himself. He knew he had to put the plane down right next to those panels on the correct airspeed. Too fast, and he'd have to go around and try again. He had spotted a crowd at the end of the runway.

Landing too fast and running over his passengers would not be good.

When the panels disappeared behind his left shoulder, Tinh rolled the plane into a turn to the runway. It was then he realized the panels were on the wrong side of the airplane. They were on the right side. He would have trouble knowing if he had landed past them.

"Dobie!" he yelled across the cockpit.

Dobie turned to him.

"When the panels are next to you, shout out! I need to land right next to them. But I won't be able to see them."

Dobie gave him a thumbs-up. Tinh focused on the two crucial items for landing now.

Airspeed. Aim point.

He looked at the landing gear lever. Above it, three green lights shone.

Gear check. Airspeed. Aim point.

Tinh sensed he was coming in high. He inched back the throttles, and the ground rushed up.

"Panels!" Dobie shouted. The plane floated. He was too fast. He should have landed. For what seemed like an eternity, the plane remained airborne.

"We're going around!" Tinh shoved the throttles forward. He had missed his aim point. As the power came up, Tinh felt the wheels kiss the dirt. Too late.

"Half flaps!" he yelled to Khắc.

The plane climbed and accelerated as the drag of full flaps eased. On a normal runway, his landing would have been fine. But on a short runway, close wasn't good enough. As a fighter pilot, Tinh had felt superior to the "trash haulers" who flew the transports, especially those with propellers. Now, he appreciated their skill in putting an airplane on a short runway at an exact point.

As he leveled off opposite the landing point, Tinh reviewed his actions. What had he done wrong? As he rolled the airplane on final approach again, he knew. He had aimed for the panels, and the plane had floated past them.

On this approach, Tinh aimed short of the panels. As the ground approached, he slowed its descent rate. Dobie yelled, "Panels!"

The main wheels slammed onto the runway! Tinh stood on the brakes.

"Get the back opened," he instructed Khắc.

Sergeant Khắc stumbled out of his seat and headed to the back. Dobie followed him. He stood at the top of the stairs as Tinh turned the airplane around in front of the crowd. He put on the parking brake and waited. The nose of the plane bumped down. Tinh knew that meant the ramp was down. Tinh felt the airplane settle as people streamed on. He nervously scanned left, then right, looking for a mob. He checked the flaps in the takeoff position.

Minutes passed. Tinh reached up and started the jets. He would need those for takeoff. Then Dobie yelled.

"Ready! Go! Go! Go!"

Tinh released the parking brake. He allowed the airplane to creep forward several feet before advancing the throttles.

"Ramp up!" Dobie shouted.

Tinh moved the throttles to the forward stop. The airplane sped up. In less than a minute, they were airborne. Tinh reached for the landing gear handle and raised it. No mysterious thumps sounded. As the airspeed increased, he raised the flaps. Remembering the steeper climb of the terrain to the west, Tinh eased into a right turn. As the plane headed south, Tinh checked the altitude. They were easily climbing above the terrain to the south. He did not need to spiral up out of the valley. He retraced his route back to the Mekong River.

As they leveled off, Khắc climbed into the right seat.

"Jimbo has supervised throwing out all weapons," he stated.

As the Mekong slid beneath them, Dobie donned the headset and keyed his microphone to call Charles.

"Pan to Wendy." Dobie paused. "Pan has departed Neverland with all Lost Boys." Another pause. "Roger. Out."

Five miles past the river, Tinh rolled the plane right and dialed in the Udorn Royal Thai Air Base navigation station. The course bar on his indicator centered, and the distance window read fifty nautical miles.

Lieutenant Colonel Tinh finally relaxed.

———·———

UDORN

———

Twenty miles from the base, Tinh dialed the tower frequency into the radio. He quickly invented a call sign to use.

"Udorn Tower, this is Tinan Zero One, fifteen miles northeast. Request landing clearance."

"Tinan Zero One, state your origin. We have no flight plan for you."

"Tinan Zero One is a Republic of Vietnam Air Force refugee flight out of Lima Sierra Two-Six."

A pause ensued. The voice of a different controller spoke.

"Tinan Zero One, say again."

Tinh repeated his statement.

"Stand by."

"Udorn, I have sick and injured on board."

"Stand by," came again.

"Tinan Zero One, do you have a prior permission number?"

Tinh was familiar with these. Non-military flights required prior permission to land at an Air Force base.

"Negative. This is an emergency evacuation flight," Tinh tried to clarify.

"Zero One, do you wish to declare an emergency?" the controller prompted.

Tinh understood the suggestion. Military controllers would allow an aircraft with an emergency to land.

"Roger. Tinan Zero One declares an emergency."

"Copy, Zero One. You are number one for Runway One Two. Cleared to land. Please state fuel and souls on board."

Tinh recognized that as a standard request for an aircraft with an emergency. He looked up at the fuel gauges. How many people did he have in the back? He could only guess.

"Zero One has one thousand pounds of fuel and eighty souls on board."

"Say aircraft type, please."

"Charlie One-Two-Three."

Tinh spotted the air base in front and lined up with the runway. The landing on the ten-thousand-foot runway was smooth. Tinh noticed a crash truck on the taxiway and an ambulance as the plane slowed. He turned off at the next taxiway and stopped. A pickup turned around in front of him. The sign on its back instructed Tinh to "Follow Me."

As he followed the pickup, a security police jeep pulled alongside the airplane. Tinh stopped when instructed, and Khắc shut down the engines.

"Now, we'll have some explaining to do," Dobie commented. "I'll do the talking."

By the time Tinh and Dobie walked out the crew door, Quyền had lowered the cargo ramp. Dobie saw another security police jeep parked behind the airplane. A policeman walked toward the ramp as a few passengers stumbled out. His mouth opened. He took a portable radio off his belt and spoke into it.

A security police lieutenant approached Dobie.

"Who is the aircraft commander?"

"Lieutenant Colonel Ngo Tinh, Republic of Vietnam Air Force, is our pilot. I am the mission commander." Dobie had his ID card out and showed it to the police lieutenant.

The policeman from the rear approached.

"Sir, you gotta see this," he said, gesturing to the rear.

The lieutenant followed him with Dobie right behind them.

A medic had stepped onto the ramp. He turned to the lieutenant.

"We have scores of ill passengers, sir," he observed. "I'm gonna need some help. And another ambulance."

He walked back to the ambulance and spoke on his radio.

The police lieutenant turned to Dobie.

"Where did you come from?"

"Lieutenant," Dobie examined the name tag, "Dobbins, we have Hmong fighters from Laos and their families, loyal allies of the United States of America. They request political asylum from Communist persecution."

Dobie spotted Marcel and waved him over.

"Their leader is Colonel Marcel Dubois."

Dobie winked at Marcel, who stopped, stood at attention, and snapped a French military salute. The lieutenant hesitated, then returned the salute.

The lieutenant looked at his sergeant.

"Sergeant, request two buses to transport the passengers. And call the major to get out here."

By now, the passengers streamed off the ramp and looked around, bewilderment on their faces. They wore dirty, tattered clothes. Everyone was very thin. Dobie turned to the lieutenant.

"As you can see, Lieutenant, our passengers direly need medical care, food, and new clothing."

"How many are there?" Lieutenant Dobbins asked Dobie.

Dobie turned to Marcel.

"Sir, we have approximately ninety men, women, and children," Marcel reported in his accented English.

"Lieutenant," Dobie interjected, "Colonel Dubois and I served together in Laos frequently over the past ten years. May we get his people out of the sun? Then I will be happy to answer all your questions."

As he finished, two buses pulled up, followed by another security police jeep. A major stepped out and hustled over to the group.

"What do we have, Lieutenant Dobbins?" he demanded.

The lieutenant gave him a three-sentence explanation. The major scratched his head. He looked at the refugees.

"Let's transport them to the theater for now."

He walked over to the medic.

"Take any in serious condition to the hospital. Request a medical response team to meet us at the theater."

The medic saluted. Another ambulance pulled up. A female nurse got out and immediately went to the group of passengers. The medic joined her.

"What do we have, Sam?" she asked.

"About ninety refugees, ma'am."

"Let's do a quick triage." She peered into the cargo compartment. "You start here. I'll check inside. Some are sitting. I'd guess they'll need immediate attention." She motioned to the drivers of the ambulances. "Bring a couple of stretchers."

The major walked back to Dobie, Tinh, and Marcel. Khắc, Jimbo, and Quyển had joined them. The major looked at them.

"Is this the entire group of conspirators?" he demanded.

"Yes, sir," Dobie answered. "They are my team."

"Consider yourselves under arrest," the major retorted. "Lieutenant, call for another jeep."

"Sir," Dobie interjected, "could Colonel Dubois stay with his people?"

"Keej can look after them," Marcel responded. "I'll come with you."

Dobie shrugged.

"Okay."

The major escorted the group to the jeeps. At the police station, he led them into a small conference room. He left for several minutes. When he returned, a colonel walked into the room with him.

"This is the wing commander, Colonel Gates. He has a few questions for you before I ask mine."

The colonel eyed the group.

"I understand you conducted a rescue mission into Laos," he began.

"That is correct, Colonel," Dobie confirmed.

"On whose authorization?"

"Colonel, we proceeded on our own initiative to rescue allies who were under the danger of imminent liquidation by the Pathet Lao."

"I understand you arrived in a South Vietnamese Air Force aircraft," the colonel countered. "How did you come into possession of it?"

"Lieutenant Colonel Ngo Tinh flew the plane to Thailand from Saigon immediately before the capture of Tan Son Nhut by the People's Army of Vietnam. We requested his services to assist us in our rescue mission."

"And where did he land so you could abscond with it?"

Dobie hesitated before responding, "U-Tapao, sir."

The colonel surveyed the group. He looked at Tinh.

"Colonel Tinh?" he confirmed.

"Yes, sir."

"What was your unit?"

"I commanded the 526th Fighter Squadron at Bien Hoa, sir."

"So, a fighter pilot shows up on my base flying a transport plane." The colonel studied Tinh. "When did you command the squadron?"

"Until 30 April 1975, sir."

"Did you know a contract pilot at Bien Hoa named Rick Guerri?" Colonel Gates inquired.

The surprise on Tinh's face was evident.

"Yes, sir, he worked closely with my pilots and me," Tinh responded.

"I heard his wife and son survived that C-5 crash."

"Yes, sir, they did."

"Rick Guerri and I flew over North Vietnam together. A fine pilot. I'm sure your pilots learned much from him."

"Yes, sir, we did."

The colonel surveyed the group.

"I presume you all have identification, so we can verify any part of your story?"

Only Tinh and Quyên failed to nod.

"I'm afraid, Colonel," Tinh began, "that Colonel Quyên and I lost our IDs before we escaped from the People's Army."

The colonel looked surprised.

"You were captured and escaped?"

"Yes, sir," Tinh stated. "A Strela hit my F-5 as I attacked the enemy east of Saigon. Colonel Quyên was a captive, too. We escaped and worked our way back to Tan Son Nhut by the morning of the 30th."

Colonel Gates eyed the rank on Quyên's shirt.

"My captors stripped me of my uniform, Colonel," Quyên explained. "I recovered this shirt on the Saigon streets."

Colonel Gates looked to the major.

"Major, intel needs to debrief our guests." He turned to leave, signaling the major to follow him.

"Colonel," Marcel interjected before they left the room. "May I ask what is being done to assist the refugees? We are suffering from severe malnutrition and disease. We have lost many in the last week because of starvation."

"A medical team is examining them now," the colonel assured Marcel. "We plan on housing you temporarily in the gymnasium. Our medical staff is setting up a ward there. The men are already donating clothes, blankets, and other essentials for them."

The major and the colonel left.

"I strongly recommend that only Marcel and I speak with the intel weenie," Dobie advised. "He has the useful info for them. Everyone else takes the Fifth."

"Amen to that," Jimbo interjected.

The Vietnamese did not understand Dobie.

Jimbo explained.

"In America, the police cannot make you confess to anything or admit to anything. It's the Fifth Amendment to our Constitution."

"What about torture?" Quyến asked.

"*Verboten*. Not allowed, in theory." Jimbo winked.

The major returned. "Intel will interview each of you individually," he stated.

"Only Colonel Dubois and I have useful intel info," Dobie stated. "So we're the only ones who need to talk to them."

The major glanced around the room. He read agreement on every face.

"Okay, let's go."

The intelligence debriefing took an hour. Dobie and Marcel returned.

Jimbo broke a few minutes of quiet.

"So, boss, what's next?"

"We'll see," Dobie replied. "But I think they have bigger fish to fry than us."

"Such as ..." Jimbo pressed.

"A major rescue operation of the general is about to launch. The intel guy was very interested in the situation on the ground around the Plain of Jars and the general's headquarters. That smoke we saw in the distance was the beginning of a battle. It wouldn't surprise me if our C-123 is gone by tomorrow to be used by others."

Jimbo whistled.

"Our showing up here with a group of Hmong must have thrown the spooks for a loop. We pulled off with little fanfare what they need to do for the general."

"Don't expect any medals," Dobie advised. He looked around the room. In a murmur, he added, "Best if we hold any conversation in a different place."

Another hour passed before Lieutenant Dobbins entered the room.

"We've called for transport to take you to the Visiting Officer's Quarters," he advised them. "In the morning, transport can take you to our modest BX to buy new clothes. The VOQ front desk has basic toiletries for you."

"I'd prefer going to the gym to be with my family," Marcel stated.

"The van can drop you there."

With that, the lieutenant led them out the door. That night, Dobie's team enjoyed showers and clean sheets. The Hmong found their accommodations an improvement over a jungle camp.

———•———

NEW BEGINNINGS

After a comfortable night in the Udorn Visiting Officer's Quarters, Dobie and the group accepted the ride to the Base Exchange. Since Dobie and Jimbo were the only ones with US currency, they paid for a fresh set of clothes for everyone. The security police escort directed the bus driver to the police building.

Their escort led them back to the conference room. The police major entered.

"Colonel Gates has ordered air transport for you back to U-Tapao Royal Thai Air Base."

He looked at Tinh and Quyển.

"Since you do not have IDs, Thai security police will escort you to the refugee camp, along with Sergeant Khắc. The Thais insist on controlling all refugees. Besides coming from Laos and Vietnam, Cambodian refugees have been streaming across the border."

"What's been happening in Cambodia since the Rouge has been in control?" Dobie posed.

"Intel reports that the refugees have harrowing stories," the major replied.

Upon arriving at U-Tapao, Thai officials escorted Tinh, Quyển, and Khắc to the refugee camp. Builders had completed the fence, and a guarded gate offered the only access. Dobie and Jimbo checked into a hotel. Dobie immediately called Ashley Peabody to report on the success of their rescue. Charles rejoined them in U-Tapao.

"Job well done!" Peabody congratulated them. "Now we have to extract our refugees from those camps. We are recruiting sponsors for them."

"We need to start the wheels in motion to rescue the Hmong," Dobie advised. "Their refugee camp will resemble a concentration camp."

"We will need a complete and accurate list," Peabody ordered. "You and Jimbo work on those in Thailand. I'll track down Clicker in Guam. He shouldn't be hard to find."

A month later, Tinh and everyone on the plane from Saigon made their way to the US-run refugee camp on Guam. Colonel Tinh tearfully rejoined his family. Clicker stayed with the Ngos during their entire stay on Guam. Another month elapsed before they transferred to the resettlement camp at Fort Chaffee, Arkansas. Clicker, Rick, and Sue helped them settle in America. Ashley Peabody organized sponsors for the other refugees from the C-123 flight.

Through the efforts of Ashley Peabody, the Hmong group arrived at Fort Chaffee after two months in Thailand. With less education than the Vietnamese refugees, their adjustment period to America spanned years. A few found that their experience in growing rice and poppies in the Laotian mountains helped them to adapt. Most remained in neighborhoods together, clinging to their tradition of strong family ties.

Direct Action magazine experienced record sales for the four issues that contained the stories.

Despite persistent reports of prisoners abandoned in Southeast Asia, only one former prisoner emerged after several years. His case faced many questions, though. Intelligence reports indicated he had willingly remained in North Vietnam. A few retired military veterans launched publicized missions claiming knowledge of remaining prisoners. However, no mission freed any prisoner. No definite proof of abandoned Americans emerged from the mountains and jungles of Southeast Asia.

Persistent rumors, however, did provide Hollywood with storylines to capitalize on the issue.

EPILOGUE - THE STARFISH

———•———

Rick felt exhausted. He had expanded on the stories in the magazine articles to fill in the details. The copies of *Direct Action* lay spread across the coffee table. His children sat quietly.

Lee picked up one photograph.

"So, this is my Vietnamese mother and American father?"

Rick nodded.

"Yes."

Lee held it close, squinting.

"Once we tried to read the name tag on your father's uniform," Rick said. "But it wasn't possible. So, Mom put the photograph away. You were our son, and it wasn't important."

Lee picked up the other photo. "And this is Mom with my Vietnamese mother?" he inquired.

"Yes," Rick replied.

Lee studied the photo. "They look so happy."

Rick leaned over to look at the picture.

"Mai had taught Mom a Vietnamese recipe. Mom was so pleased with how it turned out."

"I don't remember Mom fixing a Vietnamese dinner," Teri stated. "Did she?"

"No," Rick replied. "I suggested it once. But she said it made her too sad. And she couldn't remember the recipe."

Silence reigned for several minutes. David picked up one magazine.

"The magazine stories don't tell what happened to the refugees after they arrived in the States," he observed.

Rick replied, "Their stories weren't complete when the magazine published the issues. The Ngos remained in Arkansas. Tinh and Quyên worked for forest companies there."

"Even our story wasn't finished," Lee added.

"After Hawaii," Rick answered, "we went to Denver. The lawyer finished the paperwork, and a judge approved American adoption papers. And I found a job here in Wichita designing new business jets."

"My name was originally spelled with an 'i'?" Lee asked.

"Yes," Rick answered. "Mom and I thought you and Teri would have an easier time as kids if we gave you American names."

"My Vietnamese name is Thi, then," Teri stated.

Rick nodded.

"What happened to Clicker?" David asked. "I don't remember him."

"We lost touch a couple of years after the Ngos settled in Arkansas. He flew for a Middle Eastern airline for a couple of years. I guess the Muslim country scene offered little to a bachelor. Then, he went back to Southeast Asia to fly for an airline. The last time we heard, he was married to a Malaysian woman for a few years."

"I guess he never found a woman like Mrs. Ngo," Teri observed.

"I guess not," Rick agreed.

"The Hmong must have had a hard adjustment coming to America," Lee noted. "I have faint memories of being very confused after I came here."

"You had a couple of very rough years. But you worked so hard to learn English and go to school," Rick told him. "Mom and I were so very proud of you."

"How did Colonel Nickerson escape?" David inquired.

"He climbed onto the second-to-last helicopter from the Embassy before dawn on April 30th."

"Did Kim ever learn what happened to her fiancé?" Teri asked.

"Colonel Tinh spent years trying to find information about Truc. He learned nothing."

"Did you ever learn what happened to Calvin Reese?" Lee asked.

Rick cleared his throat.

"I heard from Jeff Nickerson a couple of months ago," Rick began. "To gain diplomatic recognition from the United States, the Vietnamese opened an unofficial channel to release information on some MIAs. Cal died evading capture."

"Did Master Sergeant Atkins ever end up back in jail in North Carolina?" David asked.

Rick gave a slight smile.

"No, he didn't. I guess his lawyer was right. The young Navy SEALS were too embarrassed to show up to testify against an old retired Green Beret who bested them all."

"Did Colonel Starbuckle ever rescue any prisoners left behind?" Teri wondered.

"Jeff told me Dobie went to Thailand twice in the 1980s chasing down rumors of prisoner sightings. He could never find enough evidence to venture into Laos."

David moved from his chair to sit next to Rick on the couch. Lee and Teri sat in chairs beside the couch. The group remained quiet for several seconds.

"Our last evening in Hawaii," Rick added, "Mom said something that made all the challenges over the years very manageable. It helped her up to the end."

His children waited for Rick to continue.

"Our time in Vietnam was very hard for her. We were there only for a short while. With the country imploding, the entire experience seemed pointless. She had been asking why we had gone there. That evening in Hawaii, we had just finished getting you into bed. Mom lingered while I went out on the balcony. Then she came out and called me to stand in the doorway next to her."

Rick paused. His emotions bubbled to the surface.

"She looked at me, then inside at you children, and said, 'Look at Thi and Lei. I understand now why we went to Vietnam. To save those two precious children.'"

He couldn't go on. Teri moved to his side, bringing the box of tissues from the coffee table. She handed one to Rick. He blew his nose and cleared his throat. He motioned for Lee to sit next to Teri.

"The next morning, the lawyer in Denver called. The lawyer said your adoptions were simple. He was working on a dozen adoptions from Hoa Sen Orphanage. We would have to come to Denver. We left that afternoon."

Rick's voice broke.

"I had never seen such joy in Mom."

Rick took another tissue. He turned to Lee and Teri.

"A couple of years ago, Mom started calling you our little starfish."

"Starfish?" Teri asked.

"Mom had read a story. It was about a little girl who found thousands of starfish washed up on a beach. If the little girl did nothing, they would all die. While she was putting one starfish after another back into the ocean, a man asked her what she was doing. What difference did it make, he asked, saving a few with thousands on the beach? The little girl placed another starfish into the ocean and said, 'It made a difference to that one.'"

Rick put his right arm around David and pulled him closer. He turned slightly to Teri and Lee. He reached out to them with his left arm. Rick hugged his children tightly, tears running down his cheeks.

They would get through this sadness together. Sue would expect that.

———•———

ACKNOWLEDGMENTS

—•—

An accurate depiction of events forming the background of *But One Reply* would not have been possible without the accounts written by veterans of South Vietnam's last days. My squadron mates of the 776th Tactical Airlift Squadron and I knew we were participating in history as we flew refugees from Saigon during its final days. We also knew much bigger stories were unfolding on the ground in Saigon. A 776th crew flew the Herk destroyed on the ground on April 29, 1975. The crew successfully escaped to a nearby C-130, which took off from the taxiway. I am indebted to those whom I peppered with questions about their memories, especially Rene Garcia and Rick Rohas. Special thanks go to Pam and Bob Munson, Air Force Academy friends who freely and eagerly relayed their adventures living in Thailand in 1975. They witnessed the end of the wars in Southeast Asia from another close-by perspective. Thanks also goes to Hiram Payne, Air Force Safety Officer and bomber pilot, for his knowledge of airplane mishaps.

Rowe Stayton, another Academy friend, provided insights from a soldier's perspective. Bill Gillin, an Academy classmate, contributed his knowledge as a rescue helicopter pilot. I am indebted to jeweler and precious metals expert Tony Kubes, who explained how to determine if a ring is genuine gold. My thanks also go to members of several Facebook groups for their answers to my questions. Among them are C-130 Hercules Aircrew, Vietnam War Veterans, and I Was Stationed at Clark Air Base Philippines. Veterans who have written memoirs deserve special thanks, as they came home to a country that only wanted to forget the Vietnam War. Many thanks go to the refugees who have shared their stories. They came to America unsure of the welcome that awaited them.

Most important thanks go to Joann, my partner for over fifty years. She was a college senior when the historical events in *But One Reply* unfolded across the globe. Our engagement at the time created a greater interest in the news than that displayed by her college friends. The few letters she saved and my pilot logbook allowed me to write a journal of the experience many years later. She joined me in the Philippines after our wedding four months after Saigon's final days. Two weeks after we arrived at Clark Air Base, I left for temporary duty in Thailand. The Air Force (with complicity from me) threw her into the deep end to learn how to be an Air Force pilot's wife. Joann's memories and Pam Munson's stories helped motivate Sue's impressions upon arriving in Bien Hoa. As I worked on *Not to Reason Why* and *But One Reply*, I monopolized the desk in our study. Maybe now Joann will have more frequent access to it.

Final thanks go to Jain Lemos for her editing and publication wisdom.

I first heard the Starfish Story while on the board of a nonprofit service organization in 2003. Internet sources cite its origin as the essay "The Star Thrower" by Loren Eiseley. At least three service nonprofits use "starfish" in their names and versions of the story for their motivation.

The Southeast Asia map was generated using R v4.2.3, a language and environment for statistical computing, R Foundation for Statistical Computing, Vienna, Austria, R-project.org, and R packages ggplot2 v3.5.1 and sf v1.0-21.

———•———

FURTHER READINGS

Brokhausen, Nick. *We Few: US Special Forces in Vietnam.* Havertown, PA: Casemate Publishers, 2018, Kindle.

Clarke, Thurston. *Honorable Exit: How a Few Brave Americans Risked All to Save Our Vietnamese Allies at the End of the War.* New York: Doubleday, 2019, Kindle.

Drury, Bob and Tom Clavin. *Last Men Out: The True Story of America's Heroic Final Hours in Vietnam.* New York: Free Press, 2011, Kindle.

Eiseley, Loren. *The Star Thrower.* Orlando: A Harvest Book Harcourt, Inc., 1979.

Elliott, Mai. *The Sacred Willow: Four Generations in the Life of a Vietnamese Family.* New York: Oxford University Press, 2017.

Grizzard, Elizabeth C. *My Journey to America: An Escape from Communist Laos.* US: self-pub, 2015.

Herrington, Stuart A. *Peace with Honor?: An American Reports on Vietnam 1973-75.* Novato, CA: Presidio Press, 1983.

Hunt, Maj. Gen. Ira A. Jr. *Losing Vietnam: How America Abandoned Southeast Asia.* Lexington: The University Press of Kentucky, 2013, Kindle.

Kennedy, Rory, dir. *Last Days in Vietnam.* WGBH Boston, 2014.

Lavell, Lt. Col. A.J.C. *Last Flight from Saigon.* Pickle Partners Publishing, 2014, Kindle.

Lee, Choua, as told to Mary Albanese. *The Girl with Ten Names: My Escape from Laos to Freedom.* United Kingdom: Oxshott Press, 2015.

McCoy, Alfred W. *The Politics of Heroin: CIA Complicity in the Global Drug Trade,* rev. ed. Chicago: Lawrence Hill Books, 2003.

Nguyen, Con. *My Last Flight Out: Last Pilot Who Escaped after the Fall of Viet Nam.* N.p.: Lulu Publishing Services, 2019.

Peck-Barnes, Shirley. *The War Cradle: The Untold Story of "Operation Babylift."* Denver: The Vintage Press Works, 2000.

Pham, Quang X. *A Sense of Duty: My Father, My American Journey.* New York: Ballantine Books, 2005, Kindle.

Vien, General Cao Van. *The Final Collapse.* Pickle Partners Publishing, 2016, Kindle.

Vu, Tran Tri. *Lost Years: My 1,632 Days in Vietnamese Reeducation Camps.* Berkeley: Institute of East Asian Studies, 1988.

White, Ralph. *Getting Out of Saigon: How a 27-Year-Old American Banker Saved 113 Vietnamese Civilians.* New York: Simon & Schuster, 2023, Kindle.

———•———

ABOUT THE AUTHOR

———•———

Robert L. Decker is a graduate of the US Air Force Academy. He served as an Air Force pilot for seven years after his graduation. Among his duties, he instructed pilots in the C-130 Herk. He also flew in the evacuation of Saigon in April 1975. After his Air Force service, he worked as an investment analyst in Chicago for over three decades. His love for flying came from his father, who served in the Army Air Corps during World War II, and from a cousin, who was an F-105 Thud pilot and Prisoner of War in Vietnam. An avid reader, he credits his mother, a high school English teacher, for his love of books. He currently resides in Texas.

———•———